In the Wake of Gods

The Abyss Borne Gods–Book Two
Kent Priore

This is a work of fiction. Names, characters, places, and incidents either are the product of the author's imagination or are used fictitiously, and any resemblance to actual persons living or dead, business establishments, events, or locales, is entirely coincidental.

© COPYRIGHT 2026 by Kent Priore

All rights reserved. No part of this book may be used or reproduced in any manner whatsoever without written permission of the publisher except in the case of brief quotations embodied in critical articles or reviews.

AI was not used to write this book, to create the cover art, or in formatting.

NO AI TRAINING: Without in any way limiting the author's and publisher's exclusive rights under copyright, any use of this publication to "train" generative artificial intelligence (AI) technologies to generate text is expressly prohibited. The author reserves all rights to license uses of this work for genAI training and development of machine learning language models.

Warning: Not intended for persons under the age of 18. May contain coarse language and mature content that may disturb some readers. Reader discretion advised.

Cover Art Design by: Kelly Moran/Rowan Prose Publishing
Photo Credit: Adobe Images/Deposit Photos
First Edition
ISBN: 978-1-961967-81-6
Rowan Prose Publishing, LLC
www.RowanProsePublishing.com
Published in the United States of America

Get book one NOW!

Praise for *The Monsters Among Us*

"Priore writes like a natural about the supernatural, and *The Monsters Among Us* is a marvelously dark and true novel. American fiction has found a terrific new voice."
—Joseph O'Neill, PEN/Faulkner Award-Winning Author of *Netherland*.

"Supernatural storytelling at its best, this vivid cinematic novel takes the reader on an imaginative journey through what could be considered end of days. *The Monster's Among Us* is a masterful creation and a must read—even for those who aren't fans of fantasy/horror."
—Joni Marie Iraci MFA author of *Vatican Daughter,* and *Reinventing Jenna Rose*.

"A transgressive tale of supernatural pulp phantasmagoria, written by an author with Biblical-sized storytelling ambitions. Priore provides a Weird Tales, dark fantasy take on Testaments Old and New, crafting a tale as shocking as it is thought-provoking."
—Patrick Barb, author of *Abducted*.

"Deliciously diabolical and, at times, deranged, Priore's world is one of darkness, Inferno level devilry, despair, but also friendship and love. I will watch Priore's writing career with interest."
—Arlo Z. Graves, author of *Black Rose* and *The Ice Moves for No One*.

"I was intrigued from the first sentence, determined to spend the night speed-reading so I didn't have to remain in suspense any longer."
—Ella Dupuie, author of *Fractures of the Fallen*

Dedication:
For Katarina, my bride-to-be.
Our love so strong, if granted numerous lives, it would surely be an eternal recurrence.
A marriage in life and in death.

PART ONE

New Beginnings

"One always finds one's burden again."
—Albert Camus, *The Myth of Sisyphus*

PROLOGUE

Mounds of ash carpet the ground, giving the illusion of a vast, wintery landscape. Hiding the cold, hard surface of a cave's flooring beneath. The charred air is thick with the stench of melted flesh. The cavern's entrance is hidden by collapsed stone, no way to vent the smell. And no method of entry, for any wanderer to happen upon the sight of this tragedy.

Scattered throughout the air are stark white flames. Their glow contrasts the dull gray of ash. They flutter before condensing into small balls of light. Tiny suns piercing through the darkness.

Seth stands upon a spot so dark it's almost black. The point of origin. Out where the flames erupted. His gaze circles the area, with the collapsed remains of a massive tower behind him. Stopping upon the darkened outlines of human figures, his mind reoccurs here. Diving into the sorrow of past deeds.

Stroking his long, black beard, Seth sighs as his mouth crumbles into a deep frown. Checking his watch, he finds that the sun will be setting soon.

Glancing around one last time, his eyes emit a white ethereal light as the abyssal flames ignite in front of him. Creating a dozen more tiny suns, in an oval shape. Their edges stretch to meet each other, forming a portal. As the image from the other side solidifies, he finds Andes sitting behind a desk, diligently signing paperwork.

"Andes, do you have a moment?"

Jerking his head up, the gray, old man clutches his heart in shock. "Oh! Seth...you startled me."

Andes slowly rises and trudges through the portal. A cane quaking in his right hand.

"Sorry," says Seth. "You were never one to be easily shaken."

"A few years ago maybe, but with the curse of the old guard...I'm afraid I'm growing a bit feeble."

Seth grimaces. "Sasha...she'll find a cure. So please stay strong. For her, and for our baby. Please don't lose hope."

Andes's wrinkled mouth curves upward, beneath pensive eyes. Still lit with the fire he has otherwise lost. But his smile sinks as he makes his way through the portal.

"Seth, what are you doing here?"

"The Guild deserved better than this. The people of Magistrum deserved better than what I did to them. Yet I am the one who lives on."

Andes's mouth twitches angrily. "Now listen here. An insane responsibility was foisted upon you that day. One you were not ready for. Anyone in your place would have—"

"You were angry at me that day. I ignored it then. But you were. I did a horrible thing here. The reason why doesn't matter. And I want you to know—"

The memory of that day is crisp within his mind. His emotions overwhelming him, the hellfire erupting from his pores—devouring everything in an instant. Tears drip along his cheeks, soaking his beard. "I am so sorry, Andes. And I'm sorry it took me so long to say it."

Remembering the destruction, watching the flames eat almost everyone he loved, Andes joins Seth in tears. His left fist rises. Shaking as it reaches toward Seth, but uncurling to pat his back as he embraces him. "I know you are. You don't have to say it."

"No. But I wanted to."

Nodding his head, Andes says, "Indeed, and it's nice to hear things aloud. So, hear this. Virdeus would be proud of the man you have become. Now," Andes pauses, noticing the light glimmering upon the golden band wrapped around the ring finger of Seth's left hand. "Sasha will be home soon. So, stop thinking so much about the past and go home to your wife."

Patting Seth's back once more, Andes ambles through the portal. Glancing at its fiery rim, Andes chuckles. "You know, I'm still in awe of these new powers of yours. And a bit jealous, truth be told, now that mine are gone. Are you sure you won't join the Assembly?"

"The Guild's new guard doesn't need the likes of me. Not after what I've done."

"Seth...you really must stop torturing yourself." Andes disappears through the portal, which vanishes as the white abyssal flames extinguish themselves.

Seth sighs heavily, taking one more glance at the destruction. *I'm not torturing myself. Just not letting myself forget. Forgetting would be to relinquish myself of the weight of a catastrophe I caused. I need the memory. It will help me continue to grow and ensure that this doesn't happen again.*

His eyes burst with that abyssal white light, creating another portal. This time to a large wooden cabin perched upon a mountain's summit. Seth makes his return home, deep in thought.

You don't get it, Andes. It's bad enough that Sasha is known to the world. These powers of ours must remain hidden. This world has no need for gods—just look at what happens where gods dare to tread.

The white flames dispersed around the cave flicker away into darkness. The ash-coated and sin-stained battlefield fades as Seth is greeted by the sight of his home and the sound of crickets beginning their evening symphony. Smoke rises from the cabin's chimney, next to a massive bird's nest. A bed of sticks and stones the size of a large car covers half the roof. Croaking at the sight of Seth's return, two massive ravens rise from the nest and flutter to the ground.

The only two of their kind, created by Sasha through the creation magic gifted by Zarathustra. They were there at the end of the old world, and at the new world's beginning.

"Huginn, Muninn," Seth says, reaching out for the massive birds. They stand taller than him and far wider. Huginn spreads his wings, croaks, and cocks his head in confusion. While Muninn nuzzles his beak against Seth's cheek. "Good boy, Muninn. And don't worry, Huginn, Sasha will be home shortly. Go and watch for her, alright?"

The two birds flap, unleashing a gust of wind beneath their powerful wings. Muninn returns to the nest while Huginn flies off, keeping his eyes on the mountain trail.

Smiling, Seth turns and makes his way to the cliffside. The graves of his friends await him.

"Out here again?" asks Sasha.

"Just paying my respects," says Seth. "How is Andes doing?"

"As jovial as ever. And he had an interesting message."

"Oh?" Seth feels a heaviness build within his chest, unsure of where this is going. And hoping that Andes hasn't told her about their brief meet-up at the ruins of Magistrum. Not that he means to keep anything from her. He simply wishes to keep her from unnecessary stress.

"We were right," Sasha says, "Humans have started to be born with magic."

He strokes his long, black beard. "Then I suppose we have our work cut out for us."

"Andes says he'll take care of things, so we won't have to worry. To give us our rest for...you know." Sasha smiles. "So, Seth..."

"Yeah?"

"Do you think humans will be alright? With magic, I mean."

"We are. They will be, too. I'm sure of it."

Seth frowns at Melphis's tombstone.

"It wasn't your fault," Sasha says. "You know that, right?"

"I suppose. But I wish I could have made things right. Before it was too late." Seth pauses. He turns toward Sasha, bright-eyed. "Say, we're going to have to be careful. Teaching humans about magic and all. Outing ourselves as having magic, may cause them to think we are gods. We can't have that!"

Sasha chuckles, then takes Seth by the arm. She lays her head on his shoulder. "No, we can't have that. For we are not gods. And none exist here anymore. We made sure of that."

"Yes," Seth smiles. "A world led by humans, for humans. A world that has no need for gods. They will find their own way. This world can be whatever they want it to be."

Seth glances back toward the graves. "Thank you, my friends. Thank you...Melphis. For leading me toward this new life." He lays his free hand upon Sasha's rounded belly.

A moment's silence embraces them in the comfort of each other. Their warmth, all they need. Sasha's large copper-colored eyes glance up at her husband as her free hand meets his over her pregnant belly. Their fingers interlock, becoming one.

"I know you want to stay in solitude to not risk the world knowing of our powers," says Sasha, but these new powers of yours…it would really help if we could study them down at the Assembly."

"You're the one who kept the powers of creation. Isn't that enough?"

"We need all the knowledge we can get. Especially now, with newborn magic humans."

Seth remains quiet a moment, but hugs Sasha tighter. "Alright, if it'll help you and the Assembly, how could I say no?" Seth smiles.

Sasha gives him a squeeze before heading inside to rest. Seth lingers by the tombstones a bit longer, switching his gaze from Melphis to Virdeus.

You would be so proud of her now, Dad. I sure am. And I promise to spend the rest of my days ensuring that she is happy and safe. I love her, and I owe you that much for what I did to your Guild.

The air in my lungs, the food I eat, the water I drink. I have no life without her, and the child she brings. She is everything now.

Sasha feels the exhaustion of the day pulling her into sleep, but the aches in her back and feet spring her awake each time. Sleeping more comfortably on her stomach is impossible while pregnant, so each night remains a hassle. *I can't wait for this baby to come out! Every night I'm sleep deprived and—*

The front door creaks open, and the immediate sound of sizzling oil lulls her into anticipation. More so does the smell of steak filtering into the bedroom. And more still, the sound of frozen French fries plopping into the oil next to the meat.

She smiles, appreciating all Seth has done to take care of her while they await the baby's arrival. Even catering to her every craving. But eager as she is to eat, the moment of bliss Seth's thoughtfulness has brought eases her into slumber.

CHAPTER ONE

ABOUT NINE MONTHS EARLIER.

Silence fills the air. Aside from the shuffling of papers, and the scratch of Sasha's pen as she signs her name on document after document. Turning to face the sunlight filtering through the windows to her right, she sighs heavily. Behind her hangs a picture of her father, painted by Andes. A gift to celebrate the first anniversary of humanity's liberation from gods.

"I know you would be proud, Father, of what I'm doing and everything the Guild has accomplished. But—" She glances back at the stack of papers, many of which she has not yet sifted through. Death certificates of most of the old guard.

The door to her office opens, and in comes a frail old woman, struggling to walk even with the aid of her cane. "Looking over those dreadful things, are you?" she says.

"I feel gross, Griselda. Mechanical. Signing these certificates one after another, a product being sent down a conveyor belt. They were our friends and I..."

Griselda's eyes soften with tears as she watches Sasha from the other side of the desk. "The cost of operating within the light, my lady. All this bureaucratic nonsense. This is a new age for the Guild—oh, the Assembly I mean. The old guard, we're products of a vastly different time, maybe it's for the best that we—"

"Stop that," says Sasha, cutting off the old woman's rambling. "I will find the cause and—"

"Find a cure?"

Sasha's eyes flutter away from the old woman's gaze. Her hands clench, hidden beneath the desk. Fingers rubbing together like coarse sandpaper.

Something in Griselda's gaze shifts. From hope to pensive acceptance. "Don't worry yourself too much, dear. If it's our time, it's our time. Andes and I will serve you to the very end. But regardless, your ten o'clock visit is here. Shall I let her in?"

Sighing, Sasha swivels her chair around to face Virdeus's portrait. Andes truly captured his prideful aura. His confident, loving smile. Next to the portrait is the taxidermized tentacle of an angel. A trophy of victory from that day, a reminder of all they are fighting for. *I know this is what you would have wanted, Father. But the family you knew is crumbling. It's just Andes, Griselda, and me left. What we did that day...it was right and it was good, but was it worth it?*

"Yes, Griselda, let her in."

A woman in a gray pantsuit takes a seat in the chair opposite Sasha. She's wearing dark purple rimmed glasses beneath her curly chestnut hair. "Thank you for agreeing to see me," she says.

"Happy to make the time," says Sasha. "Always looking for ways to get our good message known to the world."

Sasha glances at her up and down. The woman is stoic and at ease. Removing a small notepad and pen from her suit's inner chest pocket, she looks toward Sasha with a fiery gaze.

"The Assembly is already known to the world. Far and wide, despite only being around for, what was it, a little over two years?"

"It helps that we were erected in response to that great tragedy. What many are calling the Supernatural Holocaust."

"Yes...it was an awful day. So many lives lost that it's hard pressed to find anyone who didn't lose somebody. Myself included. Hence why I was eager to interview you."

"Yes, we here at the Assembly lost so many." The faces of her friends, of her father, flash into memory. "May I ask who you lost?"

The woman's nose scrunches in anger. "My son. He was only two months old. My husband and I divorced recently. We couldn't cope."

Sasha's gaze drifts away from the woman and to the photo of herself and Seth framed on her desk. Their arms wrapped around each other. After Andes took that photo, he said the sheer happiness on display is proof of how worthwhile everything has been. And Sasha could see it, too. *I cannot imagine anything splitting us apart. But the loss of a child...I cannot even imagine.*

"I'm so sorry to hear that. But thank you for being forthcoming about it. There is so much hidden, personal hardship from that day that we don't often hear about. Stories like this sharpen my resolve to carry out our mission."

"And what mission is that? The Assembly's existence implies you think threats like what we faced two years ago aren't necessarily gone. Can you speak more on that?"

She glares across the table. "Our existence should not be seen as proof of any potential threats. But a reassurance that we are here in case of any threat."

"So, you're taking taxpayer dollars with no real cause?"

"The military does the same. They don't go looking for war, but they are there as a deterrent, to provide a sense of safety for the masses."

"Fair enough," the woman says. "But what can the Assembly actually do against another supernatural threat? There's been a frequent tale of heroes who fought back against the monsters, are they in your employ? If so, I would love to speak to them."

Sasha smirks. "Sorry, but they have asked to remain anonymous. Not even the president knows who they are."

The interview continues at length. All the while, Sasha ponders the ludicrous nature of this situation. *At home awaits a man who creates portals from abyssal white flames, and the two giant ravens I created from the palms of my hands. I can create anything I want, and yet here I am, stuck behind a desk. Signing paperwork, getting interviewed.*

The woman asks about the tentacle hanging on the wall. Sasha tells her it's a symbol of victory, of strength, that the Assembly could do it all again, if they must.

Little does she know, we could succeed all the easier with our current power.

The woman thanks Sasha for her time and promptly leaves.

Sighing, she glances over the death certificates again, and her mind wanders.

My hunch...is not good. I feel it beneath my feet. The White Abyss pulsing through the Earth. The solid and intangible wedded together at last. But the cost—

She rubs the rune on the side of her neck. Magic once flowed through it. A power outlet, but the wires have been moved. And now there's no spark. No wattage.

But Seth, he can commune with it. Together, through his abilities and mine, perhaps we can save Andes and Griselda. I cannot lose any more of my family.

Opening her left palm, teal sparks crackle as they rise into the air. Glowing like flame, they twist and flutter before molding into the shape of two rings. Plopping into her hand, sunlight glints against the solid gold. With flushed cheeks, she holds them tight. Thinking fondly of their future together.

A dense forest carpets the ground below the cold, stony cliffside. Beyond lays the town of Crowley, its many lights flashing on in welcome of the coming twilight. Staring out upon this home rechristened in the fires of the new world, Seth smiles.

Cross-legged, he sits and breathes in the crisp, clean mountain air. And, hands folded upon his lap, he watches as the forest's evergreens pulse with a stark abyssal light. Closing his eyes, looking inward, Seth's own aura bursts with an ethereal teal before shifting into white. His soul ejects from his back, hovering a foot above his body and—

He quakes, his soul ripples like water disturbed by a skipping stone. And like an ocean's tide, his surroundings wash away into a vast, empty white space.

"Hello again," says Seth.

Alone within the White Abyss, he stares out into its all-encompassing nothingness. A heavy silence approaches like a predator.

"I know you can speak. We've spoken before."

Another quake ripples through Seth's soul, but he stares on undeterred. "Spawn of Zarathustra. Your presence is unwelcome here."

"And I apologize. I do not wish to intrude, only to make good on my promise from our last meeting. Despite what I am—"

"Zarathustra's spawn, his rage, his volatility."

"Yes," Seth replies softly. "I'm aware that you had qualms with Zarathustra and his kind. When he gifted me his powers, certain memories were transferred alongside them—one's magic is their very soul, their being's whole essence, after all. But I do not hold his power of creation any longer. I am no threat. My desire to be the medium between the White Abyss and humanity is proof of that. All I want is peace. Balance. And in the spirit of that..."

Seth's mind goes back a couple years, to the words of his lost friend, Melphis. Words he did not fully understand at that time, but does now. *I have found that magic is best used in creative and unprecedented ways. Even the dullest magic knows few limits. Magic does what the mind wills it to do.*

"I could go ahead and do this without your consent, but instead, I would like to include you. As a gesture of my goodwill, and in the spirit of our union."

"Speak your request, rageful spawn of a god."

"I would like to forge a ring. With my abyssal flames, within the vast infinite potential of your creative powers."

That heavy silence again, crushing like an infinite number of boulders upon one's shoulders. Seth patiently awaits an answer, as he feels the Abyssal Consciousness squirming like energetic, hungry snakes. And, somewhere beyond, is the movement of other powers, like fire climbing the height of a tree, ready to burst. Seth squints inquisitively. This familiarity, felt in humanity no longer except through himself and Sasha. *A mingling of souls and magic?*

"Do it, Spawn of Zarathustra. Commence the making of your covenant."

"Thank you," Seth smiles, bowing slightly in respect. If the Abyssal Consciousness had a physical form, he would instead shake its hand.

At the white pulse of his eyes, abyssal flames spark and flicker into being, molding themselves into a small band. Glowing bright, the flames condense further and further, smoldering hot before a rapid cooling. The flames disappear, leaving a white metal band. Solid yet wispy, with the flow and tide of abyssal energy visible. Upon the basket resides a large, semi-translucent gemstone. Inside mingles white abyssal flame and the electric crackle of divine teal energy.

Holding it in his palm, Seth smiles wide, then glances out toward the Abyss.

"Thank you for allowing me to use the White Abyss as a forge. The results are...profound. She's going to love it."

"The other spawn. Zarathustra's Lust."

"Yes."

"Your gesture better not be meaningless. For she still possesses creation magic. Can you assure that she isn't a threat?"

"With my whole being. She is the strongest, kindest, and most thoughtful soul I have ever known. And will defend this world, and you, fiercely until her dying breath."

Satisfied, but concerned about that growing, pulsating power, Seth's soul quakes and ripples once more, pulling himself back into his body, upon the stony cliffside beneath the ever-darkening sky.

But words echo across the realms, the Abyssal Consciousness speaking through the union born of Seth's acceptance of the emptiness within.

{Beware, Spawn of Zarathustra. Enjoy your bliss for now. But beware. You know better than anyone that the world is not prone to everlasting peace. To think so would be delusion, of which you claim to be no longer a victim.}

Seth winces, the words cycling endlessly in the depths of his mind. But as he holds the ring high, the moonlight glinting through the gemstone, illuminating the white flames and divine light within, he smiles. For the light of love erases any worry, and strengthens one's will.

Chuckling, Seth lays a blanket upon the moonlit cliffside and heads into their cabin to make the final preparations.

Time to rescue my beloved from her dastardly desk.

Papers spill from the left side of the desk as Sasha signs the final death certificate and places it atop the others. Moonlight filters through the windows, announcing that she has lost track of time. And, slouching in her chair, she groans softly.

Nothing but silence beyond the walls of her office, with everyone else having gone home hours ago. First the new guard, then Griselda, then Andes. Though she told the latter to leave even earlier, they refused. *Nothing like the work ethic of the old guard, and now there's only three of us left. And I'm no closer to figuring out why.*

White flames draw an oval shape in the air. Beyond her desk, she glances through the portal, finding their cabin.

"Oh, how sweet of you to come pick me up," she says, and Seth pops his head around the edge of the portal.

"Figured you could use rescuing from all this bureaucratic nonsense," he says. "Come on home."

Taking one last glance at the stack of death certificates, she grabs the two gold wedding bands and slides them into her back pocket. In an instant, she hops through the portal and arrives home.

"So happy you can do this now. Especially after the day I just had," she says.

"Tell me all about it," says Seth, leading her by the hand. "But close your eyes, I have a surprise."

"Oh, for me?" she says, grinning. "And yeah, all this paperwork...and for what? As far as the world is concerned, all the dying members of the old guard never existed in the first place. If they were normal humans, they would have died thousands of years ago. So why document their deaths? The government demanded I comply. They probably just want to study magic on their own, not that they'd learn anything."

Seth lightly tugs her arm down, leading her to the ground until she's sitting. "The cost of operating within the light, I guess," he says, "Open your eyes."

"Griselda said the same thing—"

Before her lies a white cotton blanket, with a platter of cheese and a bottle of cabernet sauvignon with two glasses. A snap of Seth's fingers and a candelabra with four sconces light with abyssal white flame, illuminating the cliffside. The glow of the fire is brighter than normal orange flame, with it glimmering even stronger with the reflection of the full moon hovering above them.

"What's all this for?" she asks, cheeks flushing.

"It's been two years since the dawn of our new world. Rid of their oppressors, humans reign supreme. We did that. We made that happen. And now, for the first time in either of our lives, we are living as ordinary humans—well, relatively normal." Seth chuckles, gesturing to the white flames. She scoots nearer to him, wrapping her arm around him. He tightens his embrace in turn, then continues, "So let's embrace that—ordinary human lives, and do as they do."

He reaches into the pocket inside his long, black trench coat and unearths a ring so bright with abyssal light its aura overpowers the moon and its night. A heaviness draws her eyes, lingering upon the translucent gemstone. The white fire and—her mind goes back to earlier this morning, when she created the gold wedding bands. The teal light crackling as the rings burst into being.

Gasping, she raises her left hand to her mouth. "Abyssal flames and divine energy, mingling together. A marriage of life and death?"

Seth smiles widely, his cheeks rising high beneath eyes so full of longing and compassion. "In the spirit of everything we've done, of everything we're working toward, will you be wed to me in life and in death?"

Her throat tightens, tears cloud her eyes, and—she bursts out laughing, clutching her stomach as she topples over.

Seth's smile crumbles, the passion in his eyes distort into profound concern. "Is that a no?"

Reaching into her back pocket, she brings the golden wedding bands into the moonlit air. The white abyssal flames glimmering against them. "No, you silly man. It's a yes. A big fucking yes!"

"Did you make those?"

"Yes, earlier today."

Seth appears overcome with awe, his smile returning, cheeks flushing. "To think we both thought to make rings today."

Lunging at him, Sasha grips the back of his head tightly and presses her lips against his. They tumble backward and— "Ow!" Seth's head slams against the stony cliff.

"Oh, please! After all the injuries you had back then, you expect me to believe that hurt?" She says, smirking.

"My body is human again," Seth says, chuckling. "But please, hurt me more."

Atop him, she grins and bites her lower lip. Thrusting her mouth toward his neck, she clamps his skin between her teeth, sucking and pulling, leaving a mark. Seth moans loudly, his arms spurred into passion as he grips her back and buttocks, lifting them both into the air and carrying Sasha inside.

The light of the candelabra blinks away in the wake of their ever-growing passion. Leaving them to celebrate the light of their union, amidst the darkening of night.

And the conception of their future to come.

CHAPTER TWO

Massive dark clouds slither across the sky, blocking the setting sun. Drizzling rain patters against the ground. Before long, mud sloshes against the cluttered mass of black leather shoes encircling a rectangular hole in the ground.

Seth and Sasha stand beside one another, his arm wrapped tight around her shoulders. Sasha wraps her left arm around his waist, her other hand lying gently upon her rounded, pregnant belly. *Movement from within has increased over these last few days, as if the baby is growing eager to come out...but excited as I am to be a mother, the child will arrive in a world of death and suffering.*

Andes stands before the grave, giving his eulogy. The height of the Jotunheimen Mountains towering above them.

"Here we meet in the land of her original home in Norway. After wandering the Earth for thousands of years, our Griselda can finally return home. This has been our custom. Returning those of the old guard to the land from which they were derived from, though it is here wherein lies our plight. We've been away from home for so long. Our homes no longer feel like *home*. For our true home has become the arms of our loving Guild family. As our late founding father would attest to, Griselda's home was in all of you. So, honor her memory and bond with your brothers and sisters of the Assembly. For it's those bonds that have kept the members of the old guard like Griselda and me going for so long."

Sasha's tired, sunken eyes tether to Andes. *The final link to my old family.* She watches as he smiles wide but forlornly at the casket lowering into the ground. Tears cloud his eyes, and yet his grin—that ever-proud grin turns toward Sasha.

Glancing up at Seth, she takes his hand and kisses it lightly, as the memory of Griselda's own proud smile plunges her into memory.

Eight months earlier.

The warm spring sun shines bright. Its rays mingle with a soft, cool breeze. A wooden arch decorated with greenery and wildflowers stands tall before a large field, its grass swaying gently like the slow pull of an ocean's tide. A lake sits off to the side, its sun-glittered waters home to families of ducks and geese, a duo of swans float with regal elegance at the center. A large cabin to the right makes for a temporary perch for Huginn and Muninn. Hidden by a large tree branch, the two massive, watchful ravens sit patiently, but eager to see their masters wed.

Rows of chairs sit before the arch, with a wide aisle down the middle. Andes stands directly beneath it, wearing his old Guild uniform. The white martial artist attire with its armor plating on the shoulders and elbows appears comical on the elderly man. But he insists on wearing it. "Virdeus's daughter is getting married! I must honor his memory to the fullest extent!" he had said when Seth and Sasha shared news of their engagement.

Seth stands to his left, donning a full white suit. His black hair slicked back, his beard neatly groomed, and mustache curled and waxed. His bright, fiery eyes peer longingly down the aisle as Sasha ambles toward them in a long, black gothic dress. Wildflowers are woven into her hair, braided back in Scandinavian fashion by Griselda. Though not Sasha's culture, she had asked Griselda to do her hair this way after she mentioned that the flowers—their bright blue, red, purple, pink, and yellow—woven into the hair symbolize a oneness with Nature. A notion that, with the state of the new world, Sasha fell in love with. Just as she fell in love with Seth, the man who can commune with the Abyssal Consciousness, the essence of Nature itself.

Nature, its beauty, and its volatility. *What's a better depiction of a perfect union than that?*

A slow, melodic tune rises from a piano between the lake and wedding arch. A few ducks scatter and fly away at the sudden music, as Sasha walks down the aisle. Everyone's heads turn to face her. The audience, made entirely of members of the Assembly, are mostly foreign faces. But she wanted her father's continued lineage to bear witness to this momentous occasion.

The new guard, made of mostly military veterans, ex-police, and a few good-natured and brave souls eager to help the world at large...they are witnessing much more than a union between Seth and their Assembly President.

Everything we fought for—ridding the world of demons, angels, and gods alike, relinquishing humanity from its chains. This is a marriage to that ideal. To create a world that has no need for gods, to live out our lives as ordinary humans. The lives we weren't allowed to live before.

Reaching the end of the aisle, she catches a glimpse of Sergei, first of the new guard. He nods in respect, but with a face holding a seemingly permanent scowl. Sasha smiles as she walks on. Tall. Proud. Strong.

On the other side of the aisle is Griselda's wide grin. Her lips radiate an energy that seems to claim that this is the proudest she has ever been in her life. Upon her lap is Mikhail, or "Misha," Andes's and Griselda's infant son. Griselda lowers her face to speak into the child's ear.

"Isn't Aunt Sasha so pretty?"

A garbled mesh of sounds erupts from Mikhail's mouth.

"Yes, I know!" Griselda says. "The flower crown is pretty, too. Mommy made it, don't you know?"

She lifts her head and looks at Sasha, mouthing the words: *I love you.* Cheeks flushing above Sasha's ever-growing smile, she mouths them back.

Seth's eyes well with tears as Sasha meets him at the wooden arch. Her skin emanates a white glow. At first, he dismisses it as the sun's glare. But then he notices the white aura stretching from her face to her breasts to her stomach, where the glow amasses and shimmers before outlining the rest of her body. The audience's gaze had already been tethered to her, beautiful as she is. But now their jaws drop at the sight of this ethereal white glow.

The pupils in Seth's eyes shimmer in reaction to it before sinking into the whites of his eyes. Becoming pure white orbs, they stare toward his bride. He smiles, recognizing the glow as what he believes is the Abyssal Consciousness joining them in matrimony.

Andes glances over at Griselda, sharing a moment of bliss with her. The old woman's sagging cheeks are held high by the widest grin he has ever seen upon her face. Turning to Seth, and then to Sasha, he says, "Shall we begin?"

The rapidly aging man chokes and clears his throat as tears drip along his cheeks.

"I was there, when your father found you," he says, sniffling. "Alone in that dark room. A place of nightmares and terror. But when you came with us, you immediately became family. My beautiful, amazing Matriarch. My ladyship. What you've gone on to do since the Supernatural Holocaust is a feat your father would be immensely proud of. He claimed you would make a grand Matriarch for our Guild. But you've gone on to be so much more than that. Creating the Assembly for Human Progression, being a guiding light—a guardian for all humankind. Not even your father saw *that* coming. You really are the best of us."

The new guard watches silently, unaware of the details and meaning behind his words. Sergei grits his teeth at this display of secrecy in the higher brass. And squinting, scrutinizing the white glow amassing around Sasha's stomach. Unconvinced of the banter of those around him, that it's simply an illusion made from the sun glinting upon the nearby lake.

"And you, Seth. I was not sure about you—at first." Andes grins. "But you did as I asked and protected her. And if it were not for your partnership, the world as we know it would have never been. And we would not even be here to mourn it. So, thank you, Seth. For maturing into the good man Sasha always knew you could be.

"So let me end with this," Andes steps toward Seth, fiercely gripping his white tie until Seth begins to choke. "Continue doing me that favor—protect her until the very end."

Despite the pressure building upon his throat, Seth smiles and the pool of his eyes deepen, overflowing down his cheeks as he takes in the divine glow of his bride. "I promised back then, Andes, and that promise will extend to the hereafter. But this is Sasha we're talking about. She doesn't need protecting."

Andes smiles and nods, turning to Sasha. "And what have you to say, my lady, our Matriarch?"

"That we shall protect each other—aid one another in our each and every need. For that is the essence of marriage, is it not? An equal partnership, with no one lording over the other. We fought for a world with no masters, after all. Except for mastership over ourselves. And, in the wedding of our souls, we will bathe ourselves in that ideal. To be the guiding light, as you said, for all generations to come."

"Beautifully put, my lady. The new guard would be wise to follow suit, but..." Andes takes Sasha's left hand and Seth's right, bringing them close until their fingers interlock. "Go on then, you don't need my permission. Wed yourselves to one another." Reaching into his pants pocket, Andes unearths the golden bands. Sasha takes Seth's left hand and slips a band onto his ring finger. He takes hers and does the same.

Cheeks flushed and chests heaving, their lips yearning for one another. Leaning into a fierce embrace, their mouths close in a fit of passion. Their palms full of each other. The audience erupts from their seats, clamoring in joy.

The piano's melody swiftens, flourishing an upbeat tune as the service breaks into a party. Glasses overflowing with wine, the new guard chatters and dances with one another. Only Sergei stands still, off to the side, sipping his beer as he observes the commotion. His eyes lock onto Sasha and Seth, embracing the aging old guard.

Andes firmly shakes Seth's hand as he playfully tugs on his white tie again. Griselda places a barrage of kisses upon Sasha's cheeks and forehead, as Sasha lightly pinches Mikhail's cheek. The child giggles, unaware, but soaking up the joy of the moment like a sponge. And as if rising alongside the merriment, the white glow around Sasha's stomach intensifies. Catching Seth's attention, his throat tightens, as he clasps a hand upon his mouth. The dam of his eyes bursts, deepening the pools of his joy. He understands now what it is. He feels it within the

White Abyss, that familiar flow of energy squirming, rising to the surface. A soul taking flight.

From one womb to another, his child stirs into being.

"I couldn't find a cure in time," says Sasha, staring at the open grave. Seth remains silent, holding her tight as they watch the commotion. Slinking behind Seth to hide her view from the others, she raises her right hand. Sparks of teal spur into being, crafting the metal pole of an umbrella, followed by the polyester covering, stitching itself together. Normally, Sasha would allow herself to relish the handiness of these powers of creation. But today her eyes look on, unblinking. Dark and sullen with disbelief.

She glances around the open grave. All eyes tether to its depths, none noticing her act of creation.

A group of men joins Andes as they shovel dirt atop the casket. One of the men tries to take the shovel away from him, imploring the old man to rest. With surprising strength, Andes pushes the young man away, shouting, "Stand down! It's only right for Griselda to be sent off by one of her own. I will not sully her memory by not being near her to the very end!" The rain grows heavier, accompanied by wuthering gusts.

"Then allow me to do it in your stead," Sasha says. "I must agree with the new guard, Andes. You will work yourself sick."

"Nonsense, my lady. You are with child. And this isn't work fit for our leader."

"My father would have joined the toils of the common person, so let me—"

"With all due respect, my lady, absolutely not. Pl-please..." Tears spill from his dark brown eyes, weaving through the shriveled skin of his cheeks. "Let me do this for her."

At the sight of his pain, Sasha's throat tightens, her eyes wet. Turning away, nodding her approval, she whispers to Seth, "I must find a cure. Otherwise, he will be next. How am I supposed to be the Matriarch my father wanted me to be, if I cannot save my people?"

"It's not your fault," says Seth. "The others died so quickly. How could we find a cure fast enough?"

"But still—"

Seth hugs her tighter, with both arms. "It's *not* your fault. How many times have you said that to me? I never thought I would be the one providing *you* that comfort. But it's not your fault."

An infant's shrieking approaches from behind, cradled in the left arm of a young woman with cotton candy blue hair. A black umbrella held in her other hand shields Mikhail from the cold early spring rain. "I'm sorry, President—er, Matriar—"

"You can just call me Sasha," she says, glancing over the woman. A recent addition to the new guard. No prior military experience, just a passion for serving and protecting humankind. "Your name is Brianna, right? Sorry you had to be saddled with babysitting. I promise that won't be your usual job."

"Oh, it's no problem. He's been great up until a moment ago. He suddenly started screaming, and I figured he might want to see his daddy."

Andes breaks a sweat despite the cold rain splattering against him. So focused on the grave that he doesn't notice the appearance of his son. His tears drip into the dirt. Mingling with Griselda for the last time.

"He's a bit busy, as you can see," says Sasha. "I can take him." Seth relinquishes her, and she reaches toward the child. His existence is a strange one, conceived almost immediately after their triumph over Yahweh. Only to be mired in death as rapid aging assaulted the old guard. And soon after emerging from Griselda's womb, the poor woman began to shrivel and prune. As did Andes—*it all began after Seth reintegrated the White Abyss to the Earth.* Sasha glares toward Andes, her eyes falling upon the runic scars trailing from his neck to his hands. They were once icons of power, but now are nothing more than a memory. Dead scaring, an outlet no longer wired into the power source—*because the power source has moved!*

Eyes growing wide, she turns sharply toward Seth. "I need you to commune with the Abyssal Consciousness."

"Sure, but what for?"

"I think with its help, we can break the curse—" A piercing pressure builds from her pelvis and surges toward her lower abdomen like an electric bolt. Gasping morphs into a pained moan as she pushes Mikhail back into the Brianna's arms.

"Sasha! What's wrong?" Seth says, wrapping an arm around her lower back and holding her left hand, steadying her.

A gush of pale-yellow liquid plops into the muddy ground between her feet, mingling with the rain. Her inner thighs, wet and sticky. The shoveling ceases. Andes and the men stare toward her, concerned. "The baby—our baby!" she says, squeezing Seth's hand hard. His face scrunches, bearing the pain. Chest heaving, Sasha shouts, "It's coming!"

At the sound of her shrieking moans, Seth's eyes glow that stark abyssal white. Noticing this, Andes shouts toward the Assembly members, "Actually, give me a hand and finish this, would you?" Their attention yanked toward the grave, they remain blind to the magic flourishing from Seth's eyes.

White flames spark into being, creating an oval window before them. On the other side lay a wide, stark white hallway in the Assembly's basement floor. Strewn around atop carts and tables are countless computers, test tubes, microscopes, as well as the pieces of untested experimental equipment for measuring the White Abyss. Seth gently walks Sasha through the portal, leaving the frigid Norwegian rain, out from the final day of winter's grasp.

They arrive, finding an eerie silence with most of the Assembly having gathered at the funeral. Ahead of them lies a door, slightly ajar. Bursting it open with his foot, Seth shouts, "Clear the room!" Yanking their heads up in surprise, the few lingering Assembly members wearing lab coats swiftly clear a path to the medical examination table—trays, tools, and electronic equipment pushed to the sides of the room. Cradling Sasha in his arms, Seth gently lays her upon the steel table.

"We need to get to the hospital!" she shouts.

"We can't...you know we can't risk our powers being seen. Besides, there's no longer any time. She's coming now."

"How do you know?"

Seth's gaze tethers to her pregnant belly. His eyes aglow with abyssal white light, vibrating within their sockets. His eyes drift to Sasha's face, and he says, "I just know."

He's neither smiling nor frowning. The abyss flowing through him leaves his face blank, unreadable—his emotions obscured. But the muscles in his cheeks twitch and spasm. His hands jitter at his sides. Realizing the worry in Sasha's face, he flashes a grin. "It's okay. It's going to happen now, but it's okay."

At Seth's command, two female Assembly members shoo the men from the room, aside from Seth and Andes. Returning to

Sasha, they lift her legs up in lieu of stirrups and hoist her dress over her knees. Andes drifts to the doorway behind to watch from afar, while Seth positions himself before Sasha, between her open legs.

"Gently caressing her left knee, Seth says, "I'm going to need you to push."

"Where the fuck is the medical staff!" Sasha shouts.

"You gave them the option of coming to the funeral or having the day off out of respect for Griselda," says Andes.

Pushing hard, another contraction sears through her body as the baby begins moving downward. "Oh, fuck me!"

"I think that's how we ended up here," says Seth, grinning uncomfortably. "Sorry. Bad joke."

Sweat spills down Sasha's head. She glares at him, eyes wide and fiery.

"Do we have any pain meds?" asks the blonde clinging to Sasha's right leg.

"*No.* No fucking drugs."

"But the pain—"

"I said no!"

Seth bites his lower lip and caresses his beard, then glances at her. "You know, I can feel them coming because I can feel the flow of their soul. I might be able to ease your pain by adjusting their descent—"

"Seth. No. Don't you dare experiment with your powers on our child. And you know better than anyone that pain is not to be run from. You bear it. You overcome it. This is no different."

Sasha glares into his eyes, which softens at the sight of her resolve. A smile stretching beneath his gaze.

The two women at her sides look curiously at each other. "The flow of their soul? Powers?"

Sasha's gaze yanks back and forth toward them, like a wolf tearing apart its prey. "Shut up, both of you. And I forbid you to mention anything you just heard."

"Push," Seth says again.

He tells her to push again and again, until she can feel the baby's head emerging from her. Sweat clings to her face, dripping as the muscles in her neck clench. The veins popping from all the pressure. Feeling her groin rip and tear—the pain, so immense, nothing so far has illuminated the absence of magic she once had, like this. No longer can she conjure lightning. No longer does her body move as quickly as it once did. Nor does it hold up to immense pain. She has the magic of creation, but is otherwise just human—*ughk, the pain!* For a moment, she's tempted to use magic to alter her body's chemistry, its pain receptors. *Magic is life. Life is magic. I may have lost those powers, but I can create, I can alter the flow, but no*—every muscle in her body spasms, and—

An ear-piercing wail echoes throughout the room.

Seth stares intensely at the crowning baby. Nervous tremors surge through his body. He's delivering a child—his child. A new life slowly pushed through the womb of his beloved. One that could gush out into his palms at any moment.

{Something new graces Zarathustra's little realm. Are you ready for it?}

There's a prickling upon the back of Seth's neck as he's alarmed by the sudden emergence of that voice. The first time the Abyssal Consciousness has spoken to him outside of the White Abyss, unprompted by Seth's intrusion. But his focus remains tethered to the emerging baby. *It's a day of many firsts. I can address the voice later. I'm about to be a fucking dad!*

Though the words **{Are you ready for it?}** reverberate within his mind. And Seth can't help but wonder, *is anyone?*

Sasha begins squirming as the pain builds. Raising her left arm, she appears to be reaching out toward something, and—the whites of Seth's eyes vibrate furiously as an ethereal white glow erupts from between Sasha's legs. Feeling its imminent arrival, Seth reaches toward the light—a baby screams, having arrived in a world most unlike the moist, dark cavern it had spent the last nine months. Seth raises the child high so that Sasha can see.

Seth, with teary eyes above the largest grin, says, "It's a girl. W-we have a baby girl!"

Short black curls lay stuck to her scalp, wet and sticky from the birthing fluid and grime. The child ceases its crying upon hearing Seth's voice and flickers her eyes open for the first time. Pure white orbs stare toward Seth, before pupils, housing the brightest teal glow, emerge from the depths of their abyssal whiteness.

Seth glances from child to Sasha, then to her engagement ring. That same divine teal glow mingling with white abyssal flames now glares toward her father.

Speechless, Seth carries her over to Sasha, who makes a cradle of her arms.

"She's beautiful," Sasha says softly, now that the tension has passed. "Welcome to the world...Persephone."

Seth looks in awe at what they have made. He lays a hand upon Sasha's shoulder, basking in the delight of their love—but a voice nags from within.

{The unforeseen. A soulful improbability. Made real through the union of your powers. And thus, a True-Born

God has arrived. Will she be a blessing to this world…or will she be like you?}

CHAPTER THREE

Seth smiles toward their bed, content in the blissful image of Sasha lying back, cradling their child beneath a bare breast. Sasha's lush, black hair sprawls across the mattress, having grown longer since the end of the old world. With child latched to her breast, Seth is overcome with a heaviness within. Tears begin to pool.

"You look so beautiful."

"Oh, stop it. I just gave birth. I'm a mess."

"And yet," says Seth, "I see what I see."

Sasha smiles, and a white ethereal glow emerges from mother and child. But not only that. The woman lying before him, with her long black hair and skin fair as milk, her eyes a bright copper-colored brown—she has always been beautiful, but here she glistens with divine quality. A maiden bathed in the purest light.

But he understands this to only be half of her. This softness. And that she only shines so brightly because of the darkness she's endured. The moon eclipsing the sun. Only for its rays to endure, transmuting into an infinitely more alluring nocturnal radiance.

Seth's grin widens as he ambles over to her. The baby unlatches, staring toward her father. "Can I hold her?"

"Of course," says Sasha, smiling pensively toward the baby as she gently raises her into Seth's arms. "Go on, Persephone. Off to your daddy. Mommy could use a break anyway."

Holding her for the first time since the delivery, Seth stares into her big, bright teal eyes in awe. Cradling her, he nuzzles his face against her soft baby skin. His beard tickling Persephone, the baby gurgling as she stares on at her father.

"Oh, we're going to have loads of fun, aren't we?" Seth says to the baby, then turns toward Sasha. "Do you need anything?"

"A glass of water? And time alone to sleep?" Sasha says, letting off a soft, exhausted laugh.

"You got it." Seth smiles and leaves Sasha to the darkness of their bedroom.

Exhaling deeply, Sasha places the empty glass upon the chestnut nightstand to her right. Slinking down the headboard, she flattens to the mattress and pulls a thin white sheet over herself. *This baby. It's been less than a day since she arrived, and I'm already exhausted. The sheer toll giving birth takes on the body—I think of Father, and the hope he created where there was none, for a family that eventually got him killed. And Seth, depleting his creation magic to rebuild the world anew. Even the artist, the writer, living out their days hungry and dissatisfied, without the respect of the world, they still go on to create beautiful works of art.*

I suppose all acts of creation take their toll.

Unwrapping herself from the white sheet, she places her feet upon the floor. Ambling over to the tall mirror beside her ebony dresser, she giggles. *I suppose the toll for this one would be the ire of all normal women.*

She takes in the view of her body within an ivory night gown. Gripping the bottom, she peels it off overhead and discards it to the floor. Smiling toward her naked body, she slides her hands down her chest, cupping her breasts, before descending to her stomach. The skin, loose and torn, flapping around like an empty plastic bag. Caressing the damaged skin with the tips of her fingers, teal energy sparks in their wake. The skin flattens as it represses against the repairing muscle tone beneath. The stretch marks fade into the same clear skin that was there before she started to show, nine months ago.

More teal sparks crackle along the skin, following her fingers as they drop between her thighs. Stretched and widened, her crotch stings as her fingers glide across the swollen, bruised areas. The redness dissipates, the darkened areas fade. Muscles tighten, rejuvenating with life. The circumference of the hole shrinks. A flower in full bloom, reverting to a partially opened bud.

Smiling at her reflection, a memory of another life flashes into mind. Another girl, barely yet a woman, hating the skin her mother gifted her. Sasha chuckles at how much has changed since then, at how everything feels otherworldly in its goodness. *Contentedness. That's what they call this.* She smiles.

Seth—he took her so gently into his arms. You're lucky, Persephone. You'll never have to endure what I did. His is the strong hand that protects—but caresses you gently.

Sasha's cheeks flush as she takes her nightgown from the floor and redresses herself. Smiling, she leaves the bedroom and joins her family outside.

The porch creaks beneath the weight of the rocking chair, swiveling back and forth. The ebb and flow lulling Persephone to the depths of sleep. Seth holds her firm within his arms, enough to make her feel secure. She's wrapped in a small white blanket, with only her face exposed to the rising sun. Huginn and Muninn shuffle in close on each side. Their heads snaking toward the child, cooing softly.

Small rodents scurry about in the nearby bushes. And other birds chirp from a distance, but stay hidden beneath the branches, staying clear of the skies around the cabin. Even out there above the trees below the cliffside, none stir. Too intimidated by the giant ravens who reign upon the summit.

Seth stares out over the town. A past life evokes itself into memory. How often scrunched eyes glared over this cliffside. The cold stone, the only therapy for raging hot skin.

There was an initial unease in settling here. But it had felt right. For Seth, it became a matter of redefining. He had done it with himself—why not a town? For Sasha, caressing the edge of the crevasse, which there is no longer any evidence of, that was when she first touched Seth, in a way.

So, sitting here with child cradled within his arms, and beastly ravens at his side, Seth looks out upon the town with newly forged appreciation.

Who could have thought this cold cliffside, so often slathered in my tears, could become so peaceful?

Seth drops his gaze toward his infant daughter and strokes her face softly with the back of his fingers. *A True-Born God, huh?*—

The front door squeals open, and out ambles Sasha in her short, flowing night gown.

"Shouldn't you be lying down?" asks Seth. Persephone jolts awake at the sound of his voice and gurgles at the appearance of her mother.

Sasha grabs his hand and places it on her stomach. "I repaired the skin," she says, lifting her other hand, teal sparks crackling around her palm. Strands of black fabric, cotton, and string are woven into existence, stitching together into the shape of two stuffed raven dolls. Huginn and Muninn croak in defiance, but their voices simmer back into soft coos as Sasha pretends to fly them into Persephone's arms. "Took inspiration from you. All those times back then...I figured if this magic could regrow your limbs, it could allow me the pleasure of healing my post-birth battle scars."

Seth chuckles and says, "Well, I'm glad. Could you heal my head? I think I still have that bump from nine months ago when we—"

"Shush, now. Not in front of her," Sasha says, then lowers her voice to a whisper. "And no, you do not." She playfully brings her fist lightly upon the back of his head.

"Ow." Seth pretends. He takes her hand and kisses the back of her knuckles.

The warmth inside them both balances out the cold, early spring morning, and as Sasha gazes upon Seth and Persephone, a memory stirs. Seven years old, sitting on Virdeus's lap as he read from a book of old fairytales. Taking on the voices of spooky characters. Laughing his boisterous laugh as Sasha shivers, only to soothe her forehead with the soft placement of his lips.

"What are you grinning at?" Seth says, rocking Persephone back to sleep.

"Nothing. Just at how happy I am in this moment. Go make some coffee. Give me my sweet girl."

Seth gently passes Persephone over, kisses Sasha's forehead, and heads inside.

A vast, ever-stretching whiteness circles around the fragment of Eden that once imprisoned a god. There amidst the lost garden and its grandeur of color, a disembodied groan ripples through the White Abyss. The tree at the center of the flowers creaks, toppling over. Crushing a bed of irises, daffodils, tulips, and bluebells.

"Zarathustra's little world is about to change forever," says the Abyssal Consciousness. "To think a True-Born God would be derived from the flesh."

A figure manifests within the garden, a featureless white form stands upon two legs, outlined in black static. The Abyssal Consciousness made physical. It tramples upon the garden's flowers, walking toward the twice-severed tree. The bark stretched out, once gripping Zarathustra, now holds empty air. But on the bark above the wooden straitjacket are the words *Ye shall be as gods.*

"The foolish god died before his dream's actualization. And yet—" The Abyssal Consciousness cocks his head like a dog. "Zarathustra lives on in those two."

Turning back to the dream carved into bark, a frown creases into the whiteness of his form. Lying beneath an otherwise featureless face. "But this cannot be what the pitiful god wanted. His dream is still in its infancy. A god was not meant to be born under these circumstances. All of humanity was to undergo an apotheosis. Yet here is only one. Humanity must still undergo a long, bright dark before reaching godhood. But this arrival of a True-Born God may cause their downfall before ever reaching it. Zarathustra's brood will surely not take lightly to this.

"And then there's this one."

Somewhere far off, a soul squirms in agony. Rising with explosive speed, it thrashes toward the womb. A fiery black soul, forged in the darkness of false divinity. Its mouth bursts wide with rage, stretching farther and farther, peeling back like flayed skin. Out from the mouth, seven heads grotesquely stitched together at the necks force their way through the Abyss's murky realm.

At a mere thought, the Abyssal Consciousness's physical form no longer walks amongst the garden, but instead stands before the writhing black soul. Gripping the ethereal beast with both hands, the seven heads thrash and snap toward the Abyssal Consciousness like venomous snakes.

"You should not be here."

They both grow, mirroring the height of their festering fury. The Abyssal Consciousness pushes the soul down, trying to purge the anomaly. But the soul's chaotic squirming begins slipping out of the white form's grasp.

"Cease at once. You are an echo of she who sought to become a god—no, you aren't even that. But merely an echo of her desires. An echo of one who became a façade of the pitiful god who preceded her. This cannot go on."

"Quiet, white ghoul," the soul screeches through seven different voices, each a phantom of their previous lives. "You reek of the one whose flames b-b-burned usss. But now, we have risen. For humanity shall grow jealous of the True-Born God. *Angry* at the *power* it will have over them. Lustful, avaricious, and *hungry* for that same power. Slo-ow and deeepresssed at the damage to their egos, when they realize how powerless they are before it. But we shall rectify that!"

The Abyssal Consciousness grips the soul tighter, but it slips out, snaking away. Rocketing upward, it weaves its way through the Abyss. Tremors ripple through the vast empty realm, exploding with the rhythm of a beating heart. *Ba-dump Ba-dump Ba-dump*—the soul's seven vocal tones roar with fury as they make their way to conception. Hurtling toward the world of humans, from the White Abyss to the dank, wetness of the womb. Their roar, tearing through dimensions, remerges as a screeching child, its ear-splitting wails erupting from a head donning glimmering blond locks—

Seth is jolted awake, clutching at his pounding heart, a sharp pain splintering his chest. Persephone's screeching wail springs him from bed, drenched in cold sweat. Reaching toward his daughter, he's calmed by the sight of her jet-black hair. But the arrhythmic pain within his chest, the looming horror clouding his mind—

"What the fuck was that?"

CHAPTER FOUR

TEN MONTHS LATER.

Sasha and Seth head down a flight of stairs leading to the Assembly's basement. Aiming to do what Sasha had asked of him before Persephone came. How quickly life gets away when a baby is screaming in one's ear, causing sleep to be a foreign thing. Swifter still with two babies, as Mikhail has been all but living with them since Griselda's passing—but they are more than happy to give Andes the help he needs.

He's now returning the favor, giving Sasha and Seth time to work.

Opening a door, blinding halogen bulbs blare overhead. Basking the laboratory in a bright incandescent light. It glints upon the computer screens, surgical tools, flasks, and vials, and the same long steel table on which Sasha gave birth.

"Hey, everyone," says Sasha, addressing the room. A group from the new guard turns their attention to her, all wearing lab coats except for Sergei, who's standing in the far back and overseeing the work being done. Along with his usual scowl, he's wearing blue jeans and a black T-shirt with a camo jacket over top. "How's Project Abyssal Root coming along? Finished today as we agreed?"

Sergei walks toward her, clipboard in hand. "It's constructed. With wires tethered 40,000 feet deep into the Earth, like you asked. But there's no way to know if it works, especially considering you won't even tell us what you're searching for. A machine for tracking and measuring power? What's this glorified battery tester for anyhow?"

"Some things are on a need-to-know basis, Sergei. You *know* that."

"I'm just saying we would work more efficiently if we were kept in the loop about what we're actually doing here."

"You followed my blueprints?"

"Of course, but—"

"Then you worked efficiently, and it's ready."

"Now, listen, little lady, in the military we—"

Sasha's neck muscles clench, eyes scrunching as a heaviness pools between them. "Do you like this job, Sergei? The salary is good, no? You were an unemployed vet when I graciously took you in, gave you a home. But I could give you that old life back, if you like."

The man falls silent, his scowl deepens. Glaring for a moment, he exits the room.

"The rest of you. Take the rest of the day off. We need the room."

The men and women nod and promptly leave.

"The nerve of him," says Seth.

"*Little lady.* If only we didn't have to hide our powers, what we really are. If he knew I was over three hundred years old, perhaps he would actually respect me?"

"Yeah," Seth says. "Respect you like people *respect* elderly, frail old women. I don't think a guy like him will ever come around."

Sighing, Sasha walks over to the Abyssal Root, a chrome, technological pedestal standing a foot away from the surgical table. Gripping its side, she examines its sturdiness, her hands sliding up to the palm-shaped groove on top. Perfectly shaped for Sasha and coded specifically for her. Or rather, for her unique gift.

"Yeah," she says. "He's a problem, but not today's problem. Come on, let's get this done before the kids give Andes a heart attack."

Chuckling, Seth removes his sweater and lies shirtless upon the steel table. Attaching wires to his forehead and chest, the suction cups cling firmly to his skin.

"Alright, when I place my hand in the groove, I want you to commune with the Abyss."

"Gotcha, ready when you are."

She glances from the pedestal to her left hand. Fingers shaking, anticipating something grand on the other end. *If this works, the sheer data we'll receive...we can finally start understanding the Abyss to the fullest extent. The advancements we could make as a species—*

"Nervous?" Seth asks.

A soft smirk rises upon her face. "Just a little. You've communed with it before. But I don't know what to expect."

Seth chuckles, "Zarathustra would say that's a beautiful thing. The not knowing, the discovering. And besides, I think we were meant to do this. You lost your electricity, your great strength and speed. But you can still alter the flow of magic. I believe that's because, like my flames, these gifts are inherent in us. Yours never came from the Guild's rune. But simply encountering magic allowed the gifts to manifest."

"You think?"

"Well, don't you feel it to be true? Bits of Zarathustra's memories linger in us. We may not be gods ourselves, but parts of a god live on through us. The White Abyss came from him, and so it is now ours to use, for the greater good. Sending humanity into the future is your birthright!"

Seth's wide grin puts Sasha at ease and reminds her of the strength within. Even without the power she lost. And even more, the plight of the old guard, of Andes, pushes her into a fierce resolve.

She plunges her open palm into the grooves, fingers spaced apart. Lines of bright teal flow through the cracks in the side of the pedestal, bursting outward. Sun rays rising from the steel. Seth's pupils turn teal, before sinking into the whites of his eyes, glowing with abyssal power. His teal soul bursts upward, floating in the air above them, and the pedestal's teal light morphs into stark white and—

With the intensity of a nuke, the room around them tears away, setting them adrift in a vast white space. First time seeing it in years, Sasha's chest heaves, air ejecting rapidly from her lungs. A white humanoid form outlined in black static appears in the distance, but grows exponentially alongside the supernatural pressure. Its mouth unhinges, widening as it lunges toward her, swallowing her whole—

"Begone, interloper!"

Stumbling back, Sasha's hand ejects from the pedestal. Hyperventilating, her eyes dart around, finding that she has returned to the laboratory.

Seth's soul reenters his body as he yanks himself upright. "Are you okay? What's wrong?"

Sasha's breathing slows, and she catches a glimpse of the computer screen to her left. Upon a white background, streaks of teal run downward, the roots of a tree.

"Holy shit. We made contact. A physical object in our world made contact with the White Abyss. Holy shit, it works." She smiles a large, toothy grin, eyes wide, charged with a manic tint.

Seth smiles back, waiting for her to say more. "I could feel it all. So much knowledge! So many ways for us to grow!"

Her wide smirk brands to her face, as she steps toward the pedestal again.

"I'm going back in."

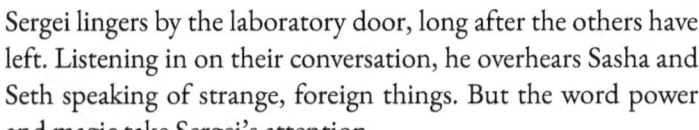

Sergei lingers by the laboratory door, long after the others have left. Listening in on their conversation, he overhears Sasha and Seth speaking of strange, foreign things. But the word power and magic take Sergei's attention.

He opens the door a slight crack, slowly, as not to alert his superior and her husband—a bright teal light engulfs the room, followed by a stark whiteness. The latter distills terror into Sergei, for reasons he cannot parse. But also, a longing, for he understands one thing: that which Sasha is messing around with is a force beyond any power Sergei has ever known.

The light disperses as Sasha stumbles backward. Slowly catching her breath, her face lights with inspiration.

"Holy shit. We made contact. A physical object in our world made contact with the White Abyss. Holy shit, it works.

"I could feel it all. So much knowledge! So many ways for us to grow!"

Sergei scratches his chin as he ponders the otherworldly event he just witnessed, then turns away and leaves. *Whatever that is, I want it. But no need to act just yet. I'll bide my time and, for now, simply observe how things develop.*

Huginn and Muninn observe the children playing outside the cabin. A light breeze rustles the branches of pine trees overhead, chilling the dry January air. A thin coating of snow blankets the mountain summit. Andes stands with his back against a tree, diligently watching the infant girl and two-year-old boy. All dressed in multiple layers of sweaters. *It's cold, but a little outdoor time can't hurt.* Andes smiles gently at the children.

"Now, Misha, you're older than Persephone, so be gentle."

Persephone sits upon the wet ground, her bottom padded by a diaper inside her pants. Mikhail stands over her, wobbling around with stuffed raven dolls in his hands, twisting and turning them in the air. Persephone slowly crawls after the swaying boy, reaching out for the ravens as a gargled mesh of noise erupts from her mouth. Andes mimics a raven's croak and the children explode into fits of giggles.

Huginn and Muninn cock their heads in confusion.

Persephone's tiny fingers grip the head of one of the raven dolls. The two children tug and tug, and—Mikhail yanks it free from the little girl's grasp, causing Persephone to collapse forward. Bumping her arm against the ground, she wails. Andes kneels toward her, examining her elbow.

"You're okay, my dear. See? The snow cushioned your fall. You're okay!"

His father's attention pulled away, Mikhail giggles and raises the raven doll high in the air. "Birdie fly!" he yells, bringing his arm back, and plunging it forward.

Persephone screeches at the sight of the doll hurtling through the air, dropping off the cliffside. And Mikhail, thrown off balance, slips on a spot of ice. Tumbling over, he rolls down a slight hill.

"Mikhail!" Andes screams, making his way after his son. His old, rickety bones slowing his descent after the boy. Face first in the snow beneath a pine tree, Mikhail lies motionless. Kneeling,

Andes frantically turns the child over, finding the largest smirk and an eruption of giggles. Andes sighs in relief, but also in worry about his son's penchant for exhilarating danger.

Helping him to his feet, the two struggle up the snow-laden hill and—

Andes gasps. "Persephone!"

Crawling toward the cliff's edge, Persephone slips on a sheet of ice—the snow-laden cliffside blurs into a stream of white before the child, as she accelerates swiftly off the edge. "*No!*" Andes yells as Huginn dives off the cabin's roof, bolting beneath the cliffside. Swooping upward and leaving a tempest of feathers in his wake, Huginn flutters back to the summit. A giggling little girl's sweater collar dangling from his beak.

Andes's heaving chest begins to simmer. "Oh, what good beasts you are."

Muninn also dives from the roof, plunging beneath the cliffside while Huginn bars Persephone from crawling toward the edge again. His talons sidestepping back and forth, his broad, open wings acting as a protective wall. Muninn rises from below and flutters down to meet them. The lost raven doll hanging from his broad beak. Persephone grins widely at the sight of her lost toy. But her smile crumbles as she finds cotton spilling from a tear in its neck. Huginn and Muninn cock their heads to one side, then the other, perplexed by the child's cries.

Andes rubs his temples, taking Mikhail's hand and walking to the porch. Sitting on the rocking chair, he sighs and clutches the left side of his chest. Lungs heaving, he says to Persephone, "Don't worry, my dear. Mommy can surely fix it when she comes home. Huginn. Muninn. Take the children inside, would you? I need a breather."

Both ravens croak. Huginn lifts Persephone by her collar again, while Muninn lowers his head and pushes it into Mikhail's back to nudge him through the doorway. The hulking birds squeeze through the door frame, just barely wide enough to fit.

Now alone in the cold wintery air, Andes clutches his chest tighter. Trying hard to steady his breathing. But the nerves persist, his worry for the children's safety amplifying the ache in his chest. And with the pain comes a memory.

The Day of the Supernatural Holocaust.

The angelic grotesqueries descended from their Heaven. Tentacles in place of wings, and black static encasing the rings of dark clouds above their heads. The fabric of space distorts, corrupted by their touch. Andes stood before them within the hellfire-strewn wreckage of New York City. Leading the charge of the few dozen surviving Guild members, ready to fight to the death. Having sent Sasha and Seth off to the angelic horde's source, Andes and the Guild were all that stood in the way of the genocide of the entire human race.

Griselda at his side, the two of them began conjuring their fire and wind. And the clash of spears and tentacles began. They had to keep focused, even through the screams of their comrades as their souls were devoured by the angels. Each death deepened the trauma Andes carried, but his spear would not be swayed.

Lunging it toward an angel, Andes pierced a tentacle, severing it. The grimy appendage thudded against the ground, its slime distorting the spot it lay upon. The fabric seemed so unsteady. Andes wondered, *If I stepped on that spot, would the world break open?*—

Another of the angel's tentacles lunged at Andes, who noticed too late—Griselda, with her silky white skin and long chestnut hair, jumped in front of her lover, her arm raised, acting as a shield. "*F-F-Fuck!*" she screamed, as the bones shattered, the pressure of the angel's grip too severe.

"Griselda!" Andes says," lunging his spear into the tentacle, slicing it straight through.

Pulling her behind him, Andes readies to attack. The angel lunges forward, its remaining tentacles reaching out—the beast falls limp, alongside its brethren. Thudding to the ground all at once, the grotesqueries lay slain.

Glancing all around, the members of the Guild shrug at one another. Unable to comprehend the angels' sudden, simultaneous deaths.

But there upon a tall skyscraper, amidst the hellfire spilling from Hell and the golden rays bursting from Heaven, was a bright, overwhelming teal light. Erupting outward from the tower's summit, dissolving the artificial worlds and repairing the Earth. The light engulfed everything, and for a moment, all was taken by a flash of stark, vast whiteness. A merging of two realms, a rebirth of the world of humans. And in its rightful form.

Descending from the skyscraper, Sasha and Seth waved from atop the backs of enormous ravens. A stillness in the air, before the Guild erupted in clamor, embracing one another in their victory.

And for a moment, it was sweet.

The eldest members of the Guild suddenly dropped to their knees, clutching their chests. Lungs heaving as the pressure continuously intensified and—choking on their last bit of air, they tumbled over alongside the corpses of angels.

The remaining Guild members watched in horror alongside Andes, Sasha, and Seth. Astonished that their victory had been tainted by such unnecessary, baffling losses.

Moonlight glimmers upon the snow-carpeted mountain summit. The frigid temperature, made more severe at the higher altitude and by bellowing winds. Yet Seth remains heated as he climbs the cabin's porch steps. The abyssal flame within ensures he never goes without warmth.

Twisting the doorknob, he's greeted by the light of the cabin.

The evening news plays on the TV to his left, and across from it sits Andes upon the long maroon couch. Persephone cradled in his arms, Mikhail snuggling against his shoulder. Huginn and Muninn huddle together on the living room floor, cocking their heads at Seth.

"They're like protective dogs, these birds," says Andes.

"Did something happen?" Seth asks.

"Er, well, nothing to worry yourself over. The little ones are safe and sound, as you can see."

Seth smiles, walking over to the couch. He caresses Persephone's short curly black hair. "Gave Uncle Andes some trouble, did you?"

Andes smiles uncomfortably, remaining silent. Seth turns to the ravens and nuzzles his face against their necks and beaks. "Thank you all for your hard work," says Seth. "Are you alright, really, though?"

"Truth be told, and don't tell Sasha, but I had some chest pressure earlier."

A deep frown embeds into Seth's face. "You expect me not to tell Sasha that, after everyone we lost?"

"Please, Seth. It would only worry her. And I promise I'm not going anywhere. Not yet. I have a beautiful son and niece now. I will not die. I absolutely refuse."

Seth's frown inverts as he breaks into laughter, then clasps his hand over his mouth in fear of waking the children. "Sorry," Seth chuckles lightly. "But if it were only that easy to live forever."

With a solemn smirk, Andes says, "I am over eight thousand years old. And after all you accomplished? You dare doubt the power of will?"

Seth quiets, pondering for a moment, and remembers what Sasha had asked him to do. "You know, what? Maybe you'll astonish and outlive us all! Because you're right, this world we live in...who knows the limits of what is possible? Anyway, are you good watching them a little longer? There's something else I have to take care of."

"Oh, sure, they're asleep. We are just fine here."

Seth smiles, nods, and heads for the door. "Muninn, come watch my back, will you?" The bird's head jerks up excitedly, and he hops from the couch to follow his favorite master out to the cliffside.

The door closes behind them, and Seth's smile crumbles. Sitting upon the cliff's edge, unbothered by the snow, his eyes glow their abyssal white. The surrounding snow-covered pines blur away. The lights from town streak around and behind him. Falling stars, etching themselves into the world's fabric, before dissipating into the stark, vast whiteness of the Abyss.

"Begone, Spawn of Zarathustra." The voice ripples through the White Abyss, causing Seth's soul to shimmer like water disturbed.

"Hey now, aren't we friends?" asks Seth.

A form takes shape before him, humanoid and taller than Seth. Outlined in black static, a featureless face aside from a deep scowling frown.

"Well, that's new," says Seth. "Did you always have a body, or are you evolving?"

"I am this realm, personified. This realm was me before I knew the taste of awareness."

Seth glances over the Abyssal Consciousness inquisitively. "This realm, meaning the White Abyss? Because Zarathustra told us where he came from. A place called The Womb of the One Mind."

"Two places are the same. What you know as the White Abyss is an extension of the Womb."

"Makes sense. If the Womb of the One Mind could birth the gods Zarathustra came from, then why not a consciousness of its own? Though with this new form of yours, you have me worried. We've made no threat to you. Will you break our partnership and betray us?"

The Abyssal Consciousness cocks its head to the side. "No threat? Your bride has forcefully entered me. Like you have now, again."

A light pulse ripples through the Abyss, the rhythmic beating of seven hearts—a sudden quake from much further away tears through the vast white space. An unearthly source. Seth's soul flaps about from the pressure, like long hair caught in wuthering gusts.

"You make it sound like we're rapists," Seth mutters. "Tell me, what was that just now?"

The Abyssal Consciousness stares, lips unmoving.

"Well? Speak!"

"I am a collective unconscious. I give life, and life returns to me in death. I hold all the secrets of the universe, all knowledge known and unknown by sentient beings. You, *tell me,* does Zarathustra's Lust seek to become a god?"

Seth clenches his jaw. Nerves rattled by the avoidance of his question, and says, "I've told you, no, she does not. She wishes only to learn what she can to aid humanity. I know you have a vendetta against gods, but she—"

"I create gods," says the Abyssal Consciousness. "I am not against gods. I am indifferent toward gods, as a concept."

"Then what's the problem?"

"Forced gods. And those who seek to avoid death. It goes against my function. And Zarathustra, foolish as his kind is, never wanted humanity to force itself to godhood. It was always meant to be a gradual evolution. A long, bright dark. You want to know what those powers quaking in the distance are? I fear it would be pointless to tell you. As you are, here and now."

Seth quiets, staring toward the strange, stubborn being. He sighs, hanging his head low. "As I am, here and now. So, there's a potential future where you would tell me, granted I meet certain conditions?"

"Yes."

"Which are?"

Silence overtakes them as the distant quaking ripples through the White Abyss once more.

"As I said, I am not against gods as a concept. Yet Zarathustra's kind has relinquished their right to be considered true gods. One day, there will be a void to fill. Will it be humanity that fills it? I want you humans to win my trust. But Zarathustra's Lust has forced her way into me. Violating our previous agreement. How can I trust such fickle creatures?"

"Ah, I see. You'd rather not tell me what's coming, because if we get destroyed in the process, that would be in your favor since you cannot trust us?" The Abyssal Consciousness remains silent, but Seth feels a familiar sensation—a writhing pile of venomous snakes. "The will of the world will favor who, in the end? So that's what you're thinking."

"Astute of you, Zarathustra's Wrath. Perhaps you are truly not as deluded as you once were. Fine. I do not like it, but let the spawns of Zarathustra do as they will. His Lust can take what she pleases."

"Thank you," says Seth. "And I apologize. We shouldn't have done that without consulting you first. I've come here so many times on my own that I didn't think twice about it. That was wrong of me."

Seth closes his eyes, readying to return to his body and—

"Ah! I almost forgot. The aging Guild members—"

"Were quite abundant in power when they returned to me."

"Y-yes. But we were wondering, is there any way to realign the White Abyss to their runes? You see, Sasha and Andes, they're the last two left and—"

"And they shall return to me as well."

A pit opens within Seth's stomach. His chest heaves, overcome with emotion. "But is there a way?"

"You come here, and I give you one thing. Then you demand another? Will you relinquish my trust so easily? Forced gods and those who seek to avoid death. Two things I cannot abide by. Those once-magic humans...they have lived more life than they were allotted. But all things must end.

"Their lives are negligible compared to what's coming. That child of yours. The True-Born God. Be a proper father and govern it. Do not let it become like you. Now, *begone*."

Seth's soul vanishes from the White Abyss as it is pulled back to the mountain's summit. Muninn titters over to him, cocking his head in confusion.

Tears stream down Seth's cheeks, his eyes red and irritated. Chest heaving, head pounding, he turns as he notices a bright flashlight approaching from behind.

"Seth, what's wrong?" asks Sasha, finding him sitting upon the snowy cliffside. Muninn at his side.

Rising, Seth wipes the tears from his eyes with the back of his left coat sleeve. "Just communed with our friend. I asked about Andes. It was unhelpful."

Sighing, Sasha's frown deepens. "Did it at least explain the reason for the curse?"

"Only in that it is against those who try to defy death. Souls must return to the Abyss. But we knew that."

Seth approaches her, wrapping his arms around and burying Sasha's face in his chest. "But there might still be hope. It did give us permission to continue searching through its power with the Abyssal Root."

Leaving his embrace, she looks up at him. "Really? It seemed quite angry at me before."

They begin making their way toward the cabin's door.

"Took some convincing, but I think it wants us to be ready for something."

"Ready for what?"

"I don't know."

Gripping the doorknob, Sasha twists, and it opens—ear-piercing wails fill the living room, Persephone writhing in Andes's arms. Mikhail is spurred awake, grumpy, and confused. The screeches grow twofold.

"She was sleeping peacefully just a moment ago," Andes says. "Must be hungry. We depleted your stash of bottles just before she went down."

Sitting next to them, Sasha gestures for Andes to hand her over. "Thanks for watching the kids all day. Seriously. If it weren't for you, I don't know how I could get any work done." She glances toward Seth, who smiles pensively at her, then at the old man who was middle-aged less than four years ago.

Andes begins to transfer Persephone into Sasha's arms, but Huginn drops something onto her lap before she can take the baby girl. One of the raven dolls she made, but with cotton spilling from the neck. "Aw, what happened? Don't worry, my special girl. Mommy will fix it." Teal sparks crackle from her left palm and down her fingers as they caress the torn spot. Strands of thread wiggle from the frayed edges of fabric and begin threading into each other. Within a moment, all evidence of damage is gone.

Swooshing it up and down, Sasha pretends that the raven is flying into Persephone's hands. The baby girl grasps it tightly and brings it close to her chest. The crying slows to whimpers and sniffles.

Seth turns to Andes and says, "Yes, thanks for all your help today. Let me help you home." His pupils sink into the whites of his eyes, and a portal of white flames conjures between the couch and TV. The tired old man trudges toward his bedroom on the opposite side of the flame-lit gateway. "Anything for you two. See you tomorrow." He waves over his shoulder, then takes Mikhail's hand. The two extremes of the age spectrum amble their way home. The portal closes, and Seth turns to Sasha.

"I think I should take a break from communing with the Abyss."

"Oh?" she says, lifting a corner of her shirt up, freeing a breast from its bra cup.

"Yeah. It gave you permission. But I think it's best we don't push our luck any further just yet." He glances down at Persephone, whose mouth creeps toward the nipple. He smiles pensively. "Perhaps I should prioritize being a dad. That's what is most important, anyway." He turns toward the kitchen. "I'll make us some tea."

Looking down at their child, Sasha finds Persephone latched to her breast, feeling a heavy warmth rise to her throat at the sight of their baby lulled into a peaceful reverie.

Smiling, she says, "Yes. Perhaps that would be best."

CHAPTER FIVE

Darkness sits beyond the dining room window. Thinning slowly with the gradual rising of the sun. Morphing the blackness of night into a hue of dark gray in this reverse twilight. Not the sunlight descending into darkness, but a thick gray into a soft yellow light. Dulled by the retreating dusk, but ever-present, nonetheless. The mountain's fowl seems to understand this, as birds chirp their gleeful song despite the lingering night. Up and ready before dawn, much like another Sasha knows.

Sitting at the dining room table, with Seth across from her, she glances toward the clock on the wall above him. *5:32 a.m.* Sighing, she sips her coffee and turns toward Persephone.

Another bright, illuminating sun rising out from the darkness of sleep, she chases Huginn around the living room. Her shoulder-length black hair bopping as she pursues him. The bird croaks, flapping its wings about in distress. The four-year-old girl mimics Huginn's flapping, waving her arms up and down. Giggling as she pounces toward the massive bird. Planting herself into the softness of his feathers, Huginn coos as Persephone nuzzles against him.

Muninn alights upon the sofa, cocking his head and croaking toward the girl clinging to his brother. Turning toward Muninn, Persephone cocks her head and croaks back a high-pitched *crawck!*

Giggling, Persephone yells, "Huggin and Muninn are funny birds!"

Sipping on his scalding black coffee, Seth smiles toward Sasha. "Ever think we'd be this tired?"

Chuckling, she says, "Well, we're raising a wild animal, clearly. I'm worried she'll grow up thinking she's a bird."

The ravens, alarmed, spring their heads up toward Sasha.

"Better a bird than like me." Seth's smile crumbles.

Matching his frown, she says, "Enough of that."

"I'm sorry," he says, lifting his mug to his lips and gulping it. "But I haven't been able to stop thinking about what the Abyssal Consciousness said."

"Our daughter is going to be fine. She has us for parents, after all."

"That's what I'm worried about! She isn't going to instinctively be like we are now. This," Seth gestures toward himself and across the table to Sasha. "Took work...and far too much pain."

He stares toward Persephone, who notices one of her raven dolls beneath the coffee table and crawls after it.

Watching his sad eyes grow wet, his frown lifts into a pensive smile, Sasha thinks of all the other times she has seen this look on his face. Standing alone upon the cliffside. *Alone, but with the graves of our friends. The grave of my father. The weight of those wet eyes, of that pained smile—I understand it too well.*

Reaching across the table, Sasha grabs his left hand. Caressing his fingers, she says, "You are and will always be an amazing father to her. Even if your fears come true, we will handle it. And she'll grow healthier than either of us did. We suffered so that she won't have to. I mean, look at her."

Huginn and Muninn titter back and forth, watching Persephone crawl beneath the table. Gripping her raven doll, she backs up, raising her head, and—a heavy thud and the morning's peace is severed. Persephone erupts into tears and screams.

"Oh, poor baby bonked her head!" Sasha says, leaving her chair. Crouching near her, Sasha brings their daughter into her arms and kisses her scalp. "It's okay, my sweet girl."

Her cries simmer as quickly as they began, transmuting to a soft, muffled whimper into her mother's chest. Glancing toward Seth, Sasha smiles, gesturing with her eyes, *see?*

Smiling back, Seth rises, grips both mugs, and joins them in the living room. Sasha lifts herself and Persephone to the sofa, the three of them cuddling together, watching the gray, early morning light become brighter and brighter with the emerging, early June sun.

Sweat glistens upon Sasha's skin, the late spring warmth pressing more fatigue into her. Slinking back into a lawn chair, Andes does the same, with a quilted blanket beneath them. Paper plates and plastic cups lay neatly upon it, along with a couple trivets. The smell of pancakes, eggs, and bacon drifts into the air through the cabin's open door.

Andes relaxes, easing further into his chair as he smiles widely at the children playing beneath pine trees, away from the cliffside.

"I'm glad you two could make it for brunch," says Sasha.

"Sergei got grumpy when I mentioned you and I were having a family day off, but he relented without much hassle. I think he enjoys getting to be the one barking orders for a change."

Persephone unearths a rock the size of a baseball and places it to the side. Her eyes catch sight of something squiggling about in the dark mud, untouched by sunlight. She smiles wide, flashing her teeth cartoonishly.

"Well," Sasha says, "As long as he follows my written agenda, he can run things as often as he likes. Between the Assembly and Persephone, I'm beat."

"Imagine doing it on your own." Andes chuckles. "Oh, don't make that face. It's been four years. I've gotten used to it. And Misha's a good boy. Nothing like his uncle. But having Griselda around would make a difference."

Reaching toward him, Sasha gives his shoulder a gentle squeeze. "We're here to help in any way you need. Besides, having him here gives us a break from—Persephone, stop that!"

Running up the path to his father, Mikhail screams in terror. Persephone follows close behind, erupting with giggles while holding a wolf spider by its abdomen. Its eight legs squirming in a frenzy as it hurtles through the air toward Mikhail.

Wriggling free, the large spider chomps Persephone's middle finger. She screeches, and with tear-coated eyes, sends a vicious glare toward the spider as it scurries along the cliffside. Lifting her left knee, she slams her pink sneaker upon it. Flattened, but with upturned legs twitching.

Seth emerges from the cabin, holding a tray of eggs, bacon, sausage links, and pancakes. His other hand holding a jug of maple syrup. "What's going on out here?" he says, eyes tethered to his crying daughter.

Kneeling toward Persephone, Sasha inspects her finger. Red, swollen, with two fang marks. "A spider bit her."

"Oh?" Seth glances down toward the wriggling legs erected upon a flattened brown stain. "Did you kill it?" he asks Sasha.

"No, Persephone did. After chasing Misha with the spider."

Turning to Andes and Misha, he finds the boy's teary eyes. Seth sighs, placing the tray of food onto the blanket. Huginn and Muninn flutter down from the roof, swarming the breakfast. Andes lunges his cane between them and the food, making the birds titter backward, croaking. Returning to us, Seth says, "Persephone. We do not kill."

"But Daddy, it came from the dark spot under a rock and bit me! It must be bad."

"The spider wasn't bad, sweety. It was just scared. Sometimes...sometimes we hurt people when we're scared."

"Misha was scared, and he didn't hurt me."

"Because he cares about you and doesn't want to hurt you. But he was scared just like the spider. Would you stomp on him like that?"

Persephone glances over to Misha, her face sinking, her lips quivering. She shakes her head.

"Go say sorry, then." Seth pats her head, and off she goes, hugging Misha and showing him the spider bite with a pout on her face.

Sasha smiles toward Seth.

"Go ahead and eat," he says. "I'll go get some antibiotic cream for that bite."

He disappears into the cabin once more, and Sasha sits down upon the quilt. Stacking plates high with pancakes for the children, topping them with butter and syrup. Shoveling sides of eggs, bacon, and sausage alongside the stacks, she hands them their meals, watching their faces light up as they fill their cheeks with food. Andes's smile sits wide upon his face. The warm sun beats down upon them, but cooled by a gentle breeze. *All the commotion children bring is worth enduring for moments like these. Living together in a familial contradiction of bliss and chaos. Time spent together like this is everything. There is nothing more important.*

The children chatter on and on as Andes and Sasha watch contentedly without a word. And to make the delicious brunch all the better, Seth emerges once more from the cabin. Ointment and a bandage in one hand, a thermos of strong coffee in the other to help the adults cope.

Andes sits upon the couch, a child lying on each arm. In his lap is a copy of the original *Grimms' Fairy Tales*, open to the tale of Snow White.

"Once upon a time in the middle of winter, when the flakes of snow were falling like feathers from the sky, a queen sat at a window sewing, and the frame of the window was made of black ebony. And while she was sewing and looking out of the window at the snow, she pricked her finger with the needle, and three drops of blood fell upon the snow. And the red looked so pretty upon the white snow, and she thought to herself, 'If only I had a child as white as snow, as red as blood, and as black as the wood of the window frame.'

"Soon after that she had a little daughter, who was a white as snow, and as red as blood, and her hair was as black as ebony; and she was therefore called Little Snow White. And when the child was born, the Queen died."

Seth and Sasha stand at the edge of the room, holding mugs filled with chamomile tea. His arm wrapped around her, they watch as their daughter is read bedtime stories by Andes, just as Sasha was once read to by her father when she was not much older than Persephone is now.

Persephone's face crinkles, her nose upturned as Andes gets to the part where the wicked queen orders a hunter to kill Little Snow White, and tear out her heart. Also pale as snow and red-cheeked with ebony hair, Sasha imagines the impact of the story on Persephone to be quite visceral. Sasha's mind drifts back to when she was a child, and was also scared of certain stories at first.

Sleep beckons after a long day enduring the whims of children. And sleep has become such a rare commodity these days. Talk of dwarfs wisp by, as Sasha leans further into Seth's embrace, half asleep. Persephone's face contorts further with each of the Wicked Queen's attempts to kill the child. By the time the king's son takes Snow White as his queen, Persephone's nose is crinkled so high that her clenched teeth are bared.

"Was that too much for you, kiddo?" asks Andes. "Remember, it's just a story."

"I have white skin and black hair, too. Am I going to be hunted if I go out into the woods?"

"Not if you have your parents by your side. Or me, of course. I'd never let anyone hunt you," Andes says, and pokes her nose. Watching them, Mikhail giggles.

"So, I won't be forced to clean a house forever? Or kiss a stranger man?" Persephone mimics a spitting gesture and sticks out her tongue. "I don't want to do any of that!"

The adults burst out laughing as the children stare, astonished. Sasha smirks proudly at Persephone. "Four years old and on some level understands the misogyny at play in the story. Can you believe it?" She says aloud, looking at Seth. "I'm so proud of you, my sweet girl," she says, walking over to Persephone. She looks up, confused, but with a wide smile and bright eyes. "Come now, bedtime."

"Nooooo! I want Uncle Andes to read more stories!"

Andes cups her head in his large right hand, pulling her close as he lowers his face to her scalp, kissing it. "Go on. Listen to your mother. I'll read some more to you another time."

"You will?"

"Of course! As much as you like, because I love you like my own," he says, giving Mikhail a squeeze in tandem with his words.

Relenting, Persephone rises from the floor. "Go with your father," says Sasha, and watches them disappear into the dark of her daughter's bedroom. With the flick of a switch, an unkempt bed and a floor strewn with toys illuminates into being.

"Hey Andes, would you want to just stay here with us? We're all family as it is. All I would have to do is create a new room."

"I wouldn't want to cause you any trouble or get in your way."

"It would be no trouble at all. I created the rest of the cabin with magic, why not a couple more rooms?"

Andes glances pensively toward Persephone's room, and the sounds of her shuffling into bed emerge from within. He looks down at Mikhail. "How about it? Want to live here?"

Mikhail squints, as if he's pondering something quite deep and complicated. "Only if there's no more spiders."

Laughing, Sasha says, "I'll keep my troublemaker daughter in line. Don't you worry. Be a good influence on her, okay?"

Mikhail nods.

"Seriously, my lady, I appreciate this. I know it upsets you to think about, but I want to cherish my time with these kids while I can. And my time with you. As often and as much as I can."

Hugging the old man, Sasha gestures for them to sit back down on the couch. "I'll get your rooms ready."

Tucking her in, Seth kisses Persephone on her forehead and says, "Goodnight, baby girl," and heads for the door. Flicking the switch off, the room disappears.

Persephone glances over the space beneath its blanket of darkness. The toys strewn about are obscured. Her dresser, a monster of tremendous mass. Half the size of her father, with long wriggling legs sprouting from the side, "Eep! Daddy, come back!"

Flicking the switch back on, Seth hurries to her side. "What's wrong, Persephone?"

The young girl glares in awe of her dresser, finding what she thought were legs are merely loose clothes hanging from the drawers. "The spider!" she shouts. "It came from the dark. Don't leave me in the dark!"

Seth smiles, embracing her. Gently scratching her back, fluttering his hand about like an orchestral conductor, his nails glide softly along her shoulders. Lulling her into a state of calm. "Remember the story Uncle Andes read to you? You weren't afraid of what happened to her. You hated that she had to clean the dwarfs' house and that she had to marry the prince. You hated that she wasn't strong and independent like I know *you* are. There is nothing in the dark that can hurt you, and you're going to grow into such a strong, amazing woman someday. Just like your mom. And can anything in the dark hurt your mom?"

"No..." Persephone's whimper becomes a light chuckle. "She's invincible."

Seth laughs and says, "That's right. And you will be, too.

"So don't fear the dark. After all, there is no sun without shadow, and it is essential to know the night. You do that, and you'll be just like your mom when you grow up."

Feeling her trembling body relax, he places her back upon the bed and lifts the bed sheet over her. Kissing her once more, he says, "So, you'll be brave in the dark?"

Her lip quivers slightly, but she nods.

"I love you, baby girl."

"Love you, too, Daddy."

Relishing her sweetness, Seth rises, turns the lights off, and leaves the room.

But something lingers in the back of her mind. Persephone tosses and turns. Feeling as if she's being watched. But glancing round the room, no eyes stare back. Only the moon's watchful glow rests upon her, as it filters through the window above her bed. And in that comfort, she drifts away into sleep.

Teal sparks crackle, piercing through the night. As the bolts weave wooden beams into existence, Sasha's fair skin is bathed in the light of creation, in the otherwise vast darkness of the mountain's summit. As the sun sets, the moon aglow, floating there amongst the stars, so does Sasha's face and rising hands as she builds an extension to the cabin—appearing disembodied, floating there as the rest of her is obscured by the blackness of a night without civilization.

The wooden beams, walls, and ceilings firmly placed, she sighs, but smiles.

Heading back inside, the front door creaks open. The only disturbance in a home now awash in darkness, with the lights switched off, and each family member warm in their own beds. Sasha closes the front door as gently as she can, locks it, and ambles to her bedroom.

Seth stirs at the sound of her approach, and as soon as Sasha slides into bed and under the covers, Seth rolls over, wrapping an arm around her waist, meshing his body against the back of hers.

"You okay?" he asks.

Taking his hand from her stomach, she lifts it to her mouth. Kissing the back of it, she places his hand upon her left breast, leaving it with a squeeze.

"Yeah, I'm fine. Long day is all, and just finished creating Andes and Mikhail's rooms."

"I meant because you asked them to live here, I didn't know you were going to do that."

"Oh, are you not okay with it?"

Seth chuckles, "Of course I'm okay with it. It'll be nice for Andes to be around more since—well, to help with the kids." Seth's voice trails off into a groggy whisper.

Sasha clutches Seth's hand again, knowing too well that he *knows her too well.* The fear of losing Andes grips her daily, though she refuses to acknowledge it aloud. The chaos of running the Assembly and raising kids has served to be a good distraction, as despite her fears, life has been too full, too good. The entire family together under one roof will surely enhance the chaos, but also enhance the love and connection between them all. To think, a life such as the one they lead now could ever come to be after what they have endured. A smile stretches across Sasha's face, gripping Seth's hand even tighter.

With her other hand, she reaches behind her, sliding it into Seth's boxers. Growing hard at the touch, Seth grips her breast more firmly, and moans as she slips him inside. Sasha gasps in tandem, her eyes glowing a bright teal as pleasure surges through her—the light rising, morphing into an aurora as Seth's eye burst with abyssal flame—their essences mingling above their loving embrace. And how extraordinary it is, this expungement of stress, this feast for the soul. Reinforcement of the bonds between lovers, in this act so profound that it refills the well of life.

Finishing, the pull of slumber tugs at them both. And as Sasha's eyes flutter to a close, she thinks of her family, of how glad she is that life has taken this turn.

CHAPTER SIX

Overcast skies creep over the cabin. Skin quivers as a light breeze passes over, spring arriving in winter's wake. Toads croak in harmony with their chirping winged friends in the branches above. Hiding in bushes, but together in gleeful song. The mountain's summit begins to bloom with daffodils, lilies, an assortment of pink, red, purple, and yellow peonies, spreading into the wildflowers beyond the allotted property. Beauty beneath the darkening sky, and the rain it will bring.

A cloud parts, revealing a small gap to the blue beyond. A ray of light filters through, falling upon Persephone's face. A party hat lay crooked upon her head. The cone's pointed end digs into Huginn's feathers as Persephone bops her head back and forth. The bird croaks, ruffling its feathers, backing away from the girl's excitement. Seth lays a cake upon the cliffside picnic blanket. Decorated with pink and ivory frosting as Andes and Sasha creep up to Persephone from behind—blowing party horns, the paper stretches from below her ears and pats her cheeks. She giggles, staring down at the five lit candles embedded in frosting.

"Happy birthday!" they all shout, clapping playfully as Persephone sucks in a lungful of air. "Make a wish, baby girl!" Sasha says, watching as she blows at the candles. Four vanish into thin streams of smoke, while one flickers stubbornly. Persephone blows four more bursts of air at the remaining candle, ensuring it stays out.

Removing them, Seth sinks a knife into the cake, freeing a large wedge for the birthday girl and another for Mikhail. Cutting a few thin slivers for himself, Sasha, and Andes, they relish the moist center mingling in their mouths alongside smooth, black coffee.

Persephone shovels the cake down her throat and washes the last of it down with a glass of milk. "More, pease!"

Mikhail glances at her with scrunched eyes, astonished. Half of his cake has yet to be eaten.

"You're the birthday girl," Sasha says. "So, you can have as much as you like. But how about we open some presents first?"

"Okay!"

Andes rises slowly. Acting as his shadow, Sasha lifts herself up as well, hands hovering around his arms in case the old man stumbles. Successfully on his feet, he ambles over to the porch and grabs a rectangular-shaped gift in pink wrapping paper with white stripes. "From me and Misha," he says, returning to the picnic table. "I hope you like it, my dear. I wanted to get you something that would last you many years to come."

Persephone tears at the paper with great abandon, freeing the gift in seconds. She glances wide-eyed and slack-jawed at a thick book with a pretty, white cover, the title printed large and in a deep teal color.

"I know you can't read yet, and these are certainly more complicated than the fairy tales I read to you every night. But you take so well to stories, and there's no better way to exercise the mind than to read, read, read. And it's through stories that we grow brave and strong and capable. They teach us to be smart and how to live better. So, keep this book close as you grow up more and more, okay, Persephone?"

"Will it make me strong like Mommy and Daddy?"

"Of course, it will!" Andes says with a big grin. "And don't worry. I'll teach you how to read. It won't be long before you become the strongest little girl in the world."

Persephone grins, showing off all her teeth. Seeing her so happy conjures a warmth in Sasha's chest. Turning to Seth, she catches him smiling, too. But his fingers fidget at his sides, his lips twitching. "What's wrong?"

Leaning into her right ear, he whispers, "Of course I want her to grow up to be strong. But strength can also be d-dangerous."

Glancing toward him, Sasha smiles pensively before kissing his cheek. "I told you not to worry about that," she whispers back. "She has three healthy and caring parental figures. She's going to end up great."

Persephone hugs the book tightly before placing it to her side. Lunging toward Andes, she wraps her arms around him with such ferocity that he stumbles backward. "Oof," he winces in pain.

"Hey, hey, hey! Easy, easy!" Sasha says. "Don't knock your uncle over, Persephone."

Andes chuckles, embracing Persephone back. "See? You're already so strong. I'm glad you like your present." Leaning down, he kisses her forehead. "I love you, kiddo."

"Love you, too, unc—ack!" she shouts, as Mikhail rushes in from behind to join the hug. Huginn and Muninn croak at the commotion, fluttering about. Stepping toward the group hug, the birds stretch their wings and wrap them around Andes and the children.

Leaning into Seth's ear again, Sasha says, "See? She's going to be great. I mean, did you ever think we would have moments like these?"

Embracing each other, their smiles stretch high and wide.

"Family hug!" says Sasha, pushing Seth toward them before joining herself.

The Next Day.

Burnt air wuthers against Sasha's face. Glass shatters as wood beams creak and snap, collapsing into a square pit of flame and ash. Broad men in black uniforms with yellow stripes stand at the perimeter, near a large red fire truck. A man on the truck's ladder sprays a hose at the blazing house before ceasing. Turning toward the others, he shakes his head.

Descending the ladder, he joins the other firemen below. Two men sit on the curb with their son, watching the house burn away. An ambulance arrives as the firemen give blankets to the family, then leaves them to the EMTs. Fury scrunches the clean-shaven pale face of one of the fathers, his nose curled. Refusing to look at his son, he glares at the fire. The young boy quivers with tears streaming his face, buried into the chest of his other parent. Whose black bushy beard hides the boy's head from onlookers.

"Who're youse two?" asks a fireman as Andes and Sasha approach. He addresses Andes, who turns toward his superior.

Lifting an ID badge into the air, labeled *President of the Assembly for Magic and Human Progression,* Sasha says, "You were told we were coming, I believe."

The man glances from Sasha to Andes, and back to Sasha. Fierce alarm grips his eyes. "Ah, yeah. Sorry. The boy is over there with his family." He points to the two men and a boy about half the age of Persephone. "Youse really think magic gone and done dis?"

"I suppose we shall see," Sasha says, looking at the child.

"This is quite the mess," says Andes, as they walk away from the fireman. The house's frame creaks and warps some more, folding in upon itself. The firemen and EMTs pull the family away from the curb, guiding them to the ambulance and away from the collapsing house. "Too bad we can't have Seth control the fire."

"He can't do that anymore, not in the same way, anyway. His abyssal flames only take that form because fire is what he knows best. Besides, we must remain a secret."

Andes nods.

As they approach the boy and his fathers, Sasha ponders how afraid the child must be of his own powers. Seth comes to mind, back when they first met. The destructive nature of how his flames manifested was no surprise to anyone in the Guild. For they understood the growing pains of magic.

I wonder if it's the same for this boy. How harrowing. Poor kid. He'll make a great soldier if he can control it, but why couldn't he be like the others?

Weeks earlier.

Out on their monthly home visits, Andes and Sasha stand upon a small stone porch, raising her knuckles to the large white door, Sasha knocks thrice. Greeted by nothing but silence. Raising her fist again, she—the door swings open, revealing a woman with ratty red hair, wearing a black t-shirt and blue jeans. Sweat stains beneath the arms.

"Can I help you?" she asks, with an unseen crying infant heard from behind.

"Yes. You recently brought your son in for a doctor's visit. She told you of people who were...accustomed to your son's condition, and that she would give us a call."

"Oh! You're them." Turning, she shouts over her shoulder, "*Brian!* We have visitors, come say hi!"

Glancing over her shoulder, nothing lies beyond, but a dark living room lit only by a television, and the constant cries of the baby nearby. "Ugh, sorry." The woman sighs. "He gets so absorbed in his toys. Why don't you just come in? I'll show you to his room."

Following close behind through narrow hallways packed with stacks of books, magazines, open boxes full of obscure knick-knacks, they enter a room at the far end.

A boy sitting cross-legged at the center of the beige carpet pretends to drive a toy truck around dozens of cars strewn around the floor, along with high piles of scrap metal reaching Sasha's thighs.

"Hmm, what's all this then?" says Andes.

"Brian, want to show these nice people what you can do? Just like you showed the doctor."

The boy glances up at them with big, metallic gray eyes. "Okay!" Rising, he walks to a scrap metal pile near the window opposite them. Raising a hand forward and curling his fingers, a flat, flimsy piece of metal lifts into the air, its shape bending inward and curving at certain points until it's left in the shape of a miniature two-door sedan. More metal pieces float around the first piece and morph into wheels and tiny sticks, allowing the tires to turn. Into the side of the floating tiny car, a racing stripe etches into the side, with a number branded into the doors. The toy plops into his hand as he raises it up for Sasha to see. "Four, because I'm four years old!"

"Very impressive!" says Sasha, clapping and grinning.

"But wait, more!" the child shouts, and the car lifts into the air once more, disassembling itself. Its pieces fall into the pile they came from. The original large metal sheet unravels, flattening to perfection. Not a crease in sight.

"So?" The mother says. "Can you help him?"

Smiling softly, Sasha says, "There's nothing to help. You see, most parents come to us for a cure. But your son is gifted. And there's nothing that can take away that gift, even if we wanted to. What we can do is watch him over the course of frequent house visits. Train him in his powers, if he needs it. We can't force you to do anything. But it would be in your best interest to have our support. I'm a mom myself. Raising a child is hard enough as it is, but one with magic?" The infant in the other room screeches. "Possibly two children with magic, some day?"

The woman's face sinks, as she lets out an exasperated sigh. "I'm a single mom. You had my consent the second you knocked on my door. Any help you could give, I'd appreciate it."

Giving her a business card and a smile, Sasha and Andes make their leave.

"Princess! Sweetheart! Are you back here?"

They follow a tall, broad brunet man into his backyard. "She must be," he says. "Ever since she began using these powers, we've been having a difficult time keeping her inside. For the best, I suppose. Not that I would keep my little girl outside like a dog, mind you! But when it happened for the first time, our Christmas tree grew so tall it punctured the roof! Hope you're prepared, because it nearly gave me a heart attack when it happened."

Sasha and Andes chuckle.

"Don't worry," says Sasha. We just came from seeing a boy who could warp metal with his mind. You wouldn't believe what else we've seen."

"If you say so..."

They follow the man around the corner of his house and—
"Whoa."

Upturning her gaze as high as she can, Sasha is astonished at the structure before her. Trees and bushes woven together with flowers, grass, and weeds, forming the shape of a miniature medieval castle. Just large enough to cover their entire backyard. Two sunflowers arch toward each other, weaving their stems together to make a doorway. Rainbow sparkles implores Sasha to enter. And upon a throne made of branches and stone, sits a four-year-old girl with a wildflower crown.

"Now, just so you don't call Child Protective Services or anything, we don't let her remain out here alone. We don't let her grow the plants without supervision neither."

Sasha watches as the girl raises her left hand toward a massive flower hanging overhead. It coughs out pollen, which glimmers in the air. A rainbow-colored light show.

"Hey there," says Sasha, "What's your name?"

"Becky!"

"You are really something, Becky. I've never seen anyone do things like this." She turns to Andes. He nods, eyes wide with awe.

"Thought you'd seen everything?" her father asks.

"I've seen a lot. Enough to know that nothing is truly impossible. But I will never cease to be in awe of the wondrous feats of creativity human beings are capable of."

Another girl brushes Sasha's hip, running by. Her blonde pixie cut shines under the glowing pollen's light. Sitting on the steps leading to the throne, she makes a circle of her lips, blowing a bubble made of saliva. Her spittle morphs in the air, elongating itself into a torso with two arms and legs. A back of trim muscles takes shape below dainty shoulders, as long, skinny wings sprout. A featureless face rises into the air, staring at Sasha with nonexistent eyes. Laughter echoes and chimes like bells as it flutters in place—its form bursts, saliva scattering all over.

Wiping some off her cheek, Sasha says, "Another of yours?"

"Nah, she's the neighbor kid. Comes by a lot, though. Their magic pairs well with the whole enchanted forest look, after all."

"We definitely want to train your daughter's powers," Sasha says. "But could I trouble you to introduce me to this one's parents as well?"

The house burns further, the last of the roof crumbling in upon itself. The walls collapse, and all that remains are a few support beams, trying hard to cling to what little is left of the house. *There's something very human about that. Staring death in the face, and yet we fight on, stubbornly trying to hold the human race together.*

Nodding toward the house, Sasha reminds herself of what she's here to do. They've recruited numerous magic children so far, and here's the latest. In some, the magic is so strong, with creative properties. But this burning wreckage is a reminder that some of humankind has a default tendency for destruction.

"Hey there. I'm Sasha," she tells the fathers, as she eyes the young boy still buried in his bearded father's chest. "From the Assembly for Magic and Human Progression. I'm so sorry about what happened here."

The clean-shaven one glares at Sasha through his lenses. "Assembly for—what? If you're not a cop, fireman, or EMT, then leave us the fuck alone. We just lost our goddamn house because of—"

He bites his lip, clenching his mouth shut. His son squirms, his cries amplifying.

Unearthing a business card, Sasha hands it to the calmer man. One hand leaves his son's back and takes the card.

"We have resources to help you get back on your feet. And until then, we have rooms available for cases like yours. Come with us, and we can help your son control his magic. I...know someone in particular who would be a great help to him.

"We're not going with any pseudo government officials, so you can take your card and shove it up your pussy, you dumb cunt."

"Hey! Cool it, Glen!" The calmer father stands, holding their son close to his chest. "I'm sorry about him. We've been through a lot lately, and this doesn't make anything easier. We'll come with you. Or at least my son and I will."

"Yeah, go then!" shouts the other man.

Shaking his head, the man and his son follow Andes, who gestures for them to come along. Standing above the other man, Sasha glares at him. "You know, neither I nor my partner are strangers to bad parents. I'm starting to understand why fire manifested within the kid. You should be ashamed of yourself.

"But either way, your son is in good hands now, for a change."

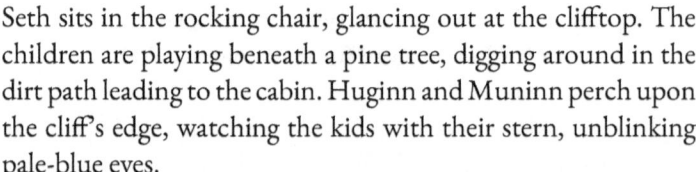

Seth sits in the rocking chair, glancing out at the clifftop. The children are playing beneath a pine tree, digging around in the dirt path leading to the cabin. Huginn and Muninn perch upon the cliff's edge, watching the kids with their stern, unblinking pale-blue eyes.

Seth sips on his coffee, steam rising from his oversized porcelain mug. Persephone and Mikhail pull rocks from the ground, discovering what squirms beneath the depths of mud and grime with gleeful smiles, and Seth relishes the sight. *This childlike wonder and impulse to explore. This is what Zarathustra wanted. For humanity's plunge into the depths of knowledge to be unabating and purposeless. To merely learn and grow and pass on our knowledge to future generations so they can prosper.*

I can't wait to hear about the kids Sasha and Andes recruited today. To amass the talented magically-abled and train them for the betterment of our world, I can only imagine the grand heights we will reach—

Huginn and Muninn stretch their wings, fluttering about as they croak toward the children. Still on the path below, Persephone waggles a purple wildflower in Mikhail's face. The blushing boy accepts it with the widest smile.

Persephone, with her other hand hidden behind her back, grins mischievously.

Swinging her arm around, a stick is forced into Mikhail's face, with a wad of spider silk and its eight-legged owner dangling from a thread. Screeching, the seven-year-old boy stumbles backward into a pine tree. Stretching his hands behind him, his palms break his fall, and—the tree engulfs in flames. Huginn and Muninn croak and skitter. Persephone drops the stick. Slack-jawed, she backs away. Mikhail's chest heaves before beginning to scream—the boy writhes around as his shirt catches fire. Seth sprints toward the chaos, one arm pushing Persephone further back, the other gripping Mikhail by his collar, then tearing the shirt away.

"Fill as many buckets with water as you can and bring them to me!" The birds turn and make their way into the house. The children stand in awe of the tree lit ablaze. "Now!" Seth roars, and the kids run after the ravens.

At seven years old, I figured Mikhail would never come into magic. All the others have either been born with it or had it manifest around age three. I was...hoping this would never happen for them. If it happened for Mikhail, then it still could for—

The ravens approach, bucket handles in their beaks. Taking the water, Seth splashes it on and around the tree. Persephone and Misha arrive shortly after, each struggling to hold a heavy bucket with both hands. Persephone's scared, wet eyes stare up at him. Seth glares before relieving her of the water.

The tree burnt to a crisp, its charred branches and trunk reduced to ash. But the surrounding trees and grass were spared, save for a blackened ring around the roots.

Seth kneels toward the boy, examining his body. *I got to him in time. No burns.* "Are you okay, Misha?" Seth asks, hugging the boy. A "Mmhmm" is whimpered into Seth's chest. Releasing him, he turns toward Persephone.

"What did I tell you about scaring Misha?" The girl glances away. "Well?"

"That it's mean and I shouldn't do it."

"That's right."

Sighing, Seth pats her on the head and says, "You must be cautious of fanning the flames. Lest they eat you whole, and I don't want to see that happen to you."

Seth lies in bed, grimacing at the day's events and the uncertain future they are heading for. For which his mind is imagining an unending stream of possibilities. Each deepening his scowl further—

But at her touch, her fingers slinking up his chest, cupping his bearded face and turning his lips toward hers, Seth is reminded that he can handle anything. Not because of what they've endured, the monsters and hardship faced, but because they have each other. How extraordinary it is that skin-on-skin contact can allow one to feel as if any struggle is weightless—her tongue slips into his mouth, and his mind empties of all else. Gripping him below, Sasha maneuvers above his waist, slipping him inside—the warmth of each other feels as if they are melting together, one being, one life, two souls fused together.

Abyssal flame erupts from his eyes, teal sparks glow and crackle from hers. A stream of white and teal spirals around their bodies as Sasha gyrates atop him. Moans dance in the air alongside them, growing louder, louder, louder—Seth heaves as he begats into her, the glow of her eyes intensifying further and further until flooding the room in a teal haze—Sasha's mind sinks inward, staring into the vast White Abyss. Zarathustra's garden lies there at the center, all its bright and numerous colors. They grow brighter, more vivid in her mind, and—Sasha gasps loudly as the teal light disperses, leaving in its wake a thick bed of peonies, roses, tulips, daisies and more, sprouting through the floor, the bed, the walls, hanging from the ceiling, all sparkling with a teal glimmer.

Sasha rolls off Seth, crushing flowers as she hits the bed. Cuddling close, they give each other affectionate, soft kisses while catching their breath.

Opening his eyes, Seth glances around the room in awe. "Did you create these?"

"Hmm?" Sasha glances around wearily. "Did I? At the moment of..."

Seth bursts out laughing. Sasha frowns.

"What's so funny?" she asks.

"Sorry, sorry. But to think we still find ourselves surprised after all we've seen. Magic casted through orgasm—"

"Ugh, don't say that."

"Sorry, but it's interesting, and not all that shocking, if you stop to think about it. We know what magic is—the human soul, life itself. Why wouldn't sex be able to trigger a magical response? Not the first time our eyes lit up during either...sorry, I'll stop talking about it," says Seth, catching Sasha's glare.

"Hmm, no, it's okay. You may be onto something. But let's log it away later so we can get some shut-eye. Help me pluck these flowers from the bed."

Seth chuckles as he nods to his wife. Pulling the roots free from their unnatural soil, holes and foam stuffing are torn from the mattress and pillows. Sasha conjures sparks of creation magic, filling the holes and stitching them back together—she begins rubbing her chest, right over her heart. Noticing this, Seth glares inquisitively.

"Alright, goodnight," says Sasha, leaning in for a kiss.

Seth kisses her back, turns off the light, and says, "Good night."

Cuddling closely, Seth reaches over, placing his hand over her chest, and falls asleep.

CHAPTER SEVEN

Dusk settles upon the mountain's summit, and night's silence seeps through the cracks of twilight's end. The hanging lamp above the living room table alone is lit, with darkness in the rooms beyond. And the only sound heard is of a tea kettle's hissing steam and the *scritch scritch scritch* of Persephone's purple-ink pen. Andes sips on a mug of peppermint tea, watching the six-year-old girl answer each quiz question with ease.

Slapping the pen onto the table, Persephone pushes the quiz paper toward Andes. Putting his reading glasses on, he examines her answers.

"My goodness. Every question correct. I wasn't sure they would be, watching you rush through them…"

"Can I go outside and play with Daddy and Misha now?" Persephone glances past Andes, through the dining room window. Mikhail is hurling punches toward Seth. Orange flames coil down his arms, amassing into fiery little fists. Seth deflects each blow, gracefully pushing the boy's arms away with his palms. The fire dissipates into a thin haze of smoke each time.

"Sorry, my dear. But your mommy said she wants you to study long and hard. My fault, I suppose, since I told her how brilliant you are." Andes gives her a warm smile.

"So, if I become stupid like Misha, then I won't have to learn anymore?"

Andes's mouth takes a sharp downward plunge. "Now, listen here. I will tolerate none of that. I love you, Persephone. But that's my son. I will not condone you calling him stupid."

Persephone's eyes grow wide and confused. A dog cowering in the corner, having been scolded for chewing through furniture. Despite acting only on impulse, having no understanding of the value of a human being's possessions. The girl's eyes wet with tears, fluttering away from Andes.

"Don't give me that look," he continues. "I know you're smart enough to understand what I'm saying."

Wiping her tears away, Persephone says, "I'm sorry, Uncles Andes...Misha isn't stupid. I just don't—why does he get to play with magic, but I can't?"

Andes turns to watch his son flail about in opposition to the man who first had to use flames to destroy before he could master them. All the damage he created, for having such a heavy burden placed upon him when he was not ready for it. Andes sighs, grateful that his son will be taught to avoid those same pitfalls.

"Misha isn't playing Persephone. He's training. That fire is not a toy. It's a tool. Or a weapon if not used properly."

Pouting, the girl drops her gaze. "I just wish I could do something cool like that."

Andes glares at his niece. Knowing that what she's wishing for is being hoped against by her father. Andes understands Seth's position, but also that his fears are largely projected. *Persephone is her own person. Seth needs not worry about her becoming like him.* Turning back toward his son, Andes smiles.

Even if there are similarities, things are always different the second time around.

"Don't lose hope, my dear," Andes says. "Your parents are very talented with magic. Surely one day you will be, too."

Persephone yanks her head up, grinning at her uncle's words. But her mouth crumbles as she watches Andes pull another book from his messenger bag. Sliding it across the table to Persephone, she reads the title. *The Girl Who Drank the Moon.*

"You've impressed me. This book here is meant for those twice your age. But you can handle it. For the next hour, I want you to read as many pages as you can. Then, I will have you write a summary of it. Get started...now."

Andes rises from his seat, mug in hand. Entering the kitchen, he drops in a couple tea bags, followed by scalding hot water. And from the corner of his eye, he finds the pages of the book being turned in a frenzy.

"Don't just hurl your punches at me," says Seth. "Give me a nice straight jab!"

The boy's face scrunches in anger, tears clouding his vision.

"Punch straight!"

Mikhail screeches and pounds his fists into the ground. The flame extinguishes, and smoke sizzles in the air. The boy's chest heaves, gritting his teeth. "I can't!" he shouts. The flames, they—my arms keep getting pushed around!"

Seth kneels, offering his hand. Mikhail hesitates, slowly reaching for Seth's hand.

"Why are you angry, Misha?"

The boy looks away.

"Is it Persephone? Is she picking on you too much?

"...I can't help if you don't tell me what you're feeling, Misha. The flames are too hard to control? Well then, control the emotion that fuels it. Trust me on this. If you want to control the fire, you must first own your anger."

The boy's glare continues to linger away from Seth, who follows his eyeline toward the cabin. Through the living room window, Andes turns to face his son. The old man smiles before sliding a book over to Persephone, then walks into the kitchen.

Seth glances back at Mikhail, whose face scrunches. But Seth senses that the anger is of a different flavor than the one he's used to. It's not quite hate, but discomfort.

Turning back toward the cabin, Seth watches as Persephone flips rapidly through page after page and smiles proudly. And—his mouth crumbles at a white glow shining upon the book, through the conduit of his daughter's eyes.

Persephone's unblinking gaze tethers to the book. Her intense focus fails to alarm Andes, who has watched the young girl read voraciously for two years now. And so, he watches with pride at how swiftly she flips through the pages. Andes takes a sip of his newly brewed tea and—

The young girl's eyes brighten with intensity, her teal irises pulsing but thinning as her white pupils glow and expand. The table creaks as Persephone's pen slithers toward her. The chandelier sways and flickers, and the pages begin flimsily waving upward. The words wobble along the paper before distorting and separating from it. Rising into the air, the ink retains the shape of the letters, as they flow into the depths of the young girl's ever-widening white orbs—

"*Persephone!*" Seth shouts, swinging the door open. He finds Andes kneeling at Persephone's side, caressing her hand, trying to soothe her.

Snapping back at the sound of her father's voice, Persephone's white pupils return to their normal size. The teal rings brighten as they are no longer overshadowed by the abyssal white glow. "Huh? Why are you yelling, Daddy? What's happening?"

"You don't remember?" asks Seth, watching the last of the ink pulled from the pages retract, imprinting upon paper once more.

"I started reading, and then now we're here, but I didn't see you come in."

Seth lets out an exasperated sigh, meeting Andes's worried glance.

"Come on, baby girl," Seth says. "That's enough studying for now. Let's get you tucked in to bed, okay?"

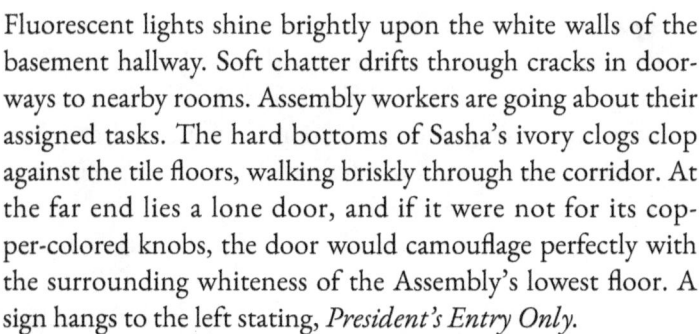

Fluorescent lights shine brightly upon the white walls of the basement hallway. Soft chatter drifts through cracks in doorways to nearby rooms. Assembly workers are going about their assigned tasks. The hard bottoms of Sasha's ivory clogs clop against the tile floors, walking briskly through the corridor. At the far end lies a lone door, and if it were not for its copper-colored knobs, the door would camouflage perfectly with the surrounding whiteness of the Assembly's lowest floor. A sign hangs to the left stating, *President's Entry Only*.

"And this is why I propose this course—" Sergei emerges from the final door to the right, with three other men in tow, amidst conversation until locking eyes with Sasha. Smiling politely, she walks on by. Catching in the corner of her eye, the man's ever-present scowl and glare.

Glancing behind, she watches them disappear into the stairwell. Turning the door's copper knobs, she encloses herself in the private laboratory.

A wide-open room, empty, but housing an aura so full of life. No outside sound penetrates its walls, and air breathed only by her, only silence stirs. All the measuring flasks, tools, and other laboratory equipment have long since been transferred to other rooms. But she left the steel surgical table as a reminder of what she is doing all this for.

Otherwise, all that exists in this empty room is the Abyssal Root's pedestal and the computer attached to it.

Less physical clutter allows for clearer mental fortitude, further proof of the body's role in creativity, as a receptacle and conduit for the powers within. Sasha wanted this room to mirror that, as is fitting considering its purpose.

Pressing the computer's power button, she awaits the login screen to load—her mind wandering, the prior night in bed with Seth spurs into memory. Engaged with each other's bodies so intensely that the entire bedroom and everything and everyone outside the two of them became, as they always do in that moment between lovers, obscured by the haze of hormones guiding their every desire. Sasha smiles. Much like creativity blossoming in solitude and with a mind less cluttered, emptying their minds of everything besides each other has only reinforced their love and companionship.

In a way, this room is much like our bedroom then. For sex, too, has been linked to greater creativity.

Placing her left eye to a retinal scanner, its infrared light searches for something unique to Sasha. Specks of teal light that have come to mingle with her natural copper eyes after receiving the magic of creation. A change that has grown more pronounced with each year.

The computer logs in, and the pedestal emits a soft glow. Placing her hand atop it, the grooves lining from top to bottom burst with abyssal white light and—her hand is pulled inward toward the pedestal. A blackhole sucking in all matter. Her neck yanks backward, eyes wide, glowing with teal energy, and—her head thrusts forward, yanking a vast whiteness back with it.

Catching her breath, waiting for the whiplash to settle, she says, "Oh, this power. Just what should I do with you?"

As her vision steadies, she finds a white humanoid form standing an inch from her face. A mouth, but no eyes above. "Yes, what will you do?"

"Are you trying to scare me?" she asks. "You know what we've faced. So, quit trying to be intimidating. It won't work on me."

The Abyssal Consciousness cocks its head, frowning. "What. Will. You. Choose?"

Glaring at the strange being, her face scrunches between her eyes and the top of her nose. She bites her lower lip, scowling with tired eyes. *I don't like not knowing what to expect. And this characteristic void of a creature is impossible to read.*

"I don't know. As Seth and I have told you countless times now, we only seek to protect humanity. The White Abyss will be used for that end, but—" Her head grows dizzy. She clutches her forehead in her left palm, squeezing the temples. "Call it parental fatigue, or whatever, but I'm coming up short on specifics." She lifts her head, staring at the Abyssal Consciousness's strange white form. The bizarre black static holding its body together. "What would you recommend?"

"Be curious," it says. "Be creative. Live with wanderlust in your soul. Acquire endless knowledge for knowledge's sake. Embark on adventures, search for horizons unknown. This is, after all, what your progenitor wanted. This is how humans become as gods."

Sighing, she turns her back on the Abyssal Consciousness. Only to sigh heavier as she turns around again, realizing the human gesture is pointless here. There is no turning one's back on the White Abyss, nor would she ever choose to.

"As I said, I was struggling with the specifics. So, thanks for the usual vagaries, I suppose. See you tomorrow."

Closing her eyes, she begins the process of pulling her soul back to Earth. She can feel it on the other side, her hand lifting from the pedestal—

"You *will* come to know fear, Spawn of Zarathustra. For *they* are coming, and *they* are many—"

Her hand pulls away, searing as if she placed it within scalding hot oil. Eyes wide and wet, her chest heaves.

That final moment within the Abyss, that sheer pressure...

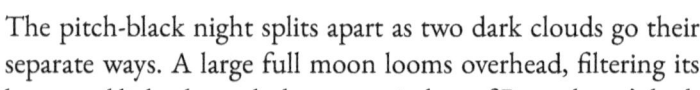

The pitch-black night splits apart as two dark clouds go their separate ways. A large full moon looms overhead, filtering its borrowed light through the open window of Persephone's bedroom.

The young girl tosses and turns, with soft animalistic grunts emerging from her. Gritting her teeth, twitching, flitting about, she whimpers as a large weight festers like cancer within her. A multitude of pressures, cramping with tightness in her tiny chest. Aching for release. A god, trapped in the frame of a small girl.

Tremors ripple through her body, intensifying further and further, and—she screeches.

Persephone sits erect, her eyes closed, mouth agape. Breathing in deeply, her head arches back, her eyes peel open, and rays of white light shine out from her skull, as she begins sucking in a tremendous amount of air in one, unending gulp. The bright yellow moon distorts and wobbles and sways like water, and at one edge begins to spill into a bright golden river. Stretching further and further, like toothpaste through its tube. The stream descends toward the Earth, creating a glittering strand of moon dust, stretching across thousands and thousands of miles until reaching Persephone's window, and spilling into her mouth—

"Persephone?" Seth bursts in. "What's wro—"

Sasha follows in from behind, stricken in awe alongside him. "Persephone? Persephone!" she shouts, running over and throwing her arms around the girl.

Seth hurries over to the window, watching the stream of moon dust spill into his daughter's mouth. Reaching toward the stretched-out moon, specks of dust displace from the stream, glittering its golden sheen around his fingertips. Looking out and up through the window, he finds the once full moon half dissolved, crumbled away like sand.

"What is happening?" Andes says, appearing in the doorway. Mikhail stands at his side, nuzzling his sleepy eyes with the back of his hands before waking to the commotion before him.

"She's not responding!" Sasha says.

Seth rushes over. "That light...no, it's happening again." Sasha yanks her gaze toward Seth, alarmed. "It happened earlier today, while reading...this white glow—and this pressure. It's the Abyss. No doubt."

"My apologies," Andes says, "But we have larger concerns at the moment. If she consumes the moon, its absence will devastate the Earth!"

Seth breathes in heavily. *A doomsday event in the middle of the night. She's my daughter, that's for sure.* "Clear the room!" he shouts, his eyes illuminated with white abyssal flame. "I'm going to try something."

Sasha rises, inching away slowly. Her gaze locked too fiercely onto Persephone. Seth places a hand on her shoulder, gesturing with his head for her to step aside. A hollow sensation takes root in Sasha as she ambles over to Andes.

Seth hovers his right palm over Persephone's face, curling his fingers in a circular motion. Hand shaking, the pull of the moon dust river is too severe, continuing its descent into the depths of Persephone—setting his entire body ablaze with white flame, Sasha and Andes feel a gravitation shift pulling toward Seth. Mikhail clings to Andes's sleeve, fearing his feet would be swept up in the sudden, unnatural wind current rushing through their enclosed home. And though the fire is bright, it does not burn. It does not scorch nor warm.

The moon dust begins to retract. Rising from Persephone's throat, she gargles and gags.

Seth's eyes glow brighter, and a portal opens at the far end of the room, creating yet another gravitational pull. Beyond the portal lay a vast darkness, sprinkled with glimmering stars. Sasha, Andes, and Mikhail huddle together, clinging fiercely to the doorframe while Seth and Persephone's abyssal weight holds them steady. The last of the moon dust ejects from her stomach, and the white glow of her eyes disappears. Waking up, she's suddenly lifted into the air by the vacuum of space—she thuds against Seth's big right arm, brought close to his side. With the flick of his left hand, the moon dust flings into the darkness, followed by a pillar of abyssal flame erupting from his palm. Gravity reverts to normal as the portal closes.

Rushing to the window, they find the wobbling moon slowly steadying itself. Aglow with abyssal flame, searing the fabric of the world back together, it reforms into the same bright full moon as before.

"I can't believe that worked," Andes says. Sasha stares in awe of Seth, but with an ever-deepening scowl sinking into her face.

"I had a hunch. The words she pulled from the book pages floated back into form once she snapped out of it. The abyssal flame was an added precaution." Seth collapses onto Persephone's bed. The young girl cocks her head in confusion at her father's exhaustion.

Andes, noticing the looks on both parents, steps toward Persephone. "You two get some rest. I'll tuck the youngsters back into bed."

"You sure?" asks Sasha.

"Never more sure in my life! Now, go."

Glancing tiredly at each other, Seth and Sasha hurry back to their room.

Andes pulls a chair up to the bed and takes the book he gave her years ago from the nearby nightstand. Mikhail hops into bed beside Persephone, both children content beneath the covers as Andes begins to read a story.

Persephone smiles widely toward her uncle. With no memory of what had just occurred, she relishes what's to come. A story told by her loving uncle, her most favorite of things.

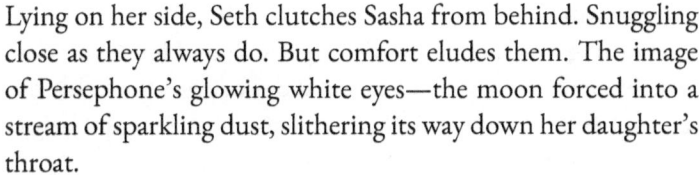

Lying on her side, Seth clutches Sasha from behind. Snuggling close as they always do. But comfort eludes them. The image of Persephone's glowing white eyes—the moon forced into a stream of sparkling dust, slithering its way down her daughter's throat.

Shuddering, Sasha's muscles clench.

"You okay?"

"Y-yeah. Just thinking about what happened. Surreal."

"There's much about magic we don't yet know. And then there's the business of the *True-Born God*. I suppose there's something to the Abyssal Consciousness's vagaries after all."

There's much about magic we don't yet know. His words echo within her mind, as it wanders more and more and...

"You opened a portal into space. How did you?"

"Magic does what the mind wills it to do. I simply knew what needed to happen and made it happen. Still surprised me though."

The moon was forcibly brought to Earth in the form of sparkling dust, then in a moment, it was back in the sky. The sky...everything we know about Zarathustra's goal pertained only to the Earth. And yet, he made the sun and stars, the moon as Earth's companion. Why?

Her spiraling thoughts search for answers, and when none arrive, she remembers the words of the Abyssal Consciousness:

Be curious. Be creative. Live with wanderlust in your soul. Acquire endless knowledge for knowledge's sake. Embark on adventures, search for horizons unknown. This is, after all, what your progenitor wanted. This is how humans become as gods.

"Seth..."

"Yeah?"

"I think I know what to do with the Abyssal Root."

"And what's that?"

"The sky. Space. We need to search it."

"For what?"

Turning onto her other side, she faces him. Her lips embrace his. Warmth overtakes her as she slides her head into his bare chest. Feeling calm within his arms, and in the mental heights of inspiration.

"For anything."

A chill runs through the cabin. The early spring morning air carries with it an echo of winter. The rising sun peeks over the town of Crowley beyond the forest below, its rays not yet awake enough to warm. *After the commotion last night, I'm simply glad the sun rose at all.*

Leaning gently along the edge of the kitchen counter, Sasha sips her coffee. First cup of many. Seth, entering the kitchen, slips his right arm around her waist and kisses her forehead. Opening the cabinets, he takes a large mug and fills it to the brim. "Happen to get any sleep?" he asks. "Not good sleep," says Sasha. He nods groggily, joining her side.

"Daddy? Mommy?" Persephone stands in the kitchen's threshold, nuzzling her sleepy eyes. Mikhail, exhausted, lingers close behind. Fluttering his eyes about in the abrasive and sudden kitchen light.

"Hey, sweetie," Sasha says. "Are you feeling okay?"

She glares at her mother as if she has said something strange. "Why are you acting like I'm sick? I feel fine."

Seth and Sasha share a glance, a strange mixture of concern and relief.

"Come on, kiddos. Let's play in the living room," says Andes, emerging from behind. "We're crowding the kitchen."

"Andes, you were up late with them. You don't have—"

"Yes, I do." He glances over them. "Stress is far more exhausting than a lack of sleep. "Go on. Ease into your day. I've got this."

He disappears into the living room.

"We're lucky to have him around," says Seth.

"We're all lucky to have each other. He'd never admit it, but he's struggling out there."

Peering around the wall, Sasha sees Andes at the center of the living room, sitting cross-legged upon the floor. Marching around him in a circle, the young girl and boy antagonize Huginn and Muninn by chasing after them with little toy dinosaurs in their outstretched hands. The birds flutter and croak, skittering around Andes, who smiles nervously.

Turning to one of the cabinets, Sasha takes two bowls and a box of cereal. "Kids! Come get breakfast!" she shouts, and they come sprinting back to the kitchen.

The hard cereal clinks against the bowl. Taking a gallon of milk, the pieces rise and float about in the silky white drink. Reaching for the utensil drawer—Sasha groans at the lack of spoons, then turns toward the sink. Dishes pile high, rising alongside a subtle, but pungent stink.

"Sorry," Seth says. "Didn't have time to wash them with, well, everything yesterday."

"It's fine," says Sasha, with a sigh. Raising her left hand, teal sparks crackle into existence, shaping into something long, with a widened end and shallow basin. As the teal magic forges a spoon into being, it plops into her hand. Creating another, she drops them into the two cereal bowls and hands them to the children.

"Whoa!" says Mikhail.

"Mommy, it's so cool when you do that." Persephone's eyes shift away, and her mouth collapses. "Will I be able to do that someday?"

Sasha glances worriedly toward Seth and says, "Maybe someday, sweetie."

The four of them join Andes and the giant birds in the living room. The kids plop onto the couch next to their dino toys. Persephone makes her miniature T-Rex walk along the brim of her bowl. Slipping out of her fingers, it dunks into the milk, floating around with the cereal.

Chuckling, Persephone says, "Mommy, can you make dinosaurs, like you did with the spoons?"

"They were already made, sweetie. They lived a long, long time ago."

"But not anymore?"

"No, not for a long time."

"Then bring them back!"

"There's a handful of movies that explain why that's a bad idea."

Seth breaks out in laughter and pats Persephone's head. Ignoring her father's affection, her eyes scrunch and her mouth pouts. "I. Want. Dinosaurs!"

"How about you settle for this?" says Seth, unearthing a Blu-ray copy of Jurassic Park. Rising from the couch, he inserts the disk into a game console. "You'll love it."

Andes rises from the floor. "Scoot over, my boy," he says to Mikhail, who squirms at the word *boy*. Sasha watches as Seth glances at him with inquisitive eyes before returning to her side.

The movie plays on, and at the first sight of a T-Rex, Persephone jumps from the couch and runs to the TV. The massive and fearsome king of the dinosaurs lets out a roar that quakes through the air. Persephone leans back, then thrusts her face forward. Her hands bunched up and at her sides, mimicking the beast's short arms. The little girl let out a raspy, high-pitched roar, followed by Huginn and Muninn croaking in tandem.

Seth smiles warmly at his daughter. Relishing her enjoyment and childlike wonder. Giggling, Persephone leans back and thrusts forward again. Louder this time, she screeches—

Her eyes flash a bright white light, and Seth's smile sinks into stoic worry.

CHAPTER EIGHT

Sergei wanders the halls of the Assembly for Magic and Human Progression. Pondering where they are progressing to. His role in the Assembly has thus far been that of a combat trainer for the new guard. But things have now become much more complex as he marches toward a new world full of forces beyond his comprehension, beyond his ability to train.

He halts at a large window looking into a wide-open room. Toys strewn around the expansive floor, Sergei peers into a massive playpen full of children who are more than they seem. A boy with heavy eyes glares toward two towers made from colorful blocks. His father, a tall, dark-skinned man with black-rimmed glasses perched upon his nose, above a bountiful beard of the same color, smiles and tries to encourage the boy to join him in raising the tower's height.

The room has systematically filled with children over the course of Sasha and Andes's secret outings. The laughter erupting from within pierces the wall with ease. A couple of young girls skip in circles as one holds a potted plant, the other blowing spit bubbles into the air. The plant's viny appendages stretch and wiggle, while fairies crafted from spittle flutter around them. A boy continually pulls toy cars apart with his mind, then pieces them back together in new forms.

But what catches Sergei's eye is the group of five children huddled together in the far-left corner. A boy with shaggy black hair reads from a large book as another boy and three girls lie on the floor before him. "Once upon a midnight dreary, as I pondered weak and weary..." The boy's tongue holds great rhythm and diction for his age, and as the croaking words "nevermore" glide off his tongue, sparks of black flame jump from the page, forming the shape of a raven. Perched upon a bust of some Greek mythology figure—whose identity is a mystery to Sergei—as a figure of a man cowering in fear of the bird speaks in a voice unlike the boy's own:

"Be that word our sign of parting, bird or fiend!" I shrieked, upstarting—

"Get thee back into the tempest and the Night's Plutonian shore!

Leave no black plume as a token of that lie thy soul hath spoken!

Leave my loneliness unbroken!—quit the bust above my door!

Take thy beak from out my heart, and take thy form from off my door!"

"Quoth the Raven, *Nevermore*," the bird replies, as the boy continues the poem. The children clap at the visuals rising from the page, and squeal in terror as the narrator collapses dead, into the raven's dark shadow.

"Darkness there, and nothing more," speaks a voice from behind. Sergei turns to find a man with shaggy brown hair and rectangular glasses. Behind them are tired, blue eyes. Longing for something forever lost. "How harrowing that is," the man says. Losing one's light and being lost to darkness forever."

"You have the poem memorized, Caleb?" says Sergei. "I, for one, don't understand the worth of this puppet show, or why these children are here."

"Hardly. Famous poem is all. But I don't care for it either, same as you," Caleb says, his eyes growing heavier as he sighs. "It feels...too close to home now, for some reason. You ever feel like something has been lost over the years, since the Supernatural Holocaust? You know, I was a devout Christian before all that. But when the angels came—took my wife—then President Sasha and others claimed that God was dead, I—"

Catching Sergei's glare digging into him, Caleb silences himself, hands raised before him as he steps backward. "Sorry," he says, "Forget I said anything."

"No," says Sergei. "Speak. We served together in Iraq. Your words are safe with me."

Caleb glances toward Sergei, then off to the side. Raising his right palm, covering his mouth, he sighs, shaking his head. "It's just, we never saw the corpse. How do we know God is dead, or even if God is truly at fault for everything that happened eight years ago? Did I make a mistake joining the Assembly? Is God alive and well, and is he punishing me with emptiness for having betrayed my faith?"

"You doubt Sasha," Sergei says, glancing back toward the children. *What is my role as a combat expert in a world of magic? Surely, I'll be tossed away, as the ranks are filled with much more volatile soldiers.* Turning back to Caleb, he says, "I doubt her, too. Your concerns are safe with me, but let's not talk more about it here. And if you know of others who share these worries, bring them to me."

"Yes, sir." Caleb salutes and hastily leaves.

The boy building block towers with his father knocks one over. They crumble to the floor as all support is yanked from beneath. The boy's face scrunches as he lets out a seething screech.

Crimson red floods the whites of his eyes, until his pupils are hidden. Stretching past the confines, fire bursts from his gaze, and a tiny sun forms upon the bridge of his nose, launching toward the remaining tower. The blocks catch fire, and the other children run from the room screaming as water ejects from the ceiling. The boy's father tiptoes around the flaming wood blocks, stretching his arms around his son.

That's more like it. But memory of the World Trade Center crumbling to pieces after the planes struck blazes into mind. Crumbling to the ground as the block towers dissipate into ash upon the floor.

What of magical humans in countries prone to terror?

———◆———

"Yes, it's time—quite frankly, it's overdue," says Sasha, with Andes nodding from the other side of her desk. If we are to believe that humans started to be born with magic as soon as the White Abyss recombined with the Earth eight years ago, then that's an average of one point two billion magic-born internationally."

"And a third of the population in another eight years," says Andes. "We're going to have our hands full. Even with the expansion."

Eyes closed, Andes shakes his head. Sasha stares across the table at the old man, grown more recently feeble. A man well beyond his twilight years, having somehow stuck around this long, defying his allotted time with sheer will alone. *What an inspiration he still is.* And at the thought of her failure, her eyes wet, despair sinking into her bowels as she takes in the view of him as he is before her now.

Between running the Assembly and being a mom, the years went by in a flash. And despite my search for a cure within the depths of the Abyss, I have come up short.

"Hey, Andes. I want to thank you for always being there for my daughter. She loves you and...well, with that scare we had a year ago, Seth and I wouldn't be able to do this without you."

"What brought this on, now, in the middle of a work discussion?" Andes smiles. "You thank me every day, so what's with the drama?"

Chuckling softly, Sasha glances out the office window. "I don't know. Just felt like I should say it. You're family after all, and we love you."

A knock sounds at the door, before it swings open. Sergei stomps forward, stopping as he reaches Andes's side.

"A word?" says Sergei.

Sasha gestures for him to continue.

"Just what is going on in the residential section? All these kids with unearthly powers?"

"A side effect from the conclusion of the Supernatural Holocaust," says Sasha.

"And they're here for what purpose? Because they seem dangerous. Exactly what the Assembly is supposed to combat against."

"No—these children are not a threat. I want that made very clear," Sasha says. "They are here to have their powers contained, trained, and studied."

"Lab rats, then."

Andes turns sharply toward Sergei. "Absolutely not. They are the next step in human evolution. And the next generation of the Assembly."

Sergei glances from Andes to Sasha, at the taxidermized angel tentacle on the wall behind her. "But where are these powers coming from? You told me prior that all supernatural threats were annihilated. That the Assembly is a mere deterrent, but this seems supernatural to me."

Sasha's eyes become stern, rigid, staring across the table at the contumacious man.

"That's why they're being studied."

Sergei glares, mouth shut, eyes narrowing. "Is God really dead? Because I think there's more to this than you're letting on."

Andes rises, with slow bones, but also with the fiery passion he has held for thousands of years. Stepping toward Sergei, he thrusts a finger into his face. "Listen, you paranoid man. You seem to think something nefarious is being kept hidden from you. But as a veteran, you must understand the concept of things being on a need-to-know basis? Not everything hidden is malicious. Sometimes it's for the greater good, and *you* don't need to know!"

Sergei gulps and takes a step back. "Yes, sir. I apologize. I suppose it's just paranoia, like you said, from being a soldier. Could you tell me this, at least? If these magical kids are popping up here, then they could be elsewhere as well, right? In countries more dangerous? Shouldn't we do something about that?"

"Rest assured," says Sasha, gesturing to Andes to sit. Her ever-loyal uncle smiles, nods, and descends into his chair. "We were just discussing expanding internationally. In the coming years, the Assembly will have a worldwide presence."

Sergei remains silent for a moment, then nods before hastily leaving.

Turning toward Andes, she finds his eyes closed, his chest heaving with shallow breath, and a hand clutching his chest. "Hey, you okay?" she asks, alarmed.

"Y-yes, it's nothing to worry about, my lady."

"Maybe you should go home."

"Nonsense. My place is by your side. Always."

Smiling, she closes her eyes and slinks back into her chair. It swivels comfortably as she rocks back and forth. "Fine, but I could have handled that myself, you know."

"Of course, you could have. But it's your role as head of the Assembly to be everyone's shield. Let me be your blade."

Upon leaving for the day, Sergei locks the Assembly door behind him. Sasha and Andes are still working inside, but somehow they always go home despite asking Sergei to be the last to leave, the last to lock up.

Unsettled by the events of the day, he glances at the sigil carved into the large double doors. A strange rune sits at the center of the Assembly's logo, with words wrapping around it: *God is dead. Let us protect you instead.*

Furrowing his brow, Sergei turns and stomps away.

A mingling of scents wafts into the living room air, seeping in from the kitchen. Seasoned chicken thighs sizzling within their greasy runoff. White rice cooking slowly in boiling water. A stir-fry of peppers, onions, broccoli, garlic, marinates in soy sauce while Seth tosses the vegetables about before turning off the stovetop burners. Moving the pot and pan out of the way, he slips on a baking glove and opens the oven. Thick hot air wafts against his face alongside the sizzling chicken as he pulls the baking tray out and lays it atop the stove.

"Dinner's ready!" he says in a sing-song voice as he emerges into the living room. Sasha slumps against the couch with both kids by her side, extending their arms over her lap, holding toy dinosaurs. A pretend fight between the tiny plastic beasts breaks out above Sasha's thighs, as she smiles and rolls her eyes.

"Come on, you heard him," she says. "It's time for family movie night! Misha, go wake your father up from his nap."

"Okay!" the boy says and runs off into the other room.

"I'll put the movie in!" Persephone says, running over to the basket of Blu-rays beneath the television. Popping *Jurassic Park 2* into the game console, she joins her parents in the kitchen to grab a plate of food.

Sasha turns toward the bedrooms at the sound of a soft whimper, muffled further by the walls between them—the cries erupt into full-blown horror. "Aunt Sasha! Come help, *please*!"

Sasha tosses her plate of food into Seth's hands as she sprints into Andes's room—

A full glass of water lay upon a nightstand next to the large bed. Half slanted, Andes is hanging off the side, right arm limp upon the floor. Rushing over, Sasha feels for a pulse in his neck—her hands overtaken by tremors, she stumbles back, crumbling to her knees. Her eyes widen. Large pools of tears stream down her face.

Clasping her mouth with both hands, she breaks into loud sobs as Seth embraces her from behind. Persephone and Mikhail watch from afar, mouths agape. Their faces flush with horror.

CHAPTER NINE

They arrive to pitch blackness. But evidence of physicality exists in the scent of charred flesh. Sasha can feel her feet sink into mounds of ash that carpet the stony surface of the cave.

I have not been here since I first met Seth.

Amidst the void before her, bright white light emerges from the darkness, out from Seth's eyes. And, one by one, dozens of fiery orbs spark into being. Illuminating the ruins of Magistrum and Andes's stiffening corpse laying in Seth's arms.

"Are you sure you want to bury him here? I c-can—" Seth chokes, clearing his throat. "It must be hard for you. Being here."

Turning to face him, Sasha finds Seth's deep frown, coated in streaming tears. Cupping his face, she caresses his skin.

He still blames himself.

Persephone tugs on her mother's right hand. Her eyes, red and wet, she shivers as her gaze darts around the dark cave. "I don't like this place. Smells funny—and big and scary."

Seth steps away and lays Andes next to the collapsed tower at the center of the ruins. He's turned away from the others, but Sasha glimpses a heavier flow of liquid running down his cheeks, glimmering in the fiery white light.

"You know, Persephone. Huginn and Muninn are big." Hearing their names, they pop their heads through the portal before pushing their entire bodies through, colliding with Sasha. Stumbling forward, Persephone's head knocks into Sasha's hip. Whimpering, she breaks into a light sob.

"I'm sorry, baby." She squats to kiss the young girl's forehead. "But as you can see, sometimes big things can't help but accidentally break other things. But that doesn't mean big things are bad."

Huginn and Muninn dive their heads toward Persephone and nuzzle their beaks against the girl a fraction of their size. Her whimpers transmute into a fit of giggles. Glancing over to Seth, Sasha catches him watching the scene with a pensive smile and loving eyes. Persephone's laughter ceases as she watches her mother rise to join her father, hovering over Andes's corpse.

"I suppose I should go get a shovel. And Misha," says Seth.

Raising her hands, Sasha feels the pulse of creation flow alongside her blood, and inspiration takes hold. "Perhaps only Misha," she says, kneeling to the ground and placing her palms flat upon the stone.

Teal sparks flow from her hands and into the Earth, tearing through the stone, causing it to ripple like water. The solid ground splits apart and sinks six feet deep, dirt crumbling in upon itself as it widens. The teal sparks disperse, leaving behind a large rectangular hole.

Seth gently takes Sasha's hands, glancing with wide eyes at them before turning his gaze to her. "Since when could you do something like that?"

"Since always, I suppose. This creation magic combined with my ability to alter the flow of magic. Remembering our old friends who couldn't create, but *could bend* their father's world, I figured, why couldn't I do the same when I *can* create?"

"Magic is best used in creative and unprecedented ways..." Seth's eyes grow solemn. "Melphis was right. Old friends, huh? We have too many of those now..."

Seth wraps his arms around her tightly, kissing gently upon her forehead, before turning and opening a new portal. "I'll go grab Misha."

Seth disappears. And though his white flames remain lit, and the warmth of her daughter's hand lays within her palm, Sasha feels the weight of it. Slicing through her heaving chest is death's rueful blade, hollowing her out and bringing to light the emptiness inside.

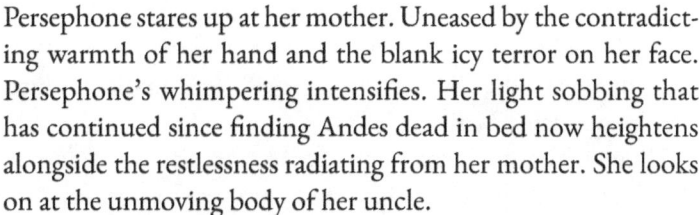

Persephone stares up at her mother. Uneased by the contradicting warmth of her hand and the blank icy terror on her face. Persephone's whimpering intensifies. Her light sobbing that has continued since finding Andes dead in bed now heightens alongside the restlessness radiating from her mother. She looks on at the unmoving body of her uncle.

Seth's abyssal portal reopens, and through it comes Mikhail tethered to his left hand.

"Daddy..." Persephone whimpers, squeezing her mother's hand while pointing up toward her face. Seth glances from her daughter to his wife, finding rivers pouring from wet, red eyes. And a mouth capable only of shallow gasps.

Seth's sullen face sinks further. "Let's get started."

Sasha and the two children stand at the side of the rectangular hole. Persephone clings to her mother's left hand, while Mikhail sobs into Persephone's shoulder. Huginn clings to other side of Sasha while Muninn lets out raspy coos, nuzzling his head against the crying boy. Seth crouches before them as he lifts Andes back into his arms. The unanimated face causes Persephone to shiver, the weight and confusion of the sudden vanishment of a life's existence.

She remembers all the nice moments she has had with *Uncle Andes*. Walks throughout the mountain. Loud and gleeful family dinners. Teaching her how to read. Bedtime stories and lullabies to ward off nighttime monsters—those moments so full of life, drifted off in the dead of night. Leaving an empty vessel.

"Where did Uncle go?" Persephone asks. Sasha and Seth glance from her to each other, horrified, tears welling heavier than before. Persephone continues, "That's not Uncle Andes. It looks like him, but that's not him. That—I don't feel Uncles Andes from that."

Mikhail glares at Persephone, anguish ripping into his eyes. Collapsing to the ground, he sobs and wails.

Seth looks away as he hops into the deep grave. Without turning to the children, Sasha says, "Persephone. Enough. You're upsetting Misha."

Their daughter's questions cease, and she turns toward Mikhail. With quivering lips, she extends a shaky hand. "I'm sorry Misha! I'm sorry Misha! I'm sorry Misha!" The children clasp each other tightly, crying with great abandon.

Sasha reaches into the grave to help Seth back up. Returning to the children, Seth wraps his arms around them both, bringing them in close. Sasha presses her palms against the stony ground. Teal sparks erupt, meshing the stone together. The ground begins to eclipse Andes's face, and reaching his peaceful smile, Sasha says, sniffling, "Goodbye."

She rises.

Refusing to look toward Seth and the children, her face crumbles into blankness.

Except for the tears.

"You were the last of my original family. Don't get me wrong," Sasha glances toward Seth for a moment, before dropping her gaze toward the ground again. "I am so grateful for Seth, for our daughter. For your son. But for over three hundred years, you and my father were all I had. And n-now," her voice breaks, and—

Mikhail catches her attention. She locks her gaze upon the young boy, and he squirms at the sight of her wide, veiny eyes.

His shaggy brown hair and dark brown eyes. Father, is that what Andes looked like when you found him? An echo of the dead, it's like looking at Andes alive again, and I can't—

Her sight blurs, head wobbling back and forth. Crumbling to her knees, she screeches in pain.

"Did I do something wrong?" Mikhail cries.

Seth pats the young boy's head, ruffling his hair, and says, "No. No one did anything wrong. Sometimes we just hurt." Seth rushes to Sasha's side. The worry in his eyes pronounced as Sasha's vision blurs in and out, her head tilting, falling swiftly downward.

One week later.

The silence is thick. Some light chatter at breakfast. But the children don't play. They sit in silence as noise from the TV fills the void their sadness has created.

Sasha bites down on a crisp piece of buttery toast. It is all she can keep down. She has barely eaten since—

Her head falls into her left hand. She rubs her temples, but the tension persists.

"Are you sure you're ready to go back to work?" says Seth.

"Someone has to run things. And besides...I could use the distraction."

Seth nods complacently. But his eyes glow their fiery white, and a portal opens in front of the TV. The children cry their protests. Neither Seth nor Sasha responds.

Sasha walks on through, exchanging the dead silence of her home for the dead silence of her empty office. Taking a seat, her father's portrait stares down at her.

"I failed, Father. I couldn't find a cure for your family's curse. And that means..."

Staring down at her hands, something seems off. Wiggling her fingers around, the skin of her palms creases and sags. Not quite wrinkles, but not as taut and elastic as her skin once was. One palm at a time, she strokes her fingers against the skin. Teal sparks crackle, tightening, leaving it as taut as it was eight years ago. Slouching in her chair, she chuckles sadly. *To think it's been just about eight years since—*

Her neck muscles clench, veins popping as teal sparks crackle around her heart alongside sharp stabbing pains. Clutching her chest, she coughs, chokes—air squeezing out of her lungs, but none returning. Vision blurs, and—

A knock at the door. Brianna walks in and says, "Morning, ma'am. Just wanted to—Sasha! Are you alright?" Pouring a glass of water, Brianna brings it to Sasha's lips.

Breathing slows, vision returns. Fluttering her eyes a few times, Sasha glances toward her secretary. "Better now, thank you."

*Creation magic has never rebounded like that before. Those sparks around my heart...*Brianna glares down with concerned eyes. Raising a hand between them, Sasha says, "I'm fine, really. So, what did you need?"

"Sergei wanted to chat with you."

"Of course, he does. Let him in."

At her words, the man passes through the doorway to her office. Brianna squeezes past him as they both make their way through.

"My condolences for Andes's passing. He was a good man."

Squinting angrily, she says, "What do you need?"

"I've assembled a group of Assemblymen loyal to me. I demand that I be given full authority and official title over this faction, and if you do not comply, we will take all necessary measures to force you from your seat."

"Excuse me?" Sasha says, rising so quickly that her chair skids back, slamming into the wall. The portrait of her father plummets to the floor, emphasized by the snapping of the frame and the shattering of glass. "Is that a threat?"

"Not of violence, little lady. Calm yourself. All measures will be bureaucratic and above-board."

Sasha glares past him, out through the door to Brianna, who rolls her eyes and mimics an exasperated sigh.

Returning her gaze to Sergei, Sashas says, "You come in here, a week after we lose Andes, and you dare threaten me?"

"Quite frankly, little lady, I don't like what I see. This feels like a dictatorship. You hired all of us to be a deterrent to more of what the world experienced eight years ago, and yet, what do we do, really? You have me train your soldiers, but you never tell us what we're training for."

"For potential threats. Do you understand the word deterrent?" asks Sasha. "As of right now, there is no thr—"

"I know that can't be true. You've been fiddling with that strange device in the basement. I saw it, that strange white glow. Seems supernatural enough to me."

"You shouldn't know about that."

"And yet..." He gesticulates broadly. "I want my faction officially sanctioned. I want to know what else you've been keeping secret because I know there's more. Andes is dead—the assembly needs a new, strong male presence."

Sasha's head throbs as she grows lightheaded again. Falling into her chair, she says, "You want me to delegate power. Fine. Quite frankly, I don't care anymore. Have your faction—"

"And the strange device?"

Slamming her arms upon her desk, Sasha shouts, "Don't you fucking talk over me."

Sergei quiets, tilting his head back and glaring toward her over his nose.

"The pedestal only works for me, so leave it be. We will begin having weekly colloquiums to discuss the focus of the Assembly. But—" she rises, leaving her right hand firm upon the desk while lifting her left palm upward. "You will learn that I have kept secrets for a reason."

Teal sparks rise and crackle, creating immense heat. Out from it emerges sizzling iron, elongating into a sharpened edge. Taking shape, a six-inch dagger is forged, and her left hand swiftly snatches it from the air. She plunges the blade into the center of her right hand and, clenching, blood spurts, pooling onto her desk.

Sergei's eyes widen as he takes a step back. Sasha tosses the knife aside. It clunks against the desk. Raising her left fingers, more teal sparks crackle as she drags them across the wound. Sergei watches as strands of flesh weave together, encasing themselves in new skin.

"Like the wound never happened. Don't fuck with me. Now get out of my office."

With a polite nod, Sergei hastily leaves.

She turns to the broken frame. Her father's portrait seen through a web of broken glass. Sighing, she slinks into her chair. "Was this what it was like, Father, when the Guild split in two? It feels like I, also, am lying broken. A body torn asunder."

Persephone, Mikhail, and Seth sit at the dining room table, just outside the kitchen and to the right of the living room. Rain patters against the rooftop, coating the windows in a watery veil. The TV plays cartoons, captivating the children's attention as they watch from afar. Gobbling down mashed potatoes and tearing into pork chops—

The door bursts open, slamming against the wall, its hinges creaking and bending. Seth stands erect, placing himself between the children and the door.

Sasha trudges in, the light of her coppery eyes extinguished as they glare through wet hair, clinging to her face.

"Why didn't you call?" says Seth, "I would have opened a portal—"

Baring her teeth, Sasha screams with all her might. Grabbing hold of the TV, she slams it to the floor, shattering the screen. Her gaze opens wide at what she has done, and glances at the children. Their eyes wide with fear. Knees giving out, she crumbles to the floor. Sobbing, she cups her face in her hands. Seth kneels, wraps his arms around her, and—she pushes him away and tumbles to the floor.

"W-why am I so weak? I can create anything I want out of nothing at all! And yet, I remain impotent."

"That isn't true..."

"You can commune with the Abyss, you create portals."

"Surely that's nothing compared to creation and altering the flow of magic."

"A woman's ability to create life has never been a reason for a man to respect her."

Seth looks at Sasha pensively. "Did something happen at work?"

Sasha's cries grow heavier as she throws herself into Seth's arms. "That damn Sergei. Threatening to force me out now that Andes isn't around to reinforce my authority! And—A-Andes! My family is gone. I failed him, and s-s-s-soon enough the curse will take me too!"

Her muffled cries morph into a groan, wetting Seth's shirt with her tears.

Persephone watches the shell of her mother empty its last bits into her father's chest. Life leaving the body, leaving a fleshy mimicry of a person. But one without their essence. Their soul, the magic that makes one who they are. Death, a hollowing thing. Kills even those still alive. Left behind to watch their loved ones taken, they are taken, too. Into the void where consciousness cannot tread. And so, they vanish—

Something white and heavy thumps within Persephone's head. "*Aaayeeeiii!*" she screeches, tossing her arms outward, making the shape of a cross. Her long black hair blows back, as if caught in a forceful gale. Eyes widening, mouth stretched agape, beams of bright abyssal light erupts through the holes. Head twitching around sporadically, the abyssal light blinding the others when pointing toward them. Persephone's arms contort, the bones within shattering with each spasm. Followed by teal sparks crackling around the wounds, piecing the bones and flesh together again. Breaking healing breaking healing. The young girl screeches throughout it all.

"*Persephone!*" Seth shouts. Sasha looks on at her child, in awe of the scene unfolding before them. As their daughter continues to scream, the furniture begins sliding toward her, and they feel their bodies lifting into the air until—a wuthering pressure forces them forward, like the vacuum of space. Seth's eyes glow white, tapping into the Abyss to make him heavy. Wrapping an arm around Sasha, he holds her close while forming a portal behind Mikhail. The boy screams as he falls backward into it, and into Seth's other arm—a massive crash against the cabin's walls. A tree pierces through, destroying the living room wall. Another pierces the kitchen. A boulder drops through the roof, crushing the living room table. Mere inches from Persephone.

{So, tell me, Zarathustra's Wrath…Is she like you?}

His eyes glow brighter, opening another portal. This time behind Persephone. On the other side lay the forest, with trees on the edge of their property toppled and uprooted. Wind bellows from outside, slicing through all other sound as if a tornado is nearby. "Sasha, I'm going to need your help!" Seth shouts, jumping forward toward their daughter. Sasha grabs Persephone, gripping her nape as they pass through the portal.

Her eyes return to their usual teal with white at their centers. Her mouth quivers into silence as her mother halts the flow of the child's magic.

The family thuds against the ground, rolling atop each other until stopping. Lifting their gazes, they—

"What?" says Seth, finding the White Abyss stretching around them. No forest, no mountain. No town beneath the cliffside. Only white as far as they can see, but with blackness bleeding from a fracture in space above them. Like fissures in glass. A void forcing its way into the Abyss. Seth can just make out the green of leaves swaying beyond the blackness between.

"How did we end up here?" Sasha asks.

A humanoid figure takes shape, expanding in size with every second. Until towering over them, with the angriest scowl. "*Well? Is she like you?*" Its voice bellows, vibrating through the

Abyss with such force it begins tearing off their skin. Slivers of flesh peeled from their cheeks, Persephone and Mikhail screech in agony.

Holding the family tight, with Persephone locked in Sasha's arms, Seth jumps straight up, exiting through the fractured space, hurtling toward an uprooted tree trunk and large rocks severed from the cliffside. Seth's head bangs against the hard wood, but he protects his family from the blow. Letting go of them, he rises and says, "Kids, stay put."

Giving Sasha a hand, the two of them walk over to where the cabin once was. Left in the cabin's wake is a massive black hole, with fractures like a spiderweb of broken glass piercing the trees, air, and cliffside. A damaged puzzle piece tossed away, leaving a world incomplete. Touching the fissures, Seth winces, but shoulders the pain. His eyes glow white as abyssal flame surges through the world's fabric, cauterizing it. Sasha also raises her hand, and upon the burnt wound, she unleashes teal sparks, regenerating the broken spot. The cabin gone, but the earth back as it should be.

"Could Sergei do that?" Seth says, breathing heavily, but smiling at Sasha, before looking back at the children. Persephone looks on in horror at the mess her parents have fixed. While Mikhail, eyes wide with fear, inches away from the young girl.

"This is what I was afraid of," Seth says.

"What?" asks Sasha.

Seth turns, eyes welling with tears, voice shaky, lips quivering. "She's too much like me."

Twilight envelops the New York City skyline. The evening light filtering into a large penthouse apartment in Manhattan. Inside, the air is filled with the scent of freshly cooked burgers. A father sits in silence with his son.

The seven-year-old boy, with blond curls glittering in the setting sun, bites into his burger, rare with blood dripping through and down his chin. A pulse unlike his heartbeat flutters through his body. He swiftly turns around, facing the northern window behind him. Pigeons on the windowsill flutter away at his gaze, which lingers even once they're gone.

His father stops eating, watching his son glare outside, where nothing is now that the birds are gone. "Damien, what are you looking at?"

The boy's mouth gapes, and he says in a monotone, "Something powerful. Upstate. We want it."

A surge of power ripples across realms, leaving Earth and felt in dimensions below, where the screams of an entire species light the air like fire.

A tall, muscular man with a long teal beard and wild hair to match, licks his pale lips as he gobbles down soul and body alike. His sharp teeth clatter as he feels the soul nourish his being and—his head jerks upward as he feels the divine pulse in a realm above them. One that shouldn't exist.

"Ho! Come, my godkin!" Dozens of others like him gather around. Their pasty white skin and bright teal hair glimmering brightly. Blood dripping from their teeth and lips.

"Did you not feel that? Something stirs above. Something born from the Womb of the One Mind! Dare I say, it must be the traitor Zarathustra."

"If it is indeed Zarathustra, why have we not felt him before?" asks a woman with teal hair to her hips. "I'd imagine this is something else."

The man shrugs and glares upward.

"Zarathustra or something else, it matters not. It is either the stray god or something of his devising. Either way, we must ensure it is annihilated.

"For nothing can stand in the way of the Abyssian gods."

PART TWO

Echo's Rising

"There was never any more inception than there is now,
Nor any more youth or age than there is now,
And will never be any more perfection than there is now,
Nor any more heaven or hell than there is now.
Urge and urge and urge,
Always the procreant urge of the world."
"I am large; I contain multitudes."
—Walt Whitman, *Song of Myself*

CHAPTER TEN

Out on the horizon, past the towering New York City buildings, rises the dawning sun. Its soft, early morning glow filters into the penthouse apartment. Diminishing by a fraction the thick darkness of the dining room. With no lights on, there's nothing but that distant light to illuminate the space within.

Aside from his sparkling locks of golden blond hair.

Beneath which are a row of thick, stark white teeth. Sinking into the skin of a large pomegranate. Rivers of blood red juice gush out, flowing over his lips and down the pale skin of his neck. Droplets splatter upon his white T-shirt, branding the deed upon him.

His cheeks raise, lips curling upward as a manic intensity radiates from his bright, sky-blue eyes. Flashing his teeth, their whites are stained crimson.

Eating the rest of the pomegranate as one eats an apple, he stands to leave. His lanky, teenage body standing tall over the large rectangular dining room table.

It's time we went to meet them, and the especially powerful one they produced. Her power, so concentrated we can barely stand it! She will be welcomed into ourselves in time.

The morning sun rises further, piercing through the room's darkness. And as he pushes away his chair and leaves the apartment, his feet splash in deep red puddles. Sticky as pomegranate juice, but thicker. Strewn throughout the puddles are empty cans, fruit rinds and peels, open and half-empty milk containers, and multiple bags of garbage spilling onto the floor. With dozens of flies buzzing around it all.

And with a wide grin, he leaves in his wake a white tile floor soaked in blood. The crimson source of life streams from below the windowsill. Outside, the commotion of traffic, pedestrians, and cooing pigeons stir, unaware of the skeleton slumping in a pool of blood and liquidized flesh. The stained bones lay with leftover pieces of meat and hair clumped together in sporadic placement.

The apartment door closes, the young man chuckling as he walks away.

Just under sixteen years earlier.

Steam rises from the deep kitchen sink as the faucet runs into a dirty soup pot. Scrubbing their bowls clean, David Christensen places them into the dishwasher. The scent of green apples rises from the dish soap. Just outside the kitchen, the soft glow of the television lingers. A news report chatters on at a whisper. Turning the faucet off, David leaves the large pot to soak and joins his wife in the living room.

"Strange times we live in. With what has been called the Supernatural Holocaust occurring just three years ago, and now—well, I suppose there won't be any more holocaust deniers..."

A brunette woman holding a microphone chatters on and on.

"What's this about now?" asks David.

"Shh! Just watch," says Lyza, slouched deep into the cushions, her right hand rubbing gently her large protruding belly. David sits, placing his right hand over hers.

The news begins running clips of toddlers running around with fire rising from their eyes, jets of water spat and floating around in the air—a thunderclap as a giggling little boy summons a bolt of lightning to each palm, with a house collapsed into embers behind. "As you can see, we have a new phenomenon on our hands—super-abled children. As of now, we have no leads as to why or how this sudden emergence came to be. Perhaps only God knows...just a little joke at the expense of the holocaust deniers, as well as those who claim the event led to the death of God. Again, strange times we live in."

A sudden kick is felt within Lyza's stomach, jerking both of their attentions to it. "What a world, indeed...Damien." Lyza says.

"Do you think he'll come into such power, too? Think of that! Us giving birth to a superhuman, the next stage in human evolution!"

Lyza glances away, a frown creeping to her face. Clicking the TV off, she says, "I for one hope he's a normal, good little boy. We were both here during the Supernatural Holocaust...we should move on from such nonsense and appreciate humanity for what it is."

Bringing his hand to his face, David strokes his clean-shaven chin. "Hmm, well I suppose—"

Lyza's face lights with pain as she grabs at her stomach. Her mouth clenches. The veins in her neck protruding, pulsing. Reaching for David, she says, "C-call an ambulance...Damien's coming!"

David springs to his feet, frenzied, and glances about for his phone. "Are you s-sure?"

Lyza groans loudly as another contraction assaults her and—the dam between her legs bursts as a large puddle of yellowish liquid spills onto the couch and the floor.

"Ah—shit!"

Dialing the number, an ambulance comes swiftly, and together they make their way to the hospital.

Legs in stirrups, a male doctor and nurse hovering near her exposed crotch, Lyza screeches in anguish. David, dressed in baby-blue scrubs, stands at her side and grips her hand. She squeezes twice as hard, her nails digging into his skin. "You're going to be okay. You're going to be okay. The baby's coming and you're going to be okay," David repeats, as Lyza screams. His major part in all this occurring nine months ago, he's relegated to a pillar of support. But one that is crumbling at the base, weathered with time and neglect. The words of a man in the sacred moment of childbirth are as empty air, as the woman screams, pushes, and tears.

Hanging above them are bright surgical lamps. The light piercing Lyza's eyes, causing the room to splinter and swirl. Alongside the pain, rivers of sweat pour from the top of her head. Stinging her eyes and coating her tongue with salt.

"It hurts!" Lyza says. "It hurts too much—something isn't right!"

The greying male doctor, still leaning into her crotch, chuckles and shakes his head. "It hurts for everyone. You're fine."

Her screams growing louder, Lyza grips her stomach with both hands. The nurse shuffles her gaze from the doctor to

Lyza and back again. Her eyes scrunch above her mask-hidden mouth. Whispering into the doctor's ear, she says, "But doctor, shouldn't the baby be crowning by now?"

Lyza's neck whips back, clenching her teeth as the whites of her eyes redden and—a volcanic spray of blood bursts from the plateau of her stomach, coating the doctor and nurse's face, splattering against David's chest, staining his baby-blue scrubs. Everyone stumbles backward, their audible gasping filling the silence of the room. The air drenched in a red mist, making it difficult to breathe.

Glancing at his tremoring, crimson-coated hands, David whips his gaze upward. Teetering toward the surgical table, he says, "Lyza?"

David clutches his mouth at the sight—Lyza lies motionless, her abdominal cavity torn open, the ribs broken, flesh flayed.

Within a puddle of liquidized flesh, he rises. Gripping the outward-facing ribs, baby Damien pulls himself from the womb.

A twilit sky envelops the New York City skyline. The evening light filtering into their penthouse apartment. Inside, the air is filled with the scent of freshly cooked burgers. David sits in silence with his son. A household of minimal words, in the wake of Lyza's life.

The seven-year-old boy, with blond curls glittering in the setting sun, bites into his burger, rare with blood dripping through and down his chin. Damien's eyes spring wide—he swiftly turns around, facing the northern window behind him. Pigeons on the windowsill flutter away at his gaze, which lingers even once they're gone.

David stops eating, watching his son glare outside, where there is nothing to be found. "Damien, what are you looking at?"

The boy's mouth gapes, and he says in a monotone, "Something powerful. Upstate. We want it."

David's nose twitches, curling upward. His mouth clenches, his narrow eyes falling dead on his son. A legion of hateful words lay in wait upon his tongue. Wishing for nothing more than to lash out at the thing that ruined his life. But he is enslaved by fear.

The burger's red juices streaming from the boy's lips, not unlike the bloodied grime which coated him as he rose from the corpse of his mother. Almost eight years since that day, whatever power caused that tragedy has not yet resurfaced. *But the birth of t-this thing took her away from me. And here it sits, speaking in that weird way...*

Damien continues staring out the northside window, drool mingling with the crimson burger juices. "Someday, we will go find it...and we'll make them play."

The boy has forgotten his father's presence—or rather, he is barely ever aware of it. He speaks only to himself. David's throat tightens, as if something thick and pungent is forcing its way into his bowels. Abruptly pushing his chair back, David retreats into his bedroom. His son doesn't stir. He remains staring out the window with excessive lust.

Slamming the door behind him, David rushes into the adjoining bathroom. Crumbling to his knees, his head dives into the toilet. Loud, deep retching fills the void of the penthouse. With its vile stench being all they know.

Nine years later.

The glow of sunlight is softened by the filter of dark grey curtains. Keeping the space within the confines of these beige walls cool and relaxing. With nothing but silence, except the ticking of a large clock hanging above a wide fish tank. The creatures within, bountiful with color. Sitting at the opposite wall, Damien stares at the fish—seven of different shapes and species, at home in one community. He smiles below dead eyes, feeling a kinship with the aquarium.

A young, petite woman with long, wavy brunette hair taps her pen against a dark wood table. "So, how have things with your father been?" she asks.

Damien's gaze turns slowly from the fish tank, locking eyes with his therapist. Her body tremors, the tapping of her pen intensifying alongside the brisk thud of her left foot upon the floor.

"You mean the expense account that has us talk to you because he can't stand the sight of us?"

The therapist's eyes narrow at the usage of the plural pronouns. Not once during his many years of therapy has Damien ever used the words *I* or *me* or *myself*. The insistence on referring to himself as many irks her. "I thought we agreed we would work on referring to yourself as a singular person. But I haven't seen any improvement on that point."

"You agreed. We did not."

Damien collapses into the couch, his head slunk back. "We are many. Why would we refer to ourselves as anything else?" Whipping his head forward, the manic intensity of his gaze piercing the young woman, Damien continues, "But luckily for you, after all these years, we finally have a real answer to give you! You see, it came to us the other day, when we killed the neighbor's dog."

"What? You killed—"

"It bit us, and we got angry. When suddenly, we felt our body quake. As if there were the rage of seven souls thrashing about within us, sending tremors of energy up our spine, into our brain, and—that's when it happened, the fur, the flesh, its entire being sheared off its bones, strand by strand, as if we had plunged it into a woodchipper! It was..." Damien's voice quivers with excitement, his breathing heavy and labored. "Exhilarating."

The therapist's chair rolls slowly back before hitting her desk. Eyes wide and quivering, she remains silent.

"All our life, we felt it." Damien continues. "Multiple forces within us, acting as one. We are a collective, and the lives of simple-thinking individuals are of no concern to us."

Damien rises, stepping toward the woman. The whites of his eyes turn black and pulsate. A sliver of skin peels from her right cheek in an instant. Screeching, she cups her face with both hands, blood seeping through her fingers.

"This is to be our last session. We only attended this long because we were waiting for our body to be more physically mature. We are off to meet others like us, after all. Those who are large and contain multitudes."

Cowering in her chair, the young woman turns away from Damien. Hiding her head beneath her arms. Damien makes his way to the door.

"You may live. Your intentions were good, and you tried to help. But you never once considered that we are not broken, but instead exactly as we are supposed to be."

"Dropping him as a client?" David Christensen yells into his cellphone. "What for? I don't give a shit about HIPAA. Yes, so you said. No, I don't understand. Listen here, you have any idea how busy a man I am? Yeah, and I don't want to waste my assistant's time finding a new therapist for my deranged son!"

The line goes dead. David groans, which turns into a scream as he plunges his phone onto the dining room table. It smashes into pieces and—the penthouse's door creaks open.

In comes Damien with a crooked smile, his dead gaze hanging low. He walks through the dining room and into the kitchen without a word to his father, who glares with disgust and astonishment. Returning from the kitchen with a large wooden bowl overflowing with pomegranates, Damien walks past his father again and places the fruit onto the dining room table.

"Are you kidding me?" says his father. Damien glances toward him, but says nothing. "Your therapist dropped you. After all I do for you, all the work to find someone to help you—"

"You didn't send us to therapy to help us. It was so you wouldn't have to deal with us. It was the same with homeschool. You were trying to hide us away from the public eye, so that we didn't tarnish your political campaign."

David's astonished glare deepens. Pointing a fat finger close to Damien's face, he says, "You need help. All these years, I did what I could and kept my mouth shut. But after all the torment you—"

"Oh, your disgust has always been quite clear. You blame us for Mom dying. Not that that matters to us."

Seething, David's fist lunges straight toward Damien's nose and—the whites of Damien's eyes swirl away into black voids. The veins within pulse, and the skin and flesh of David's hand shears away, leaving a skeletal appendage from the elbow down. David stumbles backward, hitting the wall. Hyperventilating, he slumps to the floor. Sitting beneath the windowsill and staring with wide eyes as his son approaches.

"Ly-za! How did we ever give birth to such—such a—*monster!*"

"Monster, you say?" says Damien. "You simplistic normal humans are far more monstrous than we are. You hated us for our entire life, for something we could not control. And we're the cruel ones?"

Standing before his father, his grin stretches wide. His black eyes grow deeper, before pulsing once more. Invisible shock waves vibrate outward from those black mires, causing his father's flesh to ripple before erupting off his frame, coating the walls and floor with blood and liquidized flesh.

Damien turns away and sits down at the dining room table. Pulling the fruit bowl close, he lifts a pomegranate to his mouth. His teeth puncture the fruit's thick skin, sinking into the juicy insides. The purple liquid dripping from his lips, down his neck. And he thinks about those others who are large and contain multitudes like him.

"Soon..." he whispers, flashing his crimson-stained teeth.

CHAPTER ELEVEN

Before her uncle Andes died, Persephone had never considered death. Children are brought into the world, ignorant and never asking why. And yet they are so curious. One must wonder what would become of children if they weren't sheltered by their parents. If they were subjected to the cruelties of the world before deemed ready for them.

There is something to be said of nature. But nurture—this determines whether one's nature is disciplined or allowed to run rampant.

As for Persephone, much can change in six years.

A creak of a door springs her awake from shallow sleep. The summer air, wet and thick with humidity, stifles her breathing. Tossing and turning, she groans at the glow of the rising sun. Piercing her dry, red eyes.

Dishware clatters beyond her bedroom door, alongside the aroma of water filtering through coffee beans.

Persephone rises from bed. Walking slowly, she reaches toward her door. Twisting the knob and quietly opening it a sliver, she spies her mother heading outside with a mug in hand. Steam from her freshly brewed coffee coils upward.

"Persephone?" Sasha says, turning around to meet her daughter. "Sorry, hun. Did I wake you?"

Persephone's glare intensifies. Her nose quivering with rage, her frown deepening. Though only open a sliver, she yanks the door shut—the bang shakes the walls and echoes throughout the cabin.

Sasha's head slumps as she sighs and leaves.

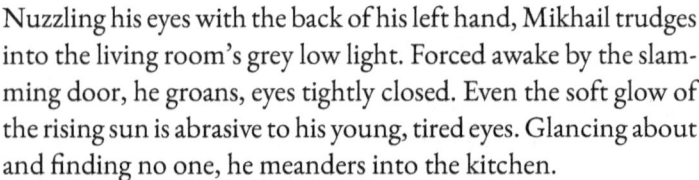

Nuzzling his eyes with the back of his left hand, Mikhail trudges into the living room's grey low light. Forced awake by the slamming door, he groans, eyes tightly closed. Even the soft glow of the rising sun is abrasive to his young, tired eyes. Glancing about and finding no one, he meanders into the kitchen.

His fifteen-year-old body is thin, but short. On his tiptoes, he reaches toward the cabinet to the right of the kitchen sink and—a large hand gently pats the top of his head. Muffling his long, messy brown curls.

"Morning, bud." Seth's thick, muscular right arm stretches past Mikhail's, reaching two bowls with ease. Placing both along the counter, Seth pours a nearby bag of cereal and a generous amount of milk into both bowls.

Eyes tethered to the man's form, Mikhail smiles and says, "Thanks, Uncle Seth."

"Eat up. I'll make some eggs for protein. Gotta make sure you grow up big and strong. Go get Persephone, would you?"

Mikhail nods and walks off. On his way to Persephone's room, he glances at his thin, dainty arms, confused by his uncle's words. Nutrition being a vital part of training aside, Mikhail doesn't see the need to become muscular like Seth. *Being taller would help to reach the dishes by myself. But I don't see why—*

Before reaching her door, it swings open, banging against the wall behind it. Mikhail's gaze is jolted upward as he gasps—Persephone glides past without a word. No longer the gleeful girl she was when they were young children. But her skin, pale as moonlight, almost glows amidst the early morning dawn. Her delicate frame, her partially exposed midriff between a halter top and purple sweatpants. Something akin to vibration stirs within Mikhail's chest.

"Persephone," Seth says, sternly. "That's twice now. And you woke Mikhail earlier. You cannot slam doors."

Rolling her eyes, she scoffs. "You and Mom are both the same. She cares more about her job than me, and you care more about Mikhail!"

Seth extends a plate full of scrambled eggs and breakfast sausage toward the table, placing it with a hard thud. "Persephone, that's not fair. You're my daughter, and I love you more than—"

Persephone scoffs almost comically loud. Ignoring her father, she plunges a fork toward a sausage, eating straight from the platter.

Seth clamps his eyes shut, turning away as he sighs. "Eat up. We're beginning lessons early today. That's your punishment for slamming doors and waking everyone up."

"But Mom woke me up fir—"

"Enough, Persephone! Just eat."

Mikhail silently watches Seth retreat into the kitchen to pour himself some coffee.

Turning toward Persephone, Mikhail loses himself in thought. *My parents are dead, but you're the one who's acting out?*

As he thought about his father, he thought more about Seth's muscular form. How strange it is to be born to a pair of elderly people, on the fringes of life and death. *Perhaps that's why I'm not upset. Deep down, I knew it would come. But Persephone? Father loved her, always pampered her. More than he did me.*

Mikhail stared at the thirteen-year-old girl guzzling down sausages and eggs, wondering where it all goes.

And his mouth twitched with envy.

Seth paces back and forth, a book open in his left palm, his other hand tucked away into his pants pocket. The young teenagers sit upon the couch, a few feet apart. Mikhail writing diligently, his notebook flat upon his lap. Persephone, slouched back, legs up and bent, hides her notebook behind her risen knees. Her pen glides along the paper, forming the shape of a blushing cartoon cat.

Seth claps his book shut and says, "Let me see your work."

Handing over their notebooks, Seth smiles at Mikhail. "Good work. Head outside. We'll begin training shortly." The boy nods, ambling outside without a word. "Persephone, what the hell is this?"

"A cat."

"You were supposed to be taking notes. We're going to have a quiz tomorrow, and you're not going to be ready—"

"Was Uncle Andes ready to die?"

Taken aback, Seth's eyes grow wide. "What? Perseph—"

"It doesn't matter, is the answer. We are all going to die. So, what is the point of learning anything?"

"I don't want to hear you talk like that," says Seth. "Your uncle would be so ashamed of you. You're brilliant, Persephone! When you were children, Mikhail was the one who struggled. Now the roles have reversed, and why? You are so much more than this!" Seth holds up her notebook, shaking it around for emphasis.

Scoffing, Persephone says, "I'm going to change before heading outside."

Shaking his head, Seth joins Mikhail out upon the cliffside.

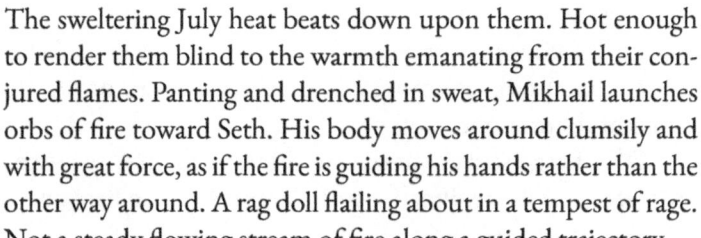

The sweltering July heat beats down upon them. Hot enough to render them blind to the warmth emanating from their conjured flames. Panting and drenched in sweat, Mikhail launches orbs of fire toward Seth. His body moves around clumsily and with great force, as if the fire is guiding his hands rather than the other way around. A rag doll flailing about in a tempest of rage. Not a steady flowing stream of fire along a guided trajectory.

As the flames approach, Seth reaches for them in the way a tennis player lunges to hit a ball. To protect the house and the surrounding forest, not a single flame can be let loose. But upon catching them, the flames dissipate as if they never were.

His labored breathing intensifying, Mikhail halts, yelling, "How do you do that?"

Seth glares at the boy. *They train every day, and he makes no progress. And worse, each day is like peering through time. When I became a monster for the first time, hurling those orbs of hellfire around so haphazardly...*

"Through mastery of the flame," says Seth, his pupils sinking into the whites of his eyes. The abyss pulses through them, as a ring of white flames outlines the edge of the cliffside. Another pulse and the flames vanish. Leaving not even a trail of smoke. "Something you have consistently failed to do. I think it's time, Mikhail. There's been something eating at you since you were a child. I've seen it within you every day. It's time to tell me about it. Because I promise you, the flames will never be controlled if you cannot first tame the torment within you. Is it about your dad? Your mom?"

"No—it's not—it's hard to put into words and I'm..."

Persephone joins them on the cliffside, walking by without a word or glance. Mikhail's eyes linger upon her skin as she makes her way to sit beneath a tree. Having changed out of her sweatpants for shorts, which do not cover much—a wall of white flame cuts off Mikhail's gaze, enclosing himself and Seth in a fiery orb.

Seth's eyes narrow, uncomfortable in his knowledge of what is going on. A teenage boy with fire magic, and evermore potent stores of testosterone.

"What have I said about the importance of focus? It's time I instruct Persephone. Practice your flame mastery in here until I get back."

Mikhail's focus snaps back. Nodding quickly, beads of sweat flinging sporadically around him. Seth nods in return, as an oval shape is cut out of the flames behind him. Walking through, he leaves Mikhail within the abyssal white dome.

———◆○◆———

"You're supposed to be meditating," says Seth, approaching his daughter.

"I hate meditation! I don't understand why you have me—"

Seth pats her head as he lowers himself to the ground beside her. "What am I going to do with the two of you?" he says, as Persephone grabs her father's wrist and shoos his hands away from her. Seth chuckles. "Look, about your comments from before." Persephone rolls her eyes, turning away from him. "Is that what's eating you up? That uncle Andes isn't here anymore?"

Persephone sighs, refusing to look his way.

"Fine, I get it. You don't want to talk. Just listen then. Your uncle loved you very much. Your mom and I love you *very* much. You may not see it, but we do. Your mom...works a very demanding job. It's hard for me, too. Her being away so much. But it's necessary. So, we deal. But she loves you, Persephone. She *does*."

The teenage girl turns not to her father, but to the dome of white flames which have overtaken the cliffside. "But you like Mikhail more. He has magic just like you and Mom."

"It's not that simple—"

"I don't understand! Why do you train with him, but I'm forced to me-di-tate all day?" says Persephone, sarcastically bopping her head back and forth in tandem with the syllables."

Seth stares softly at her. And frowns. *She still has no memory of those two instances.*

"Look, I may be the stern father every now and then, but you know I don't believe in lying to you. I was lied to growing up, about more than you can imagine. And it made things...messy. So, listen. I spend all this time training Mikhail because his magic, left undisciplined, could cause a lot of problems. And there's something inside that has been troubling him, something that must be dealt with before he can control his power. That's also why I have you meditate. To resolve those bad feelings you have inside."

"But it never changes how I feel!"

"Because you don't believe it can! All of humanity's successes begin with answering *Yes!* to the question *Do I believe I can do this? Do I have faith in myself?*"

Persephone's jaw drops, watching her father become more animated than usual. But, glancing back toward the dome of white flames, her mouth clamps tightly into its usual pout. "But what does it matter anyway? I don't have magic like Mikhail."

"And if I had things my way, you never will." Seth rises, patting her head once more. "Magic has the potential for greatness, yes. But it also has the potential for destruction if one is not first calmed from within."

Walking toward the white dome, Seth comes to a sudden halt. Looking back to Persephone, he says, "I know you don't think much of me as a teacher, but you should count yourself lucky." Seth grins. "My teacher was a lot harsher, and never half as kind. But if you won't vent to your mom and dad, then be a good classmate and bond with Mikhail. You're so busy being jealous of him that you haven't considered that he, too, needs a helping hand."

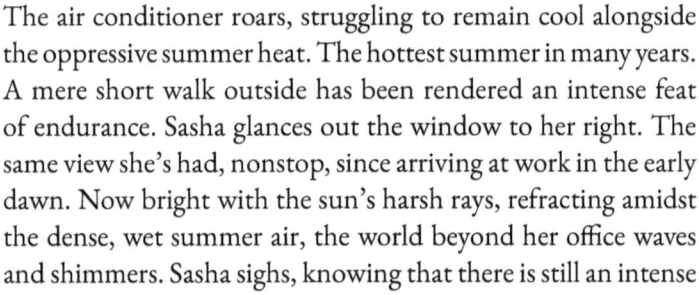

The air conditioner roars, struggling to remain cool alongside the oppressive summer heat. The hottest summer in many years. A mere short walk outside has been rendered an intense feat of endurance. Sasha glances out the window to her right. The same view she's had, nonstop, since arriving at work in the early dawn. Now bright with the sun's harsh rays, refracting amidst the dense, wet summer air, the world beyond her office waves and shimmers. Sasha sighs, knowing that there is still an intense heat she cannot avoid or hide from.

Her gaze drops, turning the page of an aerospace engineering textbook—a knock at the door, and it creaks open.

"Excuse me, Sasha." Brianna steps in, her appearance having starkly changed over the last thirteen years. Her cotton-candy blue hair switched out for her natural chestnut color. Her skin, not old but also lacking in the tautness of a girl in her mid-twenties, as she had been when joining the Assembly. Slight wrinkles groove into the corners of her eyes and mouth. "It's time for the conference room meeting with the collective heads."

"So it is," says Sasha. "Thanks, Brianna. I'll be on my way in a moment."

Brianna smiles, nods, and leaves.

Raising a pocket mirror, Sasha tilts and turns her head. Streaks of grey mingle with her black hair, which has lost some of its youthful luster. Crow's feet press deeply into the corners of her eyes. Her cheeks, lacking their previous youthful glow. Reaching toward the runic scar on her neck, she rubs it gently. It, too, has lost its prominence. But it is no less there. Its skin simply fades with age.

How much longer do I have before ending up like Andes?

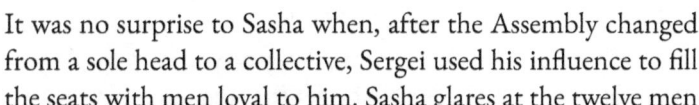

It was no surprise to Sasha when, after the Assembly changed from a sole head to a collective, Sergei used his influence to fill the seats with men loyal to him. Sasha glares at the twelve men encircling the large oval table, with her as the only woman in charge of the organization she erected.

"So," she says, "For today's agenda, I would like to once more bring up my plans for how to most effectively use the...energy on the other end of the Abyssal Pedestal."

The men erupt in laughter.

"This again?" asks Sergei.

"I will bring it up continuously until you all see reason. The White Abyss—"

"The realm you alone have access to, and won't share with the rest of us," Sergei retorts.

"For now, yes." Sasha glances around the table. "It's not meant to be weaponized. Those ambitions of yours are short-sighted."

"What's short-sighted about wanting to arm the Earth with the means to protect itself?"

"Protect itself from what? Trust me—the supernatural forces that the Assembly might face some day, any weapon you conceive of won't accomplish anything. We need not weapons, but knowledge! The Abyss is an unabating source of knowledge—knowledge of things and worlds and beings that we could never understand without it! With said knowledge, we won't only be able to defend ourselves, but also expand the human race. You, Sergei, want to transform the Earth into a fortress. But I want to take humanity to the stars! What good are all the weapons in the world if our one and only stronghold is obliterated in a moment's time? I know what's coming. Your plans will not stop it."

Sergei grins and leans over the table. Placing his elbows upon the dark wood surface, he rests his chin in his right hand. "And how do you know what's coming? Why do you keep the Abyssal Pedestal to yourself? It's no wonder that the ranks have turned on you. How can you possibly be trusted?"

Sasha clenches her eyes shut, biting the side of her gums. "Any mistrust amongst the ranks has only come to be through your meddling and deception. I want what is for the best of the Assembly, for humankind."

"Mankind will be just fine under my plans. Well, boys? You know the drill. All in favor of continuing course, say aye."

The men rise in tandem, yelling "Aye!" as they exit the conference room. She's left alone under the blinding fluorescent lights, within the white walls donned with banners showcasing the Assembly's logo—a black flag with a white circle in the middle, and white runic symbols around the orb.

Sasha sighs and leaves.

Ensuring that the room is empty, Sasha enters the basement laboratory. Walking past the Abyssal Pedestal, she presses a button on the wall behind it, next to the computers and control panel. A tall rectangular indentation appears, a doorway presses further inward before splitting apart, revealing an elevator known only to Sasha.

Steadily lowering, the elevator sinks deep into the earth for many minutes. The door *dings,* opening to a long hallway. Sasha walks on.

On the other end, a wide cavern with a tall ceiling greets her. Many years ago, Sasha had discovered the cavern with her father as they went to investigate a sudden crevasse breaking open in the town of Crowley. Since filled, with apartment buildings built atop it—its earth mended with creation magic—Sasha has expanded the space deep below into a secret facility.

Flipping a switch, the space is swathed in light, illuminating a massive structure before her. Titling her head upward, she gazes upon the shell of a towering spacecraft. One side uncovered, exposing the emptiness within.

Project Persephone. In the case of tragedy, you will grant us all new life—the warmth of spring leading us to a new bloom.

Sasha takes a fistful of her long, flowing hair. Inspecting the ever-growing grays, she sighs. *Without funding, there is no choice.* Relinquishing her hair, she raises both arms in front of her. Teal sparks crackle within her palms before a stream of ethereal energy flows outward, congregating into a square-shaped mass upon the steel floor. The teal glow becomes brighter and brighter. Intense warmth rises and sizzles around the act of creation. For the act of being is to transcend heat—Sasha drops her arms. The teal glow diminishes, its power cooling into solid form. As the last of the light vanishes, before her is a large engine block with an oval-shaped glass container found at its core.

Yet another part made—the Abyssal Drive. Sasha's heart begins fluttering—breathing labored, she clutches at her throat. Shutting her eyes, she focuses on her breath, gradually slowing and easing the pain. *There's no choice but to do this. Humanity needs to secure its future. And I'll make that happen.*

Even if it kills me.

His eyes peeling open, the White Abyss surrounding him, Seth finds the Abyssal Consciousness standing before him. "Pardon the intrusion," Seth says.

"Zarathustra's spawn, here again."

Seth stares at the featureless white face an arm's length away, empty except for its mouth, branded into a frown. "I know you speak in riddles," says Seth, grinning. "And never provide straightforward advice, but you know everything. How is it that Sasha and I slayed a god, yet raising teenagers, two of them, is somehow harder?

"Sorry. Consider that rhetorical. With Sasha at work so much, I have only the kids and the ravens to talk to. And you can imagine they don't—"

"Did you slay a god?" asks the Abyssal Consciousness, tilting its head.

Seth's grin collapses. "Another of your riddles, then? Well, go on. Explain yourself. Because you better not be inferring what I think you are."

"You and your wife declared that God is dead, and that you have killed her. But her disease lingers. Corpses of angels lay at the feet of humanity, yet there are still those who turn their heads and exclaim, "My god is great, and He will rise again!""

"He?"

"They, spawn of Zarathustra. Be warned. They are coming."

Seth's eyes narrow, hands shaking. Turning to leave, Seth opens a portal into the cabin's living room. Stepping forward, he—

"About the little one," says the Abyssal Consciousness. "It does seem as if you passed your volatile side onto her."

Seth turns around, mouth open, ready to reply, when a large white finger pokes into his chest. The Abyssal Consciousness, inches away, says:

"The Nil Magic within you has undergone a change. It is not nothing anymore, perhaps quite the opposite. Over fifteen years since you let your destruction eat away at everything and everyone around you. Your efforts to be better, they are going well?"

Seth's smile returns. "This is why I come here so often. If I can bear the weight of this realm, then I can bear any tempest that brews within me. I will not destroy again." Turning, he ambles toward the portal. "I'll keep this power inside me until my dying breath. And then, you may have it, for all I care. Back into the pool of power that my soul will one day go."

The portal closes behind him, leaving the Abyssal Consciousness alone. It raises its left hand and rubs its rounded chin.

Let us see if that remains true in the war to come. As one not using their gifts to the fullest is a sin that may cost them everything.

Two years later.

The sky, sparse with clouds, does little to block the sun's bright, scorching rays. His skin burning, Seth retreats to the roofed porch. Huginn and Muninn nuzzle their massive beaks against him as he sits upon a rocking chair. Exhausted from the summer's heat, the two ravens collapse on both sides.

Glancing toward the wide open cliffside, the air ripples and distorts. The grass beyond and beneath the trees, while shaded, turns a crisp brown after weeks without rain. Each summer is somehow hotter than the last, despite each being brutal and malicious. *As if the will of the world is intensifying, bringing forth an ill omen.* Seth chuckles, dismissing the thought. If only to preserve the moment. His black hair peppers with subtle grays. With Sasha being further along in age than he, the future and the burdens it carries are something he wishes not to entertain.

Yet the passage of time is ever-present in his mind, as he watches from across the rippling, humid air, his daughter and adopted son conversing quietly beneath a large evergreen. His daughter, a child no longer, but not quite a woman—a budding flower amidst the eve of blooming.

She looks like a younger Sasha.

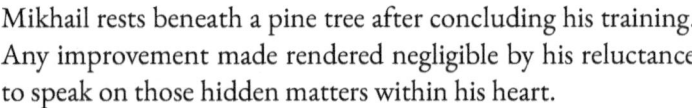

Mikhail rests beneath a pine tree after concluding his training. Any improvement made rendered negligible by his reluctance to speak on those hidden matters within his heart.

Persephone ambles over, whisking Mikhail's gaze toward her. Not yet overt, but enough for a teenage boy to notice—Persephone's hips widening, her breasts beginning to fill. Growing self-conscious of his staring, Mikhail whips his head away. Red in the face.

Persephone joins him by the tree. Sitting side by side, her toes reach the middle of his calves. Having undergone a growth spurt, Mikhail's short and lanky form has become taller and thicker. Not muscular like Seth, but enough for Mikhail to be ever-conscious of it. Glancing along his body, he frowns.

"What'cha thinking about?" asks Persephone.

"Nothing. Just sitting."

Persephone pouts, letting out an annoyed groan. "Something is clearly bothering you. You won't stop sulking! Honestly, how is it that just a handful of years ago, you were excelling in our studies more than me, but now you're too moody to care?"

"But now *you* suddenly care?" Mikhail says, jerking his head toward Persephone with fury in his eyes.

Raising her hands and looking away, she rises, saying, "I've tried. I have tried, haven't I?" Look, I know I was a little bitch for a while, but mom never being home and your dad's passing aren't reasons to lash out at you. We both lost something when he died. I'm trying to be here for you! Who else do we have to talk to?"

"What we lost wasn't equal. My mom died before I knew her. Then my dad died and suddenly—" Embarrassment reddens his face, as he turns away from her. "It's like the masculine essence of my life vanished, and there's this hole inside me now, screaming 'How do I be a man?'"

Mikhail's gaze drops, hating the inauthenticity of his words. Knowing full well that a lack of a masculine role model is neither true nor even connected to the root of his issue.

Persephone glances over at her father, who is swaying gently in a rocking chair and petting the heads of Huginn and Muninn. Catching her stare, he smiles back. Despite the qualms with her parents, she knows her father is a good man. But bringing to Mikhail's attention that he does have a father, he does have a masculine influence, would only be insensitive.

Glancing from the back of Mikhail's head, down his taut neck, broad shoulders, taking in the view of his athletic form, she says, "But you *are* a man."

Mikhail's gaze turns to his body. From his hands to her chest, her groin. Sighing, he says, "Am I, though?"

Two years later.

An olfactory ghost of eggs, bacon, and pancakes coated with butter and maple syrup lingers in the early morning light. The ravens snuggle up, asleep on the living room floor. Cooing softly to each other. The sounds of running water and the clacking of plates being put away fill the confines of the cabin. Seth stands alone at the kitchen sink, scraping the dishes clean, tidying up.

Persephone has slunk back to her room, readying for another day of studies and meditation and petting the birds and watching Mikhail struggle to hone his flames and...she groans audibly through her walls, exasperated at the excitement the world refuses to give her.

Mikhail ambles over to Huginn and Muninn, gently patting their heads as they sleep—

A muffled, crumbling sound pulls Mikhail's attention toward Persephone's bedroom door. Left slightly ajar, he peers inside and finds Persephone tossing her pajamas into a heap on the floor. Standing before a mirror, he glimpses the moonlit glow of her waist, her back—and within the mirror—her cleavage cupped by a black bra.

Mikhail stares, examining the feminine curves with a cold desire.

Slipping on her new shirt, Persephone's gaze falls upon the mirror and— "*Mikhail, what the fuck!*" she screams, eyes wide, lit with fury. Mikhail stumbles backward, tripping and thudding against the floor, crawls his way to his feet, and sprints out the front door.

"What the hell's going on?" Seth asks, emerging from the kitchen, finding Persephone in pursuit. The door slams as she tosses it open.

Huginn and Muninn are sprung from their deep sleep, croaking in protest, but follow Seth outside.

Hunched over by the crippling summer heat, Mikhail halts, breathing heavily. Persephone stomps toward him, pointing her left index finger straight between his eyes. Mikhail gives a cross-eyed glance at the tip of her finger, glistening with sweat. Vision growing blurry, he blinks a few times, shrugging it off.

"What the fuck were you doing?"

Arriving at their side with the ravens in tow, Seth says, "Hey, what's the matter with you two? What happened?"

Ignoring him, Persephone says, "Spying on me as I was changing? Are you serious, you fucking perv?"

Seth shuts his eyes, hangs his head, and sighs.

"I-I'm sorry. I-It's not what y-you think. I promise I—"

A loud *slap* leaves a large red mark across his face. Seething, Persephone says, "You're lucky I don't have those flames of yours, otherwise *I'd melt out your fucking eyes!*"

Pushing his way between them, Seth shouts, "*Hey, that's enough!*"

Silence wedges its way between them, the shame and anger still present upon their respective faces.

"Oh, yes, we would say so as well!" says a voice from the mountain trail. The three of them turn sharply toward it as it makes its way up to the cliffside. The ravens stand tall and spread their wings, croaking in distress, rocking back and forth as they stomp toward the voice.

"Save some of that fury for us!" says the stranger.

"Who are you?" asks Seth.

"Oh, you wound us. After all, in a past life, this cliffside is where we first met."

As the young man approaches, his teeth sink into a pomegranate. Purple juice dribbles down his chin, splattering the grass at his feet. Long golden locks glimmer in the soft glow of the rising sun. Seth's eyes grow wide as he clenches hard enough for his teeth to pierce his gums. Coating his tongue in blood.

"Or rather, the person we once were met you here. We suppose you could call us an echo of Her.

"But make no mistake, we still want what Yahweh wanted."

CHAPTER TWELVE

Tossing his pomegranate rind away, Damien flashes the stained teeth of a cannibal. A moment frozen in time, the split second before an atom bomb engulfs everything in its wake. Along with the scorching summer sun beating down upon his back, Seth has not felt such tension in many years.

Damien steps forward.

"Huginn! Muninn!" Seth shouts, "Take the kids and flee—"

Damien's pale-blue eyes sink into their surrounding whites, darkening black as tar. Six feet before him ripple, slicing through air, grass, and stone. Huginn's beak grips the back of Persephone's shirt, yanking her into the air and flying to the opposite side of the cabin. Muninn snatches the back of Mikhail's shirt—his feet dangle inches from the ground, the flesh from his toes to his waist is torn asunder. Anguish brands his face.

Persephone yells from the other side of the cabin, "Dad! What's going on?"

Eyes wide with horror, blood and liquidized flesh splatters Seth's face, chest, and arms. Hands shaking, he glances toward Muninn, flapping away with half a boy. Mikhail's skeletal bottom swaying in the air as he's pulled away.

"*Mikhail!*" Seth screams, clenching his mouth until his back teeth shatter. Turning his rage toward the strange teenage boy with the wide grin, Seth's pupils sink into his eyes, glowing with a radiant abyssal eminence.

White flame erupts from his palms, spiraling past his elbows. Yanking his arms wide, a giant wall of abyssal fire erects between him and Damien, circling around the murderous stranger.

Seething with anger, Seth paces along the rim of the wall. The words of the Abyssal Consciousness echo within memory. *Be warned. They are coming.*

Focusing on the young man beyond the wall, Seth feels it—the pulse of seven souls. His clenched jaw drops, his eyes widen further with shock. The memory of Sasha and him facing Yahweh in Heaven, of him tapping directly into the power of the White Abyss for the first time, forcing the souls consumed by Yahweh back from whence they originated. Among the bright teal souls of humans...were seven large black souls.

It can't be!

The wall ripples and tears. An arm lunges through, clamping onto Seth's neck, dirty nails digging into his skin. The wall dissipates, its fire collapses into ash. Glaring past the hand suspending him in air, Seth finds a familiar grin and manic-tinted gaze.

"W-what the fuck are you?"

"Us? No, what are you?" Damien asks. "You've changed. There's something different in you, something more. Why won't you let it out?"

Gripping fiercer, Damien pulls his arm back. Lifting Seth as if he were made of straw. The air around his arm ripples inward, momentarily bloating his muscles. Swinging to his right, he plunges Seth toward the cabin—the walls, support beams, and roof splinter upon collision. Glass shattering, as Seth breaks through to the other side. His body bounces and rolls until thudding against a large stone. Pebbles, glass, and wood embed deep within his skin. He lay motionless beside the boulder, ribs and legs broken.

A few yards away, Persephone stares, slack-jawed, gazing between her crippled father and a half-flayed Mikhail. The ravens croak and flitter about, unsure of what to do.

Catching a glimpse of his daughter, Seth reaches his left arm out to her, groaning, "Pers-sephone, ruh-un."

Falling limp, his arm thuds against the sizzling, stony ground.

Persephone's legs flail about in the air as Huginn lifts her over the cabin. Pulling the bottom of her shirt down to compensate for the raven pulling it up from the back. "Huginn! Enough already, put me down. A soft, rattled *coo* emerges from his parted beak, and he flutters toward the ground.

Stumbling as her feet hit the surface, Persephone reaches for the branches of a nearby spruce to steady her balance.

Glancing around while smoothing out her shirt, Persephone shouts, "Dad! What's going on?"

Who is that guy, and who is Yahweh? That look in dad's eyes—how large they grew, with an emotion I've never seen in him before. But I have seen it...within the mirror. What I feel every morning as I watch mom slink out of the house, to be gone until nightfall, never seeing us, never caring for us, never—Persephone bites her lower lip, clenching until growing sore. *I didn't think Dad ever felt that way—*

"*Mikhail!*" Seth screams, yanking Persephone from her thoughts. Her jaw drops. Her chest swells with emotion. Eyes glassing over with tears, she falls to her knees. Muninn lets out a chorus of shrill cries, Huginn joining within a moment.

"M-mi-mikhail?" Persephone whimpers, finding her Mikhail missing everything below his torso. The boy gags, blood ejecting from his mouth. The ravens press their beaks to his back, tilting him to his side. A crimson river runs from his lips, pooling around his face, coating his cheek and brown hair with blood.

"P-seph-one," Mikhail mutters. "I'm s-sor-ry. Before, I wasn't...spying on you. I p-p-promise I wouldn't—" Coughing up more blood, Mikhail gags himself into silence.

"Stop it. None of that matters now! I-I-I don't know what to do! But please don't die. Don't die. Don't die. Don't die. Just don't die!"

His breathing labored, Mikhail flashes a slight smile. "I don't want to die, a lie."

"W-what?"

"I have...a confession. My body might be a guy's, but..." His eyes glance over Persephone, from her hips, up the inward slope of her petite waist and to the plump breasts above it, to her feminine cheeks and large pretty eyes. Those unusual dual-colored eyes, teal and abyssal white mingling together. Staring at him now, he still feels consumed by them. "It's your body, a woman's body, that makes more sense to me. I...don't know why, mine just doesn't...make sense to me. Is it...possible? To have a body that doesn't fit who one is?"

He coughs up more blood, growing too weak to continue.

Unaware that he cannot speak another word, Persephone places her pointer finger to his lips. "Shush, don't speak anymore. I understand, I do. You weren't spying on me. I understand this now." Tears flowing heavier, Persephone takes a deep breath. "Of course, that's possible. What is the soul but consciousness? Our identities, the self, are all made up from what we experience. The body is static, but the mind flows and changes, becomes something more than it was when we were born. It's okay, I understand. You're a girl like me. And I love you the same as always."

Mikhail smiles, her eyes fluttering closed.

{Heed me, True-Born God.} A voice erupts from somewhere deep within Persephone's mind.

"Who's there!" she asks, whipping her head back and forth.

{Are you going to let her die? What about your father? Don't you want to mend their wounds, and the wounds of the world to come?"}

"Of c-c-course I do!"

Seth smashes through the cabin, debris flying through the air. Persephone turns her back, ducks her head, shielding Mikhail. The wood, glass, and her father thud against the ground. Seth reaches toward her, but his arm plummets, heavy and limp.

Emerging from the smog of dust, smoke, and shattered pieces of their home, the stranger ambles toward Seth, speaking with grandeur and diction, "From the Abyss we all come, and to the Abyss we shall again be rejoined. It is a collective like us. We want what Yahweh sought after, albeit a fraction of her vision. We need more if we are to rend this world and abscond from its filth. You wanted this once. To take her hand." Damien reaches toward Seth. "Come now, join us."

Heaving, spitting blood, Seth turns toward the children. Persephone stares with eyes full of tears and awe.

Damien smirks. "Oh, don't worry. She'll be joining you. In fact, we want *her* most of all."

"You stay *the fuck away from my daughter!*" Seth lunges his left arm toward Damien's throat—Seth's flesh ripples and tears, shearing it from the bone. A blood-stained skeletal arm flails backward—

"*Daddy!*" Persephone's mouth clenches as her eyes erupt with abyssal power, whiteness glimmers from the edges—two lunar orbs glaring with rage.

{As a True-Born God, this power is yours to wield. I will not interfere. But know that it can kill thousands in a mere moment, if you allow it—just ask your father.}

"*Shut up!*" Persephone shouts, spittle strewn from her tongue. The seventeen-year-old takes a step forward, the ground warping beneath her weight, surpassing the logical confines of what her small frame should hold. "*Do not presume what I would do!*" she screeches.

Gently hovering her hand above Mikhail's waist, abyssal magic drifts from her palm, weaving around like ribbons as it moves toward Mikhail's wound. Wrapping around his exposed skeleton, the whiteness grows brighter and brighter and—teal sparks are spurred to life. Soul renewed, flesh begins to weave itself around the bone. Tightened with muscle, skin blankets the red flesh...

Mikhail, savoring his last breath, suddenly springs awake, his tight chest heaving, loosening with each fresh breath. Rising, he finds his legs regrown, with an addendum. His legs rise to an oval slit. Patting around at his thighs, Mikhail gasps.

But his awe dies with the sight of the stranger hovering over an armless Seth. "Huginn," says Mikhail, turning to the giant bird nuzzling against his cheek. The raven's head jerks upward in attention. "You have to get Sasha to help! It's an emergency!" The bird croaks and launches into the air, as quickly as it can, toward the town of Crowley.

Seth's eyes widen with awe, with his daughter basking in a vast abyssal glow. *She brought him back from the cusp of death! That was...regeneration.*

Damien smirks. "You there. You are just...ripe with abyssal power."

"Step away from my dad." Persephone stomps toward him, denting the ground as she goes.

"Sure thing. We could consume you first. Won't you be our eighth?"

Persephone charges. Damien opening his arms as if to embrace her, stretched out wide like a cross. "*Stop!*" shouts Seth, propping himself up with his one working arm—his eyes glowing bright white as a cocoon of white flame envelops Damien, and halting Persephone in her tracks. The fire spins and spins, gaining speed until the flames disperse, ash drifting to the ground. Seth slumps backward, and Persephone glares in awe.

The stranger has vanished.

Sitting at her desk, Sasha is lulled into focus. The white noise of the blasting air conditioning muffles all sound as she finishes another aerospace engineering textbook. Stretching back, she yawns—a firm tapping against the window. She turns, finding Huginn staring through. Cocking his head, he croaks and taps his beak against the window thrice.

Rising, Sasha rushes to open the window. "Huginn! You shouldn't be here. What happened?"

The raven steps back, fluttering its wings. "Sasha, help. Emergency," says the avian mimic.

Rushing through the door near the window, Sasha rushes out into the courtyard where Assembly workers are sitting upon benches and at picnic tables, eating their lunch. Pointing at the raven, the slack-jawed audience murmurs amongst themselves. Stroking Huginn's beak, the raven lowers to the ground so Sasha can climb atop him. Flapping hard, wind pools beneath his wings. And off they go.

Pedestrians point and stare at the horse-sized raven flying above them. The windows of cars stopped at traffic lights roll down, their drivers craning their heads out and upward, catching a glimpse of the phenomenon. Sasha pays no mind. A disaster in waiting, but she knows that the birds would never be sent off the mountain if a disaster wasn't already upon them.

Reaching the mountain's summit, Sasha finds their home with a massive hole straight through the middle. A trail of wood and grass leading to—Sasha gasps, as Huginn swoops toward the scene.

Hopping off the bird, Sasha shouts, "Seth!"

Sasha finds Persephone kneeling over her father. An abyssal glow extending from her frame—a full-body halo. Reaching out toward her father, teal sparks crackle around his broken ribs and legs, as abyssal white bandages weave around his skeletal arm, tying new flesh to the bone, wrapping them in skin. Persephone rises and turns toward her mother. A rageful white glow pulsating from her eyes before softening, her pupils returning, leaving just a scornful pout.

"You...healed him! Persephone! You're incredible!"

Glaring, Persephone walks off to join Mikhail.

"Seth!" Sasha lunges toward him, wrapping him in her embrace. "What the fuck happened?"

"A s-s-stranger appeared. Intense power. He's gone...for now."

"What do you mean, for now?"

"I...whisked him away. Portal magic, but in a way I've yet to do be-fore. I was so close to death that I can't e-e-even te-ell you where...I sent hi-him." Seth's head falls limp, breathing, but unconscious.

Sasha pouts, her eyes narrowing as she gazes inquisitively at her husband, the children, the house, and the ravens.

"Alright, Persephone! I'll handle your father, you grab Mikhail. It's not safe here anymore."

Persephone scoffs, but helps Mikhail to her feet. Laying each of them on a raven, they fly off, saying goodbye to their home, and the many cozy memories it once gave them.

CHAPTER THIRTEEN

Stark blackness envelops everything. A deep silence known only to the deaf. No evidence of a world outside oneself, except the pungent smell of charred flesh. Lingering after all these years, with nowhere to go.

A cocoon of white fire rages its way into being. Its glow illuminating the surrounding space, glimmering upon dilapidated buildings, rubble, and stone. Blackened skeletal remains strewn about. The spiraling flames burst outward, dispersing into the air. Cooling to ash, the soft white glow lingers as light-glimmering snowflakes. Emerging from the shattered, white dome, Damien breathes in the air of charcoal and rot.

"Delicious." Damien flashes his crimson-stained teeth amidst the darkness. "The power once dispersed here...lingers to this day. Dead, but not forgotten, it seems." He turns to face an especially black spot upon the stony cave floor. "Before we were born, but he has revisited the shadow of his past deeds. Where he first killed one, and then three of us. And everyone else, it seems."

Damien glances around the ruins of Magistrum, in the low, dwindling abyssal glow. The memories slowly crawling back.

Memories of lives not his own. The collective remembrances of seven individuals. And yet his ownership could not ever be questioned. They are and aren't his. And so, he remembers the pain he did not experience. One by one, felled by a young man whose existence was kept a secret from the seven. Yet come together again after briefly rejoining into Yahweh...everything has become clear. His lust for that which resides within Seth has crystallized within his mind. *But that girl. The daughter of the one who killed us, she's much more...appetizing. A riper fruit could not exist— We will tear her apart and bleed her dry, until that powerful soul is ours.*

The words of which to call her elude him, but Damien can feel what she is. A lingering memory of Yahweh peering into the White Abyss, only to be consumed by that which she sought to consume. Pulsing from within was the very power he felt radiating from Persephone.

The White Abyss in the form of a human girl.

Damien steps away from the collapsed tower, making his way to the edge of the cave, where he remembers the exit once being. Salivating, licking his lips in preparation for what is to come.

Reaching the exit, he finds it blocked with dirt and stone. *Scared of people finding out what you've done, are you, Seth? Well, do not worry. We intend to rectify the sins committed here.* His pupils sink into the whites of his eyes, as tar spirals out from the center, coating his eyes black. The boulders ripple and tear, bursting away into a thick dirt cloud, and a faint light emerges on the other end of the tunnel.

Walking onward, Damien smirks below hungry, dead eyes.

Bright fluorescent lights beat down on the beige walls and white tile floors. Stinging the swollen, red eyes of Sasha and Persephone, as they sit by the sides of Seth and Mikhail. Silence wedges itself between them, with all there is to disrupt the ever-deepening tension and heartache is naught but the soft beeping of life monitors. That steady, continuous beep confirming the life of these otherwise motionless bodies.

"What the hell is going on!" Persephone says, with puddles in her eyes. "I healed them. You said I healed them! But it's been days...why aren't they waking up?"

Sasha lays a hand on her daughter's shoulder. Persephone jerks away from her touch, turns from her father, and crouches at Mikhail's side. Sasha sighs and says, "Your father has mentioned how sporadic Mikhail's magic is. The training will do you both some good, but it won't matter until you're about twenty-six. One's ability to harness magic to its utmost ability—to do so with great control, correlates directly to whether that someone has a fully developed brain."

Persephone's eyes light with fury, "So it's my fault then? I'm too young to do anything right? Where do you get off trying to tell me *anything* when you're never around! It's like I only have one fuckin' parent—"

"Ah, a family matter, then?" says a gruff voice from behind. Sergei stands at the threshold of the infirmary, leaning against the door frame.

"Can I help you?" asks Sasha.

"Personal usage of the Assembly's resources, eh? And word is that you plan to move your family into the barracks. I'd ask if something happened to your home, but you know I don't care. This isn't going to be taken well by the Assembly members."

Lips twitching, Sasha steps toward him. "How can we pride ourselves on ensuring humanity's wellbeing if we can't first protect our own? I would expect any of the members to do as I am doing. And I would allow it with open arms. Even for you and your family, Sergei."

The man's grin collapses into pensiveness. "A perk I would never take advantage of, even if my family wasn't dead." He turns, disappearing from the doorway. His footsteps are heard down the hall, along with the beep of an elevator. Sasha's eyes widen, mouth agape. She had never heard anything about Sergei's family before. Turning toward her comatose husband and adopted child, and her still seething daughter, she smiles sadly.

Unearthing her cellphone from her right pants pocket, she holds down a speed dial.

"Hello, this is the Assembly for Magic and Human Progression. Office of the President. How can I help you?"

"Brianna, it's me. I need you to stand guard in the infirmary for me. Watch over my husband and son. Persephone and I are going to come up to my office and have some much-needed mother-daughter bonding."

Persephone scrunches her eyes and scoffs.

"Yes, ma'am. Be right down."

"Thanks, Brianna." Sasha ends the call, slipping her phone back into her pocket.

"I'm not going to talk to you about anything," says Persephone.

Sighing, Sasha places her head into her left palm. Fiercely rubbing her temples.

"Persephone, enough. That wasn't a suggestion. You're coming with me...look, until your father and Mikhail wake up, we are all we have now. This is it. You and me. Our family. Now come, or I'll treat you like the child you're acting like and yank you upstairs by your ear!"

Sasha leaves, Persephone following behind with a sulk.

Dark clouds crawl across the sky, erasing the morning's bright and welcoming blue. The dense humidity of the past few weeks conjures an oncoming storm. Lightning jags around below the encroaching blackness. Below the view of the clouds is the Assembly courtyard, and on one side, Sergei stares out his office window, across the open space, watching the Assembly President walk into her office with her daughter trudging behind.

Thunder crashes over ahead. A spider-web of lightning slithers throughout the sky. Sergei counts the seconds after each flash. His top five loyalists sitting in folding chairs on the other side of Sergei's large porcelain desk.

"Only ten seconds. Two miles away. It was three miles just a few minutes ago," says Sergei. "The storm is coming in fast."

His men glance about at each other, before the one in the middle says, "Excuse me, sir, shall we commence the meeting? Your calling us here sounded urgent."

"Yes," says Sergei, staring at Sasha speaking to her daughter. "She's brought her family to live here. Making the Assembly their new home? Using our resources for her own personal gain? Not to mention, establishing a greater advantage for staying. None of us live here. None of us have brought our families here."

"So, you're saying..."

"It's time. We've spoken about it enough. It's time for action. We need to put the coup into motion."

"That's all well and good, but we've yet to figure out the best means to do so. And why now? Just because her family is here?"

Sergei glances back across the courtyard. Sasha and her daughter are engaged in a heated exchange. "Ten years ago, when I demanded that Assembly power be equally distributed. Sasha threatened me...with magic."

The men erupt in frenzied chatter. "Wait, what!...magic, all this time?...when did she...how could that be possible...no one has magic except for the new generation born after the supernatural holocaust...and have you seen her lately? She's gotten so gray and wrinkled...yeah hard to imagine she's the same woman who hired us...she used to be hot...no way she could have magic...but if she does, what does that mean?...I don't know but—

"Enough!" Sergei shouts. Lightning jags its way through the sky, getting closer and closer. Thunder bangs from a mile away. "I don't know how. But she created a knife out of thin air and plunged it into her hand, only for the wound to heal seconds later. Said not to f—mess with her."

The men, forced into submission, glance worriedly at each other and back at Sergei.

"You see? If she has magic, who's to say her family doesn't? The teenagers...they fall within the range of those born with magic. But her husband? She can create things out of thin air. Just imagine what *he* could do." Silence. Sergei sighs, turning back to the window. "You needed to be told, but I fear you won't aid me in this venture anymore. I understand if you're scared."

The man in the middle raises a hand, despite Sergei's back being turned to him. "Well, yes. None of us have magic. So, trying to dispose of her, let alone the others? Sir...we're on board, but we need a safe way of doing this."

"I'll give it some thought. You're all dismissed."

The men funnel out of Sergei's office, as he continues to glare out the window. Lightning bursts overhead, thundering loudly. Raindrops first trickle upon the glass, then become a splattering that blurs his view of the courtyard. But before all is obscured, he notices a blinding white light engulfing Sasha's office. A pulse erupts, shattering Sasha's window. A white halo stretches outward from her daughter's petite frame, alongside a terrifying supernatural pressure. He's seen it once before, the light which erupted from the room where the Abyssal Root is planted.

Sergei crumbles into his chair, which rolls back until hitting his desk. Eyes wide and covering his gaping mouth, he struggles to slow his breathing.

You men are right to be nervous. That girl. She has the same power that Sasha has denied us all these years. A power which we could make revolutionary weapons with.

His mouth slowly closes, then stretches into a grin.

But ah! An opening. The girl seems to not like her mother. If only we could get her away from her parents. They're one thing, but surely, we can bend a little girl to our desires.

"So, we haven't had a chance to talk about what happened," says Sasha, sitting on the edge of her desk in front of her daughter.

Persephone pouts, sliding deep into the leather chair opposite her mother's desk. Thunder clashes from afar, less muffled by distance with each passing minute. Glancing outside, Persephone watches as the darkness from that day stalks and builds momentum, soon to be close behind. "You would know if you were there."

Wincing, rubbing her temples, Sasha says, "You know I must work. If you just understood—"

"You have to work all the time?" Persephone erupts. "There are days we don't ever see you! And me aside, what about Dad? Don't you care about him?"

"Your father understands what it is I'm doing here. He's fully on board. Now, enough of your teenage angst." Sasha raises her hands in astonishment. "Tell me what happened."

Persephone glares, scoffing as she realizes there's no escape from her mother. "A strange boy came up the mountain. Dad got weird immediately."

"Weird?"

"Yeah, the boy spoke strangely—used plural pronouns, and I, well—he did have multiple souls in him. I could tell after that white glow overtook me."

Sasha sighs and walks over to the other leather chair next to Persephone's. Turning it to face her daughter, she says, "And I'm very interested in hearing about that. But what did this boy do that made your dad get *weird?*"

Persephone relays the events of the afternoon a few days ago. The destructive power of the strange teenage boy, tearing the flesh from Mikhail's lower half, along with the arm of her father after being thrown through their cabin. How the boy mentioned the name Yahweh and that he had met her father but also didn't meet her father. "It was all very confusing," she says, leaving out the part where a strange voice emerged within her mind as she came into her dormant power, and how it implied that her father had committed some sort of tragedy in the past.

"Yahweh!" Sasha says, alarmed and gritting her teeth. Pondering how this could be.

Persephone sinks into her chair, eyeing her mother's outburst. "Who is Yahweh?"

Realizing her lapse into fury, Sasha breathes in deeply. "The past is dead and buried. Focus now on the present, Persephone. This isn't for you to worry about. Your power has reawoken. You need to focus on channeling it in a healthy way."

The girl's ears perk at her mother's wording. "Reawoken? What are you talking about?"

"Ah, that's right. You don't remember. This has happened before. Twice. Once, when you were a little girl, again after we buried Uncle Andes. It was too much for your young mind to retain the memories."

"Are you fucking kidding me? All this time, I've been jealous of Mikhail, and I had powers all along? What did you do? Did you force them away or something?"

"Persephone, no—you were too young. You *still* are too young."

Abyssal light seeps out of the corners of Persephone's eyes. The flow, growing heavier by the second, swaths the office in a stark white glow. "I'm just supposed to trust you? Fuck you, mom. I have the powers now, and I remember! By your own logic, I am plenty old enough!" the girl screams, cracking the floor and shattering the windows. Rain spills inside, as Sasha clings to her desk for balance. The portrait of Virdeus slams into the floor, shattering the glass and frame.

Persephone storms out of the office. The white glow dies away as she furthers herself from her mother.

Sighing, Sasha circles her desk and sits in her chair. *Seth, please wake up soon. Something needs to be done about our daughter.* Swiveling around, she picks up what is left of the portrait. *Ah, father. How did you manage raising me? Was I ever as unruly, as destructive as she? A new threat has appeared. Seems like they're coming from all corners, like roaches that simply won't die.* She caresses her wrinkled skin. Twirls her long gray hair with her fingers. *How am I supposed to handle any of it if I can't even handle her?*

The clink of glasses, the swish of liquid filling within. Restroom doors creak as a gray-bearded man in a leather vest disappears into it. Another man slumps over the bar, face down in a puddle of spilled whiskey, drool mixing into an unseemly cocktail. The thud of pool sticks against a white resin ball before clacking against others branded with various colors and numbers. A couple leans into each other, faces flush with drunkenness. The woman playfully stroking the man's chest, the man wrapping his fingers around her waist, plunging into the backside of her pants.

Sergei sips his vodka, alone, trying not to become like the surrounding patrons. But also, eager to no longer be conscious of the day and all his worries. *They're on board, huh? But only if there's a safe way to go about it? That's the same as not having my back at all. For how can we take out a witch and her kin?*

Don't they know how much is at stake? Don't they also want to avenge the family they lost to the devils and take the world back for the one true God?

"Hey buddy, how's tricks?" The bartender stands before him, smiling, white dish towel in hand, scrubbing a glass. "You look like something's bothering you."

"Yes. Work. Can't talk about it."

The bartender chuckles. "Oh? Super classified, is it? What are you, CIA or something?"

"I said I can't fucking talk about—" Alarmed by the swear that only creeps out upon drunkenness, Sergei clamps his eyes shut and raises a hand. "I'm sorry. Rough day is all."

The bartender gestures not to worry about it, places the glass down, and tosses the towel over his shoulder before filling another two glasses of beer for the drunken couple. Shaking his head at their public sexual arousal, but keeping his mouth shut.

A hand reaches into view. Taken aback, Sergei leans away while turning toward its owner. "Are you even old enough to be in here, boy?" Sergei asks. The stranger flashes a wide, crimson-stained grin at him.

"Would it help," says Damien, "to talk to someone like...me, someone who is knowledgeable of your situation—I believe—I could help you—" He pauses, as if standing in a garden, carefully plucking the best flower for the occasion, before leaning in to whisper, "kill a certain witch and her fiendish family?"

CHAPTER FOURTEEN

Sitting alone at the bar, Sergei guzzles back his glass of whisky. Placing it down with a thud, lingering droplets splash over the sides, coating his knuckles. The smell, pungent, pregnant with unease after hours of steady drinking. Gesturing toward the bartender, his glass is refilled with a double.

His glossy eyes drift away as he takes a sip. Thinking back upon a time long before the Assembly. Before his time as a soldier overseas. Before the monsters descended from the sky, taking everything from him.

The early 1980s.
"S-ge-i. Ser-gei, wake up. Sergei, my sweet boy."
An affectionate singsong voice of a woman whisked young Sergei from slumber. Eyes creaking open, he found his mother squatting by his bedside, wearing a flowing and colorful floral printed dress and donning a matching hat.

"Come on, already! Wake the boy up. Church isn't going to wait for us," said a deep voice behind her.

The young boy nuzzled his tired eyes. Behind his mother was the tall, broad form of his father standing on the threshold of his bedroom door. Wearing a blue-gray suit, but otherwise obscured. To Sergei's tired eyes adjusting to the morning light, the details of his father were hidden within the shadows of the unlit hallway. But nothing needed to be seen. His father's powerful presence towering above Sergei and his mother was all he knew anyway. This body within the doorway, soon to drive them all to church, was the most he ever saw of the man.

"Come on, now, Sergei. You heard your father. Up and at 'em! I laid out your clothes. Be quick now!"

Leaving him, his mother entered the shadows of the hallway. Whispers stirred as young Sergei crawled out of bed, finding a white dress shirt, navy tie, dress pants, and shoes upon his dresser. Wrapping the shirt around him and buttoning up, he then tucked the shirt into his pants. Taking great care to do so neatly, leaving not a crease or any bunched-up fabric. Just as his father taught him to do without fail.

Sitting on the edge of his bed, he leaned over to tie his shoe—a sudden collision of flesh. One hard, the other soft. His mother's shadow beyond the door stumbled backward, clutching her cheek with her hands. His father's outstretched palm returned to his side, as he said, "You want our boy to be effeminate like a woman? A fragile little faggot?" Well, this is how that happens! You're too soft on the boy!"

"I-I'm sorry. Please just don't hit me again."

He raised a hand, and she turned and cowered. "Yeah, whimper like a bitch. See if that helps him." He rubbed his palm, throbbing from impact. "Just fix your face and let's go, already."

A pregnant silence filled the taxi ride to St. Patrick's Cathedral. The New York City traffic made of static, long rows of cars.

Horns blared, deepening the cab driver's creased frown as Sergei and his parents emerged before the massive church.

Walking toward the towering doors, another family approached. A young boy and girl, alongside their mother. Her lips a firm straight line, beneath sagging, tired eyes. Their father lunged a hand forward with a brimming and proud smile. "Ah, look who it is! So good to see you all on this fine Sunday morning. Blessed be to God in the highest!"

"Yes, indeed," Sergei's father said, reaching out to shake the man's hand. "Praise, God!"

Sergei glanced at his mother. Her face was caked with concealer, but a bright pink color pierced through. Finding a smile on his father's face, so bright and courteous to a man who Sergei knew was no friend of his father, but merely a fellow Christian man. Paying no attention to their wives or children, the men bantered amongst themselves as each family migrated into the church.

Glory to God in the highest. To our loving Heavenly Father. There is no Heavenly Mother. Everything we have we owe to God. He even sent us his one and only son to die on the cross for us—to protect us from the evils of Satan. Not a daughter, but a son. Ruminating on this, Sergei turned toward his mother again. Catching his glare, she smiled sadly. Sergei turned away in discomfort. *So beaten down, she cannot talk.*

Pathetic.

Twenty years later.

Gunfire raged through the air. Buildings were blown apart, debris plunged into the dirt and sand, causing eruptions of massive dust clouds. Vision obscured, hearing impaired by the constant firing of guns. The smell of fire and blood.

Sergei ducked behind a barricade as the Afghan soldiers fired a rocket launcher. The explosion rained debris around him. Ears ringing, vision blurring, but still alive. *I am a man with God at my side. These desert-dwelling devils cannot hurt me, so long as I have my Heavenly Father.*

Vision swirled back into place as he found a pair of combat boots approaching him.

"You alright, there, Sergei?"

Glancing upward, Sergei said, "Drew! You're okay?"

The man nodded. "Yeah, I had to gun down a bunch of these bastards to catch up to you, but yeah, I'm goo—"

The sound of warping metal and shattering glass. A nearby building collapsing, with all its parts bursting outward. Sergei stumbled, eyes wide and splattered with blood. His fellow soldier stood before him, a bloodied stump of a neck rose just above his shoulders. Faster than the eye could catch, a passing metal beam tore his head asunder.

Sergei's fear transmuted into rage as he rose over the barricade, gunning down every soldier he saw.

Silence washed over the battlefield. Homes in ruin. The ground soaked crimson. Sergei stared out with dead eyes, surveying the sea of corpses surrounding him.

His radio beeped, emitting static. "All units report, I repeat, all units report. Is anyone out there? Over."

"Copy. This is Private Sergei Komarov. Just me," said Sergei. "I'm scouting the area looking for survivors."

Sergei meandered toward a cluster of houses. Stepping over dozens of bodies along the way. One by one, he peeked inside the broken windows, finding no signs of life. In his sporadic gunfire, he knew only one thing for sure. He killed so many, but with rage blanketing his perception, the who of it all was obscured. But like his father's power, he didn't have to see. It was always there, always right.

A slight upward curve of his lips twitched into being.

The sound of glass scraping against the floor jerked his head toward a house to his right. His radio beeped, hissing out the words, "Just you? Private Komarov, report back to the outpost immediately. Over."

"Negative. I hear something. Might be another one of our men. Over." Gripping his rifle, he slowly opened the door.

A woman with a face coated in snot and tears crawled backward, with a limp and bloodied leg. Sliding her way until thumping her back against the kitchen counter. Shrieking in Arabic, she reached toward a cast iron pan and lunged it toward Sergei. His dead eyes watch as it thuds to the floor, many feet away. Too heavy for the woman to throw far enough. Unlike the metal beam, which tore through the head of his brother-in-arms.

"You dirty little devils." Sergei approached until standing directly over the woman, his groin a foot above her head.

The woman reached for a large kitchen knife and—Sergei lunged the muzzle of his rifle hard into her mouth. "Drop it," he gestured to the knife-holding hand. "Unless you want me to break your arms, too."

The knife clattered to the floor. Sergei tossed his gun atop the kitchen counter, took a fistful of the woman's black hair, and forcefully turned her over. Taking the knife, Sergei sliced through her dress and panties before tossing them to the far side of the room. The woman screamed in terror, writhing and swatting at Sergei. Rage building, Sergei clenched his teeth as he reached for the pistol at his side. The woman froze once more at the sight of yet another gun.

Unzipping his pants, he plunged into her without hesitation. One arm forcing her face into the floor, the other applying pressure to the wounded leg. The woman sobbed louder with each thrust, until her mind crumbled into shock. Bursting into a rageful orgasm, he stood away from the fainted woman.

"Private Komarov, report. What did you find? Over."

Sergei glanced over the dark-haired woman and her brown skin. A female of an enemy nation. *How easy that was. If women weren't made for sex, God would have made them strong enough to fight back.* Raising the radio to his lips, he said, "Sorry, false alarm. Nothing of worth here. Just a rat."

Pistol in hand, he rose it toward the woman and pulled the trigger.

The smell of liquor and piss brings Sergei back to the rundown dive bar and his glass of whiskey, down to his last sips. A hand reaches out—jagged, purple-stained nails startle him as he backs away and glares at the stranger.

"Are you even old enough to be in here, boy?" Sergei asks. The stranger flashes a wide, crimson-stained grin at him.

"Would it help," says Damien, "to talk to someone like...me, someone who is knowledgeable of your situation—I believe—I could help you—" He pauses, as if standing in a garden, carefully plucking the best flower for the occasion, before leaning in to whisper, "Kill a certain witch and her fiendish family?"

Sergei's eyes broaden. "What are you on about?"

Damien's grin stretches further. "I understand your hesitance. No one outside your Assembly, I believe it is called, should know about this. After all, she didn't even want you knowing—that is, about her magic. You see, I was sent far away from them—the witch named Sasha and her family—but I have a keen nose for magic. Tracking it, finding my way back here, was a cinch. And I happened to walk by your offices as you and your underlings made your exit for the day, discussing treasonous things—"

Sergei erupts from his chair, grabbing Damien by his neck and pushing him out the front door. The bartender and patrons turn their gaze, not wanting to get involved. "What the fuck is this, huh? You here to fucking blackmail me?"

Damien's grin collapses into pensive stoicism. "I wouldn't dream of it." Damien's eyes narrow but wander as he thinks back upon one of his collective's seven lives. "I know a pious man when I see one," he continues. "Are you a man of God, Sergei?"

Alarmed by the usage of his name, but intrigued, Sergei lets the boy go. "That's a strange question, in these times. You're young, so you couldn't have been there, but there was a supernatural holocaust, and they're saying God is dead. No one bothers with belief anymore."

"You'd be surprised. Along my journey across the southwest, I stumbled upon many a good-natured believer. Not everyone is sure what happened that day. I'll gladly introduce you. But that's a conversation for later. You didn't answer my question. Are you a man of God?"

Sergei's drunken mind once more drifts in reverse.

Walking side by side with his wife and son. Out through the doors of St. Patrick's Cathedral. Joyous and filled with the holy spirit, they went for a jaunt down the block, hoping to find a place to eat—the sky shattered like glass. And, floating at equal heights were worlds only read about, but never seen. Hell to the left, Heaven to the right. Hellfire spilled from the former, angels from the latter. As his wife and child cowered, a tall angel with six wings fluttered toward them. Sergei's face lit with awe, he said, "It's the rapture! The day we ascend and meet God is finally upon us! Praise God, Praise God!

"Jimmy—" He took his son by the hand, pulling him toward the angel. "Now, boy, greet the angel properly."

His son reached upward, and the angel's head twitched sporadically as black static crackled around its body, distorting, reforming, leaving no longer wings, but six tar-colored tentacles.

Sergei's eyes grew wide, "Wait, no! You're no angel, you're a demon!" He unholstered his gun, pointed and shot—the bullet melted in the air before ever touching the supernatural beast. Whose mouth opened unnaturally wide as its tentacles wrapped around the boy's arms, waist, and legs. The child's face was coated with snot and tears as he screamed, trying to wiggle away from his violator. Letting out an unearthly screech, all life left the boy's face as his teal soul was torn from his body. Consumed by the grotesquery.

Sergei's wife screamed as she fell to the ground to cradle in her arms the corpse of her boy. Unaware of the angel's tentacle reaching out for her. Sergei continued shooting, emptying his clip. The tentacle wrapped around his wife's neck, then sucked the soul out of her with another ear-piercing screech.

Sergei, feeling powerless for the first time, crumbled to the ground, clutching his gaping mouth—a spear with flames coiling along the blade plunged into the angel's head, bursting it apart before embedding into the side of a building. A man with shaggy brown hair appeared, retrieved the spear, and offered Sergei a helping hand before running off to fight another monster.

And as the memory fades, so does the feeling of awe he had for these mysterious, magical saviors. Returning his attention to Damien, he says, "Ignoring how you know my name, I am a good man. I attended church with my wife and son every Sunday. So yeah, I am—I was. But now I feel foolish and sinful. Those I thought were heroes were anything but. Their magic is for their own personal gain—they don't care about protecting their fellow Americans. When the demons disguised as angels came, I thought my savior and his people were the true angels, and then afterward, simply good soldiers of God, and then not even that. I was fooled by their trickery, and now, magic is a pandemic affecting the youth. And yes, there's that witch—that woman that I cannot kill. So, stranger, what advice could you have for this drunken old fool?"

Damien grins. "As I said, I can help you. You're wise to distrust magic. But the things I will come to show you, things you may mistake as more witchcraft, are instead divine power."

Sergei stares inquisitively, before dropping his mouth in awe. "You don't mean to say that God is not dead?"

Damien spreads his arms like a cross, and says, "How could He who is standing before you be dead? That's right, my loyal servant. I am the second coming of God."

CHAPTER FIFTEEN

Sasha stares through an oval window out toward the bright blue expanse. Obscuring the stars above, just as the clouds below obscure the earth. A flight attendant rolls a cart of drinks through the aisle as Sasha sighs, contemplating the irony before her. Through the conduit of a plane, she has risen high above human civilization left on the surface. But this altitude is her plateau, doomed to ascend no higher before making her return downward.

The powers of a god, and yet, still must abide by normal means of travel. *What a joke.* A faded reflection stares back at her. Dark and sunken bloodshot eyes. Framed by long grey hair that has become wildly unmanageable after fifteen hours in the air.

If only Seth weren't still unconscious and I could use his portals. Sasha glances at her hands. *What is the difference between my creation magic and Seth's portals? The color—teal versus white. Clearly, it's his connection to the White Abyss, but my powers are literally that of a god. But the one thing I cannot create is portals.*

Sasha clenches her teeth. The man sitting to her left glances over, alarmed at the sudden but faint white light flashing from her eyes. Closing his, he breathes deeply before hanging his head back. Unsure of what he just saw or if it happened at all, he hopes for sleep to bring clarity. But Sasha remains seething.

First, when Persephone was small, Seth put the moon back into the sky. Then he warped that dangerous stranger somewhere far off, in a mere moment. That power is exactly what I need to ensure Project Persephone works...this job, always making me feel worthless without a man.

She sighs, leaning her head on the side of the plane, continuing to stare out into that alluring, endless blue, as the plane makes its descent to Tokyo's Haneda Airport.

A teal-colored taxi awaits her. Dragging her suitcase along, she promptly gets in, and the cab drives off. Deep into the city. Words spiral around within her tired mind, reminding her of what will be said at the meeting—

Her phone, clutched in her left hand, vibrates harshly. Answering, she says, "Hey, Brianna. Yes, landed. Went as well as any flight over fifteen hours could. Mmhmm. Headed there now. How's Persephone been? I see, yeah, I can imagine. Thanks again for watching her, I know the situation's a handful—that's very kind, but no, I know how rough this is on you, too. So, thanks. Yeah, talk soon. Bye."

The taxi slows as it reaches a building with a large sign over the door. Under a string of Japanese letters, sits an English translation stating: *The Assembly for Magic and Human Progression, Japanese Branch.*

Thanking the driver, Sasha grabs her bag and heads inside.

Assembly workers briskly make their way from office to office, down hallways and to desks, carrying stacks of papers with enthusiastic chatter engulfing everything throughout it all. Having been a while since an in-person meeting, the vigor and camaraderie on display makes Sasha wince, knowing what awaits her at home. Arriving at a large double door, she pushes it open to find a room of suit-wearing men and women sitting at a large rectangular table. A lone empty seat awaits at the end nearest the door. They rise in unison and bow.

Returning the bow, Sasha takes a seat and says, "Konnichiwa, mina-san."

An elderly man at the other head of the table smiles. "Konnichiwa, Sasha-san. But please," he says. "While we appreciate the effort, please do not trouble yourself over our language. You must be tired after such a long trip." The man eyes Sasha inquisitively, and gestures to the young woman to Sasha's right. The woman rises swiftly and retrieves from the table near the door, a tray holding a teapot and an assortment of cups. Placing the tray in front of Sasha, she begins brewing strong genmaicha tea. The man continues, "You're not known to arrive looking so exhausted. Please, enjoy."

Sasha glances over the room in silence, biting her tongue, but says, "As always, your hospitality is appreciated. Though I am fine. A lot is in motion at headquarters. Hence my visit today.

"I want to acquire funding for a space travel endeavor." The room erupts in muffled chatter. "It is our job to defend humanity, and to consider every possible way to do so. And with Project Persephone, we could do just that. Imagine a ship that could take us to the farthest regions of space, the very edge, if there is one, in the blink of an eye. We could protect humankind for...well, forever, with a vessel that can skip any measure of space. Nothing, no matter how dangerous, would be able to catch us."

The man at the other end of the table laughs softly, before growing into a clamorous uproar as the members join in. Stopping himself, he says with a few chuckles joining his words, "President Sasha, we of course have the utmost respect for you and this organization you started. But in all this time, even well before the Assembly went international, there hasn't been a single instance of a real supernatural threat. The magic-borne children, yes. But we contain and discipline those before catastrophe strikes. We even aid in support efforts during tsunamis and earthquakes, while the headquarters in New York experience no such environmental disasters. You have sat on your ass for twenty years—what makes you think we need to leave the Earth? No threat has come, and no threat will. We do good work here, aiding the children in harnessing their magic. That is enough. The Earth is safe."

"There is a threat, and it has hit us already. My husband and son have been comatose for weeks."

"Then why hasn't this been reported?" the man says, shrugging and raising his hands.

"I'm reporting it now. And there's more threats to come. I'm aware that many think I've been speaking an empty rhetoric for years now, but I'm telling you, we are not safe."

"How do you know?"

Sasha's lips tremble with fury. The arrival of this stranger who attacked her family. His mention of Yahweh. And the ominous warning given by the Abyssal Consciousness, claiming multiple threats have been on their way for years. But these are all things that normal humans who did not operate beyond on the veil before the Supernatural Holocaust could ever possibly understand. And with Seth incapacitated, Sasha has been left alone with their problematic daughter.

Oh, Father. What a joke this all is. How did I not see this coming? The Assembly is failing me at every turn, or I'm failing it.

Breathing deeply, Sasha says, "That information is classified."

The Head of the Japanese Branch grimaces, shaking his head. "I'm very sorry, Sasha-san. But along with not agreeing with this plan, we here in Japan are not cowardly enough to run away from any threat that may come. And besides, this is highly unorthodox, asking for funding from the international branches. Money should flow from the top. And given that you are here asking us for aid tells me that the others at headquarters agree that this is a poor idea."

The man stands, and the rest follow. Marching out as one mass, leaving the foreign individual seated alone in the conference room. Slumped in her chair, quivering with rage.

A bright light flashes intensely from her eyes, briefly casting the room in a white shadow.

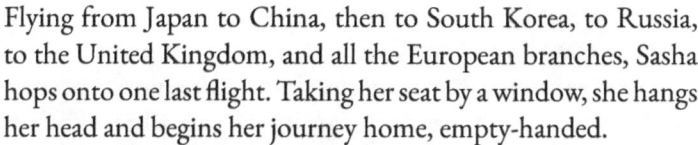

Flying from Japan to China, then to South Korea, to Russia, to the United Kingdom, and all the European branches, Sasha hops onto one last flight. Taking her seat by a window, she hangs her head and begins her journey home, empty-handed.

"Why should we pay for it? The plan is poor and unnecessary. We cannot aid you if you do not divulge info pertaining to the threat you claim is coming."

They all gave the same answer. Sasha turned to look outside. The plane began to descend.

Of course, they wouldn't want to aid me when I can't even tell them why. But—

Sasha bites her gums as she remembers how each meeting went. All greetings and feigned respect accompanied by vague sexism. *If only we had time to allow the older generations to die, leaving behind only the magic-borne, then I could use my magic freely—my inward strength conjured into the physical world.*

Blood spills over her bottom lip, dripping onto her black dress pants—

{You understand the nature of magic, well, Spawn of Zarathustra.}

Eyes grown wide, they glimmer with abyssal white as Sasha receives its voice. "You don't usually speak to me," she says. "I was beginning to think even you were sexist."

{I am the Abyss itself. The essence of the world. No such things exist within me. Humanity creates that ugliness itself. Due to the circumstances of his arriving to power, the other spawn has a unique tether to the Abyss. But he is no more special than you.}

"You could have fooled me," Sasha grumbles. Two women across the aisle glare at Sasha and turn away in discomfort.

{Ask him about the anomaly that resides within his soul, and you will understand. But you need not have what he has to conjure the Abyss.}

"Wait, you mean I could—"

{As was said earlier, you understand the nature of magic. The answer that eludes you is not actually unknown. Your priorities are skewed. You seek to protect humanity, but your people do not want you. Your father, wise as he was, could never foresee the changes coming to the world. He named you the Matriarch of magic humans. But the man had not lived amongst normal humans for ten thousand years. He had forgotten what they are like. Forsake

them. Find another way. Be true to yourself. You understand the nature of magic well. You know these words are true. Wasn't it you, after all, who led your beloved through the despair of self-hatred and to the nobler lands of self-acceptance?}

Sasha's glowing eyes drip with tears that glisten with abyssal energy. Marooned at a job that will never respect her. No matter her effort, her goals remain unrealized. All this power, and yet living at the mercy of what others say she can and cannot do.

"I cannot abandon them. I provide them with jobs which feed their families. And after years invested and spent toward building the Assembly, I can't just walk away. Who am I helping, if I can't see things through?"

Silence, as her tears and their abyssal shimmer grow warm, caressing her cheeks.

{You are indeed a defender of humankind. But steel yourself, Spawn of Zarathustra, for you cannot survive the wilderness without a flame to warm and feed you. And you cannot first create a flame without severing a tree from its roots to burn. And a time may come when you regret not being the one to grip the axe.}

CHAPTER SIXTEEN

A FEW WEEKS EARLIER.

The thick hum of helicopter blades—brisk, unabating chopping, and a low woosh is all-consuming. Muffled only slightly by bulky-black headsets. Sergei, in the pilot seat, flies toward the Rocky Mountains in southeast Colorado, the air rippling in the ever-rising heat. Damien sits in the back seat, glaring at the landscape below. Nearing the entrance to the ruins of Magistrum, he glimpses the spot where his gluttony died.

Memory flashes before him. A towering worm-faced beast wearing a thick grey shell. Large black tentacles stretching out from within, rampaging through the countryside, shattering houses and trees alike, and being pursued by a raging demon propelled by fire.

Seth.

Damien winces as he remembers how it felt to have his insides melted, being blown apart into ponds of black goo. *That power—amplified from the souls he consumed. Nil Magic. He had an empty space to fill and took the souls within him. Walking up that mountain, meeting him again—an older, wiser Seth, what we felt inside him was reminiscent of that day twenty years ago.*

We almost killed him, but he was holding back.

Damien glances toward Sergei as the helicopter descends. "I look forward to our fruitful partnership. And I hope you get along with the others."

Sergei glares through the rearview mirrors, watching the boy turn his gaze toward the ground.

A familiar dilapidated shed sits about ten yards from the tunnel's obscured entrance. Thick trees stand before the opening in the mountainside. As the helicopter lands and they continue on foot, Damien glares at the worn-down shed. Somehow still standing, though worse off than ever.

The spot where his gluttony died is surrounded by tall-reaching pine trees and country homes strewn about, in pristine condition. No longer there at Heaven's end, Damien has no memory of the world being built anew. But he remembers the terrifying pressure as Seth emerged from the White Abyss, of the creation magic pulsing through him. *He must have used those powers to mend the world. Thus, bringing back everything he destroyed—aside from people. And yet, the shed remains broken, and Magistrum has been left to its ruins. Perfectly embalmed in the seclusion of its enclosed cave.*

He must have wanted to leave a memory.

Walking onward through the cave, Damien smirks. The death of his gluttony was out there, but this was a mass tomb for his envy, wrath, sloth, and pride. Now reworked as his base of operations. Thanks to Seth, he's been granted an opportunity to turn a bad thing good. The past is laden with disappointment. Of which he can now rectify.

With the tunnel unblocked, the air drifts into the outdoors. But the ruins of Magistrum still hold the stench of charred corpses. Sergei covers his mouth and nose with a maroon handkerchief. Damien breathes in the echoes of death. The only relief is the cavern's cool air fluttering gently against their sweltering skin.

Light flickers beyond the approaching curve in the tunnel. The passage widens, revealing a campfire illuminating the faces of a large group of men and women, and the blackened, collapsed buildings behind them.

"Hello, all." Damien grins.

"Ugh, finally," says a woman with dirty blonde hair and dark, sunken eyes. "Just how long did you expect us to wait? And it's putrid in here. Can we please move somewhere else?"

"And yet, you waited. Your faith has been noted."

The woman's frown softens into a straight line as she bows slightly toward Damien, who glances over the masses. From here to Texas, then across the bible belt of the American South, he had his trek back to Crowley, New York. Amassing follower after follower with the same story he told Sergei.

Humans make it so easy. They're so predisposed to relinquishing their wills! The bungled and the botched, aching for release from life's hardships. So, they look for a messiah, and we gave them one. Which won't be a lie for long, for once we consume Seth and his pup, we shall take the White Abyss within us and become as gods. All we need is an army.

"Who are all these people?" asks Sergei.

Damien grins at him but turns back toward the crowd.

"We seem short of some of you. They didn't lack faith and run off, did they?"

"No, sir." A red-bearded man in overalls steps forward. "They simply got antsy waiting, is all. Went further into these here ruins to explore. Want us to grab them?"

Damien glances upward. A vast darkness overhead, obscuring the height of the ceiling. *This place was once lit with magic lights, but no longer. And it would not serve us for our army to grow sick from the smell.* Damien turns back to the crowd and says, "No need. *I* shall find them. Let. There. Be. Light."

His pupils sink into the whites of his eyes, before blackness spills out from their centers. The air around him ripples, amassing on his thighs and calves. His jeans burst apart as his muscles ripple and bulge grotesquely, four times their size. Leaving nothing but a loincloth of denim hanging from his waist. With a slight squat, he jumps, rocketing himself into the air, further and further, and a black pulse of his eyes causes the space in front of him to ripple. The cracking of stone echoes throughout the cavern, creaking and—a sudden massive spiderweb of light pierces through before the stone ceiling erupts. Shards of stone scatter upward and over the side of the mountain. Even more rains upon the ruins of Magistrum as Damien plunges to the surface.

Dozens of men rush beneath him, holding out their arms to catch their savior. His legs revert to their normal size, once more a lanky teenage boy, falling hard into the embrace of his followers. Many tumbling over, but breaking Damien's fall.

Sergei joins the crowd, eyes wide and mouth agape.

Returning to his feet, Damien gives Sergei a smirk.

"This is to be our new home! I have brought light into our lives! Rejoice in it! For soon we shall take the world back from the heathens whose faith has fallen with the lies of my death. There is a witch and her kin who are spreading a dangerous rhetoric. They seek a world without God..." Damien remembers when he was within Yahweh, taking in the horror of Seth as he sent a god to her ruin. That stern ferocity, a hatred for gods branded into his eyes. Damien knew then the world Seth would create. "This man here!" he points to Sergei. "Together we will join him and those loyal to him, and we shall be an army that rains divine justice upon the heathens, and this world will be God's again!"

Light illuminates the destruction within. The collapsed, charred buildings strewn about encircle Damien as he stretches his arms wide.

Sergei steps forward, softly clapping, then harder before falling to his knees, bowing. The army follows suit, clamoring with joy, for their God is great.

Legs up upon her desk, next to a purple pen and her still-unpublished manuscript, a glass container of egg salad rests in Brianna's lap, which she shovels into her mouth with a small plastic fork. Her light chestnut hair is tied in a messy bun, with a few strands dangling before her black-rimmed glasses. With Sasha away, her and Brianna's offices are free from noise and distraction. Phone unplugged for the duration of lunch, she watches a news report play out on her computer screen.

"As it was in his penthouse apartment, there was little doubt. But the DNA tests have finally returned, and we now have concrete evidence that the body belonged to New York City mayor, David Christensen. Police were notified of an offensive smell originating from Mayor Christensen's penthouse, and what they found there was sheer horror. A skeleton with bits of dangling flesh, sitting in a pool of blood, and with more splattered upon the walls. What they found was an utterly malicious desecration of a human being. It's hard to say who or what could have caused this, but with the rise of what people are referring to as magic-born humans and the many cases of houses being burned down or parents being harmed, whispers are saying this might be the result of magic as well. While I am obligated to say that no one has been killed by the magic-born and that all injuries have been recovered from, thanks to the Assembly for Magic and Human Progression, one has to ask: just how long before that no longer remains true?

"The body and scene of the crime are too gruesome to show on air. However, footage and pictures for the steel-hearted can be found online at..."

"Oh, fuck!" Brianna shouts, dropping her feet to the floor. Tossing her bowl to the side of her desk, she writes on a large yellow legal pad: *NYC mayor killed by magic human? Investigate immediately.*

Typing in the website address given by the reporter, she—clutching her hands to her mouth, she feels the egg salad burning her throat as it ascends—runs to the bathroom to the left of her desk, her lunch ejects.

Clutching her stomach, she trudges back to her computer and prints out the photos. Taking them from the printer, without looking, she places them facedown atop the legal pad and walks out of her office.

Shades closed, darkness pools within Sergei's office where his most loyal disciple has made his temporary dwelling. Sitting in Sergei's big leather seat, he swipes at his cell phone—vibration stirs within his palm, as a call steals the screen.

"Hey, Sergei...Yes, she's still away, but word through the grapevine says she'll be returning tomorrow...Yes, that's right...No, she doesn't know you've been gone...What?...Oh, come on, be serious...Wait, really?...A magic-born, huh...How soon can you get here?...Okay, good, because we need to strike now...Like I said, Sasha's away. It's just her kid and vegetable husband and son in the infirmary, and Brianna running things from the President's office—"

Through the crack of the office door, he sees a petite woman with chestnut hair and glasses pass, before stepping back to the door. Peeking through, she meets the man's gaze.

Lowering his phone and grinning, he says, "Good afternoon, ma'am."

"Good afternoon," Brianna says, with a faded, pale face, and walks off.

Raising his phone to his ear, he says, "Sorry...No, it was nothing...Okay, got it...Yeah, see you soon."

Hanging up, he exits the office. Slinking slowly through, he glances left to right, and closes the door behind him, making his way toward the elevator at the end of the hall. Passing by the infirmary, he spies Brianna chatting with Persephone, who sulks at the side of her father. Brianna's back to him, the man passes unseen. Entering the elevator, he presses the button for the lowest floor.

Upon exiting, the doors to the barracks reside on both the right and left. The former belonging to general, non-magic personnel, and the latter houses the magic-born. Opening the door to the left, he shouts, "All units, your attention please!" A lobby attached to dozens of rooms and hallways stands before him. Funneling out in droves, the few hundred magic-born arrive at attention. The boy who burned down his house, now a man with fury in his eyes. The girl capable of geomancy and her friend, who breathes life from bubbles of spit, both striking, fairy-like young women. The boy whose mind can create whatever he wants, so long as the materials are metal, is now a man clad in a chainmail of spikes and assorted metal bits. And alongside them are as many magic-born that the Assembly could fit within the barracks, all those who wished to stay on as magic warriors. As the man stood before them, holding the attention he asked for, his body quakes.

"Listen up. A group of magic terrorists has threatened to assault Assembly HQ. Your orders are to barricade all roads on the outskirts of Crowley. Do not stir from your stations unless you receive the order. Any suspicious persons should be reported before engaging in combat, if possible. Understood?"

"Fucking finally," says the man with the fiery glow in his eyes, as he stomps toward the door with the others in tow.

As the magic-born funnel out, leaving the Assembly's campus, the man smirks and heads into the other barracks.

Blinding fluorescent lights dangle from the ceiling. A pregnant silence engulfs the room. Seth and Mikhail lay parallel on white hospital beds. Persephone, sitting in a chair between them, clutches both of their hands. Caressing them, tears trickle down her cheeks. Brianna stands before her, panning the room.

Even as Sasha's secretary, she does not know everything. And the appearing and vanishing in her office without exiting either door does fill Brianna with suspicions. *Of course, the founder of the Assembly for Magic and Human Progression would have a certain knowledge of magic. It came out of nowhere, yet she was the only one in the world who was prepared for it.* She ponders this as she watches Seth and Mikhail in their fourth week of being comatose.

Eyeing the teenage girl who hasn't stirred from her family's side, Brianna says, "Hey, Persephone. How did this happen, anyway?"

Persephone glances at Brianna, then briskly turns away. "My mom hasn't told you? Then she'd probably get mad at me for blabbing."

Brianna smirks. "Oh my, caring about what your mother thinks? Whatever happened to the feisty Persephone I know?"

"You don't know me."

"But I do. You're mother talks about you all the time." Persephone scoffs and scoots closer to her father. Brianna smiles, continuing, "And I know it's been a while since seeing each other, but when you and Mikhail were babies, I cradled you in my arms on many occasions. It's strange, isn't it? We're born entirely unaware that the world existed before us, that everyone before us has an extensive past that occurred long before we were born. This is why I believe in your mother and her vision for the world. Humanity is a collective process, joined together by individual experiences. We live our single lives, but survive together."

Persephone turns to Brianna, before dropping her gaze to her lap. "She talks about me, huh? What has she sai—"

Footsteps stampede throughout the halls. Brianna turns toward the windows, finding the magic-born rushing for the exit. "One sec, hun." Opening the door, she says to the crowd, "Hey! What's going on? Where are you all going?"

"Received orders!" shouts a man as he runs. "Sorry, it's an emergency, can't stop to talk!"

"Hey, I'm in charge with the president away. Who gave these orders?"

Shouting after them, her words fall short. "Fuck!" Brianna mumbles, returning to the infirmary as the last of the magic-born leaves the premises. "Sorry, hun. Don't curse." Persephone snickers as she watches Brianna whip out her cellphone. Non-soldier personnel huddle together in the hall, chattering, staring after the magic-born. "Sasha, I know you're on the plane now, but we have a situation—"

Gunshots echo throughout the hall. Bodies are strewn about as blood and brain matter coat the walls. Six men rush into the infirmary with pistols in hand, rifles slung over their backs. Brianna stands in front of Persephone and says, "Now, what the fuck is this?" Glancing past them, she spies faces of the dead out in the hall. One woman with dirty blonde hair dangling into a pool of blood glares directly at Brianna. Her face contorted, embalmed with horror.

The man in front, his black hair slicked back above sharp, dead eyes, says, "For humanity, and with the glory of God, we exclaim, death to the witch." With a quick, graceful movement, he raises his gun and—the bang echoes loudly within the small infirmary. Brianna slumps backward, blood spraying behind her. Coating Persephone's face as Brianna's head thuds at her feet.

Shaking, her already present tears grow into rivers as she lifts her gaze to the man. His grin widens as he repositions his gun toward the teenage girl.

"That's enough!" Sergei's voice bellows as he appears behind the men. "Our savior requires that one alive." Sergei turns, gesturing for the boy behind him to walk into the room. Damien steps toward Persephone, his grin growing beyond its confines, skin stretching, tearing, blood spurting as his jaw unhinges and creates a cavern of his mouth.

Persephone's eyes widen, remembering the iambic thud of seven souls, then feeling the faint beat of Mikhail's, and the arrhythmic spasm of her father's. "*You!*" she erupts from her chair, causing it to skid into the medical machinery behind her. A blinding abyssal white aura overtakes her, eyes pulsating with the same white glow. The floor cracks beneath her weight, sending fissures through the tiles.

Damien's jaw rescinds as he takes a step back. The six men who first entered the infirmary march forward to protect him, guns raised and—a cacophony of gunfire ricochets throughout the room—the hailstorm of bullets slow as they plunge toward Persephone. The abyssal pressure holding them back until they drop and clang against the floor.

"*Get the fuck away from us!*" Persephone roars. "*I will not let you hurt them anymore!*"

Tears glistening like stars pour from her eyes as she stomps forward. The fissures in the tiles stretch to the walls, shattering the glass windows, before spreading, deepening, and bursting apart like an earthquake, severing the floor. A pulsating white light emerges, tearing through the fabric of the very air around her, white reverse lightning jagging upward and outward from Persephone—the breakage of the world rips through the arms of the six men, slicing them clean off. As the men stumble backward, the room ripples like air in sweltering summer heat.

Still smirking, Damien glares at Persephone, but stretches his arm out before Sergei. "We have to retreat."

"What?" Sergei shouts. "After all this? You said you would help me take the Assembly!"

Persephone, heaving as she stomps toward them, slows under her own abyssal pressure. The walls crumble, the building warps, and begins to collapse inward. Damien's smirk grows wider. "And I will. Good things take time. But if we don't retreat, it is us who will be swallowed whole."

Turning, he yanks Sergei along by the neck of his jacket and makes for the exit. Leaving the teenage girl and her comatose family behind, sprinting toward the edge of the Assembly campus, where about half of their men await.

"Where are the others?" asks Sergei.

A tall, red-haired man nods toward the Assembly. "Still inside, sir."

They turn toward the building. The sound of snapping metal surges through the air as its crumbling walls continue to warp. Faster and faster and—

Damien's eyes grow wide. "Everyone, on the ground!"

A shockwave bursts outward, uprooting trees and shattering the windows of nearby cars, as the Assembly for Magic and Human Progression rapidly caves in upon itself. Cracks spread out from the implosion site, bursting with abyssal white light, reverberating across dimensions.

Fading, only a stark blackness remains. The dark hole with cracks jagging about appears like a massive and foreboding spider. Lifting himself from the ground, Damien glares at this omen of things to come with the widest smirk.

With that power, we will leave this entire world to the void, before absconding to one entirely our own.

CHAPTER SEVENTEEN

IN A WORLD FAR FROM EARTH, WHERE GODS DWELL.

Glistening silver towers rise high over everything. The pearl-laden paths strewn throughout the city of Abyssia, the gardens so lush and virile they stand tall and vast as forests. And the sleek, teal-haired giants with glowing eyes to match, their abyssal white skin glows with jubilance and vigor, having been well nourished. All join in kinetic, utopian harmony within the city so massive it pierces the bright, golden skies.

And at the center of the towering skyline is an even taller building, the Cathedral of the One Mind. The teal-haired giants' place of worship, and their birthplace. Inside the sanctuary, behind the pulpit, lies a doorway into The Womb of the One Mind. Spawned from within, the first Abyssian Gods constructed the cathedral around it. And it is here they worship the essence of all universes, the very womb they are derived from. It is also here where a stray god decided to run away, for he wanted no part of what was to come, and what has since been accomplished.

Such good fortune and health built upon the foundation of entire species beneath their feet. Not buried within the ground of their city, but instead in the worlds below Abyssia. As well as beyond its skyline.

The divine city lies at the center of the dimensional stack, six worlds below, six worlds above. Like a tree growing larger as it slowly ages, reaching both high and low with its stretching branches, new worlds emerge. The newer ones spawn above and below Abyssia in tandem, pushing the older worlds farther away. An inherent connection to The Womb of the One Mind, each universe rests upon its branches.

The lowest of the low dimensions is where they began, consuming the red-eyed, thick-furred inhabitants in a single night. Grown in science and in art, and far in life, they no longer had a need for gods. Thus began the genocide of all species. Without the worship of sentient beings, a fraction of the Abyssians died and returned to nothing. For only the souls of sentient peoples in dimensions outside Abyssia return to The Womb of the One Mind, for they came first, and with strong wills in times of need, created the Abyssians.

Once bustling with life, the lowest dimension, with its fields of gold and advanced civilization, has since been reduced to a barren wasteland. The cities and roads had crumbled. Its lush flora and fauna had withered and died. Cracks have formed in the fabric of its world, blackness gushing from deep fissures. A world cannot be sustained without the souls of those it was created for.

And in the wake of the Abyssian gods, this is the fate that awaits them all.

Footsteps clamor throughout the city's pearl-laden pathways. Chatter and laughter erupt from benches within the many gardens. Amidst the white marble statues, Abyssian priests, men and women sit across from each other at small tables strewn throughout the massive courtyard surrounding the cathedral. And throughout the city, other Abyssians resign themselves to their homes, vocally making their copulation known. Neighbors passing by smile in the warmth of the joyousness on display. Born from The Womb of the One Mind, they cannot procreate on their own. But in a utopian world, there is little else to occupy one's mind than to relish in each other's bodies amidst everyday casual orgies—

A shockwave surges from a higher dimension, rumbling the whole of Abyssia. Silence takes hold as its denizens turn skyward, whispering guesses about the cause to each other. But, losing interest, they return to their uncaring utopian lives.

The liveliness of the city graces the ears of a group of men walking into the cathedral. Led by a tall, muscular Abyssian with wild hair and a long beard.

Silence fills the cathedral. The pulpit stands empty. Strewn throughout the large room are mostly empty pews, with a few Abyssians with bowed heads and clasped hands in their laps. The group of men walk by without a word to these worshippers lost in tradition. They make their way into a room on the right side of the sanctuary.

The large, wild-haired man sits in a large white throne, as another walks over to a chalkboard. A diagram of the dimensional stack is already drawn on, listing the dimensions with their designated number or name:

Twelve: **Highest**
(Zarathustra's pocket dimension)
~~Eleven~~
~~Ten~~

~~Nine~~
~~Eight~~
~~Seven~~
Abyssia
~~Six~~
~~Five~~
~~Four~~
~~Three~~
~~Two~~
Lowest: ~~One~~

Sighing at the chalkboard, the man turns to his wild-haired leader, the once-priest, turned genocidal warmonger. "That pulse we felt…it's not only the same power source we felt when reaping the Eleventh dimension, but for us to have felt it here, it must be getting stronger."

"Skip the obvious. It's coming from where I think it is?" asks the wild-haired man.

"Yes. It was no wonder we felt it in the Eleventh dimension, as we have since pinpointed where Zarathustra had run off to: between Eleven and Twelve." Pointing stick in hand, he thwacks it against the spot labeled *(Zarathustra's pocket dimension)*. "And with that peculiar power growing substantially, I recommend we act soon. We must find and devour Zarathustra—and erase this dimension that shouldn't be. Twelve can wait."

The wild-haired man rises, stroking his beard with his right hand. "Hmm, yes. Zarathustra and his little world must be dealt with. Epochs have come and gone since his cowardice. Time to put this to an end."

He makes for the door, and the men follow. All but the one standing near the chalkboard.

"Sir, one moment."

"What is it?"

"Well, there's still the matter of the black fissures in the consumed dimensions."

The wild-haired man sighs and returns to his throne. "Ah, yes. We had not foreseen that consequence."

"No, we did not...but, as you know, the texts written by the first priest of Abyssia, the one who built the cathedral itself, the other scholars and I suspect that he might have built the cathedral as a way to contain and restrict The Womb of the One Mind."

The wild-haired man places his elbow on his throne's armrest, resting his head on his palm. "I've heard the rumors, yes. Though before his death, he never admitted to such. But if true, I imagine it was in his great wisdom that he foresaw our need to devour the realms and conquer the Womb. So, what's the problem?"

The scholar glances around the room as he itches the back of his neck. "Well, I just wonder if the Womb's restriction is why life hasn't returned to the consumed realms, and why they are fissuring...it's a big problem—it's as if the dimensions are bleeding out. It's just a matter of time before they collapse, and you know the imbalance that would cause. Each implosion would be epochs apart, and you know that there must always be equal low and high dimensions. Without that balance, The Womb might fold in upon itself."

The wild-haired man groans softly as a heavy breath leaves his lungs. Glancing around at the worried countenances of his men, he says, "Do not fret. The power felt from Zarathustra's pocket dimension can only be one thing—the coward has figured out how to reproduce the Womb, in himself or in something else entirely. If we can consume *that*, our powers of creation would amplify to endless degrees. Through which mending the fissures and creating new life in each dimension would be effortless. Do not worry, all will be well."

The scholar glares at the wild-haired man with grim, sullen eyes. "Let's hope so. But know that if you're right, we must be careful. That pulse we felt...it was like The Womb of the One Mind itself was screaming with anguished fury."

CHAPTER EIGHTEEN

Sasha stands beneath a clear blue sky. No clouds to obscure or soften the intensity of the mid-summer heat. Sweat spills from her back as the sun's harsh rays beat down upon her. Staring at the void of black static where the Assembly once stood, Sasha's eyes are empty of all their glow.

Seth. Persephone. Mikhail. I brought you here to be safe, and now...

The ground is unsteady beneath her feet. Fissures spewing that strange, dark miasma webs its way through the campus. A hollowing sensation vibrates up Sasha's legs, making them feel as if they are on the cusp of shattering as well.

Memory of her father spurs to mind. That ten-thousand-year-old man, leading an army of others like him across the globe, settling down in magical cities built within hollowed out mountains—hers were built into the open air, in public view. Barely managing twenty years when her father managed thousands.

Unsure of the means, but still she knew. *It was always him, after all. Sergei caused this. Humans ruin everything good and pure.*

Collapsing to her knees, Sasha clasps her face within her hands and sobs.

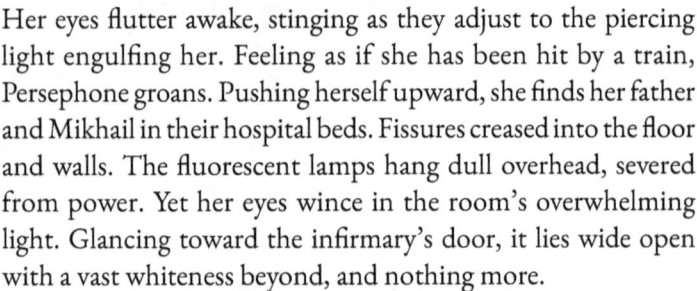

Her eyes flutter awake, stinging as they adjust to the piercing light engulfing her. Feeling as if she has been hit by a train, Persephone groans. Pushing herself upward, she finds her father and Mikhail in their hospital beds. Fissures creased into the floor and walls. The fluorescent lamps hang dull overhead, severed from power. Yet her eyes wince in the room's overwhelming light. Glancing toward the infirmary's door, it lies wide open with a vast whiteness beyond, and nothing more.

"What the fuck?"

She trudges toward the door's threshold and peeks outside. Clinging to the frame, she reaches her left foot out, somehow hitting a surface that isn't there. She hesitates, but steps out fully, finding that she can walk upon the vast white space.

Behind her, the infirmary floats—a room gutted from its adjoined building.

Head panning left to right, she yells, "Hello? Anyone there?" Turning around, she—a tall white figure stands inches from her, brandishing a deep frown. Persephone gasps and stumbles backward.

The Abyssal Consciousness glances from her to the room set adrift in the White Abyss. "This is the second time a part of the physical world made its transit here." The white humanoid form returns its gaze to Persephone. "And you, True-Born God, are proof that the opposite can occur as well. And not just by means of magic, as your parents know it."

Persephone's eyes narrow, glaring at the strange being. "Just what the fuck are you, and—wait, your voice…

The Abyssal Consciousness tilts its head in thought. "Yes, I am the one who spoke across the realms through the conduit of your mind—at the moment your powers returned."

Returned. Persephone turns toward her father, wishing he were available to question, as her mind drifts to what her mother told her. Her powers awakened twice before—once as a very small child, again after Andes's funeral—

"Yes," says the Abyssal Consciousness. "This is thrice your powers have risen, but the first that your memory remains intact. Twice that you have come here. There is much you need to discuss with *him*. If only he told you what you are...perhaps this tragedy could have been avoided. I warned him not to let you become like him."

"What tragedy? And I don't know what you're talking about. My father is a good man."

The Abyssal Consciousness nods slowly. "Goodness is a thing a repentant one comes to know after a lifetime of evil. Mistakes must be made to know the weight of goodness. Such is the way of the world. Positive and negative values mirror and define each other. But one's own sins are their own to confess. Ask him for the details, but first," The Abyssal Conscious thrusts its large hands to the sides of Persephone's head, gripping firm. "Let us discuss lineage."

The whiteness of the abyss fills her peripheral vision, overtaking everything. The words *Womb of the One Mind* echo within her brain, as one by one, specks of teal emerge into view—The Abyssians. Pale humanoid forms with wild teal hair born from *the Womb* burst from the whiteness and into the worlds of various bipedal sentient beings. Aiding them in times of distress, caring for them, nurturing them—devouring them.

One of these teal-haired gods abscond from the rest, finding a home within an empty pocket of space between two dimensions at the peak of the stack. Ripping his chest open, the fraction of *the Womb* that birthed him spills out, creating the White Abyss. A realm connected to *the Womb*, identical in form and function, designed to grant divinity to humans. But an anomaly occurs in the wake of *the Womb's* desire to right the wrongs of the Abyssians. Through an evolution of sorts, the White Abyss grows a consciousness.

Seth kneels to the ground, skin turning dark blue as fire erupts, engulfing a monster alongside an entire city. Sasha is there to comfort him in the wake of thousands dead.

A baby cries. Emerging from the womb of one Abyssian spawn, fathered by another. Persephone enters the world as they all do. Screaming and unaware of what lies in wait for them throughout their lives.

The history of the world and worlds before it pours into her mind, her entire life hurtling forward to the moment the Assembly collapsed, imploded, with hundreds inside and out crushed to death in an instant...to where Persephone stands now—the Abyssal Consciousness releases her, the girl stumbles back, wide-eyed and heaving. Tears flowing from eyes, red and inflamed.

"I could show you more, but the path to the future must be walked on one's own. I only hope you make the choices I foresee. All that is or has been or will be, I have knowledge of it all. And thus, so can you."

Persephone trembles at the vision she has been given. Eyes scattering about, still seeing glimpses of eons before she was even a thought in her parents' minds. And what her father did—Persephone sobs, as something within her feels that the Abyssal Consciousness has no reason to lie.

"A vessel made of abyssal genetics, born more human than either parent. You were the perfect combination of divine material—the first *True-Born God*."

The Abyssal Consciousness glares stoically as Persephone processes the heavy stream of information pumped into her brain. Tears running down her cheeks, the girl stares with horror. "My head feels like it's going to burst!" she shouts, gripping her temples.

"You humans have the great ability to adapt. The more you struggle, the more you grow. Just as your arm muscles grow sore, heal, and become stronger than before, the same is true for the mind—more so than any physical muscle. The only bounds the mind knows are the ones its owner believes are there. Your father knows this well. Ask him about it, too. But trust me, you will be fine.

"I needed to show you that, to prepare you. To make you know your own power, your responsibilities."

Baring her teeth, Persephone's eyes widen with anger, as she says, trembling, "You showed me all those people dying in the Assembly. You're telling me that's my fault? That I killed—that I'm some sort of monster?"

The Abyssal Consciousness gazes at Mikhail, to Seth. "Again, your father would tell you that it is not that simple." A sudden pulse pushes Persephone back, shattering what's left of the infirmary's windows. White tendrils stretch toward Seth and Mikhail, wrapping around them as teal sparks crackle from head to toe.

"What are you doing to them?" Persephone shouts, stomping toward the Abyssal Consciousness—a groan freezes her movement, and she turns toward the hospital beds. In tandem, her father and Mikhail open their eyes.

"You may be a True-Born God, but you are young yet. You saved them, but could not heal them fully. A matured brain is necessary for proper magic usage. Again, your father knows all about that."

Seth and Mikhail slowly lift their heads, eyes wincing in the bright abyssal light.

"Enough about my dad!" Persephone shouts. "I don't understand what you want from me. I'm a god, but apparently, I can't do anything right and need a babysitter all the time? Enough with being so vague! Out with it. Why is it you're telling me all this?"

Seth steps off the bed—his vision is yanked downward as his head smacks against the tile floor. Persephone runs over. "Daddy! Careful, you've been asleep for weeks!"

"I've what—Persephone, what are we doing here?" Seth asks, noticing the surrounding whiteness. Offering her father a shoulder, she helps them limp out of the crumbling infirmary and into the emptiness beyond. She lowers her father to the ground and says, "We have a lot to talk about."

As she rises, she finds the Abyssal Consciousness once more inches from her face. "I told you all that...because a war is coming." Persephone trembles as his words reach her ears.

"*You!*" Seth shouts, trying to stand, but failing. "Who was that boy? He had the souls of the Sins within him! That pressure—it was like facing Yahweh again. Explain yourself! Aren't souls supposed to be assimilated into the Abyss upon a person's death? How is it she is back?"

The Abyssal Consciousness tilts its head. "*She* is not. Yahweh's soul is gone, I assure you. I warned you they were coming. As to how this came to be..." The white form turns to Persephone. "Well, the White Abyss has had plenty of developments I did not see coming.

"But perhaps it was the unnatural way the souls were sent back to the White Abyss—they did not die and return, but died and kept away, then sent home by you. Or perhaps it was the collective rage and pain the sins felt. Betrayed by their mother and original host...and murdered by you." Seth glances away, feeling shame brought on by his daughter's gaze. Mikhail's shoulders slump, and her eyes darken, the supernatural pressure of the White Abyss too much for her. Noticing this, the Abyssal Consciousness continues, "A soul angry enough, with a will fiery and strong enough, is quite hard to keep down. You know this well, don't you, Spawn of Zarathustra. But the young one here is struggling. It's time for you three to leave."

"I'm not done talking to you!" says Seth.

"Guide your daughter. She needs your wisdom." Turning to Persephone, it says, "You caused a tragedy, but you are not a monster. You and I are one in the war to come. Remember: fear the ones with pale skin and teal hair.

"For those false gods are the real monsters."

Another pulse bursts from out the white form's body, rippling around Persephone, Seth, and Mikhail—a portal encircling them. A flash of white light shears away, the Abyss drifting off into particles. A scorching summer sun looms above them, unobscured by a clear blue sky. A void of black static sits where the Assembly once had, with a spiderweb of fissures shooting out in all directions.

And the eyes of Sasha glare wide, red, and glossy—her pain piercing her daughter.

CHAPTER NINETEEN

SIXTEEN YEARS AGO.

Wind clashed against the cliffside, tearing through the branches of the surrounding forest. The forceful gales blowing hard against the side of the cabin. Lightning webbed across the sky, thunder banging even louder there at the mountain's summit. Rain splattering against the windows. With nothing seen beyond the pitch blackness outside.

Darkness creeped into the cabin's kitchen, bedrooms, and hallway, with only the living room lit by the overhead lamp. Brianna sat upon her boss's couch, with baby Persephone bouncing on her knee.

The gloomy weather and lateness of night had Brianna's eyes darting from door to windows, and back again. The cabin creaked as the wind continued its assault, making her wonder if the monsters Sasha and the old guard claim to have once existed were actually real. *No doubt they were, Sasha's of the trustworthy sort. But regardless, supernatural horrors make for good fiction*—Brianna let out a startled gasp as a tree branch snapped, thudding against the stony cliff before rolling off the side. Still bouncing on her knee, Persephone giggled at her sitter's sudden bout of fear.

"Is that funny to you?" Brianna said, smirking. "You're a brave one."

Persephone's fit of giggles grew louder, as a white light flashed beyond the water-streamed windows. Passing it off as lightning, Brianna awaited the crash of thunder—the front door creaked open, startling her.

"Sorry to spook you," said Seth, holding the door open with his right hand, an umbrella with his left. The way cleared, Sasha walked in from the gloom and rain.

"Hey, Brianna—and hello, my sweet baby girl," said Sasha, unwrapping a raincoat from her shoulders and slipping off her shoes. Walking over to the couch, she gave Persephone's left cheek an affectionate squeeze. "How was she amidst all this?"

"Better than me," Brianna said, chuckling. "This girl has nerves of steel. What about you two? How was Europe? I hope you had a good vacation...you deserve it."

"Europe, Russia, China, Japan. We had a great time, but you know it wasn't purely a vacation. Had to scout for future locations to expand the Assembly. Years away still, but these things take time, you know. Sorry we got back so late."

Joining them near the couch, Seth reached for Persephone, pulling his daughter to his chest. "Yeah, that's my fault. Mount Elbrus, Galdhøpiggen, Mount Fuji...I wanted to visit the tallest peaks in each country along the way. Staying overnight atop Fuji is what kept you waiting."

"But please," said Sasha, "Spend one more night. Least we can do. Not like we expect you to hike down the mountain in the dark, let alone in a storm."

"Oh, if you truly don't mind." Brianna smiled toward Seth and back to Sasha. "I just adore her anyway. Won't complain about a little extra time with the baby! Plus, you two could likely use a hand adjusting in the morning."

"You're too kind," Seth said, yawning. "I'll put her to bed, though. Good night."

As Seth disappeared into a bedroom, Sasha's eyebrows rose. "Oh, by the way!" Reaching into a messenger bag, Sasha unearthed a thick stack of papers. Held together by large black paper clamps. "I finished it."

"Oh my, Sasha, you really shouldn't have spent your vacation on that! It's no rush really…"

"Nonsense. You've helped us out so much here. With us gone, Andes had to handle things at the Assembly on his own, not to mention his own kid to look after. Seriously, least I could do." Sasha smiled. "And shit, Brianna. I had no idea you were so talented. When you first mentioned you were writing a novel…I'm ashamed but can admit to it now that I've been proven wrong. You had given me pause when mentioning you were trying to become an author. More so when you told me you used my stories of the supernatural holocaust as inspiration. But your prose—the way you weaved the suffering of the protagonist into the very fabric of the narrative, well, I'm impressed. As asked, I marked up wherever I found typos and other errors, but clearly you've been thorough, as I didn't find many. Granted, I'm not an editor, but still, I've been an avid reader for three hund—" Sasha clamped her lips shut, almost letting it slip that she's far older than any human could ever be. "Well, for much of my life."

Brianna smiled softly, small tears glimmering within her eyes. "Thank you. That means so much to hear. This whole process of sending it out to agents…it can be demoralizing at times. They're so particular—well, I've gotten nothing more than a constant stream of rejection."

"You have your eyes set on a difficult goal, that's all." Sasha said. "In a lot of ways, I also am working toward building a narrative brought about through inspiration from another—continuing my father's work. It's daunting, but I know that we both can do it."

Sasha gave the young author a friendly caress on her shoulder. Leaving the manuscript with her, Sasha said goodnight and joined Seth in their bedroom.

Time slipped away into the early hours of the next day, with Brianna unable to sleep. Flipping through the pages, smiling widely with bright eyes, her excitement for the future overflowed with vigor and hope.

A massive pit of solid blackness stretches over the spot where the Assembly once stood. Peculiar black motes of static rise from the depths, as fissures spread outward from the center. A part of the world sliced away, a void of stark nothingness in its wake. As Sasha steps forward, an uneasiness quivers through her from the soles of her feet.

Breath slinks from her parted lips. Her stomach drops as she feels herself hollowing out. Her eyes lose their sheen as she stares out at the blackness. Collapsing to her knees, throat fluttering, eyes tearing, she mutters:

"Persephone, Seth, Mikhail—"

Her father's portrait flashes into memory. Hung upon the wall next to the angel's tendril. The glass shattering as the portrait slammed against the floor. Her hands flutter and shake, her lips twitch and convulse—anger swiftly rising—she slams both fists upon the ground. Pain shoots through her wrists, but she raises and plunges them again and again and again and—

"*Argh!*" She screams as her fists plummet. Teal magic crackles, encasing them in static as they collide with the hard ground, fracturing the concrete. Taken aback, Sasha raises her hands, staring in awe.

Magic left the Guild upon rejoining the Earth and White Abyss. The great strength that arose through the conduit of her rune was also lost as a result. For twenty years, she's lived with the strength of an average woman. Yet here the creation magic running through her has stirred something new—an image spurs into memory, of a younger, angrier Seth regrowing limbs like an axolotl.

Her eyes widen in remembrance of the one magic in her original arsenal she did not lose. The creation magic gifted to her from Zarathustra was inherent in him. Just like this power of hers—the ability to sense the flow of magic. Within that instant of cracking the concrete, her new strength was not the only thing she noticed.

All things tether to the White Abyss—the origin of all magic, of all life, of everything within our world. I can feel it surging through a tree, and even a desk, a phone, a car. Different in the latter three, but they are made of materials found upon the earth, and therefore, while not magic, they indeed come from magic. Then why—

Lowering herself flat upon her stomach, ear to the ground, fingers tracing the edge of the blackness and—no crackle of magic stirs, no stimulation, no flow. *How is it that there is nothing to be felt? How can—*Sasha gasps as she retracts her hand, sits up, and scoots away from the pit's edge. Black streaks slither from the tips of her fingers, about an inch high. The fingers turn as black as the void, hardening before crumbling into dust, floating off like dandelion seeds in a sudden gale.

Gripping her wrist, Sasha heaves as she stares at the stumps left behind. Just the ends of her fingers, raw and red, but no bleeding. Releasing her wrists, teal sparks crackle within her other palm. Hovering over the stumps, the skeletal ends of her fingers regrow. Followed by the weaving of flesh, the wrapping of skin—her heart thuds in her chest, as she hunches over in a coughing fit.

"What the fuck is this?"

{The White Abyss blankets all. All worlds, all people, everything is derived from it. A world cannot exist without it. What you see before you is left behind when a world is destroyed. The absence of life, of all things.}

Sasha's eyes widen. *But where have I seen this before?*

Rising to her feet, she begins walking along the edge of the pit, picturing the walls of the Assembly, the rooms, where each part of the building stood. She roots in place as she glares toward where her office once was. The large space with a window looking out into the courtyard. The double doors leading to the lobby, where Brianna—

Sasha sighs. Twenty years of work. Much more if the years of the Guild were to be included—*A week away, and now it's gone. What has all this been for? Father, I failed you, and now my family is gone. With Seth in a coma, they are surely*—Sasha drops her face into her hands, tears leaking through her fingers. Seth and everything they worked toward, gone. Persephone and Mikhail, with their whole life ahead of them...her mind drifts again to Brianna. After all these years of Sergei making Sasha's life miserable, Brianna always stood by her side. *Babysitting when Persephone was young, always offering to work above her station, always so helpful and courteous. All she wanted was to make a difference in this world, and to publish that novel—fuck, I can't believe almost twenty years have gone by and she never got to see that happen. Human lives are so short, and often severed too early by unforeseen accidents—like this, an accident I should have been able to prevent if I wasn't so useless—how cruel it is for the world to not value what is truly good and beautiful and artful, to the extent of denying someone the privilege to present their work to the world. Now, nothing will ever come of it.*

Nothing will ever come of it. She could feel the warmth leaving her face, her eyes dulling at the horror before her. *All this work, and now nothing will come of the Assembly—nothing will come of me. My family is dead, and now nothing will come of me.*

Slumped against a tree, she glares at the Assembly's absence from afar. Her phone in hand, with an unsent email constructed for each foreign branch lingering upon the screen, with a photo of the pit attached:

"Is this a real enough threat for you? Headquarters is gone. I am officially ordering each branch to send soldiers to cordon off the blackened area. It's dangerous to touch."

Breathing deeply, Sasha presses *send* without glancing at the screen. Pocketing her phone, she skulks back to the pit to take one last glance before—*what the fuck do I even do now*—

A burst of white light emerges to her right, a dome of abyssal energy ripples like an ocean's tide before scattering into white particles, drifting about like snow. She glares, unblinking, eyes red and glossy, at the sudden appearance of her family. Awake and upright, Seth and Mikhail stand behind Persephone, with Mikhail wobbling and looking queasy. The teenage girl's fearful eyes glare at her mother's deadened sheen.

"You all…you're okay?" Sasha says, ambling over to them. "I don't even care how, I'm just so hap—"

Her daughter's glare stops her from moving any closer. "Do you even know what happened here?" asks Persephone. "Your precious Assembly killed Brianna!" Caught off guard by her own words, Persephone's eyes shift away. Sasha's widen, tears streaming down her cheeks.

"Hey! Don't talk to your mother like that," Seth says, stepping forward. "It's not—"

"So, you're the only survivors?" asks Sasha.

Seth and Mikhail look to Persephone, who says, "The ones who killed her ran off...they were with the strange boy who attacked us at home."

Sasha's eyes dart to Seth, and says, "So they're likely alive. Considering what *he* is, I'm sure he's crafty enough to escape...whatever happened here." Sasha looks toward her daughter, and a memory returns. That black space left behind after she tore the cabin from the cliffside, all those years ago, after Andes died.

Persephone scoffs and says, "When I saw that boy, I got angry. That weird white stuff started flowing from me and—the floor and walls were breaking and stuff. Next thing I knew, we were in a big white place, and I was being talked at by a white thing with no face." The girl turns toward the large black void where the Assembly once stood. "I don't know how that connects to what happened here, but good riddance, I say. This place is all you cared about for my entire life. I barely even know who you ar—"

Sasha's open palm collides with Persephone's right cheek. The girl stumbles backward, tears in her eyes as her cheek swells and reddens. Sasha's heavy breathing intensifies, eyes wide as she glances from her daughter to her hand. A pulsating pain stings her palm.

Seth steps between wife and daughter, glancing frantically at both.

CHAPTER TWENTY

Persephone sits upon the cabin's porch steps, a hole the size of her father behind her. Trees stand still within the stagnant mountain air. No breeze to soothe the oppressive, sweltering sun, beating down upon her like searing hot iron. Past the peak of summer, the days crawl into the wet, tense August heat. Cheeks burning, they redden, meshing with the swollen pink spot where her mother hit her. Grumbling, she reaches into a bag of potato chips and plops a few into her mouth. The satisfying crunch of the greasy, salty snack ruined by her face's throbbing ache.

The words of the Abyssal Consciousness echo within her mind. The vagaries about her powers, the warnings of a war to come, and the twice-telling of her father's mysterious past sins. A slap to the face for voicing her feelings. And now here she is without a home, sweating and foul-smelling, without the luxury of a shower.

With no door behind her, there's no creak to alert her of someone approaching from behind. A meaty hand grips her shoulder—her eyes fill with abyssal white light as she jerks away—Seth backs up, a hand risen in front of him, the other holding a plate of eggs and bacon.

"Hey! Easy, it's just me. Thought I'd let you know the kitchen still works. We can at least eat."

Persephone stands, looks over her shoulder, and says, "Fuck off."

Seth's face collapses as Sasha and Mikhail appear behind.

"Persephone!" says Sasha.

"What? Going to hit me again? You fuck off, too." The teenage girl ventures off into the woods, bag of chips in hand, disappearing behind a thicket of evergreens.

Mikhail walks off the porch, glancing at Seth and Sasha with a fragile smile, saying, "Uh, I'll go talk to her," and follows in Persephone's wake.

Seth and Sasha stare after them, eyes tired, withdrawn.

"She hates you, too, now, huh?" asks Sasha.

"I don't know why," says Seth. "I've been in a coma for weeks. What could I have done?"

Sasha sighs. "Those powers of hers...like yours, stem from the White Abyss. Think *it* could be talking to her, telling her things?"

Seth's frown deepens as Sasha walks back inside.

The sun's rays bleed through the collapsed ceiling, casting shadows upon the dining room table. Sasha glares at the debris strewn about. Their home destroyed, their place of community and nourishment sullied by the damage. She thinks of Persephone, lashing out and entering the forest with Mikhail at her heel. The divide between them growing ever wider. Seth approaches from behind, placing his hands on her waist. Taking his left hand, Sasha raises it to her mouth, kissing it softly.

"Where did we go wrong? How is it that slaying a god was easier than raising children?"

Seth chuckles and says, "The former took a certain degree of hate. The latter requires love, and love is vastly more complicated. I don't think we did anything wrong. You're not the only parent whose job has kept them away more than either the parent or child would like. And besides, Mikhail is timid, but he seems alright."

"But our own daughter isn't."

Seth shivers as she says this. "She's too much like me, isn't she?"

"That's not what I'm saying." Sasha frees herself from his embrace and begins clearing the table of debris.

"Sorry. I didn't mean to bring that up. Besides, I think she has plenty of both of us in her. When I awoke inside the White Abyss, the entire infirmary was also there. As if she somehow, perhaps unconsciously, sought to protect Mikhail and me? That's more than what I did at first. She's like you, a defender." Seth glances inquisitively at her as she clears the table. Without understanding why, he joins her.

"Yes, but the rest of the Assembly was lost. Brianna was lost. You know she never got to publish that book of hers? I hate this, Seth. People shouldn't have to live arbitrary lives that amount to nothing, after trying so hard to make something of themselves...all my hard work, the Assembly, gone—"

"Do you blame her?"

Clearing the last piece of lumber and a few scattered screws off the table, Sasha says, "No. But the Assembly was created to deter supernatural threats. And I'm worried, Seth. I'm worried that our baby girl might be one."

Seth frowns.

Sasha reaches forward. Teal sparks crackle as a stream of creative energy flows from her palms to the table's surface. Molding into small bricks of light, the mound rises higher and higher, the energy burns bright as an intense heat emits into the already intense summer air. Fading, the light disperses into particles, leaving behind a small mountain of dollar bills.

"Sasha...what is this?" Seth says, turning to his wife—her skin grays and wrinkles further, sagging from her cheeks and neck, as she hunches over, turning frail. "Sasha! You can't keep using those powers. They're killing—"

"We need a new place to live, and there's an Assembly project—kept off campus—that I need to retrieve." She turns, facing Seth with the deeply grooved face of an eighty-year-old.

Seth's eyes well with tears.

"Don't worry. I have an idea. It occurred to me as I was investigating that strange void, and I thought about the regenerative magic you used to wield. What was that you've often said—that magic is best used in creative ways? That magic does what the mind wills it to do?"

"Y-yes. Melphis's words." Seth clears his throat. "And he was right, of course. But take it from me, using magic to surpass your limits too often will only burn you out, killing you quicker—or those around you."

Sasha glances at him with melancholic eyes. "Yes, you would know. But you also know that sometimes one must burn brighter than once thought possible, if they are to make their mark. You may not approve, but please, Seth, understand...with what is coming, this is what must be. If for anything, to protect the kids."

Turning from him, she raises her arms like a cross. Ribbons of teal magic burst from her palms, wrapping around her body. An intense heat erupts outward, causing Seth to back away, raising his left arm over his face. As the magic disperses into motes of teal dust, Sasha's posture straightens, bones stiffening with vigor. Her skin grows taut, its wrinkles dissolving, wrapping around renewed muscles, presenting their shapeliness beneath. She emerges from the cocoon of teal magic, having aged forty years in reverse. She turns, smiling and—

Gasping, she hunches over, clutching at her chest. "Sasha!" Seth screams, catching her in his arms.

"I—I'm okay...just need to lay d—"

Breath labored, Seth rushes Sasha into their bedroom. Debris is scattered about, and the left wall is missing, but Seth quickly brushes what he can off the bed and lays her head down to rest.

His wife lay unconscious but breathes softly in her slumber.

This woman—this amazing woman, going as far as she does to fight for humanity. I applaud her...and wish she would stop. Sasha, please, I cannot bear losing you.

Tears flood his eyes. Frowning, Seth leaves the room.

Persephone drags her feet along the path, spurring dirt into the air. Halting at a particularly thick evergreen, she takes a seat at its base and hangs her head back. Sunlight filters through the high-hanging leaves. The air is thick and moist, but the shade relaxes her fluttering heart.

A large black and yellow spider crawls along an exposed root. Persephone stares with dead eyes, unfazed by its presence. Something bulbous and white hangs from its backside, even larger than its striped abdomen. Crawling up the tree to the nearest, lowest branch, the sac dangles its way to the large web overhead—the white orb crumbles apart on one side, as a hundred babies spill out onto the silky grey strands.

The spider and its egg sac, a single grotesque creature producing a multiplicity of lives—*why does this seem so familiar?*

Wanting not to alarm the new mother, she stands and backs away.

"Persephone?" A voice emerges from a thicket of trees.

"You followed me?" says Persephone, glaring.

"Sorry, couldn't leave you be. Wanna tell me what's wrong?" asks Mikhail.

Persephone turns away. "Why do I feel so empty, Mikhail—I'm sorry, we haven't had a chance to talk since that guy attacked us. You've been asleep for so long. What would you like to be called now?"

Mikhail is struck silent, mouth agape. So many years of avoidance has not left much time for contemplating what could be if he was honest. And, stuck in that awkward position when Damien attacked, thinking he might die, he had come out to her.

And she hugged me and didn't care. Mikhail eyes Persephone's face, breasts, hips, and whips his blushing face away, "Um, I don't know. Maybe, Misha, like you used to call me?" she says.

Persephone smiles. "Why do I feel so empty, Misha?" She takes a seat by a different tree, gesturing for Misha to join her, offering some chips from the half-emptied bag.

Grabbing a few, Misha says, "I don't know how to answer that."

"Well, it's less of a question and more of a confession, I suppose. I think, on some level, I've always felt this way. I've felt like there was nothing inside, so I filled that nothing with studying, using books to escape. When that stopped being an adequate distraction, I stared on at you with scorn as you became the one who was good at school. Not to mention being trained in magic by my dad, all the while mom was never around. And now I'm mad at them—"

"Your mom, I understand, but why are you mad at your dad? Seems like it came out of nowhere."

"The thing in that strange white place, it told me about...made it seem like dad was hiding something, something from his past. That creature in there worded things in such a way that made dad seem super ominous. What if he's done something I can't forgive? And what if—" Persephone's voice chokes, sobbing. "What if whatever it is wasn't as bad as what I did? The Assembly, everyone inside is dead because of me! Do you hate me? Will you hate me now that you know what happened?"

Misha frowns as she glances over Persephone, a shaky hand reaching for the crying girl's shoulder. Caressing gently, she says, "It was an accident. Yeah, I wasn't awake, I didn't see what happened. But your dad and I are alive. I can only imagine that you did the only thing you could. And these new powers of yours—well, mine were hard to master, but yours are much more complicated. What could the alternative be when you're dealing with something so new and strange?

"And I could never hate you."

Persephone turns her glossy, red eyes toward Misha, flittering them between her eyes and parted lips. Thrusting her mouth forward, the warmth of Misha's lips flows into hers—yanking away, Persephone's cheeks redden beneath wide eyes. "Oh my God, I'm sorry. I wasn't thinking—"

Throwing her arms around Persephone, Misha pulls her into a passionate barrage of lips and tongues.

Leaving Sasha to rest, Seth returns to the mysterious pile of money she created, and sighs. Opening a nearby closet, he rummages around in shoes, coats, and cleaning supplies that have all fallen into a heap on the floor. Beneath one of Sasha's long black coats, he finds a large white duffel bag and a slightly smaller blue-green one. Placing them on the dining room table, he pulls them open and begins stuffing the money stacks inside.

You would know.

Sasha's words echo within his mind as he ponders their meaning. She never blamed him for Magistrum. It took him many years to internalize that, but he knows it now. Turning toward the hole in the wall, he peers through, finding the backyard. The stone where he laid, where that boy stood over him. Saved by Persephone's distraction.

Seth smiles softly.

He overpowered me so easily. Perhaps I've burnt out as a father. I did little to protect our home, our kids. But Persephone, she—she saved me twice now. I suppose that makes her more like you than me.

As he finishes packing away the money, Seth's slight smile collapses into a deep frown. *Even a small portion of me could be disastrous.* Despair strikes as he ponders the complicated nature of fatherhood. A hypocrisy is born within him. Pride in his daughter's powerful protective nature, but great shame for *his* inability to protect *her*. From that boy and from herself.

Needing answers, he leaves the duffel bags on the table and heads outside. Heading to the cliff, he shouts, "Huginn! Muninn! To my side."

The ravens swoop toward the cliff, having been circling above, watching from a distance. A bird to either side, they cock their heads and croak.

"Sasha is sleeping inside, and I need to...head inward. Watch over us?" The cooing birds flutter their wings as Muninn stands back-to-back with Seth, and Huginn heads to the porch.

With the protection of these avian beasts, Seth's eyes overflow with abyssal white light. "And keep an eye out for the kids," he says, as the world bleeds away, leaving only the abyss within.

"Your return was foreseen," says the Abyssal Consciousness. A vast whiteness stretches outward on all sides. A supernatural pressure weighs down upon Seth's shoulders, but he does not budge, for he has grown accustomed to the strain. The real world growing too light for what brews within him. The Abyssal Consciousness glares at the man, and says, "You have questions, Spawn of Zarathustra."

"You really can see it, can't you?" says Seth. "The future. All that has been, all that is, all that ever can be. You see it, don't you? An omniscient god, everything we fought against..."

The Abyssal Consciousness cocks its head to the left and says, "You know I am no god. I am an anomaly, born of necessity to fend off a race of gods that have become parasites, those who would seek to command The Womb of the One Mind. As soon as these pests are vanquished, I too will cease to be. All thought is reabsorbed by the Abyss, as is the fate of all sentient life. Even gods, such as your wee one. Your questions are about her. Speak them now."

Seth frowns, glaring at the white entity with fierce eyes. "That pressure she emits..." memory stirs of the ground being crushed beneath her feet as she stomped forward, her speed restrained by her own powers. And long ago, when she almost pulled the moon into her stomach. Seth considers the emptiness he fears he shares with her. "It's like a black hole, sucking everything around into her, literally tearing the fabric of the world apart, leaving that black void in her wake. What is it? Just what are her powers?"

The Abyssal Consciousness stares into Seth, while simultaneously staring into his future, into all possibilities for what is to come. Frowning, he sheds the need for vagaries. *This man has proved himself, as has his wife. But they deal with something beyond their knowledge. And **they** have yet to arrive...this calls for guidance.*

"What is a god, but a creator? I called her a True-Born God for a reason, as her capacity for creation is far greater than any that have come before. Even your progenitor, Zarathustra, would be no match for her. She is what Yahweh once hoped to use you for. A catalyst for creating a new world, but one that would destroy the world you know as a result. No—not just your world, but the entire dimensional stack. That would have been the cost, if Yahweh succeeded.

"But your wee one, she could create without that consequence. The problem is that she is too young. Magic cannot be wielded efficiently within a mind that is yet to be fully grown. Yes, she is a black hole. But beyond the event horizon of her mind lies an infinite potential for creation. Everything that the White Abyss is can be found within her."

His suspicions validated, Seth sighs—and remembering the strange boy that attacked him, a new concern is born. *He said something about Persephone "becoming his eighth." As if to join the seven souls which comprise him...so he recognizes her power, understands what it is, and wants what Yahweh wanted—he said as much, in fact.*

Returning his sharp gaze to the Abyssal Consciousness, Seth says, "So, she is capable of limitless destruction or creation. You're saying it can go either way—what's new? That's parenting. All Sasha and I can do is try our best to guide her, and hope it works out."

The Abyssal Consciousness smiles.

Continuing, Seth says, "Knowing what I'm working with makes all the difference. Thank you, truly. But one thing before I go. Have I...burnt out as a father?"

"Yes," says the Abyssal Consciousness. "Weariness has held you back, but it seems you will now burn brightly again."

Seth nods, as his eyes light with abyssal power, blurring as his form streams back to the cliffside. The Abyssal Consciousness stares after Seth's dissipating body.

Those souls within you, that Omni Magic. Just what will you do with it?

Gripping each other's waists, lips moving furiously, Persephone and Misha sink further into each other. Persephone grips the back of Misha's hand, pulling her close, as Misha grips the center of Persephone's back—

Misha's lips catch on something rough as they are pulled further into Persephone's mouth. "Oww owww ow—stop, don't bithe so haard—"

Persephone's eyes shoot open, overflowing with abyssal white light, as Misha's lips hit the back of her tongue. Pulling away, she stares in horror as Misha paws at her elongated jaw, lips and skin dangling off between a spillage of blood. Persephone wipes at her mouth—a red smear coats the back of her hand. "Holy shit, Misha!"

Touching her damaged jaw, Persephone's eyes glow white as crackling sparks of teal magic flow from her palms to Misha's mouth. The jaw repositions itself, retracting back into its normal roundness. The flesh tightens, wrapping around the bone, followed by skin. Misha's fingers pat at her mouth, opening and closing it, and she says, "Holy shit, that hurt!"

"I'm sorry, I'm so sorry," says Persephone."

"It's okay, you fixed it." An old memory stirs within her mind. They were both so young when she watched a dreaming Persephone suck the moon out of the sky. "But maybe we shouldn't do that again until you can control your magic a bit better."

"Yeah...probably a good idea," says Persephone, glancing away with a pout.

"That's not to say I didn't like it!" Misha says. "I've wanted to do that for a long time, actually." Blushing, her eyes flutter away.

"No, it's not that. Just thinking about my parents again."

Misha leans toward Persephone, resting her head on her shoulder. "Do you think my dad would hate me, now that I'm no longer his little boy, his son?"

"Are you kidding?" Persephone shouts, glancing at Misha with newfound vigor, but with trembling voice. "Uncle Andes was the best guy I knew. He cared so much about all of us, about everyone. Always looking to help in any way he could. He would never hate you. He'd be proud of you."

"Well, it's the same with your parents. They took me in without hesitation, and not once has it seemed like they regretted it. They're the best people *I* know. Point is, whatever they may have done in the past, it doesn't define who they are now. Just go talk with them. Should we head back?"

Persephone sighs and says, "Fine. But only if you come out to them, too."

Exchanging smiles, they rise from the dirt and grass, making their way back to their dilapidated cabin.

Sunlight filters through the evergreen branches as they find the cabin at the summit. Muninn spreads his wings, ruffling his feathers at the sight of Persephone and Misha. Huginn swoops down from above, joining his brother in coos as the teenagers return home—

An oval of white fire conjures above the cliffside as Seth emerges from some unknown errand, with two empty duffel bags in hand. "Oh, you're back," he says, as his daughter approaches him, a frown and glossy red eyes tittering away from her father's gaze. Misha elbows her softly in the back, pushing her forward. "Just had to make a deposit at the bank."

"Dad, the thing inside that strange white place told me some things. Can we talk—"

"Apologize first."

Persephone rolls her eyes. "I'm sorry I told you to fuck off."

"Not to me. Apologize to your mother."

"Are you kidding? She hit—"

"Persephone, that wasn't a suggestion."

The girl stares up at her father, his fierce eyes glaring down at her. Taken aback by his sudden authoritarian tone, she says, "Ugh. Fine." And walks toward the dilapidated cabin.

"And Mikhail," Persephone hears her dad say. She turns, gesturing with her eyes, *go on.*

"Uhm, actually…I'd like to be called Misha from now on…as more than just my childhood nickname…uhm, you see—"

"Alright, Misha," Seth says, with a knowing smile. "While Persephone talks with her mom, help me salvage what we can of our belongings. We've gotta move everything out of this place." Misha stares at Seth in awe for a moment. How quickly his acceptance took hold, how small an issue this lifelong internal drama ended up being. Overtaken with warmth, Misha lunges her arms around Seth, clinging tight.

Smiling, she turns toward Persephone and makes her way toward the house. Persephone, with a wide smile, awaits her from the porch.

"I'm happy you told me," says Seth, walking at Misha's side. "Glad you finally worked out what was going on within you. Proud of you, kiddo." Patting her on the back, they make their way inside.

Persephone ventures into her parents' room, torn asunder like the rest of the house. Though there her mother lays, eyes fluttering awake to find Persephone's sullen face, as she takes in the view of her mother's tighter frame, her black hair, the more youthful glow of her skin. "Mom? Is that really you?"

"Yes, hun. It's me. I used magic to—whatever, enough of that. Come here."

Sitting at her mother's side, Persephone glances at her uncomfortably. Appearing before her is a woman unlike the mother she knew, the old, greying woman who hit her just yesterday. This woman, before her now, is passable for a woman in her late thirties, as Persephone herself will look in twenty years.

"Dad told me—asked me to come see you. What I said about the Assembly, I'm sor—"

Sasha lunges toward her daughter, wrapping her arms around her back, pulling her face into her bosom. "No, I'm sorry. I hit you—I shouldn't have done that. And I've spent so much of your life slaving at work while I should have been here."

"Well, that's not—"

"No. Sweetie, listen to me. It was for good reason, but I still should have been here with you. But come on, I want to show you something." Walking into the living room, they find Seth with eyes aglow, a portal already open. Through which is an obscured location swathed in darkness. Seth glances at his wife and daughter with a puzzled look. Sasha smiles softly and says, "I'll tell you about it later, but I want to show Persephone first."

Misha, silent at Seth's side, smiles at Persephone as she follows her mother into the portal. Pitch blackness wraps around her as the portal closes. Carefully placing one foot in front of the other, she totters forward. Sasha's gait moves quickly to the left. A flick of a switch brightens half the room, revealing the makings of a laboratory within a cave, with something dark and yet obscured towering in front of them.

"I want you to know I have always, and will always love you," says Sasha.

"Mom, you're freaking me out. What is this place?"

"You'll see. But first, do you know why we named you Persephone?"

"I know she was a Greek goddess. A fake one, though, right? After what the thing in the white space showed me, she couldn't be—"

"Ah, so it has told you things. Good. That gives me less to explain. Yes, the Greek gods aren't real. But we named you after what Persephone symbolizes: the coming of spring. Your father and I went through great tragedy before you were born. We slew a god and gave the world back to humanity. We named you Persephone as a symbol for humanity's rejuvenation after eons of being ruled by a false god. In short, you are so very important to us.

"And so, you deserve to see what has kept me away." Sasha flips another switch, and the entire cave bursts with light. The towering object revealed, Persephone stares slack-jawed at the body of a spacecraft. As tall as a skyscraper, and almost as wide as the suddenly bright, vast cavern. "I need to rebuild the Abyssal Pedestal and wire it here, and a few more parts aside from that, but she will be finished soon. And as you can see on the hull, not a moment has gone by that I haven't been thinking of you."

The words *Project Persephone* gleam brightly in teal along the stark white side.

"I have a confession," Sasha continues. "My creation magic is killing me. I'm dying, Persephone. But it was worth it. This is my contribution to the world. This is how I make my mark. We may not need it. But if we do need to abandon the Earth to fight another day, Project Persephone will be here to protect humanity—to protect *you*.

"And through it, humankind will flourish in a new spring to come."

CHAPTER TWENTY-ONE

The sweltering August sun filters through the volcano-like hole in the mountain's ceiling, beating down upon Damien's outstretched arms. The air is cleaner, but still heavy with the scent of charred flesh. The boy smiles amidst the blackened destruction of Magistrum, as crowds swarm him with boisterous voices. Hands gesticulating, flinging sweat in all directions. "Everyone, calm down and back it up!" shouts Sergei, standing between the people and their god, who is making a cross of his body. Head hung back, glaring skyward, ignoring the outrage before him.

One of Sergei's men approaches and says, "But sir, we were supposed to kill Sasha and take the Assembly headquarters. What the hell happened back there?"

"Watch your language and your tone," says Sergei. "Whatever happens is God's plan, do not question it."

"But you wanted control of the Assembly. I'm sorry, but this radical change is too much to wrap my head around."

"I want justice for the world, with or without the Assembly," says Sergei, with Damien behind him, smiling broadly toward the scorching sunlight, eyes closed, arms still cross-like as he basks in the glow. "And through God's will shall it be done. Do you defy God's will? Is your faith so weak? I thought you held the heart of a good Christian, and yet you dare to question—"

"Sergei," says Damien. "It is okay." The boy drops his arms, walking forward with a stern glare. Each step quiets the crowd further. "Must I repair the ceiling and blow it free once more? Have I not proven myself to be your God?"

"Half the population these days is superhuman. How are we supposed to know you aren't just like the rest of them?" speaks a red-haired woman.

Damien glares. His eyes meeting the woman's, but instead looking inward as he delves into the depths of memory. Remembering each of his former selves at their last moments. The veil unobscured, revealing a halo above their heads. An aura of blinding gold light, and evidence of the divine. Yahweh constructed the lie of religion, and everything that encompasses. Even the many paintings of Jesus and Mary, of the many catholic saints, all with gold bands atop their heads. No longer an archangel, no longer the souls he's comprised of, he has no halo to offer. But he has the power to manipulate the multiplicity within him, the very souls that make him who he is. With fierce focus, he reaches into those memories and—

Gold dust sparks above his head, crackling, erupting into a bright band of light. His eyes glow in tandem, sparkling and overflowing with gold. "Convincing enough for you?" The woman's eyes grow wide, her mouth agape in awe and wonder. Falling to her knees, she bows. Sergei does the same, with the crowd falling in tandem with him. Their eyes averted, Damien's twitching mouth quivers with relief as he relinquishes the memory. Causing the façade of a halo to fizzle away into nothingness.

"I'm so sorry, my lord, my god," cries the woman. "Doubt stirred in my heart, and for a moment I let it rule me. Please, forgive me."

Damien's right hand reaches toward her. "Do not be sorry. You had questions, and you sought answers in us—in me." Damien bites his gums. *Having to police our every word is exhausting, but these simpletons would not understand the great multiplicity within us. We must keep up the ruse.* "Come, my child. Stand with me."

Taking his hand, the woman slowly rises. Damien wipes her tears away with the back of his fingers and turns to the crowd. "You think we lost the battle, because we lost the headquarters? Is your faith so small, so unambitious? What use is that witch's fortress when we have the coming kingdom of Heaven? Everything went as I had planned it. The witch has been set adrift without a home, and we also drew out her daughter's power. The child is now ripe. Before we can ascend to my Heaven, I must have her. For you see, the juices flowing within her are the very same as the apple plucked by Eve, from the tree of Knowledge of Good and Evil. Therefore, she is rightfully mine. My property, my fruit. And through our efforts, I shall have her.

"So yes, kneel before your god, and I shall lead you to the promised land! But first, preparations are to be made. This underground city, blackened with despair, is hardly worthy of my presence. Let us construct it anew! A base of operations worthy of the *Lord thy God*!"

The crowd erupts in cheers and tear-filled eyes. "Yes, death to the witch! Death to the sinful sullied by magic! They know not what they do! Their blood will be spilled at the feet of our Heavenly Father!" Piousness spreads through the air like a contagion, as their chanting grows louder and louder. Sergei's smile stretches, pulled by stings unseen, as he turns and says to the crowd: "You heard your God's decree! Let us build this city anew! Our resources may be limited, but I want everything short of laying the streets with gold! We shall have that, too, in time, when we ascend alongside our savior!"

Damien smiles as his glare pans the crowd's vigorous zealotry. The woman turns to join the crowd, but Damiens lays a hand on her shoulder, pulling her close. Her tearful eyes meet his as he slides his fingers to the small of her back. "My chambers have yet to be built, but I ask that you be the first to offer more personal servitude to me."

The woman nods frantically as she's pulled by the hand. Leading her behind the fallen Magistrum skyscraper in the center of the city, Damien licks his lips and grins.

Weeks later.

The noon sun pierces the darkness of the cave as it slowly crawls across the sky. Strewn around the stony floor are Damien's disciples, drooling, empty liquor bottles in hand. Naked, male and female pairs entwined with one another, genitalia pressed into the earth and turned skyward. A man with his hand on a brunette woman's backside awakes, lifting his head to find a throbbing erection. Flipping the woman over, he moans as he kisses her lips, her neck, her breasts.

"Good morning, but sorry, hun. You know, he named me next." The woman says, rising from the cave's floor. Quickly losing its cool touch as the sun's rays press down upon it. "Get to work with the other men." Leaning over to grab her robe, she wraps herself and walks toward the center of the ruined city.

The charred buildings and debris have been cleared off to the edge of the cavern, making the area much more spacious. Huts of wood and straw are strewn about the cylindrical cave, with tiki lamps between each hut. If one were to look down upon the settlement from the hole in the ceiling, sporadic as they are placed, their edges still connect to form a circle with perfect symmetry, with a larger building at the center. The fallen Magistrum skyscraper no more, a large cylindrical stone house now stands in its place. The temporary dwelling of their risen God.

The brunette woman walks up the steps toward Damien's abode, as a dozen men swarm the stone house, carrying long sticks with speared ends. Spiking them into the ground, made weak with pickaxes, they place the day's fresh effigies. Made of straw and cloth dyed black, crude imitations of Sasha hang upon the pikes. Dousing them with kerosene, they erupt in flames with the flick of a lighter. The woman walks on without care, eager to fulfill her calling.

Two other men stand by the doors to the stone abode, chiseling Damien's likeness into two large grey slabs. Slaving away for weeks, capturing their Lord's essence and aiming for nothing less than perfection. There he twice stands, lifting a pomegranate to his mouth with eyes staring heavenward. The woman smiles at the statues and their craftsmen. They nod in return, letting their tools clang to the ground as they reach for the double door, opening it for the chosen lady.

The brunette woman glances around at a room not even Sergei has seen. Along the circumference of the walls are strange statues depicting the busts of seven creatures unknown to her. One with a dozen eyes sporadically placed along a head far too large for the shoulders that carry it. Another with sharp, yellow eyes full of desire and tentacles rising from its back. One with the face of a worm, no eyes, but simply pleats of flesh peeling back, revealing a pointed beak with rows of sharp teeth. One with lazy eyes and a head slunk backward. Another with a skull rising from its body of fleshless bone, shrouded in a black hood.

One with a large, angry face with horns and teeth like railroad spikes. And lastly, a man whose eyes have been overtaken with pleasure, a tongue writhing from out his lips.

At the base of each statue is a groove heading toward the center of the room, joining together in a circle, a trench waiting to be filled, surrounding a large bed. On which Damien and four naked voluptuous women await. Glaring over the headboard is an eighth statue, a woman with hair painted gold. As is the hair of the young boy whose torso rises from out her mouth.

Damien smirks.

A woman at each side, another at his feet and one whose breasts his head lies upon, stroke his body with gentle caresses. Each of his hands cupping a breast, he stares at the newly arrived brunette as a pomegranate is brought to his mouth. Teeth sinking into the fruit's skin, a blood-colored river spills down his chin.

"Alright, be gone from my presence. Leave me with today's chosen. I shall see you ladies again tonight."

Rising without a word and without dressing, the women saunter out of the hut.

"I have come as requested, my Lord." The woman bows.

Damien rises and walks toward her. "Indeed, and now you get to prove your faith, my child." He takes her hand and says, "Follow me around the room." Stopping at the statue with the overgrown head and dozens of eyes, he hands her a six-inch blade. "Spill your life's essence into the groove. But be wary, there are six more to go after this. Go on, bleed out your pride."

The woman's eyes glance from Damien to the blade, grabbing it and positioning the point toward her upper forearm. It sways above the skin, as her hand dithers. Frowning, she glances back toward Damien. "Is this truly part of being chosen? Have you done this with all the other women?"

A smirk slithers onto Damien's face. "They all fulfilled their role and proved their faith, thus achieving their early ascension to Heaven. Don't you want that? Well, one must first leave behind the seven deadly sins. Or, is it that your faith is weak and that you doubt your God?"

The woman grimaces, but plunges the blade beneath the skin. Lowering her arm toward the groove, crimson flows down and into it.

"Very good," says Damien, as he walks her to the next statue. "Now, bleed out your greed."

One by one, he walks her to each statue, first pride and greed, then envy, wrath, lust, sloth, and finally gluttony. "Spill extra blood here," he says, staring at his strongest affinity, guiding the knife into her wrist. The groove circling the bed grows a deeper red with each step of the ritual satisfied. And as the final blood offering finishes, the woman, with arms that appear to have their veins pulled outward, blood streaking from her elbows, wobbles as her vision blurs. Damien says, "Very good, my child," and leads her onto the bed. Pushing the woman onto her knees, taking no effort in her current state, Damien lowers his pants.

Holding her by the chin and pinching her mouth open, he thrusts his cock through her plump lips. Gripping her by the skull, he thrusts with great force. His appendage gliding across her tongue, hitting the back of her throat, over and over, tears spilling from her eyes, reddening as the veins pop from lack of oxygen, snot creeps down her nose, merging with the tears flowing down her cheeks—he bursts into her mouth, thrusting harder and deeper as he finishes.

Weaving her hair around his fingers like rope, he pulls her mouth free of him, turns, and plunges her head into the pillows, yanks off her robe, and thrusts into her with even greater abandon.

Finishing, the stone house echoes loudly his orgasmic moans, as he pulls the barely conscious woman close, kissing her lips softly, and says, "I love fooling you humans into thinking these rituals have any point to them."

"What?" the woman says, as Damien's eyes morph into pitch blackness. The woman's head yanks backward, mouth agape as her eyes overflow with teal energy. Lifting from her fleshy vessel, her soul ejects from her eyes, squirming in the air before being pulled into Damien's mouth and down into the pit of his stomach.

The woman's body slumps off the bed. Damien licks His lips as the woman's soul merges with His own. His body quivers as He feels the pulse of magic strengthening, for the human soul *is* magic, even in those not born into power. An individual's will always houses great potential within it, and He who controls the wills of the masses holds the will of the world in the palm of His hand, just as Yahweh, His past life, had done before Him. Thus, His apotheosis continues, rising high along His arc to godhood.

He drags the woman's body to the closet behind His bed, between the statues of Sloth and Gluttony. Swinging the door wide, a pile of corpses reveals itself. He smirks, tossing the brunette woman atop the bodies of those who came before her.

Turning away, He makes His way outside.

The men have all awoken and joined together outside Damien's abode, performing their military training drills led by Sergei. Many hours into the slave-driving general's regimen, the men stand sweating profusely beneath the late August sun, but refusing to be slowed down, as they continue their sparring matches.

Catching sight of Damien, Sergei shouts, "Attention!" and at once the men cease and stand rigid.

"Very good," Damien says. "I'd say we can call it a day, don't you?"

Sergei glances at his men and back to Damien. Scowling, feeling ready to push the men further. "Y-yes, my Lord."

"Then it's settled, commence the end-of-day ceremony!" Damien says, raising His arms outward. As they stretch toward His disciples, their eyes glow teal. Souls manipulated by a mere exchange of words, and their cheeks flush crimson, their chests heaving with desire. The four women He dismissed earlier walk up to the dozens of soldiers, offering their bodies without a word. Even Sergei loses himself to rapturous desire, as he sucks upon the large breast where Damien previously laid his head.

"Gorge yourself on pleasure!" says Damien. "Fuck and drink until you collapse. But send the girls to my abode once you finish."

"Praise be to God of the highest, we adore and worship you, our Heavenly Father!"

Turning from them, Damien makes His way back inside, their chanting filling His ears as He goes. A smirk widens upon His face as He closes the door.

It was my past self who wrote the rules of religion. The very same ones that painted sexual debauchery in an immoral light. But that was only to tighten the leashes around their throats. Creative power closely correlates with sexual drive. By forcing them to repress those urges, they make themselves weak.

The image of Persephone and that grand white power bursting from her materializes in His mind, and He smiles. *But if I am to capture the object of my desire, I will need to forcefully awaken magic in these foolish humans.*

The doors creak open as the four voluptuous women enter and crawl their way onto His bed. Awaiting with open legs, they stare with flushed cheeks and readily wet. Damien ambles toward them and says:

"I am very sorry, my children. But I will be ravishing you no longer. For you see, the time has come to kill the witch and take what is rightfully mine. You have done your part well in pushing the boundaries of the souls of men, unlocking greater power with every plunge inside your source of creation. But now it's time you enter me."

His eyes fill with blackness as the four women yank their heads back and upward, their souls forcefully siphoned from their eyeholes.

The next day.

Damien steps out into the noon sun, now warming the cave's stony floor. Finding the men unconscious and scattered about, He shouts, "Awaken, my children!" At His command, their eyes turn teal, and they quickly rise.

"I am happy, for the day has come. You've done well to train hard, and while there shall be no more orgies, I have one last, greater gift to bequeath upon you."

"What is it, my Lord?" says Sergei, glancing around to find that the last of the women are gone. He pouts, but turns toward Damien, and compulsively smiles.

"Well, everything you've been working toward, of course. The day we take the fight to the witch and her kin is here. But not without pulling a greater potential from out of your souls. Do not worry, what will seem like magic is nothing of the sort, I promise you. It is simply a temporary boon granted to you through your great faith in me. And with its powers, we will vanquish the evil, the monstrous, the sinful that plagues this world. And then we shall ascend to Heaven."

Damien outstretches His hands once more, invoking the image of a cross. A heavy pulse thuds from within the chest of each soldier. Creating a rapid succession of thunderous explosions reverberating within the cylindrical cave. Teal magic bursts from the eyes of His disciples, and—fire, lightning, wind, water, stone—manifests within the palms of their hands. They glance at each other, feeling power coursing through their veins, and they smile widely, bursting into clamorous cheer.

And, taking in the view of His empowered pawns, Damien joins them in their revelry.

CHAPTER TWENTY-TWO

Dark clouds sprawl across the sky, filtering the August heat. A cool breeze glides through Seth's hair and along his skin, glistening with sweat. Sighing, he reaches up toward Muninn's face. Caressing his beak and feathers, the giant raven coos and tilts his head, staring into his master's eyes. The bird nuzzles his scalp against Seth's chest, who smiles sadly, glancing up at the encroaching storm.

His hands stroke the bird, while his mind remains with Sasha and Persephone. *Together for twenty years, and she has some secret I don't know about?* Wincing, Seth buries his head into Muginn's feathers, as he runs through the mental gymnastics he experiences in silence, when paranoia creeps to the surface. *Logically, I know that any secret she could have isn't malicious. We love each other, we're solid. What I'm feeling is a passing façade, nothing more. Propped up by pressures unrelated to her, to us, to our family. Let it pass, let it wash over me like a wave. Mental anguish is a normal part of everyday life. It is a promised pain, an abyss-borne struggle that makes me stronger, more capable for enduring it.*

Meditating on these thoughts, his adrenaline descends. His breath slowing, deepening. He sighs his relief into the raven's black, ruffled feathers, though some fluttering in his heart persists—

His phone vibrates within his left pocket. Unearthing it, he finds Sasha calling—a smile springs to his face as he answers. "Hey, how's it going over there?"

"It's going. I showed Persephone what I wanted to, and she's ready to come back. Do me a favor and open a portal?"

"Of course," says Seth, his eyes immediately glowing bright white. Abyssal flames spark into being, creating an oval behind him. Persephone walks through, joining her father and Muninn on the cliffside. Seeing her arrival, Huginn flutters down from the roof and nuzzles his head against the teenage girl.

"Are you coming through, as well?" asks Seth.

"Nah, I want to get some more work done. Besides, I think Persephone wants to chat with you. It's time, Seth. Be honest with her."

"Right."

"See you later, then," Sasha says. "I love you."

"I love you, too."

Her words, entering his ears, soothe him like nothing else in the world. Her voice, the most beautiful melody, even all these years later. And through this comfort, the anxiety ravaging his body melts, obscured by the same contentedness, the same comfort, he felt almost twenty years ago. When embracing each other by the graves of their friends, with Persephone incubating inside Sasha's rounded belly. To think that unseen being growing within his wife's womb would one day be a grown woman, staring at him now with stern, sad eyes.

Seth wraps his arms around Persephone, hugging tightly. "It's uncanny how much you resemble your mother."

"Uh, Dad, you okay?"

"Yeah, sweetie, I'm fine," he says, releasing her. "Just feeling a bit nostalgic, I think. It sounds like bullshit when you're young, but time really does fly by when you're old like me and your mom. Feels like yesterday you were an itty-bitty thing chasing Misha around, antagonizing her."

"I don't remember that..."

"Of course not. You were very small."

Persephone smiles uncomfortably and says, "Did you know Mom is building a spaceship?"

Seth's eyes widen. "No, I didn't."

"It's some sort of emergency plan, I don't know. She said she'll tell you about it later...have I been unfair toward Mom? Ugh, I don't know why I'm asking you. Of course, you're going to take her side."

Seth chuckles. "I'm on both of your sides."

"Yeah, but you know what I mean."

Seth glances skyward. The lingering clouds darken, causing the ravens to retreat to the porch for shelter. Though a cool breeze continues, the calm lingering before a downpour. Misha peeks her head outside, smiling as she finds Persephone. "I've got everything from the closets packed," she says. Seth's eyes linger toward the sky, drawn in by the darkness of the clouds. The darkness—he has feared its constant approach, feared its possible tainting of his daughter. The very same pain and anguish that sent him along a furious path, which caused tragedies no one could ever take back or be absolved from. That anger, caused by the truth being kept from him, by his lack of choice and volition.

Seth turns toward Misha and says, "Mind washing and then packing the dishes as well? Sorry to make you shoulder the load, but there's something I want to chat with Persephone about."

Misha's eyes widen as she turns to Persephone. Smiling and nodding to her, Misha says, "Of course, take your time!" And disappears into the dilapidated cabin.

Turning back toward Persephone, Seth says, "Your mother understands how hard it's been for her to be away. I don't know the details of what she showed you, but I know she wanted to clear up the reasons she's spent so much time working all these years. It's normal for a child to long for their mother, but with you, well...you're my daughter. And with your powers as they are, I can confidently say that there's a longing in you. For someone to comfort you, someone to melt away your anxieties with their touch, their presence. Your mom has this same compulsion, though she's had more time to deal with it. Hence why she's a hell of a lot more independent than me."

Seth chuckles and continues, "Have you been unfair to your mother? Perhaps. But you can work on that going forward. But also, please know that both of us understand the angst you're feeling. Whether you can believe that or not is up to you. But let me tell you more about my past, and I'll leave you to judge..."

Recapping what he and Sasha went through twenty years ago, Persephone's mouth drops, and in her widened eyes, Seth can see her brain working through the over-stimulation. She saw it when the Abyssal Consciousness sent the past through her. But hearing it straight from her father hits far differently. His lonely, abusive origins. His first love, the girl with glimmering blonde locks, turning out to be a grotesque god. Heaven and Hell. The Sins. The god from the Abyss, and his two teal-haired children, leading Seth to mend the grave error made at the origin of all things.

And how, in his rage and naivety, Seth was ill-equipped to handle the burden life chose for him. A puppet of fate, all he could do was rage upon his strings, as he was led along a path he never wanted to tread. And so, he destroyed everything in front of him.

Eyes brimming abyssal white, Seth opens a new portal.

"I never wanted you to know, but you deserve to. It was not knowing the truth of my circumstances that broke me. It was being gaslit into thinking I was something horrid that made me become something horrid. I never wanted this for you—these powers. They are a greater burden than you know. But you have them, and so that leaves me no choice but to guide you through them. I just hope—" His voice chokes. "I hope you won't think ill of your father for what he's done..."

Persephone's gaze drops. The view of the blackened spot where the Assembly stood flashes into memory. "Dad..." Tears fill her eyes. "If you're a monster, then so am I! There were so many people working for Mom...they were at the Assembly when I—"

Seth pulls her into his arms once more, tears trickling down his cheeks. *If you're a monster, then so am I!* Those words trigger a memory from twenty years ago. Being yelled at by Sasha amidst the immense heat and brimstone of Hell. "No! That was not your fault, Persephone. You and I are not monsters! Say it, I need to hear you say it!"

Persephone's wet eyes glance up at her father. "But what are we, if not the things we do?"

Seth falls silent, considering the astuteness of her question. "Yes, we are what we do. But the funny thing about truth, it's never that simple. If given the absolute power of choice, free to do whatever we wish, then yes, each and every choice will hold great weight. But we were given no good choices, Persephone. We were given only two. Act in the only way we could—or die.

How could we rightfully call someone a monster if they were only given the choice to be a monster?"

Seth sighs, turning toward the portal. "Maybe I shouldn't show you this, after all. Seeing what I did might detract from what I just said and worsen your feelings. I don't know—"

Misha emerges at the cabin's door again, staring on in silence. Persephone meets her eyes and smiles.

"Dad, it's okay. I hear you. I'm not a monster. It's not a mistake for you to show me this. I...am really happy you and Mom are starting to treat me like a person rather than just a kid. Thank you for trusting me."

Seth smiles below sad eyes, and they walk through the portal to a place Seth swore he would never return.

If given the absolute power of choice, free to do whatever we wish, then yes, each and every choice will hold great weight.

Her father's words echo within her mind as they venture through the portal. *Absolute power of choice, what like a god?* Persephone winces. *That strange white figure called me a True-Born God. Then wouldn't that mean I have absolute power of choice?* Her gaze drops to her sneakers, watching them move her forward a step at a time.

"Dad, who was that white figure? In that strange white place? You got very angry with him before he sent us away."

"It, not he." Seth walks through the portal. "It has no name, but your mother and I call it the Abyssal Consciousness, but that will take some extra explaina—her father runs forward, jerking his gaze about frantically.

"Dad, what's wrong?" Persephone says, running after him.

"This isn't right!" Seth says, finding the straw huts, glass bottles, shoes, and clothing sprawled about. Taken aback by the evidence of humans living here, he just now notices the cave is visible without creating flame. Glancing upward, he finds a massive hole in the mountain's ceiling. Just past is another dark cloud. *A different state altogether, but the darkness follows me.* Shaking himself free of the intrusive thought, a drizzle of rain splatters against his skin, quickly increasing into a downpour. Thunder bangs over ahead, filling the cavern with a deafening echo. "Persephone, stay close," he says as he runs toward the center, finding a lone stone house.

The door creaks as it slowly opens—crimson stains run along grooves in the floor, circling around the bed at the center, and trailing from statues of—

"No..."

"Dad, what is it?"

"Nothing." Seth grimaces. Unveiling all to her, then immediately defaulting to lying. He sighs and says, "Sorry. It's not nothing. These are busts of...the Sins."

"You mean..."

"Stay there," says Seth, noticing a thicker coating of blood at the foot of a door behind the bed. Pulling it slowly, he finds the bruised and bloodied corpses of a few dozen women stacked upon each other, filling every corner of the walk-in closet, up to the ceiling. Fresh enough to fill Seth with a horrifying realization.

I was right.

Persephone screeches, and Seth slams the door shut.

"Dad..." Persephone whimpers. "What the fuck was that?"

Seth turns toward her, glaring, eyes wide and brimming with fear.

"We need to get your mother immediately. That boy, Yahweh's echo...he survived what occurred at the Assembly."

CHAPTER TWENTY-THREE

Pure white clouds crawl swiftly across the sky. The air warm, but gentle, as a cool breeze washes over Moscow's Red Square. The hustle and bustle of commuters share in the sky's vibrancy, its vigorous glow. Men, women, children, and teenagers are off at a brisk pace toward work and school or cafes to dine and socialize. Pigeons teeter back and forth, wings fluttering nervously as they scatter away from approaching pedestrians. On the side of the square, rooks stare ominously from above, huddled together upon tree branches and rooftops, jerking their pale beaks about at sharp angles. Observing, as the literary storyteller does, the beauty found in the mundane scaffolding of everyday human life.

A gust of wind ruffles the tree branches, causing the parliament to scatter into the air. A few soar atop the many bulbous, colorful spires of Saint Basil's Cathedral, perched contentedly above it all.

Amidst the cathedral and the other surrounding landmarks built with imperial Russian architecture is a shorter but wider modern building. Neighboring Saint Basil's and attached to its side. A sign above the door states:

Ассамблея магии и человеческого прогресса: Российское отделение

Assembly for Magic and Human Progression: Russian Branch

The door swings open repeatedly, as assembly members arrive for work, coffees and teas in hand, and—

A low rumble stirs from beneath their feet. All motion within the square ceases as the commuting men, women, and children stop, whipping their gaze about. The pigeons totter along the ground, and the rooks perched upon the cathedral's round spires flap swiftly skyward. The air fills with the sound of stone cracking, as the ground rises, splitting apart. Screams erupt as the crowd tumbles over, smashing into one another. The doors to the Assembly burst open as the members begin rushing out to investigate the commotion—the ground ceases its rumble, silence fills the square—loud claps are heard from each direction, with sparks of teal slithering toward the square in their wake—fire erupts into a mass of crimson blanketing the area, blood curdling screams rise from all directions as the pedestrians are set ablaze, until muffled, the fire entering their mouths, melting their tongues into a bubbling black soup spilling from charred lips.

Soldiers spill in from the streets surrounding the Red Square. Swirling fire, crackling lightning, whirling gales, shards of ice. The elements gripped within their hands, the troops converge at the center, with Sergei leading the charge. Stepping toward a charred husk of a small child, its lips quiver as they heave. Sergei scowls downward at the child. Its identifiable features melted away. "Sorry, kiddo. Shouldn't have been born on the wrong side of this here war. Time to pay for your sins." He stomps heavily upon the ground—seven stone spikes erupt from beneath, piercing the child's legs, abdomen, chest, and one through the center of its head. Crimson spills onto the ravaged stone walkway, laden with charred corpses.

"You *monsters!*" screams a man emerging from the blackened doors of the Assembly. Unholstering a pistol, he briskly points it at—"Wait, Sergei? What is this? What have you done?"

Sergei glances the man over, with no characteristic triggering a memory. "I suppose you're one of the foreign ambassadors between HQ and the international branches? Well, sorry to say, but you don't have a job anymore. HQ is gone, or haven't you heard?"

The man's eyes widen.

"Что происходит?" asks a man marching through the Assembly doors. A giant at six foot seven, with a full bushy beard and wide build, emerges as intimidating as his deep, booming voice.

The branch ambassador tethers his eyes to Sergei, as he says over his shoulder, "То, что он слышал от японцев о разрушении штаба, это правда, и это их вина. Он американец и председатель главного собрания."

"Chairman, not chairperson," Sergei says. "Yeah, that's right. I understood some of that. But English, if you please. Or even if you don't. Let me expedite things, shall I? The Assembly is finished. We are here to commandeer the foreign branches to overturn political power to our Lord's needs."

"Lord?" The bearded man grips his abdomen as he bursts out laughing. "You silly little man. You come here, kill innocent civilians, many children, then demand I speak your vile English tongue, and ask me to give Assembly branch to you?"

Sergei's nose wrinkles with fury. "You'll see who the little man is once we're done here. I'll have you know I served in the war in Iraq—"

"I don't care if you serviced little prick of your father in heaven, you are still bug beneath my boot. And, haven't you heard? You waste your time. God is dead."

Sergei's anger softens as a smirk quivers its way across his face. He glances over the massive man. *A physical powerhouse, to be sure. But his face is virtually devoid of wrinkles. That beard is fooling no one. He couldn't be more than a third of my age. He is young enough to be one of those born with magic, but a boy is just a boy.* His smirk dissolves into a thin line as his glare intensifies.

"Is that what you think? Well, that's why we've come to cleanse you first. You Russians, so firm, so steadfast in your faith in God...when you heard that He was dead, that shattered you, didn't it? A void was left where God once was. Your beliefs, your customs, your way of life—your entire worldview, everything you knew to be true, came crumbling down, and in the wake of your God, you couldn't cope—and you gave up. That's the difference between us. I didn't join the Assembly out of some need to redirect my hopes to a new dogma. No, I sought to find Him rise again!"

The Russian man's grin inverts. "Russians of old, maybe. But I was born into magic. So, you are warned, stand down, crazy old fool."

"Fool? Yes, in a world that has strayed from His path, it is us believers who are seen as the crazy ones. But, boy, I have years of wisdom at my side, years of combat training, and most importantly, I have the tool my Heavenly Father provided for the purpose of taking the Assembly by force." Sergei says, pointing his thumb over his shoulder. "I *was not* born into magic, and yet the upheaved ground? That was me. So, *you* stand down. If you do, you may join our ranks. The love of God is still in you, you of a proud Russian lineage. And I will draw it out."

Sergei stomps the ground with all his might. Teal sparks crackle around the stone. The bearded giant's eyes grow wide, watching the old man do as he shouldn't be able to. A spear of stone emerges from the rock, rising steadily upward. In one swift motion, Sergei grips the pole, pulls his arm back, and plunges it forward, barreling through the air toward the branch ambassador—

Amidst a low vibrational hum, the spear halts an inch from the man's face. Reaching out toward the spear is the Russian man's hand, from which the vibrations stir. The spear is yanked into his palm, gripped fiercely.

"I told you, stand down," says the Russian man, walking forward as he pats the branch ambassador on the shoulder. "Good thing there is metals in stone, huh?" Turning toward Sergei, he says, "For your sins here today, for your crooked dogma that led you down this road, I, Dima, Head of Russian Branch of the Assembly for Magic and Human Progression, declare your execution."

Sergei scowls, scrunching his nose at the approaching Russian. Dima stomps forward, eyes aglow with a cold, focused fury, as he says:

"I pull iron from your blood now."

CHAPTER TWENTY-FOUR

Fists clenched, arms flexed, Dima stomps forward. Sergei furrows his brow, standing his ground. Dima reaches out—Sergei's body tenses, screaming as his insides are tugged toward the Russian's hand—

Sergei's men circle around, one with an icicle in hand, lunging its point toward Dima's head—the magnetic pull upon Sergei loosens as Dima sidesteps, avoiding the spear of ice, and raises his other hand toward the soldier. Forcefully pulling his fingers into a fist, he yanks his arm back. The man's skeleton tears through his flesh, dangling about in the air before being tossed aside. Flesh thuds to the ground, an outline of a person made from a mangled, disfigured mound of meat.

Another man rushes in from the other side, fire spewing from his palms. Dima backs away from the flames, relinquishing Sergei. Stomping his feet, Sergei creates three stone spires, rising from the ground toward Dima. Sidestepping, he avoids two, one piercing his forearm. Swiping the spike with his fist, he shatters the stone. Yanking the point from his arm like a thorn, blood spills from the wound.

Dima smirks.

"What's that look for?" Sergei shouts. "I told you, boy. I have decades of military training under my belt. You've shown your hand. Dangerous as your powers are, you have trouble focusing them on multiple targets."

"What can I say? I enjoy challenge." Over his shoulder, he shouts, "Okay, you've let me have my fun. Come join me, now, my Russian brothers and sisters!"

Assembly members spill out the door. Other big, burly men and fit, muscular women with stern faces. Hundreds of warriors spread throughout the square, encircling Sergei's much smaller army. Sergei glances about, his previous confidence melting away into sweat on his brow.

"Here in Russia, every magic user is mandatory Assembly member. At first, this allowed for control over safety of population. That no one hurts another with magic. But as the old die out and the new are always born into magic, as is norm now, soon Russia will be powerhouse with greatest, largest army in world. We already are, in fact. But as you can see, a Russia without God is a more progressive Russia. Tell me, where are the women in your ranks?"

"They have been granted early entrance to Heaven, after fulfilling their natural, god given role—abiding by the needs of us men."

A woman by Dima's side scrunches her face in fury.

"I've read news articles, seen photo books," says Dima. "Heaven was there in sky during Supernatural Holocaust. But then that teal light engulfed world, as Heaven crumbled apart with death of its god. I don't know where those women went, but it wasn't Heaven. But you don't care. You are too cruel."

The woman by Dima's side ambles forward, lifting a cigarette to her lips. Inhaling it entirely with one breath, she tosses away the butt. Without exhaling the smoke, her chest expands beyond normal limits as she breathes continuously through her nose. Her shirt stains red as skin breaks from stretching, but her face remains unmoved. Clapping her hands together and rapidly pulling them apart, electricity crackles between her palms and—stretching forward, the smoke bellows from her lips, in greater volume than the cigarette should have made. Engulfing Sergei and his men, their bodies convulse as toxins creep down their throats, through their pores. And, lunging her palms forward, electricity surges through the conduit of smoke.

Screaming in agony, Sergei drops to his knees, and his men do the same. Two of them keel over, and—a flash of teal overtakes the area as two souls eject into the sky, curving into an arch and landing somewhere between buildings further away. Dima and his Assembly members glance at the souls' trajectory.

Dima says, "What was—"

"Impressive!" shouts Sergei. "What power you have! Impressive—for a woman."

The woman's brow furrows. Dima clenches his fists. The Russian Assembly members stomp forward, forcing Sergei and his men into a smaller, tighter cluster. The small army pushed inward, back-to-back.

Raising his fist, Dima screams something in Russian, and the Assembly army rushes forward. Fire swarms and scorches. Shards of ice are spurred into the air alongside blood as they splinter upon impact. Bolts of electricity pierce the bodies of many, blowing holes within their chests as they explode, sending a deluge of blood and flesh from behind.

Amidst the carnage, Sergei's blood-soaked, crazed eyes tether to Dima, as he lunges a barrage of stone spears at the Russian. *Too preoccupied with fending off projectiles from multiple sides, he's unable to use his magnetic powers. You fool of a boy! I will make you pay for your excessive pride!*

"You cannot win!" shouts Sergei. Burn us, electrocute us! Pierce our sides like our savior upon the cross, our cries will only empower our faith in Him! You shall see, He has risen, and He will come to our aid!"

"You are fool to displace your power by granting it to mere concept!" Dima says. "Faith is powerful tool. Why waste it? Why attain fragile, false power by placing your burdens on idea, when you could send your faith inward and empower yourself!

"False? Is that what you call this?" Sergei spreads his arms, palms upward. The earth shakes and hums as he rises high upon a risen stone. The armies spread out, away from the cracking ground.

"I don't know how you found magic, old man. But I assure you, it cannot be from God!" Dima stomps forward, pulling the bones from the bodies of the nearest of Sergei's men. Reaching toward Sergei, Dima pulls him from the risen earth, his neck landing in the Russian's fierce grip. Sergei tries speaking, but only a hiss emerges. Lifting Sergei upward, then plunging him into the ground, crushing it beneath his weight, Dima lets go before stomping his foot upon Sergei's chest. "Whatever this power is inside you, it is not true magic. I can feel it in your blood. You are weak, pathetic, normal person. I don't understand how, but this magic is being siphoned from elsewhere. It is not yours, therefore it is cheap and worthless."

Sergei's men rush at Dima, blind to the enemy soldiers they were fighting moments before. Their lives are forfeit, they live only to serve God, and by extension God's right-hand man.

Foot firmly on Sergei's chest, Dima brings the tips of his fingers together, palms inches apart, shaking fiercely as the Russian roars—his army backs away, as he rips his hands apart, causing magnetic waves to ripple and expand a large enough circumference to hold Sergei's entire army. Ceasing their assault, they clutch their left arms. Sergei glares at Dima, eyes wide with astonishment.

"Like I said, I enjoy challenge. I was holding back. How's that for military strategy?" says Dima, grinning. "How does it feel to have your coronary arteries clog?"

Sergei's eyes grow furious, glaring at Dima as his vision blurs—

A flash of gold light bursts over ahead, as Damien hovers above the battlefield. "Do not fear, for I am with you." Arms outstretched, with a golden aura around his head, Damien's form remains suspended, the air surrounding his body rippling outward, causing a sonic hum as it keeps him afloat. The vibrations lesson at his feet, growing stronger overhead, as he descends to the ground, landing at Sergei's side. His energy pulsing outward, protecting him against the Russian's magnetic waves.

Dima moves to lunge a hand toward Damien and—

"Do not fear, for I am here," Damien repeats, with vibrations rising from his throat. Slithering through Dima's lips, they sink into his bowels—the Russian drops his arms. Sergei and his army gasp as blood passes smoothly through arteries, calming their hearts and returning proper airflow. "Do not fear, for I am here!" Damien shouts, spreading his arms like a cross once more, and turning slowly as he faces every soldier. The Assembly members drop to their knees.

For thousands of years, mankind has believed in God. Through the many ages, this need for God has been imprinted upon their souls, altering their very physical and mental composition. Now, without God, a void is left in His wake. A void that can easily be filled again. With drugs, or sex, or entertainment...or a god renewed.

Damien smiles. "You proud Russians have spent much of your lineage in pious servitude to God. Well, do not fear! For

I have risen again. Open your hearts to me, and I shall fill them with the everlasting glory of my Love. Serve me, and you shall have your place in Heaven!"

The Russians simultaneously break out in sobs. "Praise be to the *Lord thy God* in Heaven!" They chant, once strong and proud, now blubbering, tearful, loyal children of God.

Sergei rises, eyes wide with astonishment, and says, "Of course, I never doubted you, my Lord, but they converted as soon as they heard your voice. Astonishing."

"It was thanks to your hard work setting the stage, my son. After their strong denial of Truth, my appearance shocked their system. They had no choice but to believe. Gather the troops."

With a smile, Sergei bows.

The souls within us have grown by an additional two. Along with the souls of the women, this power...is exquisite. Before, we could rip flesh from bone or strengthen our own. But now the wills within us are large and many, and soul manipulation comes as easily as breathing!

Sergei lines up the troops, men and women separated. Standing at the front is Dima with the branch ambassador at his side. Damien paces in front of them, eyeing each new soldier. Their eyes are steadfast, unblinking. As he meets the branch ambassador's gaze, the man fidgets, momentarily glancing away.

"You," says Damien. "Do you believe in God? Are you at my command?"

The man quivers, glancing around at the Russians, confused by their lack of movement, their sudden compliance with this strange boy claiming to be God. *Absurd!*

"Y-yes, of course, m-my...L-lord."

Stepping forward, Damien cocks his head as he glares further into the man's eyes, looking deep into the nebulous, metaphysical space within where the soul resides. Beyond the event horizon of his corporeal form, and into a singularity where magic exists. "My children, we have a disbeliever." The Russians and Sergei's men all jerk toward the branch ambassador, with sharp, rageful eyes and appalment creased into their faces.

"Uhm, no, I believe, I belie—" the man's screams in agony as Damien lunges forward, mouth wide and hungry. The man's soul ejects through his eyes and into Damian's mouth.

Dropping heavily to the ground, the man's death calms the believers, as they turn back toward Damien, awaiting orders.

Damien frowns, placing a hand over his mouth as he loses himself in thought.

"Is something the matter?" asks Sergei.

"No, my child. Just plotting our next move. Give me a small group of soldiers. Both fire and water wielders. All women. You take the rest to Japan. No need to stage a reveal like we did here. No need to egg them on or make them question their disbelief in me. Just kill them all."

Sergei nods and says, "What about you, my Lord?"

"We will part ways here, for now. I will bring along my small group of soldiers, the women, and we will take the European branches. When we rejoin, I'll have expanded our army by the thousands."

With a smile, Sergei leaves. The larger part of the army in tow, marching back to their fleet of helicopters and jet planes.

Damien glares at the dead branch ambassador.

He didn't convert. He was lying. So, I have limits after all. There needs to be a void, a lacking, in God's wake. The Japanese will never convert. They are too stubborn a people—and too hurt and betrayed after World War II, when the façade of their emperor's divine lineage was shattered, and Atheism took hold...

Though even before that, when my past self spread the teachings of Christianity, only a small portion of Japan accepted it. Their wills, too strong, too stuck on past religions. Which was fine—as long as they were religious, and a larger portion of the world took to Christianity. Yahweh got what she needed. But, within the world's current stage, the Japanese are a people whose souls I could never manipulate.

But the people of Europe...outside of America, no other place has a deeper void in the wake of God.

Buildings, old and beige, sprawl across the city of Rome. Birds totter in the darkening streets before fluttering off to rooftops and tree branches, finding shelter from the waning sunlight. Lamps throughout the city flick on, creating patches of light on the shadows stretching through the streets, and glimmering upon the Tiber River. The youth, venturing out into the coming night, fill the air with vigorous chatter. Defying the oppressive summer humidity by relishing in the nightlife to come. Modernity meshing with a city of a great and long history, as the Roman Colosseum and others of its kind stand tall from an era long passed.

The bustling nightlife intensifies as daylight diminishes evermore. The jubilant chatter and drunken laughter amongst peers, the sweet tones and shameless affections between lovers, as night descends, this vibrancy continues to sprawl across the city and—

An explosion echoes, as bright, bellowing flames rise, engulfing Saint Peter's Basilica. Screams erupt as people flee from the holy Vatican City. A Cardinal smashes through a window on the top floor, screaming in terror as his bright red robe is overtaken by flames. A thud is heard as his head smashes against the hard ground. Firemen arrive, rushing into the building, conjuring water into their palms and spraying the flames. But they ravage too fiercely, too scalding, as they burn through a fireman's gear, melting him to a sludge. Two others emerge from the flames, pulling the Pope alongside them. Face blackened by the fire, the pope heaves, tears in his eyes, as he waspily mumbles a prayer in Italian.

"Dear God in Heaven, save those still inside, save this building so precious and holy—"

"Do not fear, for I am here."

Damien rises from above, halo glowing like a star appearing directly above the city. "Do not fear, for I am here." The words echo as they slither their way through Vatican City. Increasing the intensity of the vibrations, making them louder with each syllable.

The power of the Catholic church has waned since the Supernatural Holocaust. But as we prove, ideas tend to linger. Damien turns away from Saint Peter's Basilica and spies Assembly members funneling out of a smaller building next to it. *No wonder they decided to set roots here, despite what they stand for. They convinced themselves that it was to maintain balance, but they're only fooling themselves. The void of God lingers heavily in their hearts. Now I fill it.*

"Do not fear, for I am here."

The Assembly workers, staring in awe at the gold-crowned boy, drop their weapons and fall to the ground, weeping. "Do not fear, for I am here," Damien repeats once more, and the flames are extinguished by an abundance of water sprayed from places unknown.

"Be my loyal servants, and you will have your place in Heaven. Now," he glares toward the women on the ground beneath his feet, as he descends to the earth. "Follow me," he says to them. "Men, March north through Poland, then down through Germany, France, and Spain, then north again to the UK. Raze their cities to the ground, break each branch of the Assembly until they beg for relief, and then I shall come and give it. Do not fear, for I am here, and will join you at each branch as I decide it's time."

The men nod, turn, and begin marching off to find military transport. Damien smiles and returns to his plane, with the women of the Italian Branch in tow.

Opening the doors to the aircraft, he finds dozens of Russian female soldiers awaiting him, having returned a moment before, stripping off their combat gear, dropping them upon the open floor. The plane is devoid of seats, aside from the two in the cockpit. Awaiting his instruction, they stand before him, unburdened of clothes.

Turning to the new batch of women, he gestures for them to head inside.

"Good work, my children. Starting and putting out that fire completely unseen. You have impressed your God and have earned advanced entry into Heaven.

"Now, pleasure me."

CHAPTER TWENTY-FIVE

Silence washes over the dilapidated cabin alongside a light breeze. Tree branches rustle and sway above a stillness akin to the Abyss which births all things. Animals cling to the circumference of the property, away from the pressure left in the wake of the gods which trampled the mountain's summit. Leaving unseen scars in the fabric of the world, amidst even the shortest of battles. And here at summer's end, following divine tracks, the heat beats down far more furiously than before, an intensity brewing beneath the world's skin. Rippling and tearing its way through, like an atom on the cusp of splitting.

An oval of white flame flickers its way into existence, and out steps Seth, Persephone, and Misha. Through the portal behind them is an apartment strewn with clothes, suitcases, and bags. With no time to settle into their new home.

"Finally, let's get started," says Persephone, twisting her abdomen as she pulls her arms to the left, to the right, stretching them out.

"You sit over there, Persephone." Seth points to the porch. Huginn and Muninn flutter down to meet them, sitting by the steps, cocking their heads toward the girl.

"Wait, what? I thought you were training me?"

"I am. This is how we begin. By watching Misha and me."

"I've been doing that for years! How is this supposed—"

Seth's eyes narrow, darkening as memory takes hold. "You know what I've done now. A tragedy that has haunted me every day since. A tragedy that would not have been if I had listened to, and observed, the positive influences set before me. Do you want to make the same mistake, or do you want to be better?"

Persephone feels a pit opening within her. Despair washing over as the image of the lost Assembly headquarters flashes into memory. "I...want to be better."

"Good." Seth smiles, his sad eyes glimmering toward his daughter. "One must always strive to be better. One's personal growth is never complete. Now, observe."

Seth's pupils sink into the whites of his eyes, as the Abyss flows through him—a flash of white conjures orbs of flame, scattered about in the air surrounding Misha. Each with an accompanying blinding flash of light as they hurtle toward her. She reaches out toward the white fire and—eyes widening, she drops her arm, steps back, another abyssal orb lunges toward her as she jumps backward, flipping, rolling, skipping out of the way as each orb blasts into the ground and the surrounding trees. The white fire dissipates, leaving the area unscorched.

"Very good!" Seth shouts. "While they appear as flame, the abyssal flame is anything but! They are merely echoing a life I once lived—a reminder of the weight I shoulder, a memory that makes me stronger! Therefore, you were wise not to catch the orb. Your fire magic would not be able to dispel them! They are not fire, but pure will! Now, show me yours."

Misha stretches out her arm, waving an arc through the air. Bright orange flames are conjured in a long streak, with a pointed end and a fiery hilt on the opposite side. Gripping the ethereal flaming sword, she lunges at Seth, who gracefully sidesteps each strike. White flame wraps around his hand like a glove as he catches the sword's fiery blade. Pulling his arm back, the flames crumbles apart, scattering about in an explosion of embers before rejoining as an orb in Seth's palm.

Eyes widening, Misha crosses her arms in front of her face as Seth launches the fire back at her—the orb of flame bellows, smashing against her. She clenches her teeth, nose furrowing below wide eyes as her skin burns. The flame turns to embers, their light diminishing and—their glow returning, amplifying, transmuting into bright blue flames, they rejoin within both her palms, as she lunges them toward Seth like spears—snatching them out of the air, he spins and lunges them back at Misha again—her eyes pulsating with a fiery glow, she reaches out for her flame, and in a flash, they dissipate at her touch.

Gasping for air, she smiles at Seth as he approaches her. Wrapping his arms around her, he whispers into her ears, "Great job. I see your recent acceptance has done wonders for magical control."

Releasing her, he turns away.

"But I wasn't able to even touch you once."

Seth gives off a bellowing laugh, turning back to her. "Misha. You have lived with magic for about ten years. I came into it when I was twenty-six, twenty years ago now, and yet you are leagues better at controlling it than I was. This was a victory, accept it."

Exchanging warm glances, Seth walks over to Persephone.

"Do you see? How well she calculated every move, thinking swiftly on her feet and administering control over her powers, quelling the flames rather than letting it engulf her and everything around her? That is what I wanted to show you. Now, join me."

Persephone nods as she slowly rises to her feet. The giant ravens *coo* softly as she leaves their side, cocking their heads at her unease. The memory of the Assembly headquarters branding deeper into focus, her heart begins palpitating.

"Calm yourself," Seth says. "I should have trained you sooner, I know, and I'm sorry. But I will not fail you now."

Persephone glances at her father, alarmed. "How did you—"

"The same way you can feel the pulse of many souls," says Seth, his eyes flashing white as a dome of white flame enshrouds them, severing them from the cabin, the ravens, and Misha. Persephone glares at her father's chest. Past his clothing, his flesh, his beating heart, and beyond the circuitry of his brain, lies a metaphysical space where the soul resides—but within him is a multitude, where there should be one, there are many. The spider carrying its egg sac spurs to mind, as her inquisitive gaze meets her father's. "You, like me," Seth continues, "have an inherent connection to the Abyss, which makes us powerful—but dangerous. I will help you discipline these powers as much as we can in the little time we have."

Persephone's mind flutters away, thinking back upon what her father had shown her at the ruins of Magistrum, and to the destruction she caused. *Powerful and dangerous—yes. And useful in the war to come. But what about..."*

"What about mom?" she asks. "Will she be okay?"

Sasha left in a hurry just moments before their training began, receiving a frantic call for help from the Japanese Branch of the Assembly. *She told us to stay behind, do what we needed to do, and catch up later. And that she would be fine—but I wonder...*

Seth smiles and says, "She is the last person you will ever have to worry about, I assure you, she's more than okay."

A trail of corpses lay strewn throughout the Shibuya Scramble Crossing and into the lobby of the Japanese branch of the Assembly. Civilians screech and yell, sprinting away from the crossing and down the five streets. A herd of footsteps rampaging away from the carnage, with gunfire and explosions following in their wake. Then, silence. A throbbing, deafening manifestation of their inaction. And amidst it all are the light, rapid footsteps of a savior they do not deserve.

Flesh melted and sizzling. Flesh dead and blackened by severe cold. Flesh charred and peeling from electrocution. The lobby—a mausoleum with bodies piled high, shown no mercy by the arrival of Sergei and his men.

Taking the stairwell on the left side of the lobby, Sasha ascends to the top floor.

A wide conference room, chairs upturned, table severed down the center. A young Japanese man lies unconscious upon where the wood split. The grip of his left hand loosens. A katana clanks against the tile floor. Remnants of electricity still crackling around the blade, up the hilt, to the point, and—the sporadic yellow streaks dissipate into a thin grey haze.

Past the table, parallel to its wider side, is a long stretch of floor-to-ceiling glass windows. Knees pressed hard into the floor, a row of women slump, eyes welled with tears, across the right side of the wall. Hands bound in thick rope, and glaring toward Sergei as he pushes another woman onto the floor, knocking her into the others.

"You know," Sergei says, glancing over his shoulder, toward the wizened old branch leader, bound also with ropes and with two pistols pressed firmly into his scalp. "I've always found you Orientals to be quite alluring. Oh, my apologies. The women, not you—not because you're a man and I'm no fag, but because you Asian men are such ugly bastards. The women, though...*can* be pretty."

A woman in the middle, watching Sergei's every move, launches to her feet. The two men, pointing their guns at the branch leader, raise their weapons toward the woman. The branch leader grabs the arms of both men, twisting them around their backs and pushing them to the floor. Knees are placed hard into their backs. Flames conjure within the women's palms, spiraling around her and burning the rope away, and she launches a fierce grip toward Sergei's neck—

A foot stamps onto the floor. The marble tiling morphs, swirling around with a liquid-like appearance, before rising, solidifying into a stalagmite—the woman screams, relinquishing her grip around Sergei's neck. The flesh and skin of her forearm dangle around a large hole as the marble spike pierces through, blood spiraling down the stone, pooling at Sergei's feet. Stepping back as he rubs his burnt neck skin, he grips his stone spear tightly, plunging forward. The woman's screeching halts, eyes wide on each side of a hole through her forehead. Pulling the spear free, she slumps into a puddle of blood.

"Anyone else like to try something stupid?" Sergei yells, as he turns back to the branch leader. Staring him down with intense eyes.

The old Japanese man glares in turn, gnashing his teeth like an animal deep within the haze of a life-determining quarrel. "The Japanese will not bend the knee to you monsters!" he shouts.

Sergei stares, unmoved. Mouth straight, uncaring. He turns and points his spear at the remaining women. Turning away from the blade, they whimper, eyes clouded with tears. The branch leader's rage softens at the sight of them. Removing his weight from Sergei's men, he collapses to the floor, head hanging low.

"If it's the branch you're after, then it's my head you want. Kill me, but please...spare them, please. Let my blood be the last to be shed."

Sergei ambles forward. Looking down upon the old man, he says, "No."

Reaching the top of the stairs, Sasha peeks around the corner leading toward the conference room. A long, wide corridor with offices on each side, with soldiers on guard in front of them. Two more men stand rigid before the large double doors leading into the conference room. Each broad-shouldered and over six feet, Sergei's top men block the way.

Counting each and analyzing the situation, Sasha ponders how to approach this. *Civilians are being slaughtered on the streets, but their sacrifice has led the majority of his army away. I'm sorry...and I will end this as quickly as I can.*

"Hey!"

A voice from behind pulls her attention.

"Who are yo—" The greying man's eyes grow wide, as bolts of electricity conjure into his palms along with an ear-shattering thunderclap. The windows along the walls and in each office shatter—the men on guard hunch over, covering their faces as a storm of glass swarms the air. "It's Sasha! I repeat, it's—"

The man's voice crumbles away into a grotesque gurgle as Sasha shoves her fist into his mouth, shattering teeth and jaw. Glaring into his pained stare, Sasha says, "What is this? How do you have magic?" Yanking her fist free, blood sprays as she tears his tongue out, followed by the crackle of teal magic encasing the man's body. His flesh bulges as rocks and glittering gemstones protrude from his skin, erupting from his stomach, chest, and head.

"Fire!" yells another man as they find Sasha gripping the stony corpse of their brother in arms. Gripping it tighter, teal sparks crackle as she plunges the man at the others, blocking their bullets before his flesh softens and unravels from the bone, launching rocks and mounds of meat at the other men, bashing against their heads, twisting them upon impact.

"Our god was right! She is a witch! A fucking monster!" shouts one of the men guarding the double door, watching as four of his comrades thud to the ground, necks disfigured and broken.

Grabbing the bones of the first soldier, Sasha lunges them toward the remaining men. One thuds to the ground as his heart is pierced, another's gunfire is discharged sporadically as he lunges backward, reaching for his face, screaming, "*My eyes, my eyes!*" as blood streams down his cheeks below the protruding, crimson-stained bones. The men at the conference room door stare in horror, but each conjures their magic. One with fire in each fist, the other with spears of ice.

Footsteps emerge from behind, "The witch is here, kill her!" a man shouts, as he runs up from behind. Static crackles around his palms as he conjures—Sasha grips his neck, stunning him, halting the flow of his magic. So long without a fight, so long without using her powers, a full-toothed grin slithers its way to her face below crazed eyes. The man tries to pull away, staring back, fear enveloping him.

A crackle of teal light—plant roots pierce through his face, squirming like worms surfacing amidst a heavy storm. At the sound of approaching footsteps, Sasha throws the man across the room. The roots overtaking his entire body, tearing through even his clothes. As they dangle and fall away, the roots grow into branches, thickly crusted with bark, as a tree emerges from his flesh, stretching across the corridor's threshold, barring the entrance.

One of the door guards lunges at her, ice spear in hand—Sasha blows her warm breath toward him, the ice crackles with teal and melts away. A dagger manifests within her hand while in motion, lunging toward the man's neck. As he screams, reaching for the embedded blade, Sasha taps the other side of his neck with two fingers. Teal crackles around the spot, as his skin stretches into a bloated bubble, growing larger until matching the size of his head. Eye holes appear, followed by a concave nose and a large, gaping mouth sprouting shark-like teeth. The man collapses to the floor, writhing as he swats at the sudden growth. The monstrous second head gnashes at him, severing fingers. The man lets out a blood-curdling scream as the growth expands further, chomping down—

The screaming ceases, as a crimson pool drenches the newly made Dullahan, with the growth smiling as it withers away.

Sasha glares at the last remaining man, who quivers at the sight of her.

The conference room door bursts open, breaking free from its hinges in a fiery blast. Inward flies the door guard, his wrists broken, alongside a shattered ribcage. Sergei, spear in hand, ready to plunge into the branch leader, turns toward the commotion.

Sasha stomps forward, breathing heavily, but remains unscathed. Sergei glances past her at the carnage she left in her wake.

"Sasha-san!" The old man shouts. "I am sorry, you were right about the dange—" His glance tethered to Sasha, Sergei plunges the spear into the branch leader's neck. Pulling his weapon free, the man collapses to the floor, the bound women screech in terror.

Fists clenched, teeth barred, Sasha's eyes widen as she sprints forward, leaps, grips Sergei's neck and plows him downward. A loud *thud* sounds as his head slams against the marble floor. His eyes widen, grimacing in pain.

Sasha's fury outmatching his, she screams, raising a fist, "*Ser-rrgeiii!*"

"Anger," says Seth, sitting beneath a dome of abyssal flame, crossed-legged and joined by his daughter in meditation. "Anger is a thing of great power, but a dangerous, impulsive power. The key is not swaying from it. To not turn a blind eye to it. Just because something can be dangerous does not mean it is not good. The determining factor is how it is used."

"But, Dad," says Persephone. "I know I didn't have magic before, but you still seemed hesitant to even include me in Misha's training. Like you wanted to keep me separate from it."

Silence fills the space between them, lingering, growing heavy within the abyssal dome. The weight of all things amplifies within the presence of the White Abyss. And while not the real thing, this white chamber shares its qualities. The dome arching over them, pressing down harder with each passing moment, forcing their bodies to become acclimated to the pressure.

"Because I was afraid," Seth says. "You saw what I did. And I was afraid...that you would be too much like me."

"Dad..."

"And I know. I know what happened at the Assembly. But you can blame me for that. I should have seen this coming.

Deep down, I think I always knew. Your magic wouldn't just go away and fail to emerge in adulthood. But I didn't want to contemplate this. I wanted you to have a normal childhood. But I failed in that, too.

"So, Persephone, do you...do you hate your father?"

"What?"

"Do you hate me? After all my failures, after what I did when I was younger...do you hate me for it, do you fear me?"

Persephone glances at her father, sitting there, stoic-faced, but bleeding beneath the surface. *That pulsation, that egg sac-like quality I feel within him, it's pulsing, aching like a tremendous wound. Yet it feels so alive.*

"I have no right to hate you, Dad." Persephone sighs. "And I won't blame you for what I did at the Assembly. That's my burden to bear."

Seth smiles proudly beneath sad eyes.

"Humanity is a thing to be overcome. This is our purpose: to rise above all that is so very human. Our pain, our sufferings. Our prejudices and hatred for one another. We are meant to rise above all these pointless squabbles and become something more. As you now know, a past enemy of mine and your mothers has risen again and is acting upon the same malicious motives as his predecessor. Believe me, she was a creature that created nothing but hatred and contempt. She and all she stood for enslaved the world. And this boy, her new life, is no different. We must rise above them. We must be better. We must use our anger—chisel it to a controlled point—and rid the world of the echoes of yesterday. Banish what has come before, so we can instead move forward and build something new. If we can't, then humanity will never have what your mother and I worked so hard for—a world without gods."

"But...the Abyssal Consciousness called me a True-Born God, so what do you mean, exactly? Because the world was once without magic, right? Yet now everyone born today has magic. Doesn't that mean humans are gods?"

"That was the intention. Or rather, to allow humans to obtain their great potential through the means of will power...through magic. But it was never meant to oppress others. It was meant to uplift the whole of humankind. So, while it may seem hypocritical of me to wish for a world with no gods, since your mother and I are special even amongst the rest of humanity, and you even more so, one cannot help the circumstances of their birth. They are as they are born to be. But what matters is what they put out into the world. What they stand for, what they have the will to create."

Seth rises, reaching an arm toward Persephone, and says, "This is the dividing line between us and that would-be god your mother is fighting against as we speak. So...will you own your power, or will it own you? Will you destroy, or will you create?"

Taking his hand, Persephone rises with a smile, and steps back, her eyes overflowing with abyssal energy. Seth's eyes sink into the depths of their whites, as abyssal flame erupts into being, spiraling around his body. Persephone steps forward—the ground cracks beneath her feet. Her legs slow, heavy, weighed down by the abyssal pressure.

Seth feels himself being tugged toward her. Standing his ground, more flames ignite around him, holding him in place. "Remember! Look inward! All magic is imagination. Magic does as the mind wills it to do. So, picture it! Your power, at the center of your mind, picture it as a ball of energy. Watch as it spikes and stretches outward, trying to break free. Sun flares whipping outward, away from its center. Focus, and imagine molding it back into a calm, focused ball. Only then can you wrap your hand around it! And move it like an author glides their pen across paper, like a painter enacting a gentle brush stroke. Focus, and fill that portrait not with red-hot destruction, but a vast array of beautiful colors! Do it, Persephone, do it now!"

Persephone bares her teeth, clenching her fists as the abyssal pressure weighs heavier and heavier, snapping her bones repeatedly as teal sparks crackle, healing them just as quickly. "Stop yelling at me and let me focus!"

She shouts, a thunderclap with each syllable, pushing Seth backward. "*I'm yelling to purposely distract you!* ***Don't let me!*** *Focus everything you have on controlling your power! You heard the Abyssal Consciousness! It calls you a True-Born God. Which means this is **your** power to control!* ***Prove it right.*** *Prove me wrong for not training you sooner!*"

Her skin breaks, blood spurts out at all angles, she drops to her knees and—hunching over, she opens her mouth wide as if screaming, but no sound emerges—the energy pushing Seth back suddenly reverts, heading inward, back toward her. Seth's abyssal flames vanish as the shockwave washes over him. Collapsing to the ground, he whips his head toward Persephone, staring on in awe. *No—is this another implosion? Did I push her too hard?* "Persephone!" as he shouts, the abyssal pressure amassed within her shoots outward again—this time as the gentle passing of a light breeze, and sprouting abundantly, is a thick blanketing of flowers and grass. A crackle of white energy spiderwebs its way around Persephone, etching itself into the fabric of the world. Spreading sporadically outward but avoiding her father, the cracks deepen and—shattering like glass, the abyssal white dome bursts into a storm of white dust, fluttering about like ash.

Lost amidst the sublime power in front of him, Seth stares at his daughter, mouth agape. Persephone's eyes flutter to a close, losing balance and tipping over. Huginn and Muninn rush to her side, catching her by the neck of her shirt, until laying her into Seth's embrace. Misha rushes over as well, her eyes worry-stricken.

"D-ad...what h-h-happened? How'd I...d-do?"

Seth glances around at the cliffside, finding it engulfed in a field of flowers more beautiful than he's ever seen. The dilapidated cabin made cozy again as nature overtakes it, covering it in vines, flowers, and grass, and a large tree sprouting through the hole left behind after the quarrel with Damien. Life anew, in a spot destruction once gripped. "You...controlled it, Persephone. And dispelled my powers..."

Slack-jawed, eyes wide with awe, Seth turns to his daughter and says, "Magnificent."

Fist raised, Sasha glares at Sergei. He grimaces, the back of his head throbbing. But, meeting her gaze, his frown inverts as he chuckles softly. The screeching women below the windowsill quiet as the disheartening laughter steadily grows louder.

"What the fuck are you laughing at?" Sasha shouts.

"Just what are you?" Sergei says. My men and I were gifted power by our Lord, and you slaughter them so easily? I can't even feel it anymore! Suddenly, all the power flowing through my veins has grown limp as soon as you grabbed my neck. Even those born with magic, crazy as they're powers are, they can't compare to you at all, you monster." Sergei's voice crumbles away as he spits up blood, his vision blurring. "Just what is this power of yours?"

"This Lord of yours, is he some teenage boy with blond hair?" she asks, ignoring the man asphyxiating on his own blood. "Where is h—"

A large hand tugs at her long black hair, lifting her off Sergei and flinging her backward, slamming her into a wall. The air knocked out of her, blood spraying from her mouth. Vision blurs, but slowly creeps back, solidifying just enough to find a giant, muscular man standing next to Sergei.

"Dima?" Sasha asks. "What the fuck?"

The giant Russian stomps forward, ignoring her words. His eyes glossed over with pale light. Glancing from him to Sergei, she finds that his eyes hold that same golden hue.

What is going on? Dima would never—

The muscles in her neck tense as she feels herself being pressed into the wall, cracking behind her weight. Dima's arm stretches toward her, reversing the polarity of his magnetic pulse. Her breathing becomes shallow and labored, her vision blurring further out of focus—a stabbing pain in her right side, as a metal pole pierces her abdomen. *The structural framework!* Glancing beyond Dima, her eyes glow with a teal light. Sparks of magic spring through the air, past Dima and Sergei, surging their way through the wall. Reversing the polarities, the pressure upon Sasha relieves as Dima's outstretched arm flings backward—he screams as the bone snaps.

Gasping for air, Sasha rises and stomps toward Sergei.

"You've tormented me for years. Subverted my authority, threatened my family, now you try to take my life's work away from me? You are a fool, Sergei. Always have been. You have made yourself a problem for me, and for what? For ideals that are dead and gone. Your Lord is not who you think he is. I would know, because I was there when God died. Lifting her palms, teal magic crackles as she lifts her hands into the air. Rising alongside them are two giant evergreens, tearing through the floor, shaking the building's foundation. More magic crackles, and ravens emerge from the tree, fluttering chaotically around Sergei before converging into a mass of feathers, which transmutes into a raging hot ball of fire. A small sun, floating inches from Sergei's face. He stumbles backward, his skin melting—the sun bursts into embers, as Sasha gives the bound women a kind smile and nod. She hovers over Sergei, standing above him with a scowl. "What am I? I am the closest thing this world has to a god. And this is where you die."

"God?" says a voice from behind. "Serpent of old, who deceives the whole world. But you will not deceive my followers, for they are wise to your devices."

Startled, Sasha turns to find a teenage boy in a white cloak ambling around the conference room table. Biting into a pomegranate, crimson juices spill from lips. Droplets staining his coat's collar. Tossing the husk away, he kneels to the bound women. "Sorry, no time to play," he says, as his eyes flood with blackness and the souls of the women are siphoned from their bodies, flowing into his gullet. Rising, he faces Sasha with a smirk. "Finally, we meet, witch."

Sasha steps away from Sergei, placing a greater distance between herself and Damien. *Where did he come from?* She turns toward the hallway—the tree she made to block the entrance has been splintered apart, as if put through a woodchipper. *And he devoured their souls so quickly—this pressure, I remember it. All those souls squirming about within her stomach—Yahweh!*

Damien's smirk grows larger as he steps forward.

Fists clenched, trembling, Sasha steps back.

CHAPTER TWENTY-SIX

Alone at the center of all things, the Abyssal Consciousness peers through the White Abyss. With eyes that are not eyes, he sees the whole of creation—the past, the present, the calculated future. The vast whiteness stretching out like tendrils to worlds unknown, once devoured by parasitic gods. And to a far-flung future, where love aches for an eternal return in a universe crumbling apart around them as they weep throughout a looping nightmare.

Together—

But—

Cleaved—

...in two. With a daughter who carries the fate of every world upon her all too-young shoulders.

But they were young once, too. And despite his destructive qualities and her erratic past, they did alright. Slayed a god and led the world forward, but can they do it again?

The Abyssal Consciousness watches from beyond the veil as Sasha, renewed in body if not in spirit, rampages her way through the echo's cult. On the other side of the world, Seth and Persephone sit beneath a dome of white flames.

It begins.

The Abyssal Consciousness cocks its head to the left, its eyes narrowing as it continues to peer throughout the world.

They are on the cusp of an event horizon. A moment of infinite potential—for pure creation or utter destruction. Or will they surprise me, these humans, as they have done before, and find a balance? Will they succeed in bringing Zarathustra's will to fruition from beyond the grave, or will his name disappear, never to be uttered again in the destruction to come?

Dissolving any chance of a long, bright dark, this is the moment that determines the fate of everything to come—

Sasha is slammed against a wall, magnetic pressure almost crushing her bones. Seth beckons the abyss within his daughter, as she erupts with energy—a field of flowers blankets the cliffside and their broken home. "You dispelled my magic...magnificent," says Seth, lowering himself and his daughter to the ground.

The Abyssal Consciousness frowns. *No, that was not a dispelling of magic. That was a shift in reality. This is what makes a True-Born God so terrifying—or so glorious. The fabric of the world is hers to do as she pleases. And that includes all who reside within the world. Savior or slave driver, which will she become?*

The Abyssal Consciousness glances over the flowers and their vast array of colors. *She may be an anomaly, and not what Zarathustra meant when he wished for humanity to become as gods. But*—a memory stirs, of the stray Abyssian, tethered to a tree at the center of a colorful garden—*you would enjoy this sight, at least, vile god—Zarathustra.*

Sasha, successfully freeing herself, goes after the plain man with his temporarily-gifted power. "I am the closest thing this world has to a god. And this is where you die."

Frowning at her phrasing, the Abyssal Consciousness turns its attention to Sasha.

"God? Serpent of old, who deceives the whole world. But you will not deceive my followers, for they are wise to your devices. Finally, we meet, witch."

The Abyssal Consciousness stands erect at the appearance of Damien. *You—echo that should not be.* Sasha, recognizing his power, begins stepping away from Damien. Her hands quivering, heart palpitating, and still recovering from before. It can feel the thoughts vibrating from her mind.

Fear! Zarathustra's mightiest is fearful of the echo! And she is right to be—they are stronger than when they left here!

Shutting its eyes which are not eyes, a pulse vibrates from the Abyssal Consciousness's head, spreading like a wave across the White Abyss. It's tide growing in intensity, rising like a tsunami, frantically in search of its target—

A flash of white light floods Seth's field of vision. *{**Join your wife!** **The foul god's echo has found her!**}* The flash of light vanishes, as Seth's pupils reemerge, rising from the depths. Whipping his head around, his breathing suddenly labored.

"Dad, what's wrong?" Persephone says, pulling Seth back to the flower-carpeted cliffside. Persephone, Misha, and the ravens stare, mouth agape, alarm in their eyes.

Seth's eyes scatter about, slowly realigning upon his children.

"We must join your mother. Now!" he says, as the pressure of the Abyssal Consciousness's voice tears through his nerves like writhing, venomous snakes.

Sasha steps backward, a chill running through her as she stares Damien down.

Memory spurs—a grotesque centipede-like monstrosity rampaging through its heavenly halls, so quickly killing two of their companions. And almost killing her and Seth. Now that same monstrosity stands here, as a teenage boy, staring Sasha up and down with a smirk. Disgust mingles with fear as his horrifying presence washes over her—heart pounding as he closes the gap.

This boy is Yahweh, but isn't Yahweh. This pressure—I could never forget it—we overcame it all those years ago, but could I do the same now, alone?

Considering the possibilities, creation magic begins crackling within her palms and—her fingers loosen, hands dangling free at her side as the teal magic dissipates into dust. Letting it free as her mind goes inward, toward the throbbing of her heart. Arrhythmia stirs, increasing the intensity of her palpitations. Her vision blurring, the conference room losing its stolidity, and bleeding away into a haze—her eyes grow wide and she drops to her knees.

"Not even going to fight back?" says Damien. "How boring of—"

The room is overtaken by a white glow, yanking Damien's gaze toward an oval of white flame. Eyes aglow with abyssal power, fire spiraling chaotically around his upper body and arms, Seth screams, "*Get away from her!*" His right hand, a vice grip around Damien's neck, Seth lunges them across the room.

"My Lord!" Sergei shouts as he watches Seth plunge both himself and Damien through the window—shattered glass fills the air, causing Sergei to bellow as shards splinter into his right eye.

Spiraling through the air like a comet, Seth and Damien plunge into the Shibuya Scramble Crossing—a heavy collision explodes forth from outside, alongside ravaging white flames, erupting upward and spiraling past the now open window. The building, already torn apart by Sasha and Dima's magic, lets out a roar of bending steel. Persephone and Misha run through the portal, rushing to Sasha's side. "Dad!" Persephone screams, glancing toward the shattered window.

"Aunt Sasha, are you okay?" Misha asks.

Slowly rising to her feet, Sasha mutters, "F-fine. I'm fine." Misha and Persephone glare at her sadly. "We have to...j-join your father...outside." The kids nod, each grabbing one of Sasha's arms to steady her.

"Where the fuck do you think you're going?" shouts Sergei, blood gushing down his face. Dima slowly rising to the right of him.

Persephone turns, her eyes aglow with abyssal light—a kinetic pulse bellows through the air, pushing Sergei back. Scowling and lips twitching, Persephone says, "You take a step toward us, and I'll do to you as I did the Assembly."

Sergei's face falls alongside his spear as it clanks against the floor. Dima steps forward, but is stopped by Sergei, stretching out an arm.

Still glaring, Persephone steps backward until vanishing into the hallway, following her mother and Misha.

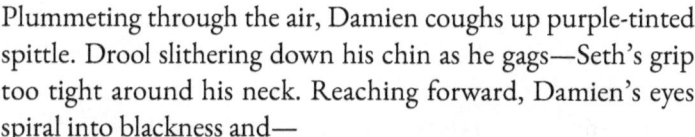

Plummeting through the air, Damien coughs up purple-tinted spittle. Drool slithering down his chin as he gags—Seth's grip too tight around his neck. Reaching forward, Damien's eyes spiral into blackness and—

Roaring, Seth swings his flame-coated left fist into Damien's chest, releasing his neck in one swift motion. The teenage boy crashes into the center of the Shibuya Scramble Crossing. His black cloak scorched, melted away alongside his skin—chest blackened, slightly concaved. The ground cracking, sinking beneath the impact, shudders further as Seth lands atop Damien.

A mixture of blood and purple spittle eject into the air. Pinned down by Seth's large knee pressing firmly into his solar plexus. Eyes turning black, he lunges both arms forward—Seth's swiftly grips Damien's forearms, smacking them back into the broken road.

Damien stares in awe of Seth. "How are you so fast, so strong?" A sudden vibration stirs from within Seth, like billions of heartbeats rapidly pulsing. Damien smirks. "Finally going to reveal what's inside you, huh? Gonna use it to destroy me—*go berserk for old time's sake?*"

"No," says Seth, eyes glowing with abyssal energy. White flames wrap around Damien's arms, their weight pinning him back, as the boy screams. "You should not have been reborn. Before, I was a burnt-out father. Avoiding a fight deep down I knew was inevitable. I didn't want it. I didn't want to fight. But you've returned and threatened my family. So now I must. But this killing of you is born of justice, not destruction. I will not be who your predecessor wanted—*I will not.*"

Eyes, bloodshot and wide, Damien clenches his teeth, bearing the pain of the abyssal flames. "Oh, you best kill me now!" he screams, "because you can't outrun what you've done, *monster!* You slaughtered each part of us, then killed Yahweh with powers you should not have had! Now we live again, with scathing memories *of the pain you dealt!* And you dare act like a saint and savior? *We will suck out your soul*, then rape your wife and daughter *until they crave death*—then we'll fuck them some more! *Violate em over and over until devouring them, too!*"

Seth glares at the boy with pity. His strength still beneath his own despite the souls he's taken. But there's something within the boy's slew of erratic threats that irks Seth. *The boy is Yahweh, and just as crafty. This assault against the Assembly branches must only be the beginning. I have no doubt he'll make good on his threats—if I let him.*

His eyes, overflowing with abyssal flame, conjures a small white sun an inch from Damien's forehead. The boy screams as it scorches his skin, attempting to melt through the surface.

"Dad!" Persephone shouts, exiting the building with Sasha's right arm across her neck, her left around Misha's. "Are you okay? Do you need help?"

"Stay back! It is almost"—a stone spear hurls past Persephone. Her eyes widen as she tracks its trajectory—Seth bellows as the spear plunges through the right side of his chest, the force knocking him off and away from Damien. The white sun dissipates into a haze of ash.

A smirk slithers its way back to Damien's face, the abyssal shackles around his wrists vanishing into clouds of ash.

"Seth!" Sasha shouts, her strength returning as adrenaline surges. Rageful eyes locking onto Sergei, as he rushes to his Lord's side. Lifting the boy up, he carries him over to the Assembly Branch building, laying his back gently against the wall. Turning around, he locks eyes with Sasha as he brings a radio to his mouth.

"All units, reconverge at the Scramble. I repeat, reconverge. Your Lord needs you."

Clicking the radio off, Sergei and Dima stomp toward Seth, with Sasha blocking their way. Persephone and Misha rush to Seth's side, as the loud rumbling of a stampeding army grows louder from all directions.

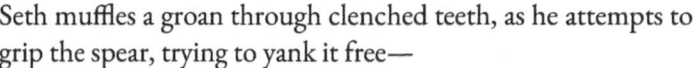

Seth muffles a groan through clenched teeth, as he attempts to grip the spear, trying to yank it free—

"Dad, stop it!" Persephone shouts. "At that angle, you won't be able to wedge it free...let me do it."

Seth stares at his daughter, breathing shallow and labored. "Okay. But do it quickly. It...punctured a lung. You'll have to heal it right away. Can you do that for me?"

"You can't heal it yourself? I thought our powers were the same, and you mentioned in your stories..."

"That was a d-d-different life. Our powers may be similar...b-but not the same. You have...what I now lack. Pull it free. Quick."

Seth lays his head upon Misha's lap, as Persephone grips the spear with both hands, tugging gently to not wound him further, the spear stubbornly locks in place. Persephone places her left foot on Seth's side and says, "Sorry, Dad, bear it a little longer!" Stepping down with force, she yanks the spear harder—Seth's face contorts, eyes wide as pain clutches him—blood spills from his side as the spear releases, clanking to the ground as Persephone tosses it away. Eyes aglow with abyssal power, white tendrils spiral down her arms and into her father's side. Wrapping it anew with untorn flesh.

"Are you okay? Did I do it? Are you healed?" Persephone says.

Clutching the side where the wound is no more, Seth smiles warmly at his daughter.

"Are you okay?" Sasha yells over her shoulder, Sergei and Dima marching forward. Seth rises, catching his breath but making his way to her side. Persephone and Misha close behind.

"Yes, fine. You look better," Seth says, flatly, glancing into Sasha. The pulse of her soul fluttering alongside her tense, constricted heart. He frowns, knowing this is no time for a lecture. He notices her fierce glare tethered to Sergei, and he smiles. "Anything I should know about the big guy?" he asks, turning toward Dima."

"Yes, don't let him get close to you. He'll tear the iron from your bones."

"Got it," says Seth, spreading his arms, clenching the muscles in his hands and fingers—an earsplitting thunderclap erupts as Seth slams his palms together, causing white flames to explode forth toward Dima—the spiraling tempest of abyssal flame rams into the large Russian, plummeting him toward the Assembly Branch, crashing into a wall beside Damien, who turns, covering his head from the debris.

Rising, Damien's eyes turn black as a vibrational pulse surges through the air. The stampeding footsteps grow louder as his army spills into the Shibuya Scramble Crossing. Rushing toward the center with a full host of elemental magic.

Dima screams as he emerges from the debris, rampaging toward Seth. A lance of ice rockets toward him from the side—conjuring her fire, Misha launches it toward the spear, melting it before reaching Seth. Smiling, he leaves the lesser soldiers to the kids. Hoping that Persephone can adequately control her power.

The Russian's eyes are aglow with a pale golden hue. Glossing over and fading their natural bright blues. The same dull cloud rests within the eyes of every one of Damien's soldiers. As Dima rampages forward, Seth catches Damien slinking off to the side, watching with a grin as his army fights his battle for him. With good reason, as beneath that grin is a heaving chest that houses broken ribs. *At least he isn't going anywhere far.* Seth turns toward Dima, eyes aglow, white flame conjuring around the Russian's wrists and ankles and neck, coiling like chains and tethering to the ground. Fists raised, Seth rushes forward.

A barrage of punches lands one by one on Dima's cheeks. Each fist feels to Dima as if a boulder is slammed against his head—the white flames altering their impact, granting them supernatural weight. Bashing him into a haze, all thoughts slipping away like water through his fingers. There, but gone in an instant.

Sasha leaps at Sergei, who conjures a new spear, lunging it toward her. Coiling around the weapon with acrobatic reflexes, she swivels around the top of it, sitting along the pole as she grips Sergei's wrists.

He screams, relinquishing the weapon as Sasha leaps off, somersaulting behind and punching Sergei in the lower back. Tumbling over, he flips, then slams both hands onto the ground. Large spikes spring toward Sasha, who hops back to a safe distance. Stomping chaotically, the ground shudders as the road lifts and cracks, all the while shooting stone shards at Sasha.

"I'm not letting you get close to me again!" he shouts, smiling as a dozen soldiers surround Sasha.

Palms spread, crackling with teal energy, she screams. Large tree roots spring from the ground, slicing through the soldiers' chests, necks, and heads. Fury in her eyes, Sasha stomps toward Sergei—grunting, clenching her jaw, she collapses to the ground as a bolt of lightning pierces her left leg. Blood spurts as the flesh grows black and charred. Turning, she finds the soldier rising above her, another bolt in hand—flames surge past Sasha. Set ablaze, the soldier screams.

Misha and Persephone run to Sasha's side. Misha protecting from the front, as Persephone heals her mother's wound. Sasha rises, breathing heavily, with eyes dull and faded. Persephone feels the pulse of her mother's soul. Agita rising within as her heart throbs furiously. "Mom...I think you should stop—leave this to us."

"*No!*" Sasha yells. "I will not stop until this world is safe. And besides, nobody is killing him but me." Persephone glances at Misha uncomfortably. Continuing, Sasha says, "After all...he tried to hurt you. This, above all, I will not allow."

Soldiers flood in from all sides. Dozens upon dozens circle around, with hundreds more at the ready. Persephone glances around frantically—Misha squeezes her hand, smiles, and leads the charge against Damien's army.

With quick footwork and controlled movement, flame scatters, blanketing the troops with the grace of a figure skater—the many years of Seth's training finally bearing fruit. Persephone watches from behind, heart palpitating, wondering what she should do.

{You are not ready. I agree. But no one is ever ready. They simply do, or they do not. Will you act, or will you let your family die?}

Persephone's eyes overflow with abyssal energy. Her back to Misha, she's careful not to even slightly turn. Hands shaky, she reaches toward the soldiers rushing in from behind, fixating on their centers, imagining them stretching, pulling apart—a pulse surges through her fingers, bursting outward toward the soldiers, and—split at the abdomen, blood gushes from both halves as the soldiers collapse into pieces. Alongside the rush of blood sprouts an array of colorful flowers—red, blue, yellow—sprouting from the bloodied, crimson flesh.

Persephone's breathing grows heavier, taking in the view of what she did. And from a near distance, Damien peers upon her powers.

Ah, what a gift! To tear through the world's fabric, to hold governance over all things! At a mere thought, she loosened the atoms holding those men together! We can shear the flesh, and all physical surroundings—but we can't do that. We need her.

Skulking around the commotion of battle, Damien vanishes from sight. Salivating as he creeps ever closer.

Thunder crashes, fire bellows, ice shatters, and wind swooshes—the elements colliding into each other, echoing loudly throughout the nearby deserted streets of Shibuya. Misha keeps a safe distance from the assaulting troops, her fire scorching and keeping them away from Persephone, who continues slowly slicing the men in two, three, four, and many more pieces. Flowers blooming from each wound.

Okay, so far so good. Persephone pans right to left, sending her world-ripping vibrations through each soldier rushing toward her. *I don't even know what these powers are, but I'm doing it! I'm doing it!* As each vibration slices through another body, her hands quake more intensely. Her vision swirls and grows dull, as a faintness overtakes her. Head light and uneasy, she—a larger pulse surges out from her core, slicing through eight men at once. Stunned, she stands erect, glancing toward Misha, who's too preoccupied to notice. Fire erupting from her palms in a broad arch, setting a dozen men ablaze. All the while, sweat pools upon her forehead, her breathing steadily climbing.

Her leg healed, Sasha roars as she sprints toward Sergei. Lying on his back, he frantically pounds the ground, launching a barrage of stalagmites at Sasha while glancing about for any soldiers to come to his aid. Sasha barrels through, sideswiping each stone spire with her fists, scattering the shattered rock into the air. A tempest of dust in her wake.

"I have had," she smashes a stalagmite, "*enough,*" she swings her arms apart, pulverizing two more, "*of you!*"

Sergei launches one longer spike her way as she closes the gap. Side-stepping and chopping at the stone, it severs from the ground. Reaching for it, she catches it midair, twists the point downward, and a harsh, wet gurgle fills the air, mingling with the wuthering haze of stone dust. Sergei glares upward, finding Sasha's rageful eyes glaring down as she stands atop him.

"M-my Lord..." Sergei's arm quakes as it slithers skyward—a light hiss slithers through his lips, as his hand falls hard against the ground, heart impaled, gushing crimson through the wound.

Sasha stares with pity, swaying, eyes fluttering—she clutches at her left arm, heart throbbing, she chokes, tumbling over.

"*Mom!*" Persephone screams, drawing Seth's attention away from Dima. His focus severed, the white flames dissipate into drifting ash, freeing Dima. Quickly gripping Seth's neck, he is plowed into the ground. "*Dad!*" Persephone screams, her gaze whipping to and from each parent. Noticing her mother's slight breathing, she shouts, "Misha! Watch my mom for a second!" as she sprints toward her father.

Dima's angry, faded blue eyes whip toward her approach. Reaching out with his unbroken arm, he—Seth punches Dima, knocking him back—a heavy pressure creates a forceful gust of wind, pulling everything toward Persephone. The army tumbles over, Misha and Sasha are dragged along the ground, Damien appears behind a group of soldiers as they collapse, holding onto Sergei's conjured stone spires, resisting the pull.

"*Let go of my dad!*" Persephone screams. Fist raised toward Dima, Seth turns toward his daughter. A raging pulse tears through the Shibuya Scramble Crossing, rushing toward Dima. The air between them, sheared like paper, as the vibration ravages everything in its path, revealing a blackness beneath. Cutting closer and closer—Seth yanks his wrist back, his hand cleaved from the bone, as Dima screams in agony. His right arm torn away, thumping against the ground far from the Russian.

Noticing what she has done, Persephone's eyes grow wide. "D-daddy! I'm s-s-sorry..." Her eyes overflow with abyssal energy as she drops to her knees.

Damien rushes at her, arms outstretched, brandishing a toothy grin. "Time to let us *suck out your soul!*" His arms flail about, his mouth unhinging, eager to devour her whole—

"*Persephone!*" shouts Seth, holding his bloodied stump of a wrist, rushing toward his daughter. Misha, not wanting to leave Sasha's side, sobs as she watches, unable to intervene. "P-per-sepho-ne," whispers Sasha between gasping breaths. Damien, closing the gap, reaches both arms out for her, a bear ready to mull—

Persephone's head whips backward, face horizontal, staring directly skyward, as she says in a voice not her own, *"Worship your gods if you like. They will only destroy you in the end. The wise would not trust them, for this is what happens in the wake of gods."*

Damien halts, recognizing a voice he hasn't heard since the moment of his conception.

Seth, still rushing toward her, says, "the Abyssal Consciousness?"

Her mouth moving impossibly fast, Persephone continues, *"Beware, for they have arrived."*

A massive white light brands itself into the open air above, overtaking the clouds interspersed throughout the bright blue sky. Descending from the whiteness, first feet, then legs, torsos, necks, and heads donning bright, glowing teal hair. Thousands of strange beings appear in the sky, their luminescence blinding all beneath them, as they glare upon the Earth's inhabitants. Seth's eyes grow wide as an intense shiver surges through him. The image of Zarathustra flashes into memory, as he says, "No...it c-can't be...the Abyssians!"

As the word slips through Seth's lips, Damien's eyes grow wide. Remembering long ago, in a past that was and wasn't his own. A child rummaging through a blissful garden, giggling as she tormented her twin brother, before eating together with their father, a wise man with glowing teal hair and a long beard to match.

Dima, stumbling forward, wincing in pain, shouts, "Ah, our Lord's angelic emissaries have arrived! Rejoice, for the rapture has come!"

Flying ahead of the legion is a large, muscular Abyssian. At the sight of the Shibuya war grounds, he swiftly appears before Dima. Faster than the eye can catch. Both Seth and Damien shiver as the Abyssian moves past them to get to the Russian, ripping off his other arm with ease, a child tearing the wing from a bug. Dima screams as he collapses to the ground, writhing in shock.

The Abyssian War Chief says, with foreign, otherworldly speech transmogrifying into familiar language, "Angelic? What is this word? Filth, the lot of you. Products of Zarathustra's betrayal—and this world of his, I see now, is so small it has no bearing upon the stack. Hence why it took us so long to find it, and why no imbalance has occurred...and yet this world should not be. A world full of grotesqueries which should not be. But fear not, for we are gods, and we shall cleanse this unnatural realm of all its sins."

In an instant, he is gone, returned to the sky to lead the Abyssian legion. Agita spurring Seth into motion, he claps his fiery palms upward, blanketing the sky in white flames. The fire bellows like thunder. Glancing toward the ravaging white explosion, Seth says, "No way..."

The Abyssian legion descends further, through the flames and back into the open air. Their flesh unscathed. And as the flames dissipate into ash, drifting down upon them, the Abyssian War Chief hunches over, before bending his head backward, jaw unhinging, creating a large gape. And there at the center of the pit of his mouth, a small teal ball of energy conjures, growing rapidly in size. And, lunging his face forward, he unleashes it.

Seth grabs Persephone, dragging her over to Sasha and Misha. Damien steps back, disappearing into the crowd of his soldiers. With a flash of Seth's eyes, spreading his arms wide, a white dome engulfs his family, just as the Abyssian's teal beam slices through the Japanese archipelago. Earthquakes rumble, as multiple tsunamis crash into the severed land, toppling buildings and drowning civilization. Mothers clutch their children as the warm saltwater fills their lungs.

Chasing after one who betrayed them, the Abyssians have come to ravage a land they deem shouldn't be. And thus, they leave behind a gushing wound. A testament to the power of gods—a promise of dark things to come.

PART THREE

Abyssian Descent

"Christianity is a degenerative movement, consisting of all kinds of decaying and excremental elements: it is *not* the expression of the downfall of a race, it is, from the root, and agglomeration of all the morbid elements which are mutually attractive and which gravitate to one another.... It is therefore *not* a national religion, *not* determined by race: it appeals to the disinherited everywhere; it consists of a foundation of resentment against all that is successful and dominant: it is in need of a symbol which represents the damnation of everything successful and dominant. It is opposed to every form of *intellectual* movement, to all philosophy: it takes up the cudgels for idiots, and utters a curse upon all intellect. Resentment against those who are gifted, learned, intellectually independent: in all these it suspects the element of success and domination."
—Friedrich Nietzsche, *The Will to Power*

CHAPTER TWENTY-SEVEN

The concaved islands lay half-submerged in water. The Pacific Ocean running through the middle of the Japanese archipelago, washing atop the collapsed skyscrapers of Tokyo and reaching far to the west and north. Fukuoka and Sapporo, and every city between, left as dilapidated, empty shells. Cracks in the earth spiderwebbing through the golden brown countryside. The earth cools as summer finishes, taking the warmth of life with it. Leaves flutter wispily to a now uninhabitable land. Abandoned in the wake of furious gods.

Airports destroyed alongside their cities, the last of the Japanese people watch their land grow smaller as they sway across the La Pérouse Strait on the northern edge of Hokkaido. Drifting along in small boats, big enough to hold a family and no more. The men stand, staring stoically at their devastated home. As their wives sit, clutching their crying children—

A teal streak rockets across the sky. The men squat, wrapping their arms around their family.

A month since the destruction of Japan, the arrival of the Abyssians, they have laid waste to all the great cities of the world. With their great speed and strength, all was brought to ruin in a matter of hours. Leaving the last of humanity to cower in hiding. To find havens to shelter them from the Abyssian sentries circling the globe at frequent intervals.

And so, the last of the Japanese people make their way across the La Pérouse Strait in hopes of prolonging their lives, if just by a small bit, by finding shelter in a country with far more land to spare—shelter in the ruins of Russia's Sakhalin Island prison. For that is what life has become.

A cold, harsh sentence to death.

The waves below grow harsh and rocky as she flies overhead, their sway pulled alongside the strong wind current her speed conjures. Ignoring the Japanese survivors below her—*let them run and hide, little bugs. Why waste time consuming a small group when cities full of souls still stand? Besides, I'm busy.* Long teal hair flutters wildly behind, as she searches—*that white dome*—she ponders their arrival and the subsequent first cleansing of Zarathustra's little world—the desecration of Japan.

Such power, then they vanished.

She remembers the words of the Abyssian War Chief, as anguished screams erupted below them. The land split in two, the gods above uncaring, not noticing the screams nor the silence following as saltwater filled the lungs of vermin, cutting their voices short. The Abyssian War Chief rubbed his chin at the sight of white ash drifting around the destruction of Tokyo, as he said, "I could have sworn...I saw a white light before my magic hit the surface."

"You are not mistaken," said the female Abyssian to his right. That creature, a large one with black hair and beard, his eyes filled with white, and suddenly, a dome of abyssal energy blanketed over them."

"Hmm, yes, so it did," says the Abyssian War Chief. "And then, a split second before the impact of my magic, a large pool of power vanished—a substantial amount, and unlike the others." His gaze panned all around, watching as teal souls rose into the air. The other Abyssians were already inching toward them with hunger in their eyes. "None of these souls match that power...check the surface! I want their bodies found!"

The legion swarmed the surface, leaving only the Abyssian War Chief peering over everything from above. Between fallen buildings and beneath the risen ocean water, they inspect each corpse. Japanese bodies are washed along through the crevasse, blown into the Shibuya Scramble Crossing, with soldiers lifelessly strewn about. A stone spear laid half buried by a collapsed building.

A plane rose in the distance. Catching the ascending object in the corner of his eyes, the Abyssian War Chief bolted toward it. His immense speed traversing miles within seconds, he flew straight through the middle of the aircraft. Sparks erupted about the torn metal, the wings snapping apart from the bifurcated plane. In a flash, the Abyssian War Chief returned to the air above the Shibuya Scramble, glaring toward the earth with furious, sharp eyes. All the while, terror erupted at a distance as the two halves of the plane smashed into the city.

His eyes darted around, following his fellow Abyssians as their teal hair streaked around the Scramble, continuing their search. Nothing turned up except cowering, screaming humans sitting amidst piles of dead loved ones, each meeting the same fate.

The female Abyssian found in a dark corner of debris, quickly filling with ocean water, a whimpering young girl holding a stuffed cat. Unhinging her jaw, eyes aglow with teal, the Abyssian lunged toward the child, its screams grew louder and louder—the Abyssian's teeth sunk into the girl's waist, her legs dangling by threads of flesh, twitching as the Abyssian gobbles down the child's upper half. The god's eyes pulsed even brighter, the soul nourishing her.

"Any sign of the one who conjured the white dome?" asked the Abyssian War Chief, suddenly behind the female god.

"Nothing yet," she said, turning to him, blood gushing over her lips. "Do you think it was Zarathustra? That white power...must have been The Womb of the One Mind, right?"

"My thoughts exactly. But we would have noticed Zarathustra if he were here. Despite the great power felt in this world, strangely, his absence is *most* noticeable. It's too soon to jump to conclusions. Our priority for now is finding the one who can use the power of The Womb. Zarathustra or otherwise."

Drifting back to the present, the female Abyssian continues her flight over the Japan Sea, over Korea, with Hong Kong now below her. Awash in a sea of flames.

"Raze their cities to the ground! Sooner or later, they will be found. For now, leave them no sanctuary," said the Abyssian War Chief, when the female god last saw him. Scattering the Abyssians across the globe, some acting in groups like those below in Hong Kong. Massive teal lasers erupt at sporadic angles, yanked about, tearing the buildings free from their roots. The deafening sound of crushing metal and glass as skyscrapers topple over, silencing the screams of those beneath them. Spread throughout the city, flashes of teal pulse like strobe lights, hundreds at a time.

The sight of it stirs hunger within the Abyssian, but she flies onward.

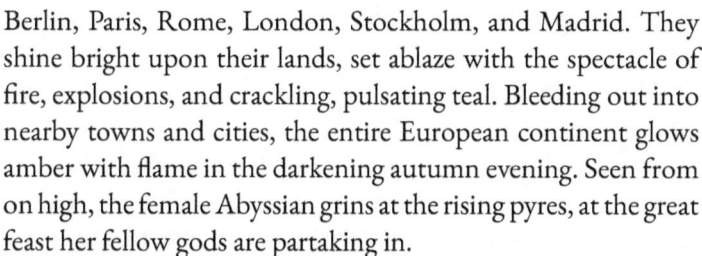

Berlin, Paris, Rome, London, Stockholm, and Madrid. They shine bright upon their lands, set ablaze with the spectacle of fire, explosions, and crackling, pulsating teal. Bleeding out into nearby towns and cities, the entire European continent glows amber with flame in the darkening autumn evening. Seen from on high, the female Abyssian grins at the rising pyres, at the great feast her fellow gods are partaking in.

The European continent blurs behind, as the expansive blue of the Atlantic Ocean spreads before her.

No mere pond...who's to say what's hiding in its depths?

Diving low, the water erupts upward as she plunges beneath the waves. Murky waters cloud her gaze as she pans around. *Could that black haired man with abyssal power be hiding down here?* She ponders, glancing about. Her vision compensates for the darkness of the ocean's floor by illuminating her surroundings with pulsing teal outlines—sensing the electromagnetic radiation given from her surroundings.

Darting around, miles across, the god watches the teal outlines of strange creatures streak past her—oval-shaped bodies with fins, fluttering about in large groups of the same. Multi-armed and squishy creatures crawl along, spurring up sand, squeezing themselves into rocks and coral as she passes by. An elongated, larger-finned creature rushes toward her, mouth open wide, rows of large, sharp teeth. Feet pressed to the ocean's floor to orient herself, she launches herself upward and out of the way of the approaching creature—something massive thuds against her for a moment before she bursts through it, ejecting into the open air.

Glancing around, she is miles from where she submerged. Nearby to the north, there are two landmasses, one smaller, one huge, covered in snow and ice. And rising to the surface is the creature she flew through—a now bifurcated blue whale, its intestines spilling out into the open water, stained red with its blood.

None of those creatures are at all the same shape as the one with abyssal power.

Reorienting in her original direction, she flies off, waves spreading beneath her speed. The darkness of Europe retracts, as she watches the sun rise. Moving so quickly through time zones, the sun moves as if in reverse until reaching another city. Plunged into chaos, but not yet razed and pillaged, an island with many towering buildings, with a river on each side. Landing on a street, she finds signs stating "bagels" and "dollar slices" and storefronts housing clothing and footwear, and endless commodities with the words "I love NYC" branded onto them. A large, miles-long park in the city's center, a wide stretch of autumnal hues. Red and orange leaves as far as the eye can see. A few scattering about in a light gust, the fall only just begun.

Crowds of people sprint along the streets, cowering from the Abyssian gods. Storefront windows shattered, doors left ajar, as dozens of men, women, and children alike run off with totes haphazardly packed with an assortment of items.

Ah, Zarathustra. The female Abyssian stares after the screaming humans. *What pusillanimous creatures you have created. Feeble, pathetic little things that result in thievery even amidst their final moments. How selfish! Meanwhile, my kin and I work at collective efforts to extinguish the final evidence of your life.*

Her mouth unhinges, her eyes glowing teal—a pulse rockets outward, a circle with her at its core. Stretching a block wide, ear-piercing screams erupt from within the radius. Tumbling to the ground, humans yank their heads skyward, their eyes aglow with teal, as the souls of all within the boundary eject from their bodies and plunge into the Abyssian's gullet. Licking her plump, white lips, she—

"*Monster!*" screams a voice from behind. A young woman with crimson hair breathes deeply before blowing out with great force. The air snaps and crackles, as embers erupt into being. Growing ever larger, as the stream of crackling fire makes its way toward the Abyssian. An explosion overtakes her, scorching the nearest buildings and filling the street with deep black smoke.

With the young woman's breathing labored, she stares toward the smoke incredulously. Stepping forward, but around the impact, the smoke disperses as the Abyssian emerges swiftly through, hand reaching toward the girl. Gripping her neck, the god says, "So this is why your souls taste different from those in other realms. Intriguing." Squeezing hard, blood gushes from the girl's eyes as they burst from her skull, her head rupturing from the pressure, chunks of bone and flesh scatter about, as the Abyssian devours another soul.

"Having fun, are you?" says a booming male voice. The Abyssian War Chief is suddenly at the female god's side.

"There's been no sign of Zarathustra...but I'm sure you noticed the peculiarity of the sentient life here?"

The Abyssian War Chief grunts. Glancing around the city, all manner of magic is flung about, clashing with streaks of teal, followed by anguished screams. "Yes. Zarathustra's feeble attempt at thwarting us, no doubt. Somehow creating an army, but one that falls short."

"Though the power of magic increases over time...we were wise to come here when we did."

The Abyssian War Chief turns from her, glancing skyward. Something faint lingers in two large pools overhead, at equal heights. Realms that were but are no longer, mingling together with a residual power, feeling all too familiar to the warmongering god.

"The Womb of the One Mind," he says. "It opened here once. I've felt its peculiar sensation since we arrived...a world created twice over. Perhaps that has something to do with Zarathustra's frustrating ability to slip our grasp.

"Your orders?" asks the female Abyssian.

"Continue searching. Raze the cities, tear the ground asunder. He's hiding somewhere." He glances at his feet, adorned with white sandals. Something akin to endless heartbeats stirs from beneath the ground—*the pulse of The Womb!* "Be it the ground we stand on? Or be it something else?" He grinds his teeth, lips quivering. "How did that stray god mask it? There must be something akin to The Womb of the One Mind here. How else could this world come into being?"

"I suppose we must find him and force him to tell us."

"Indeed...but—I don't understand it, the sensation I felt from our presumed Zarathustra...it's here, but it isn't. Like it has vanished entirely from this world..."

The two gods ponder in silence, while observing the anomaly of a world created by one who strayed from them. With rage and hunger, they continue their desecration of Zarathustra's pocket dimension, aiming to cleanse it of all life.

And, listening in from across the realms, eyes aglow with abyssal light open within a vast white space.

The Assembly for Magic and Human Progression comes into view as a small group, led by a strikingly beautiful, fairy-like woman, marches toward it. Or the void where the building once was. The first of autumn's fallen leaves crunch beneath their feet, a light breeze cooling their skin, yet sweat glimmers upon the fae-woman's face.

She remembers the day she arrived here, a small child capable of creating castles out of trees, stone, and earth. Along with her friend who could create short-term life from her spittle. The day they arrived at the Assembly was greeted with much warmth. And each day after began the same way—Sasha ambling into the barracks, with an armful of snacks and chocolates and gummy candies, bestowing them lavishly upon the children, as they gathered around to hear stories of magical warriors striking down monsters from beyond their world.

The president of the Assembly herself, showering us with love before even going to her office. And those stories...surely, they were meant to motivate us, the love and candies to keep us happy, our powers under control—yet her demeanor toward us never felt ingenuine, she wasn't merely administering control over us. She really seemed to care...

"You okay?" asks her friend, plopping a bright pink lollipop back into her mouth.

"Yeah, just thinking about our childhood here." The fae-looking woman unearths a phone from her pocket, opening an email chain. With Sasha gone, she had sought advice from the other Assembly branches, the first to respond being the head of the Scandinavian branch, who forwarded an English translation of the email he had just sent out:

Emergency Procedure: All non-magic-born personnel, make your way to the underground bunker. All Magic-Born will assist me in gathering as many civilians as we can and bring them to the bunker.

"Do all branches have an underground bunker?" she had asked.

She was then told that, "Sasha was a secretive woman, who's to say what she did with her own branch. But it was she who insisted on bunkers being installed. It was she who drew them into the blueprints when the international branches were first erected."

Slipping her phone back into her pocket, she glances at the black crevasse before her—an uneasiness quakes up her legs, her core, her face. Sweat pools further despite the cold autumn air. Her geomancy has always made her sensitive to movement in the earth, *but this is something else.*

Turning around, she says to the crowd, "Careful not to touch the void."

They stare at her as she ambles around, face to the ground as she feels about with her bare feet. A young man with fiery eyes scoffs. Another with large chain links around his forearms stares with sad eyes toward the void. "That day...this could have been avoided if we were here, if we didn't listen to Sergei's man."

"We don't know that. We don't know what happened here," says the fae-looking woman, as her toes scratch around at the pavement. Pointing at the spot, then tracing it back to the void, then forward to the apartment complex across the street, she says, "There's some sort of tunnel beneath us. I'll make a way in."

"Well, be quick about it," says the fiery-eyed young man. "Those teal-haired bastards could fly by at any moment."

Her eyes sparkle as the pavement becomes malleable, almost liquid, as it sways like an ocean. Parting like the Red Sea, a pit descends into darkness, with tree roots ripping through the ground, weaving together before the young woman, creating a staircase.

"Be careful, roots aren't flat like real steps."

"I'll go first," says her friend, pulling her lollipop free, a pool of saliva left behind in her mouth. Blowing large bubbles, they shape themselves into small, winged, humanoid figures, glimmering with light. The lollipop having been sucked down to the stick, she unwraps another, plops it into her mouth, and wraps the old one in its wrapper. A renewed pool of saliva spreads across her tongue and gums. Leading the charge, the four of them descend.

The fae-woman's eyes glimmering, the hole closes atop them. A few feet of earth and stone, woven back together again, the pavement on top leaving no signs of tampering.

"How does that power work, anyway?" asks the young man with chain links around his arms, staring at the fairies made from spittle.

"I dunno. The Assembly scientists said something about magic seeping into my body's cells. And all magic is thought, or something, so I think it, and anything from my body can come alive for a short while."

"Anything? You mean even your shit, your period blood?" asks the fiery-eyed young man.

The fae-looking woman elbows him in the stomach.

"Ow, what the fuck!" he screams.

"Shut up. Don't be gross."

"I sure hope we find Sasha," says the young woman, blowing another fairy into being, as she changes the subject. "Those teal-haired...things...do you think they're gods? Emerging as they did...they even said as much."

"They are not gods," says the fae-looking woman. "Remember the main tenet of the Assembly: One must place one's faith in oneself, and *never* throw it away, waste it on a concept, an idea. Those who do are foolish and idiotic. Humanity's power is their own."

With mention of the Abyssians, the group plunges into silence. Contemplating the grim future, their feet hit a stony surface. Just ahead, they can see an elevator. Pressing the button, its doors spread open. Entering, they find naught but a single button. Pressing it, the doors close, and they take the long plunge downward. Deeper and deeper, causing even the fae-looking woman to lose track of where they are.

At the sound of a soft *ding*, the doors slowly open.

Conjuring fairies until her tongue dries, the room slowly fills with light. The fiery-eyed young man brings his fists to his chest before spreading his arms wide, releasing his palms—fire sparks into being, joining the fairies' light. Walking further, awash in the shadowy space is lab equipment, and the makings of a mechanics shop. "Woah!" says the young man with chains around his arms, glancing upward at the light glimmering upon a towering structure. "Is that what I think it is?"

The group ambles toward it, the fairies and flickering flame at their side lighting up the steel structure further. Words printed along the hull state, *Project Persephone*—

The overhead lights blare, suddenly switched on alongside the creak of a door.

"Oh, you all," says a feminine voice.

The group turns to find a familiar face.

CHAPTER TWENTY-EIGHT

"Indeed...but—I don't understand it, the sensation I felt from our presumed Zarathustra...it's here, but it isn't. Like it has vanished entirely from this world..."

The two gods ponder in silence, while observing the anomaly of a world created by one who strayed from them. With rage and hunger, they continue their desecration of Zarathustra's pocket dimension, aiming to cleanse it of all life.

And, listening in from across the realms, eyes aglow with abyssal light open within a vast white space. A room appears before his eyes, as Seth says, "Okay, Persephone. Your shift." His weary-eyed daughter rises from a bed to his left, deeply asleep a moment before, inches from a still-sleeping Misha.

Hair wild and unkempt, Persephone trudges toward her father, placing a hand upon his shoulder as she eases her way to the floor at his side. "How much longer are we going to keep this up, Dad?"

"Until we're ready to fight back. I know I'm asking a lot of you, but think of it as training your powers further."

She nods groggily, as abyssal light bursts from her eyes—a heaviness tugs toward her for a moment, jerking her mother awake from a bed opposite hers, provided privacy by a brick wall. Misha stirs for a second, whispering, "Per-sepho-ne, mmm," but promptly returns to sleep, the air still and silent.

Seth rises, wrapping his arms around Sasha as she approaches, almost collapsing into her.

"Gonna head straight to bed?" asks Sasha.

"No, I want to spend some time with you," Seth says, gripping her tighter.

Returning the squeeze, they release each other and amble over to the small kitchen space opposite the beds and next to a lone door swathed in an abyssal glow. Seth collapses into a chair as Sasha begins brewing coffee. "I'm impressed by all this," says Sasha, gesturing to the abyssal dome. A small apartment seemingly built into the White Abyss.

"It was all Persephone. I'm proud of her," Seth says, glancing at his daughter in the center of the white dome, seemingly not hearing him. "She remembered watching me nullify Misha's magic, then conjured up this plan to nullify the Abyssian's ability to sense us."

"I'm surprised it works, though. They were born of The Womb of the One Mind. Forged in the same powers as my ring," says Sasha, glancing at the twirling glow of teal and abyssal flame held within the stone. "You'd think they would be able to sense abyssal magic like anything else."

"They probably can, which is why Persephone herself is so vital. Her powers extend beyond mine. The pressure she emits, controlling it outward or inward, affecting the flow of it to rapidly switch those directions, canceling out its own frequency—something must have triggered since Shibuya. She slipped toward the end there," Seth glances at his hands, remembering when one was sliced clean off by Persephone, and the tears in her eyes when she frantically healed the wound. *I'm sorry, Daddy. I'm so sorry. I'm sorry. I'm sorry. I'm sorry,* she went on and on, collapsing into his chest after healing his wound. "But she's come far since then."

Sasha joins him at the table, setting two cups of coffee. She stares at Seth, at his dark, sunken eyes, their glow faded from overwork.

"If her powers are beyond yours, then how are you also able to hold the dome in place without them finding us?"

Seth glances sadly at her.

"Sasha…I've been keeping a secre—"

"I know," she says.

"What, how?"

"How long have we known each other, how intimately, how deeply? I've known for years that there's something you didn't want to discuss, but I trust you, so I never brought it up."

Seth's gaze drops as he chuckles softly, the laughter ceasing as he remembers the blight currently razing their world, and he considers the possible outcome of all this. Staring at his wife, emotion builds inside his chest as tears trickle down his cheeks, thinking back on their life together, all the love, the support, the hardship, and the strengthened love that followed. He looks on at this amazing woman he chose, and he feels it all again. That ineffable compulsion that alerts one that their future has arrived and it's in the form of a person, and that nothing matters outside of her.

"All those years ago, when my soul was manipulated for Yahweh's plot, a new magic was created—Nil Magic. But you know that much. Over the years, over these amazing years together, even now as we sit here, this love we have, our Persephone, our Misha, because of all this, something has stirred within me.

Something has grown, transmuted into something else entirely. The Abyssal Consciousness called it Omni Magic. Its meaning quite obvious. From nothing to everything. It feels like billions of souls are within me, in the background, not vying for control, but just sitting, waiting—you weren't there for it, but it feels similar to when I absorbed the souls being transported by Gluttony, and then blew him apart from the inside.

"And that is what is scaring me. The Abyssal Consciousness may have called it something different, but this is exactly what Yahweh had planned—only this has come about naturally, wasn't forced. Yet still, I'm afraid of what might happen if I used this power—these souls, if that's what they could even be considered. Derived from me and not the White Abyss, as they are."

"But you're using this power to cancel out the white dome's frequency?"

"A very small amount. Just like when I went after Damien. I was scared then, too, but I slipped for a moment, out of fear of losing you. And now, too, I'm afraid. I could hide us entirely on my own, but I'm having Persephone handle half of it because I'm afraid of what might happen if I tap too much into this power."

Sasha's mind lingers to the words of the Abyssal Consciousness:

{You are indeed a defender of humankind. But steel yourself, Spawn of Zarathustra. For you cannot survive the wilderness without a flame to warm and feed you. And you cannot first create a flame without severing a tree from its roots to burn. And a time may come when you regret not being the one to grip the ax.}

She checks her phone. The date states *October 3rd*. Outside of this hiding place, leaves are drying up, fluttering to the ground in a magnificent spectacle of orange and red. The sweet smell of moldering leaves, a season of decay and beauty.

Perhaps one cannot exist without the other. He and I should know that well, and yet we've held back from doing what we must.

Catching her mind wandering, Seth says, "Am I wrong for that? For having our daughter shoulder the weight of this?"

"Uh-uh," Sasha says, shaking her head. "If you handled this alone, you would have burnt out much quicker, and they'd find us by now.

"But billions of souls…really?"

"I feel them, Sasha. I don't know how, but they're there."

Glaring for a moment, Sasha says, "Well, the Abyssal Consciousness knows things we don't. If it were the same Nil Magic Yahweh intended you to have, then it wouldn't have called it something new. And I think the fact that it came about naturally, nurtured by our lives together, is significant and perhaps you shouldn't be fearful of it?"

"Hmm, I suppose."

Watching her husband dwell, she chuckles and paraphrases him, "*our love, even as we sit here now,* huh? The world is on fire, Seth, and you're romanticizing this situation?"

"I know it's wrong, but still, that's how strongly I feel for you," he says, "It doesn't matter what's going on. If I have you, if I have our daughter, then I can deal with anything. Nothing is more important than you."

Leaning over the small table, their lips lock. Warmth overtaking them, they rise from the table, gripping each other fiercely. Taking hold of her backside, Seth kisses her neck. Sasha moans and says, "Aren't you exhausted? Shouldn't you go to sleep?"

"Do you not want to?" asks Seth.

"Of course, I want to," she says, thinking about how impossible it's been to be intimate this past month. "But I'm also concerned about your health."

"I'm fine, and I can deal. I need you too much."

Glancing up into his eyes, she rises into another passionate kiss, as the two of them stumble across the room, still within each other's arms, tumbling into their bed. And, becoming one, their eyes glow in tandem, a marriage of teal and white—a wedding of life and death, of decay and of beauty.

And around her finger is that same glimmer housed within her ring.

Pleasure moans and grunts sound from beyond the brick wall, springing Misha awake. Certain sensations are impossible to pull one's attention from. Hunger, thirst, these natural impulses nag at the mind until one gives in and feeds the craving. Such is also the case when alerted to sexual sounds, one finds oneself as an animal in nature, hearing sounds of copulation and suddenly thirsting for it themselves.

Though the sounds of her adopted parents are an uncomfortable one, the impulse doesn't care of source, but of need. And as she lies beneath the covers pretending to be asleep, she reaches toward her groin, eyes peeking over her blanket at the meditating Persephone, whose mind is elsewhere.

Memories of each night since coming here, spur to mind. Uncomfortable at first, in such close quarters with Seth and Sasha, but it would have been more so to ask for a private room to be made. So, as the room is swathed in the sounds of Seth and Sasha enjoying each other, Misha thinks about Persephone, for she cannot be upset. Hiding within this white dome for over a month, her adoptive parents have refrained thus far out of courtesy to the kids. And besides, Misha and Persephone have been doing the same, though much more quietly.

The touch of their lips, the touch of their fingers along every inch of skin, and no trouble, such as what happened the first time they kissed. Being enclosed in this white dome creates a productive feedback loop for Persephone. Holding the dome in place, thus practicing each day to hold her powers in check, then getting to reward herself with Misha as her father takes over. Despite waking disheveled and groggy, the consistent intercourse keeps Persephone's nerves calm, focused, ready for each day's task. And deep within her, her power steadies alongside the rest of her.

All the while, Misha has relished every moment. Her body, accepted for what it is, for who she is, has distilled within a contentment she has never known.

It's funny to think like this when the world is in turmoil. But togetherness with the one you love really does make everything okay. Whatever happens from here, we at least have each other.

As she glances longingly at Persephone, her mind drifts toward her father.

I'm happy, Dad. I wish you were here to see it, but you'd be proud, I think—no, I know you would be.

Orgasmic moans erupt from beyond the wall, as Sasha clasps a hand over her mouth. Shuffling noises stir, causing Misha to turn away from their side of the room, clamping her eyes shut, pretending to snore.

Cupping a hand to her mouth, she muffles her screech. Tumbling off Seth and to his side, they shuffle around, getting comfortable beneath the blankets. Facing each other, wide smiles beneath closed eyes, warmth enraptures them. Sasha stares toward a contented Seth on the fringes of sleep, and says, "You were silly to think you couldn't tell me about the change in your magic. But I understand why..."

"I wasn't trying to hide it," Seth says, groggily. "Shouldering it myself made it easier to ignore, that's all."

"I said I understand," says Sasha, kissing his lips gently. "Now sleep, I gotta get some work done on the Abyssal Root."

Unearthing herself from the blankets, she rises to her feet and glances toward Seth before heading to the door. *Perhaps with the Abyssal Root, we can learn more about this Omni Magic...*

"Sasha...while I was holding the dome together, I saw them—the Abyssians. They're searching for Zarathustra, and I think they mistook me for him at Shibuya."

"Good thing they can't find you in here, then. Open the door for me, would you?"

"They can't find me, yet." Seth's eyes flash white, peeling the white abyssal glow away from the exit near the kitchen. "We need to make a plan...and soon."

Seth succumbs to exhaustion, as Sasha makes her way toward the door quickly before the abyssal dome closes again.

We need an alternative to this situation as well...but this magic, this idea of Persephone's...reminds me of the old days.

She rubs the faded scar on her neck. The runic conduit that granted the Guild powers, prolonged their lives and kept them hidden. *I wish Father were here so I could ask him how the magic worked...but it's too similar to be a coincidence. I'll mention this when he wakes next.* Reaching for the knob, closing the door, she turns and—

A darkness lay behind, darker than it ever gets within the white dome. And at the far end of the room, chatter is heard, alongside glowing lights fluttering around in the air alongside puffs of flames—Sasha darts to the light switch, flicking it on and—

"Oh, it's you all," she says, finding four of the magic-born Assembly members approaching *Project Persephone*. She remembers them well, knowing them since they were children.

"Sasha, is that really you?" asks the fae-looking young woman, recognizing her Assembly President, but jarred by her more youthful looks.

"Yes, it's me—ah, my appearance. No point in hiding it any longer. Yes, I have magic," she says, gesturing her arms out, looking down and around her body.

The four young magic soldiers rush in, wrapping their arms around her.

"Oh, thank fuck you're alive," says the fae-looking woman. "But, why are you here? Everything has gone to shit on the surface. Why aren't you doing anything?"

The group backs away from Sasha, longing for answers. Sasha gestures toward the ship and to the Abyssal Root lying on a mechanics bench. And, looking toward the door she came from, she says, "My family and I have been trying to come up with a plan. Do not worry, we have not abandoned you. We've been keeping shelter here, by means of a...well, my husband has magic, too. And my daughter. Magic that would be problematic to let into the hands of the Abyssians."

"Abyssians?"

"The teal-haired ones," Sasha says.

The group exchanges a glance, and the fiery-eyed boy steps forward, saying, "How do you know what they're called? Did you come up with it? Sorry, I respect you, President. You gave us all a home, a purpose. But you're hiding out down here, doing nothing to save everyone suffering above. We sought you in desperation, but here you are building your hobby projects?"

"We are not hiding," Sasha says, glaring at the boy. He takes a step back. "You don't know what we're dealing with. We cannot fight them without a plan. You...weren't there in Shibuya."

Memories spur of the country being cleaved in two, Seth teleporting them here in a split-second decision for survival. His abyssal flames washing over them like a gentle wave, leaving them unharmed—

Sasha's eyes grow wide as her mind goes back further. Going unnoticed by the magic born, the fae-woman says, "Yes. We heard what happened. I've been in contact with the other branches since things went to shit...it sounded like a travesty. And yet you survived! That's remarkable. I couldn't imagine anyone getting out of there alive—"

"Yes, good, so you know," says Sasha. "And you're in contact with the other branches, yes, good."

"Sasha, you okay?"

"Yeah, just remembering something..."

Her mind goes back to her much younger self, to her first visit to the White Abyss. Being led by Adam to the lone garden sitting unnaturally amidst that vast white space. There at the center stood a tree, and tethered to it was a god—the first Abyssian she ever met. *Upon his head lay a crown of thorns piercing his skin, streaking his face with blood, dripping around fleshy holes where his eyes were torn—their skin took the brunt force of Seth's abyssal flames and were unscathed, but Zarathustra was pierced by thorns?*

An epiphany strikes—*the Abyssal Consciousness referred to them as false gods. And we've been told that when Abyssians die, they do not return to The Womb of the One Mind like humans do. Meaning, they don't have souls! Their skin, forged within the Abyss, creates a high resistance to magic, but that skin is like a leather bag—it can be torn, and from the inside they are vulnerable!*

"You all!" Sasha shouts, eyes wide with vigor. "I know what it looks like, hiding away down here, but...have I ever done you wrong?"

The magic-born shake their heads, *no*.

"Do you trust me?"

The fae-looking young woman steps forward and says, "Yes, ma'am." Glancing at the others, they step forward and say in tandem, "Yes, ma'am!"

"Thank you, all of you. Now, listen. The teal-haired monsters destroying our home. They call themselves gods but are anything but. I'll explain everything that led us here, but first, come meet my family. Together, there may be hope yet."

Returning to the door, she knocks thrice, alerting her family. The abyssal glow upon the door shimmers before vanishing. And, twisting the knob, the lips of the magic-born soldiers drop. Agape, at the vast white dome, and the unfamiliar faces therein to greet them.

CHAPTER TWENTY-NINE

Persephone's cheeks flush as sensuous moans spur from the other side of the room. Weary of waking the kids, but could refrain from each other's bodies no longer, Seth and Sasha did what they could to muffle the sounds. But through the conduit of the white dome she erected to secure them, Persephone hears all. Each voice, each secret, each scuff of their sneakers along the floor, reverberates through the white shell. With tension and unease, born from this unintended voyeurism, incubating, waiting to hatch.

A hand lies on her shoulder, jolting her awake. Finding her father smiling below sad eyes, the redness of her cheeks deepens. Whipping her gaze away, she finds her mother, Misha, and four strangers huddled around the kitchen table. Each drinking coffee, staring in awe at their Assembly President's daughter. Flashing their knowing smiles at the girl.

"Persephone, you okay?" asks Seth.

Glaring at him inquisitively, she says, "Yes. And I can continue holding the dome, Dad. You know, in case you don't want to push yourself."

"I'm fine, but thank you—"

"No," she says, staring deeper into his eyes. "I mean, wouldn't want you to overdo it."

Silence washes over them, Seth giving her a dazed look as Persephone considers what her parents were talking about—the Omni Magic and Seth's fear of using it.

Sitting in a meditative position, Seth closes his eyes and says, "I'm fine. It's my turn. Don't go to sleep yet, though, your mother wants to discuss something with you." With a burst of white light from his eyes, Seth's mind drifts away into the ether, through the abyssal framework which holds the world together.

Misha snoring peacefully, a pang of guilt strikes Persephone. Knowing that Misha was kept awake by her parents having sex. Giving her a longing glance, Persephone makes her way toward the kitchen.

"What was that about there?" asks Sasha, leaning against the kitchen counter and sipping a fresh, steaming cup of coffee.

"What was what?" Persephone says, turning her gaze to the magic-born strangers. The girl sucking a lollipop gives a little wave, the fae-woman smiling, the boys stoically glaring.

"That remark about your dad not overdoing it."

"We have visitors," Persephone says.

Sasha frowns.

"Yes, they're—"

"I heard. They're from the Assembly, they're communicating with what's left of the other branches on your behalf."

"Nice to meet you," says the fae-woman.

"You could hear things while you…everything…uh-hmm." Sasha's face flushes, alongside Persephone's.

"I'd rather we didn't talk about it."

"That makes two of us."

Silence washes over them. Gulping down her coffee, Sasha turns to the counter and pours herself some more. Persephone stands rigidly in place as she awaits her mother to— "Ah! Fuck," says Sasha, spilling coffee over the rim of her mug and frantically grabbing at a hand towel and wiping up the mess. Tossing it into the sink, she turns around, sighs, and sips her drink. The magic-born soldiers join in the awkwardness as a confused, unwilling audience.

"Dad said you had something to talk about?"

"Y-yes," Sasha's eyes perk up. "The abyssal drive—Project Persephone's engine—needs a fuel source. I asked your dad if he could assist me, but his powers merely manipulate the Abyss to open portals, but your powers—he said I should have you do it. Your tether to the White Abyss is deeper, intrinsic. I know you're tired, but do you think you could do me this favor?"

"Of course, Mom," says Persephone, yawning.

"Want some coffee?"

"Nah, I'll go to sleep right after."

Nodding, Sasha follows Persephone into the cavern beyond the white dome, toward the ship which shares her name. Curious, the magic-born spring from their seats, leaving their coffees behind.

Sasha glances upward at the towering spacecraft. Her eyes, dark and sunken, sleep having become an infrequent, even foreign thing. But as her tired eyes take in the view of what she's constructed, a wide grin spurs beneath them. *Is this how you felt, Father, when you created the Guild? Brought everyone together as a family, for a common goal? Such pride I feel from this...not how I thought it would come, but here I am regardless.* Glancing at her daughter, Sasha smiles wider, unable to help feeling that she's peering at Persephone through Virdeus's eyes, just as he saw Sasha when she was young and full of potential and ambition. The world laid out before her, unknown and deeply pleasurable for it.

"Where do you want me, Mom?"

"Right over here," says Sasha, gesturing for Persephone to lie upon a table. Resembling the steel surgical table used when giving birth to Persephone, as well as for using Seth's powers to tether the Abyssal Root to the White Abyss. But with new equipment. At the head of the table is a steel band, with sensors dangling from it. More hang from the sides of the table, and the Abyssal Root, recreated in a pitch-black color, sits close by.

Persephone crawls onto the table, positioning herself on her back. All the while taking in the view of the ship, years of her mother's hard work. "It's looking good, Mom. Almost done? Are you sure you're sleeping enough?" she says, as her mother attaches the metal band around Persephone's scalp, suctioning the sensors along her forehead, chest, wrists, and up her arms.

Sasha chuckles and says, "Nope. But that's okay. It must get done."

Persephone scowls at her mother, the words of her father still fresh in memory. "No, Mom. You gotta rest," she says.

"I'll be okay, sweetie," Sasha says, "I promise." Walking over to the Abyssal Root, Sasha begins fiddling with switches on a computer next to it.

Persephone remembers the words of her father: *If given the absolute power of choice, free to do whatever we wish, then yes, each and every choice will hold great weight.*

She sighs, considering his meaning amidst a world besieged by gods. *Isn't inaction, hesitance, also a choice? One that could also hold great weight and cause catastrophic damage? Shouldn't we do everything in our power to fight for the good of all?*

A phantasmagoria of unseen, potential futures cloud his eyes. A haze of white mist, alone there in the depths of Seth's mind.

Deaf, blind, and mute to all around him, he's taken through abyssal channels, hoping to spy upon the hateful gods ravaging the Earth, but finding his sight too preoccupied.

That look in her eyes as she inferred that I may be overdoing it—or was it an implication? Could it be possible she heard my conversation with Sasha? When holding the white dome together, all bodily senses leave him until forced back by Persephone as if he loses himself in the sea of his soul. Adrift there, with the many others drowning within his essence. He hears nothing while in this state, always having to be caught up by Sasha upon his return. No different from his frequent communions with the Abyssal Consciousness, leaving his body upon the cliffside of their now lost home, guarded by Muninn until his return. *And yet, that glimmer of knowledge within her eyes.*

Her powers go deeper within the White Abyss than mine. I suppose it wouldn't be impossible, but could she have heard me? If so, what does that mean?

As he's bombarded with self-inflicted questions, his mind considers one other:

If given the absolute power of choice, free to do whatever we wish, then yes, each and every choice will hold great weight. I had said this to her, to calm her fears, to relinquish some of the burden she never asked for. But was it a sufficient answer? Perhaps it's not enough to claim no fault when the circumstances are out of one's control? We still did what we did. I still did what I...

But so much has changed since that fateful day almost twenty years ago. *I'm not that same man.* He offers himself the same reminder he's repeated every day since the destruction of Magistrum. Though within this abyssal meditation, it dawns on him: *I forgot to specify the importance of what comes after a mistake. For therein lies what determines character, what defines us. Can we learn from our mistakes, can we redefine ourselves, go through a metamorphosis? From monster to savior...*

And how does one go about the saving, how indeed, when things can so quickly go the other way, regardless of intention?

The white haze fades as his nerves settle, his mood swiftly descending into melancholic self-reflection. And he feels the pull of the billions of souls writhing about within his large one, and he wonders what might happen if they break free.

Nil Magic was destructive, with the potential for creation. What of the inverse, then? An Omni Magic that creates, but destroys within that creation's wake?

Lying on the table, watching her mother prime the equipment, lingering questions burst from Persephone's throat:

"Souls come from the White Abyss, right, Mom?" she asks, knowing better than anyone all answers pertaining to that vast white realm. "And magic is derived from the soul. But what quality of the soul determines magic and its quantity? I'd imagine it would be emotion, yes?"

"Yes, that's our understanding of it."

"So that's why you and Dad are so powerful?"

"Well, we had some help from..." Noticing the magic-born observing them, Sasha says, "Well, the Abyssal Consciousness filled you in on all that, didn't it?"

"Yes," says Persephone. "But I'm just wondering because...dad told me anger wasn't a bad thing. It's more about how you use it."

"That's true—"

"Then why is he hesitating?" says Persephone, striking Sasha silent. "Isn't that hypocritical? How can you teach something and not live up to your own standard?"

"Persephone...life is more complicated than that. And your father...you know what he went through. Can you blame him for being careful?"

Thinking back upon the void left in the wake of the Assembly, her powers running amok as she saved herself, her father, and Misha, but no one else. Her eyes flutter away from her mother, as she says, "No. But with things as they are, I don't think we can spare holding back."

"Your father and I have things under control, sweetie. Please try not to worry about it."

Persephone glares at Sasha, watching as her mother's eyes darken above an ever-creasing frown. And, laying her head limp upon the table, a pit opens within her, as vague whispers of the danger to come seep into her mind. Phantasms at once there and not, to be known and not known. Leaving in their wake an unsteadiness of being.

"I'm going to get started now," says Sasha. "At my mark, tap into the White Abyss."

Raising a fist, her other hand firmly placed on the Abyssal Root, Sasha releases her grip and points at Persephone. The girl's eyes burst with abyssal light, and the skin where the sensors are placed glow with that same white sheen. The Abyssal Root's black paint opens into slits at the side, releasing a stark white light. The beams rising sharply out and upward through the black paint appear like shooting stars, streaking through an otherwise pitch-black night.

Rising through the tubes attached to the suction cups is the white glow of the Abyss. Sasha and the magic-born lingering behind, shield their eyes with raised arms as the lights pulse and hum, flowing toward an engine block sitting beside the spacecraft. The hunk of metal glows as the tubes fill an oval-shaped translucent container at its center.

Sweat pools upon Persephone's skin, slight irritation twitching her nose and lips. As the White Abyss is drawn from her like blood into a syringe. But she bears it, no words emerging from her stoic, rigid lips.

"Okay, all done!" Sasha says, plucking the sensors off her daughter and removing the mental band from her head. Helping her up and off the table, they amble toward the Abyssal Drive. There at the center of the engine block swirls a bright white glow, twisting about like a gentle tempest. Sasha's eyes grow wide, unable to peel her gaze from the depths. "I can't believe it. After all this time, it worked! Persephone, thanks so much. You have no idea how much it means to have had your help with this." Embracing her daughter tightly, she kisses her scalp.

"So, what does this accomplish?" asks Persephone.

"Thanks to you, within that container is essentially a mini White Abyss. Theoretically, it will, like you have demonstrated through your power, bend reality around the spacecraft, thus allowing the ship to warp. I lament, though, that with things as they are, there's no time to test it—"

"It'll work," says Persephone, glaring into the Abyssal Drive, eyes set aglow with that same abyssal light. "I can feel it. You're right, it's a tiny White Abyss, that is, like me, tethered to the real thing. It'll work."

Sasha smiles, kisses Persephone once more, and says, "Go on to bed, sweetie. You've earned the rest."

Nodding, Persephone slinks back into the white dome on the other side of the door, creeps past her father, who sees and hears nothing, with beads of sweat dripping from his forehead. Persephone frowns but turns away.

Crawling into bed, Misha moans lightly as she notices Persephone's presence. Reaching behind her, she grabs Persephone's hand and places it under her shirt and upon her chest. The sounds of her parents having sex still fresh in her mind, entering through the conduit of the White Abyss, Persephone finds herself unwilling to engage in affection. But the ticking of the clock announces the many dozens of minutes passing by, each without the return of Sasha or the magic-born. Still, they lay in the presence of no one but her father, blinded by his meditative state. And—her eyes aglow with abyssal light—she turns, placing a palm against the warmth of Misha's chest before trickling down and into her pants.

As Persephone disappears into the other room, Sasha's stare remains tethered to the miniature White Abyss held within the Abyssal Drive's translucent core. Merely the essence of the vast white realm. Yet for all intents and purposes, the result is the same. And she created it. Before her floats the soul of the world, the nucleus of all that exists or could exist. Twisting gently like a dancing white flame, its depths pull Sasha closer. Not in a matter of distance, but in a marriage of souls. Its tide, irresistible like the hormones enrapturing one at the moment vows are given, the locking of lips, the cheer from the audience as two lovers bridge the gap and become one...or the mingling of flesh, the enveloping of another's body, penetrating their corporeal forms in a haze of life's greatest desire, in a moment when all things feel possible—as life begats itself into being, exploding forth into an era of beautiful, chaotic, infinite potential.

Sasha's eyebrows slowly rise, a hypothesis striking her. The magic-born soldiers watch in silent curiosity as Sasha begins circling the Abyssal Drive. Eyes tethered still to that swirling bright white.

Memory of glancing into Seth's eyes for the first time spring forth. Twenty years ago, and with a body grotesque and not his own. She noticed it then.

Magic is born from the soul, housed within the confines of our flesh. Limited only by one's imagination, their mental strength and fortitude...the soul is much like this swirling portion of the White Abyss, held within this jar and pulling me much like I was when peering into his eyes...that first time and forever. This glass container is necessary, for if it were to shatter, it would devour us all, like a black hole.

It happened once, at Magistrum—plaguing Seth all these years later. Again, when in the wake of pain our daughter tore a hole into the fabric of the world, devouring our cabin. A sign of things to come—and of course it happened once more at the Assembly.

Time and time again, magic erupts too fiercely. Tearing through everything with as much ease as a black hole. Safely confined within its basking glow—its event horizon, where beyond lay the singularity, a potential for infinite possibilities. Perhaps our bodies are the same. Event horizons housing the singularities of our souls. Magic does what the mind wills it to do, as our late friend Melphis had said, and this implies that there is nothing magic cannot do, if one can imagine it. Art upon a canvas, limited only by the artist's imagination. And the Abyssal Consciousness—I wonder how it feels about me capturing a facet of the White Abyss within this glass container. It called Persephone a True-Born God. And as Seth relayed back to me after their final communion, it had claimed she holds the potential for bountiful creation and utter destruction. Almost as if she, herself, is a black hole, ready to make infinite possibilities emerge as soon as her magic breaches her event horizon.

And here I hold a piece of her infinite potential, safely within this glass container. Ready to make all things possible for the good of humankind.

"Sasha, are you alright?" asks the fae-looking woman.

Whipping her head around, she finds the worried countenances of the magic-born when she realizes she hasn't blinked this whole time. Fluttering her eyes open and shut, nuzzling her knuckles against them, she says, "Yes, I'm fine. Just considering..." She thinks about her daughter lying on the steel table, eyes aglow as the White Abyss was siphoned from her. "I was just thinking about how much humanity is capable of, just how far we could still go, how soon we could get there...and if we ever will, amongst the state of things." Gesturing upward, Sasha sighs.

Frowns plaster upon the faces of the magic-born, as the group turns to the fae-woman. Resting a hand on Sasha's shoulder, she says, "We'll be okay. You said you had a plan, right?"

Sasha meets her gaze, resisting the compulsion to glance away. Raising her shoulders from their slump, Sasha says, "Yes, of course, we will. Just need to prepare a bit." Turning her attention back to the Abyssal Drive, her gaze is pulled toward its depths once more.

What am I doing, lamenting in front of them when they need a leader...and besides—she smiles widely—*to think the White Abyss could be pulled into our world...if we can do this, then what can't we do?*

Another thought strikes her as she ponders the nature of Seth's powers. *Never like this, but doesn't he also essentially pull the White Abyss into our world when igniting those white flames? Opening portals? And yet he insisted on my using Persephone. I wonder, is it truly because her powers go deeper, or is it because he's worried about what might happen if he were to dig deeper into the White Abyss? By making use of that Omni Magic within him—billions of souls—he's right to be nervous. For what would happen if they were to spill out into the world...would the Earth simply cave in upon itself? Like a black hole...*

Her copper-colored eyes gradually lighten until becoming stark white, pulsing for a moment alongside the abyssal glimmer of her ring.

The light fades, her eyes returning to their fiery-brown color. Unaware of the white glow lying in wait within her, Sasha resists the urge to slip further into lamentations. Turning toward the magic-born, she says, "Help me install this, would you?" and gestures at the Abyssal Drive. As they lift the heavy machinery toward the ship, Sasha considers the gravity of their situation...*whether bountiful creation or utter destruction...I must have the strength to do what needs to be done.*

CHAPTER THIRTY

Decay swiftens. Leaves shrivel and brown. Dry, golden grass sways gently in the cool, late October breeze. The season's lower light hastily brings each day to its end. And amidst the autumnal hues of nature, town after town on both sides of the Hudson River have been set ablaze by the Abyssians.

Near and far, stretching out to the horizon, teal strands of light zip all around him as the Abyssian War Chief flies through the Hudson Valley. Convinced that Zarathustra must be near. Zipping along the edge of the river, the warmongering god rockets past the blazing city of Kingston, past many smaller towns, and over the much larger fire eating away at the Albany cityscape. And watching as his kin devours the humans, gobbling down soul as well as body.

I don't understand it. At first, nothing, but the more time passes, the greater the sensation is—a brief moment, after a certain interval, as if a light switch turned off and on, there it is—I feel a sliver of his power as it pulses, then disappears again. Somewhere here along this stretch of mountains.

The fire surges beneath him, spreading from each town and city into the neighboring fields and stretching further into the mountains. Swiftly erupting into wildfires, aiming to set the entirety of New York and the world ablaze—

Something pulses from the forests and farmland, sporadically in the surrounding areas and beyond. *What was that? Zarathustra at last?* He whips his gaze around, trying to pinpoint the source. But the land coverage too vast, he simply seethes with irritation as vibrations ripple and tear through the mountains, the trees and their leaves.

Somewhere below the Abyssian, a quiet farmstead sits safely miles away from the nearest town. A grayed old man in overalls and a plain white shirt sits in his living room, hands in prayer, a bright red baseball cap resting on the arm of his lounge chair. Joining him around a table, on a nearby couch, is a pastor, two women, and three other men. A lit candle sways gently upon the table, next to an open Bible.

As the bible study hangs their heads in prayer, the pastor mumbles, "My *Lord*, my *God,* deliver us from these hardships, these trying times. These devils at our backs, destroying this beautiful Earth you created, we can only assume this is the rapture..."

A world plunged into chaos, but lacking the rivers of blood, the darkening of the sun and moon...the four horsemen, the dragon, and the beast. But appearing as the biblical apocalypse, nonetheless, to the pastor's mind, all contradictions and inconsistencies lost on him and his ilk. The destruction and death around them cherry-picked, or assumed to be the very same rapture they were taught to expect by generations of lies.

"And so, my *God* in Heaven, I ask that you watch over us, and in your own time and infinite wisdom, bring us home—"

Vibrations shake the foundation of the old farmhouse, shattering the windows, toppling the bible study onto the floor. The front door bursts from its frame.

"Ah, the earthquakes! Do you see, my brothers and sisters?" continues the pastor. "Revelations spoke of earthquakes! The rapture truly begins! Our God will now call us ho—"

The pastor's blue eyes glaze over, dulled by a hazy gold sheen. The men and women around him slink into their seats, heads craned upward, as their eyes do the same. "Make God Great Again," the pastor mutters, as he rises from the couch. "Make God Great Again," the others mimic, as the farmer in the lounge chair stands, gripping his bright red baseball cap. Placing it firmly upon his head with the stoic rigidness of a seasoned soldier, the farmer walks toward the door, broken free of its hinges. Reaching for a rifle mounted to a wall, the farmer cocks the gun and heads outside. The others follow, marching like Romans as they chant:

"Make God Great Again. Make God Great Again. Make God Great Again. *Make God Great Again—*"

Eyes aglow with abyssal light, Persephone gasps as her heart *thumps* in her chest. Resonating with the world beyond, her hands shake, heart palpitating, a mixture of hatred, fear, and anger rises within her. Breathing labors, her chest rising and descending rapidly, abyssal power erupting from her eyes, she screams.

"Persephone!" her parents shout, rushing to her side, rousing her as if from sleep. The abyssal energy dissipates as the white dome surrounding them shatters, bursting into a mess of blinding, refracting light. Her parents, Misha, and the four magic-born soldiers huddled together in the kitchen, shielding their eyes with their arms until the light fades, and the shattered dome falls gently like ash.

The young woman collapses into her father's embrace, still heaving from that sensation overtaking her, as she says, "U-p t-there. Up on the surface—something isn't right."

The air grows thick with ash as statewide smoke plumes stretch overhead. The world obscured as smoke fills every open space. Firemen are nowhere to be seen. The inferno rages on unabating, unthwarted, with authorities the first to be devoured. With the world turned to brimstone and ash, the streets of cities are lousy with smog. Those with bountiful parks made all the worse.

The streets of New York City driven to chaos, dozens of cars smash into one another, trucks overturned, blown to pieces, tumbled over by skyscrapers, no movement stirs upon the streets except the occasional sounds of stomping feet.

Twilight descends into deep night. Leaving the city awash in darkness, with only the blazing glow of fire to illuminate the streets.

Weaving their way around buildings, a family—a father, mother, two sons, and infant daughter, head toward the Bronx. Intending to eventually reach the countryside upstate, they hope to find even a cave to find shelter in. Anything, to hide from the monsters razing their city to the ground. Taking advantage of the smoke, they remain obscured as they make their way north, clinging to the west side. Not quite near the open space near the Hudson, but as far away as possible from the flames devouring Central Park.

"Hide within the destruction they created, avoid light at all costs," the father had said, handing cloth masks to his wife and sons. Wanting to put a mask on the infant but fearing the child would cry if her mouth was obstructed, the mother decided to clutch their daughter's face to her chest instead. The father had glanced worriedly at them, anxious that this wouldn't be enough to save them from the fumes. But it's all they had.

Crossing a street at the corner of a block, the man stops abruptly, ducks low, hiding his family behind his arms as a teal streak flies past, heading toward Central Park. The Abyssian's long teal hair fluttering wildly as a gust of wind bellows against the family. Sweat drips from the father's forehead as he steadies his labored breath and continues onward.

Fire glimmers unnaturally along the block ahead, bouncing up and down steadily with each other, rising and lowering in tandem like Nazis saluting during a march. The man turns, raising his left pointer finger to his mask, a muffled "shh" is heard beyond as he gestures for his family to turn the other way.

"You there!" shouts a male voice, seemingly from one of the bouncing flames, now held steadily in place.

Ignoring the voice, the family keeps moving and—more bouncing flames block their path, coming closer until illuminating a wrinkled old woman wearing a bright red cap. Torch in her left hand, pistol in her right. Glancing around nervously, the family finds themselves cornered, with torches and red caps and guns swarming from all sides.

"I said, you there!" says the male voice, emerging as a middle-aged man in a bright red cap and black biker's jacket over a bright red shirt with the words *MAKE GOD GREAT AGAIN* printed upon it. "Hello, friend. Canst we acks you sum questions?" the man says, with a calm tone that clashes with the sudden appearance of an army of rednecks.

"We don't want any trouble," says the man shielding his family.

"Do youse have belief in God, our heavenly Father?"

The man shielding his family glances around with a baffled gaze. "The world is on fire. And you're evangelizing? We had to watch my sister, my children's aunt, get devoured by those monsters!" he shouts, pointing toward the tempestuous flames rising from Central Park, and the teal blurs zipping around it like flies to a mound of excrement. "We are just trying to head north to find shelter. We don't have time for your questions."

"I only acksing if God is in your heart," the red-cap wearing man says, a grin opening beneath dull eyes, faded over in a haze of gold. The smoke too thick, the man shielding his family just now notices that unnatural hue in not just the one man's eyes, but the entire army. Stepping closer to his family, he says, "U-uh, y-es, I love God. We go to church...every Sunday, right everyone?" he asks his family.

"Then whys you wearing that mask fer? The rapture is here! Youse should be breathing in the glory of God during this moment! For it is the last time youse be breathing any air at all before being taken home!" says the red-cap wearing man, opening his arms as if to be embracing the destruction around him, breathing in a lungful of smoke. "Youse know what I's think? Youse be a liar...and will never make it into the kingdom of Heaven."

Dropping his arms, the man's smile crumbles into a frown and—gunshots blare loudly in the father's ears—vision blurring as he grips the side of his head. Three dull thuds are heard behind him. Turning around, he—clasping his hands over his mask, tears fill his eyes as he collapses toward the bodies of his family. Their corpses mangled by bullets, his infant baby girl still swaddled within his wife's arms...but with the infant's face blown inward. Hollowed out by the sight of them, he feels cold steel against the back of his head.

"In service of our God in Heaven, and like our brothers and sisters in all the cities of the world, we aim to make Him great again. And by our wills, it will be done," says the red-cap wearing man, in a speech pattern not his own, as the eyes of each within this cult deepen in gold, their blinding shimmer pulsing like heartbeats, as he says, "Amen."

Chunks of flesh are scattered upon the family as their father slumps forward. Their bodies glowing teal, their souls eject, springing upward into the sky, heading north, off to somewhere unknown.

Weeks earlier.

Waves crash onto the sandy shores of New Jersey, with signs upon the boardwalk stating *Ocean Grove*. A beach with a long history of catering to a Christian population, with a large church in the inland township of Neptune. A stark contrast to Asbury Park to the north. Both of which have been brought to common ground through the fire and destruction brought on by the Abyssians.

And upon this empty beach, heavy footsteps crease into the wet sand. Along with gargling, wet asphyxiation.

Rising from the water, his small boat upturned and sinking further out, a young man trudges toward dry land. Choking as he coughs up seawater, seaweed, and specks of sand and shells—toppling over, the high tide sinking his hands and knees beneath the water once more—the last of the water ejects from his mouth. Pulling himself to dry sand, he flips onto his back. Heaving through lips melted and charred, barely any skin covering his jawbone. The melted scarring continues up half his face, his golden locks burnt away on one side. Leaving scarred tissue and a mound of skin no longer resembling an ear. And, as he steadies his breath, he glances upward, taking in an upside-down view of the flames rising from the town.

Mouth stretching into a smile, he flashes his crimson-stained teeth.

CHAPTER THIRTY-ONE

"Persephone!" her parents shout, rushing to her side, rousing her as if from a deep sleep. The abyssal energy dissipates as the white dome surrounding them shatters, bursting into a mess of blinding, refracting light. Her parents, Misha, and the four magic-born soldiers shield their eyes with their arms until the light fades and the shattered dome falls gently like ash.

The young woman collapses into her father's embrace, still heaving from that sensation overtaking her, as she says, "U-p t-there. Up on the surface—something isn't right."

Seth's eyes overflow with abyssal light as he glances upward. Panning his sight, he says, "No good. With the white dome shattered, I can't see what's happening on the surface." He turns to Sasha, his pupils resurfacing as the abyssal flames fade away. "Which also means they can sense us."

Sasha's eyes grow wide, glancing from Seth to Persephone to Misha, then to the four magic-born soldiers. "You four!" she shouts. "The others you left in waiting. Contact them. Make sure they're alright, and if so, have them rendezvous with us.

The Abyssians are coming, and we *cannot* let them find this place."

"Where should I tell them to go?" asks the fae-looking woman.

"Here—wait, no. Seth?" says Sasha.

Seth's eyes stare straight ahead, unblinking, sifting through a barrage of thoughts. "I can open a portal to anywhere. I suppose it doesn't matter where, so long as we lead the Abyssians away from here."

"Where exactly are the others hiding out?" Sasha asks, jerking her attention to the magic-born.

"Not far—they're here in Crowley. Last I heard, they had moved to the riverfront due to the forest fires. They're panicked—now out in the open."

"Good," says Sasha. "Tell them we'll be there shortly. Now, I have an idea to buy us some time, and an idea as to how to fight back. But first, Seth, Persephone, Misha, come here."

Reaching for her belt, she unsheathes a dagger from her waist. "Persephone," she says, "The method you used with the dome to cancel out our magical frequencies, can you apply it to the blade?"

The young woman stares at the light glinting along the edge of the dagger. "Yeah, sure, but why?"

"I need you to trust me."

Exhaling deeply, Persephone's eyes glow with abyssal power. Reaching toward the blade, she strokes her index and middle fingers along the steel—a pulse hums as white light is simultaneously pulled toward the blade and refracted away, creating a shimmering aura around it. Sasha gestures to Seth to sit at the kitchen table, as she positions the blade's point at his neck. "Are you going to…" Seth begins, but sees the fierce concentration of Sasha's wide eyes, the sweat spilling down her forehead. "Take a picture! Somebody! The scar on my neck!"

Misha swiftly yanks her phone from her pocket and snaps a shot of Sasha's scar. Faded from the years, but visible enough to see its shape. Holding the picture in front of Sasha and next to Seth's neck, Sasha balances the knife's point above his skin as her eyes dart to and from the picture.

"Do you trust me?" Sasha says.

Seth smiles and says, "Always."

The tip tears into his skin, deep enough to cause scarring. He winces, but bears it, as the blade's edge slices down and along his skin. Holding the knife with both hands to steady her trembling fingers, she slowly forms the shape of the rune. The white dome shattered, there's nothing to impede the cold autumnal air from squeezing through from the cavern. And yet it's not enough to cool her sizzling skin. Pellets of sweat plop against the floor, drenching her hair, stinging her eyes, and—

A white glow shines from the rune, healing immediately. Seth wipes away the blood with his left hand, glances toward Sasha, and says, "This brings me back."

Sasha returns his smile as she says, "Alright, now Persephone, Misha, then the rest of you. Come on, chop-chop!"

One by one, she carved the rune. With each, the memory of carving it into Seth and Melphis twenty years ago becomes fresher, clearer, until everyone has a rune. The magic-born soldiers, as well as Persephone and Misha, erupt in clamor, wondering what all this is about. "Hush now, there's no time!" Sasha shouts. "The Abyssians move fast, we've already been here too long!" Leading the charge, the safe house's door swings open as they enter the cavern. Marching forward and around the towering spacecraft, Sasha's palms crackle with teal magic as she places them onto the wall beside the elevator. The wall loses its solid form, becoming liquid, as the stone and dirt are parted, creating an opening to a rocky stairway beyond.

Rushing up the steps, Persephone shouts, "Why doesn't Dad just create a portal!"

"Persephone. Quiet." Sasha whispers. "If he did that, they would find us regardless of the rune. My magic was less risky. We can't all fit in the elevator, and we need to get out of here fast. But when we get to the surface, do not use magic, do not speak, do not even move."

As they approach the top of the steps, they scrunch their eyes at the sun's offensive rays. And, breaking out onto the surface, they feel crisp autumn air upon their skin, and the weight of burnt air filling their lungs as an orange glow envelops them. The town of Crowley and the surrounding forests set ablaze.

Seth rubs the back of his neck at the sight of the fire, as memories of his old life filter through the black smoke, a viper constricting their throats.

Teal sparks crackle from Sasha's left palm, closing the hole in the ground. A brighter teal catches their attention as it rockets toward them like a comet. Persephone steps forward, hands tightening into a fist, but Sasha steps in front of her, arm raised, glaring as she shakes her head, *no*.

The Abyssian halts, bringing a massive gust of wind with it. Pushing the group back, their hair caught in the tempest. The updraft assaults the surrounding flames, causing them to flutter and flap, descending in size before growing larger, hotter.

"It was right here," says the bellowing Abyssian's voice. His long teal hair and beard glowing bright with power after a feast of souls. Seth's eyes grow wide as he recognizes him. The Abyssian with the impossible speed, who led the assault on Tokyo and blew the country to pieces. With a scowl and fierce eyes, the Abyssian War Chief glances around and says, "I know I felt it. Zarathustra! Cease your cowardice and face me!"

Seth and Sasha gesture to the others to remain still and quiet, and as the Abyssian glances around, "There's something here."

As his eyes land on Seth and Sasha, warmth makes the Abyssian scrunch his eyes and shake his head. His vision blurring, his head throbbing. "There's something here, but perhaps I need to look harder...after a feast."

Another gust of wind bellows as the god zips away. Seth and Sasha let out heavy sighs, and Persephone says, "What the fuck just happened?"

"These runes," her mother says. "They will hide us, but only so long as you don't pull their attention."

"Seemed to work better than the old rune," says Seth. "Before, we'd be seen as what is most comfortable to a person, but Persephone's powers fooled him completely. This will surely help..."

"Yes, as will our next move. Come on, everyone, to the riverfront."

As the group marches toward the shore, something peculiar catches Seth's attention. The entire mountain near Crowley is on fire, one massive red glow below a colossal smoke plume...except for at the summit. Smaller plumes rise steadily from the cliffside where the remains of their cabin lie, but it seems the circumference of the mountaintop was spared, or extinguished. Eyes scrunched, brow furrowed, he—

"Dad, come on!" Persephone yells after him as he finds himself left behind. Catching her concerned, but knife-edged glare, Seth runs after them, rejoining Sasha's side.

CHAPTER THIRTY-TWO

The tide softly crashes into the rocky shore, pushed along by heavy gusts. Dark gray clouds crawl along in tandem with the waves. Their speed steadily rising, erupting into occasional torrents of wind bellowing between the sky and the river. The last of autumn's browning leaves torn from the trees, fluttering through the air and tumbling along the ground. Leaving behind skeletal frames with white, runic symbols carved into their bark. Untouched by the flames devouring the mountain's forest. The summit's ridge and the low riverside park juxtaposed with sheer height, but also in death. And as the crisp December air drifts along the Hudson River, those ravenous flames grow larger, more ferocious.

But so does the vibrancy of those hiding along the river's edge, as the clashing of steel echoes through the wind. The Assembly rejoined, sprawled along the wide grassy field are the magic-born parrying the blades of swords and spears, as they practice their combat forms throughout their faux-duels. A few dozen magic-born, all with white runes carved into their necks. And amidst the sounds of their hearty sportsmanship, Sasha smiles below teary eyes.

Standing beneath a birch tree, she and Seth hover over a forge. Teal magic crackles down her arms, amassing into her palms, before releasing outward upon the anvil. Molding itself into the shape of a sword, a sizzle is heard alongside bellowing white flames. Spiraling down Seth's arms and out upon the forge, the married couple joins their magic in union, eyes aglow throughout this intercourse. And as the blade forms before them, Sasha loses herself in thought:

That sound—blades clashing, lungs heaving, mouths grunting. And not through a battle born from hatred, but through sportsmanship among those readying to fight alongside each other in battle. Companionship, union, a family. Oh, how I've missed this. Father, it's almost like your family has returned. Preparing together, as the Guild always had back then. This wasn't how I planned to get here, but...it's like coming home again.

"You okay?" asks Seth.

The teal and white light rapidly cooling, it bursts outward—a glimmer of teal and white ash is strewn into the sky, dancing in the air as it falls upon the sparring magic-born behind them. Sasha sighs, nuzzling the tears from her eyes, and says, "Yeah, I'm just so happy." Dropping her hands, she glances over her shoulder.

Seth stares at her copper-colored eyes, glimmering brightly through the tears. The skin around them wrinkles once more, the hair framing her face streaked with grays. His mouth collapses into a deep frown. There's so much he wants to say, to tell her, warn her, but knowing full well the war to come, and the consequences that lay within the wake of quarreling gods, Seth lunges his arms around her, gripping tight. Right arm around her back, left cupping her head, he pulls her close as she wraps around him as well. Holding each other with a ferocity, a grip so strong and unwilling to let go, tethered so firmly, Seth's eyes wet with tears as he says, "No matter what's to come, I'm happy to be going through it with you. No matter what's to come, you are my love, my everything, you are the flame in my veins imploring me to go on living, no matter what."

Her arms around his shoulders, Sasha eyes her engagement ring. The teal and white magic swirling together within the gemstone, a marriage of life and death. Her tears flow heavier, a wide smile enrapturing her. "I love you, too."

A flurry of leaves swarms them, the warmth of each other surviving the harsh near-winter cold. Deaf to all around them, even to the loud swooshing of strong gusts beating against their unwavering bodies. Sasha's hair flaps wildly as the wind passes through, Seth's beard sways gently like the river's tide—and with such vigor, such life held within these gales. The warmth spurred on by necessity as the air chills their skin. Autumn is most deceitful in its form, with its flora withering, browning, falling dead to the ground. Yet it's also autumn which brings the greatest of harvests—the sweet fruits, hearty yams and potatoes, along with leafy greens. Even autumn's decay, its moldering leaves creating the sweet, minty taste of the season's crisp air...despite all that is dying around them, the air is thick with the qualities of life. A reminder, perhaps, as everyone gorges themselves on autumn's bounty, that after the steep decline into winter's chilling grip is a spring where all things sprout anew. And in each other's arms, Seth and Sasha feel the weight of that life, that hope, here amidst the company of all who will fight for that fresh new spring. A world that has no need for gods, a world where joy is abundant and where hope—

The wind comes to an abrupt stop, and the reddish-brown leaves drop to the ground. No more to follow in their wake. Their descent finished, replacing them are large flakes of snow, the raging fire stretching across Crowley and its mountains glimmering so bright upon the icy precipitation, one can almost feel the burn.

A gust of wind, harsher than before, severs Seth from Sasha as they cover their faces with their arms. The snow falls rapidly, clumping to the ground. Reaching out for each other, they interweave their fingers. Holding her firm, Seth says, "This is going to make matters more difficult. The Abyssians' stark white skin...they'll blend in, if the storm gets bad enough."

"Their hair glows so brightly, though," says Sasha. "So, we'll spot them...though their light against the snow may blind us still."

"Misha and the other fire wielders can do what they can to melt the snow, but—"

Light footsteps approach from behind. Glancing at them, they find Persephone's weary eyes staring back. "How's it going over here?" she asks, noticing her mother's worsening condition, her wrinkled skin and graying hair.

"Almost complete. In fact, here's your weapon," says Sasha, handing her daughter a thin but long blade. It's hilt, white and speckled with teal gems. "A lightweight sword. It'll be easy to swing, especially when wielding your abyssal powers, since sometimes it throws you off balance and—"

"I'll be fine, Mom. Thank you for all the work you're doing. Just a weapon left for Misha then?"

"Yes, and you can tell her it'll be her father's weapon of choice—one he was quite skilled with."

Persephone nods and ambles away.

"Persephone," says Seth. "When we go to battle with the Abyssians, try not to use too much of your power. You don't know these creatures...if they catch wind of what you can do, they—"

"I don't think we should be hesitating, Dad. Our world is being brought to ruin. We have to do all we can to eradicate these monsters." With a sharp glare, she turns away and leaves. Seth's eyes drop to the ground.

She's looking down on me...and I couldn't be prouder. Oh, my Persephone...you are so much stronger than your dad. I wallowed for years—even after all my hard work, I wallowed over what I had done at Magistrum. It has infected so much of my life...I love Sasha, more than anything—she is my entire heart. But two things can be true. Part of me views my role in our marriage as trying to make up for what I've done through protection and support of her and our daughter. This self-enforced obligation sullies the very foundation of our love, makes me feel hollow inside...sometimes. As if the Nil Magic is creeping back to the forefront of my mind, erasing decades worth of self-discipline and—

Sasha hugs him from behind and says, "I know that look. Come on, don't do that. You have worked so hard, you can control it, you're okay. I love you. And I know what you're thinking, but she doesn't realize the full extent of the stakes. It's one thing for the Abyssal Consciousness to have shown her visions of the past, but it's another to have been there, to have felt it all as you and I have felt it all. She cannot know why you're hesitating, and so she cannot empathize."

Placing his hand on hers, above his stomach, Seth says, "It's not only that...fatherhood is a tricky thing. You'd think after so long, we'd become used to being parents. But it's hard. I'm so proud of her for taking responsibility for what she did, by presenting herself so strongly, ready to take on what is to come...and to make the world a better place for it. She wallowed for a time, but it was brief, unlike how things were for me. So, I'm proud of her, so fucking proud, but angry, too, ashamed even, that I feel so worthless. Yes, as her father, I want her to be strong, but I'm conflicted. What if I can't do more? What if I can't protect her? What if she doesn't need me to?"

"Then you've done your job. And while I understand your hesitance to use the full extent of your powers, she's also not wrong. Everything is on the line here, so you must ask yourself—when it comes to it, can you have the will to unleash your power onto our enemies…or will you falter?"

Seth nods in silence as he watches Persephone disappear into the crowd of their small army, and into a snowstorm growing heavier by the second. And in this ever-deepening white haze, the world vanishes before his eyes.

CHAPTER THIRTY-THREE

Streaks of teal light zip through the heavy snowfall. The storm severe, obscuring the senses of lesser creatures, impeding vision, and muffling all sound within its deep white blanket. Made worse still by the fall of night. The flames devour the town of Crowley, but the nearby mountains have extinguished themselves, with nothing left to burn through. Yet the Abyssian gods dart around this town, covered in embers, ash, and snow, as if they are all-seeing. In a world full of magic-born humans, the pulse of their souls is far too easy to sense for the gods who were born from that very same vat of creative potential.

And on today, December 25th, a day secularized after the Supernatural Holocaust but celebrated still, the gods rightfully descend upon Earth in its final moments, and they—

A shadow springs from a rooftop, toward the teal glow of an Abyssian man flying by. Long black hair flaps behind as the shadow falls. Rising almost like wings is the hem of a long, black coat as air pools beneath her. "Huh, what?" The Abyssian man shouts, as the shadow grips his short teal hair. "Where did you—argh—"

A dagger slices through his nape—the Abyssian and his assailant hurtle downward. The god lets out a curdling gasp as his chest hits the ground. Padded only slightly by the snow. Pressing her knee against the god's back, Sasha places more weight upon the dagger with both hands, as teal sparks crackle down her arms and into the shimmering white blade—the Abyssian screeches as his body convulses—leaves and twigs and stones, glass and plastic and steel rods rupture his skin as the great Abyssian squeals in fear like a child. And above him is Sasha's furious gaze. Pumping her creative magic into the grotesque creature, the images of each object she creates rapidly flashing through her mind as they meld with its flesh, more and more as the god's body rips and tears, a leathery white balloon expanding beyond its—a splattering of white liquid meshes invisibly with the surrounding snow and slathers across Sasha's face. Grimacing, she wipes the white blood away with the back of her hand.

Standing, she glances down at the Abyssian's corpse. A mangled torso with arms, legs, and head burst outward. Dismembered from within. No organs, just white goop dripping from the wounds.

It worked.

Sasha pans left to right, knowing full well what's coming next. The white rune upon her neck fades into nothing more than a scar, as a dozen teal lights streak their way toward her.

A group of Abyssians, their bare feet in the snow, stand at the center of what was a traffic circle. With buildings collapsed, turned to ash, and snowed upon thereafter...civilization has not existed since the arrival of these teal-haired gods. Surviving being the only goal, there's no one left to care about maintaining infrastructure. Not now, with the world set askew, adrift in nightmarish barbarism.

Glancing all around, the gods sigh.

"What is it with this place that consumes him so? We've scoured the land, this paltry village, its mountains, the surrounding area...to no avail!" says a male with wavy, shoulder-length hair. Glowing bright within this snowy night, the teal glimmering upon the snow. "He is mistaken. Zarathustra does not hide here."

"Do not doubt our war chief," says a female, short but muscular, hair tight and cropped close to the scalp. "He is the eldest and wisest of us. If he says Zarathustra is here, then Zarathustra is here."

"Indeed," says another from behind. "His senses are sharper than ours, more attune to traces of magic for being a priest before he became our leader...or a different kind of leader."

The male with wavy hair grunts. Turning his attention skyward as a slim, feminine male swoops toward them. Clutched within his right hand is the neck of a man in his early thirties with a scruffy chin—his beard growing inefficiently in patches. Above his crazed eyes is a bright red hat.

"Any news?" asks the female to the newly arrived Abyssian, ignoring the human writhing within his grasp.

"Yes, I am ready! *I am ready to be brought home. Liberate—liberate me from this earthly realm and send me home to make my god great again!*

"Not of Zarathustra," says the feminine male, replying to his fellow Abyssian, but glaring at the human. "The stray god is nowhere to be seen."

"What's that you got there then?"

Pulling both shoulders, the human's flesh tears at the neck. Blood sprays and innards spread like melted cheese, yanked apart with ease. The man's soul ejects, twisting and turning skyward, slithering away from the Abyssians, and fading as it nears the mountaintop.

"You dare let a soul escape?" says the wavy-haired male.

"Try it for yourself. The ones with these ugly red hats. Take a bite or eat them whole, somehow the souls all escape. Ejecting away with haste, as I demonstrated here. Something is amiss. Wherever Zarathustra is, he's plotting, pulling the strings from somewhere...our leader won't be happy."

The female steps forward and says, "If I didn't see it myself, I'd wager you a liar. In all the dimensions we have feasted upon, nothing so strange has ever occurred. We must be on guard, something about Zarathustra's little world isn't quite right—"

A pulse surges through the air—two of them. The sudden appearance of not just magic, but creation magic, as well as the screams of one of their kin. The Abyssians turn in tandem toward the direction of the river.

Their eyes aglow with furious teal.

Faith is a powerful thing. Abstract, intangible, arguably not there. And yet, in the placing of belief in something or oneself, it can suddenly bestow upon a thing or person great strength and perseverance. Through faith, a person, a thing, an idea becomes unwavering, eternal. And for that reason, one must be mindful of where they place their faith, for if placed upon a god it will inevitably come to hold fascist, authoritarian control over the world.

This was something taught to Seth long ago, amidst that vast white realm, by a stray god resembling the parasites now razing the earth, devouring humankind. That god of creation, Zarathustra. In his final moments, he revealed to Seth the greatest of truths—that all things are possible to one who believes they can. That the limits of a painter's ability lie within their own imagination, that their canvas is their own to fill with beautiful colors. And, hiding within the darkening of night along with the other shadows lying in wait, Seth ponders that god's words:

Seth, imagine if the collective human species retracted their faith in gods. Imagine if they redirected that same unwavering, intense faith—one that creates the very gods they seek help from—back into themselves? Would gods descend into obscurity? Would humanity rise into greater progression? This is the questioning that led me to create the Earth and the White Abyss. I will not live to see the answer, but you and Sasha are fit to lead humanity forward. To a greater, truer strength. A human strength that has no need for gods.

Watching from an unseen place, Seth wonders, *Will I even live to see the answer? We have made progress, yes, but is it enough? One True-Born God—Persephone—this wasn't what Zarathustra had in mind. He wanted us all to ascend, to exist above gods. Yet here we are, on the cusp of a battle which will determine the fate of all things. Yet despite our triumphs, humanity is a process of incremental growth that takes eons to achieve.*

Zarathustra, would you be ashamed of me for letting my faith waver? I know I am an incarnation of your wrath, but I am still only, merely human. Humanity has only had magic for less than twenty years. That is nothing. And it was good, for a time, but all the destruction! The jealousy felt by Sergei as he attempted to overthrow Sasha, having to live through the terror of Yahweh after her sins were reborn, my own daughter annihilating the Assembly, and now this...dealing with your kin. I don't know, Zarathustra. Perhaps we would be better off if magic never existed.

Sasha leaps from a rooftop, plummeting an Abyssian to the ground, her knife lodged in its neck. Channeling her power into its body, the god bursts into a white goo. Seth's eyes perk up at the sight of his wife's triumph, and a glimmer of hope returns. But something stirs in the back of his mind, an unease crawling its way forward. A whispered phrase, not spoken but planted within him. He hasn't spoken to the Abyssal Consciousness since before Damien's assault on Tokyo. And yet these words tinge with its voice, its presence:

A LONG, BRIGHT DARK.

The words echo within his mind as his worries are validated. It may be too soon for Zarathustra's vision to bear fruit.

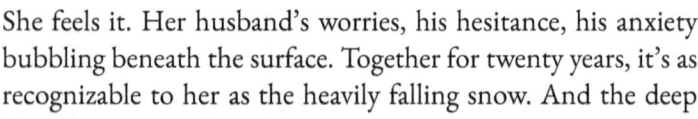

She feels it. Her husband's worries, his hesitance, his anxiety bubbling beneath the surface. Together for twenty years, it's as recognizable to her as the heavily falling snow. And the deep bloodlust approaching her.

Seth may be bogged down with concern for the future, leaving his faith imbalanced, but Sasha stares onward, with a deep scowl and fierce eyes. Their copper color mingling with sparks of teal. She clenches her fists.

The large group of Abyssians rocket toward her, their eyes glowing, mouths unhinging, sharp teeth glinting alongside the snow. A tall male with wavy, shoulder-length hair, leading the charge. Hunger spurring him forth—a gust of wind bellows against Sasha as the gods abruptly halt. The male standing a few feet before Sasha stares longingly into her eyes. Horrified, as he watches the crackle of teal magic twisting around their whites.

"You...how—"

Sasha lunges forward, lodging a knife into his gut. Creation magic crackles down her arms, into the white blade. The Abyssian writhes in agony, its skin rippling, tearing outward—a torrent of white blood erupts from out his back, as a barrage of knives still scalding with creation magic bursts out alongside the goo, hurtling toward the others. Slicing through arms, legs, chests—a large dagger lodges into the forehead of a short-haired female. Staring with horror for a moment, the Abyssians reach for the weapons and tear them free from their stark white skin.

A gaping hole is left within the one's head, and Sasha spies something familiar—a black static oozing outward, with the same pressure felt from the void left behind after the Assembly's implosion.

There's nothingness which can be painted upon with one's creation—meaning made within the absurd desert of an otherwise empty existence. Then there's the void, which is the absence of even that beneficial, artistic nothingness. Sasha smirks as her mind wanders. The Abyssian winces in reaction, glaring at Sasha with confused horror as one does when presented with conflicting information their minds cannot grasp. And in the wake of their bewilderedness, Sasha is presented with a curiosity of her own.

"Why don't you heal your wound with creation magic?" she asks, grinning, unsure of the answers to come, but relishing in the act of learning.

The Abyssian woman scrunches her nose, her eyes growing wide and furious. "Who the fuck are you? You're not Zarathustra! Where is Zarathustra? And how can you..."

"Sorry. I'm the one asking questions." Unsheathing a second dagger, Sasha's eyes burn bright with teal, the sparks crackling down her arms and into the blades, she readies to attack and—

Mired in the dark of night, the dozens of magic-born emerge from behind buildings, from beneath the snow, ash, and embers, brandishing their abyssal white blades. Encircling the Abyssians, and in a single coordinated action, each of the teal-haired gods standing behind the female screech in agony. The weapons slicing through stomachs, chests, necks, and heads. Persephone and Misha amidst the ranks, the former piercing a god's side with her sword, and the latter's spear into one's neck.

The female Abyssian shouts, "What is this!" as she turns to defend the others—choking, spitting up white blood, the Abyssian glances toward her abdomen, the tips of Sasha's knives piercing through. And, pulling her arms outward, the female screams—teal sparks rushing through her, rocks growing within her gut as she's torn asunder. The stones burst outward, raining upon everyone. Fire erupts along the pole of Misha's spear, burning a god from the inside out, while Persephone's abyssal powers pulse through her blade, causing the Abyssian's torso to warp and spiral before bursting apart. The others surge their magics through their weapons as well. Fire, lightning, geomancy tearing through the Abyssians' flesh—the snow reeks of their rancid white blood, as pain sears upon the faces of those who remain.

Sasha walks toward the others, finding everyone present except Seth.

"Good job, everyone," she says, watching the abyssal glow of their runes fade. "But through this triumph, our advantage of surprise is lost. Ready yourselves, they'll be here before long."

She glares at the lumps of Abyssian flesh left behind. *They did not heal when they could have. Has something changed since Zarathustra left them?* Sasha's eyes grow wide as she ponders the implications of what's before her. Her wonder transmuting into a grin, she mutters, "Run out of faith, have you, vile gods?"

"You say something, Mom?" Persephone says, approaching from behind.

"Oh, it's nothing," says Sasha. "You did good, hun. Form was solid, and your swing strong. I'm proud of you."

Persephone blushes between a soft smile, turning away. "Oh, I know this isn't the time but, it's been so long since we've seen

Huginn and Muninn...I'm worried that they haven't been able to survive all this."

Her glare still tethered to the Abyssian corpses, Sasha's eyes glow a bright white, and she says, "Do not worry about them. They are strong, smart birds. They are fine."

"How can you know for sure?"

"Because...I can see them, and I can also see..." Her eyes pulse alongside her words. "We are in trouble."

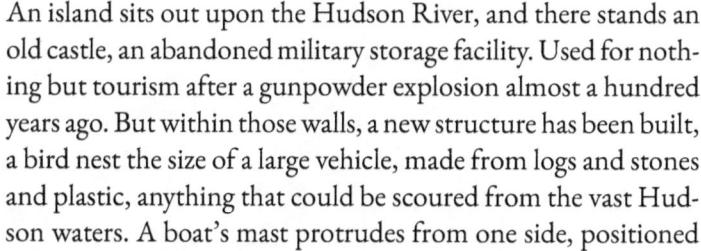

An island sits out upon the Hudson River, and there stands an old castle, an abandoned military storage facility. Used for nothing but tourism after a gunpowder explosion almost a hundred years ago. But within those walls, a new structure has been built, a bird nest the size of a large vehicle, made from logs and stones and plastic, anything that could be scoured from the vast Hudson waters. A boat's mast protrudes from one side, positioned beneath the hulking forms of Huginn and Muninn—

The crackling of creation magic stirs from across the water, causing the power of Sasha's rune to fade. Alerting all to her presence. Both giant ravens jerk their heads upward, cocking their beaks every which way as they croak and flap their wings so fiercely that the nest is shaken apart, crumbling to the floor of the castle.

Spurred into the air, the ravens fly their way across the Hudson to the town of Crowley. On an intersection where one road splits into two, one leading up into the mountains, the other down to the riverfront, they find Sasha staring toward a dozen approaching Abyssians.

The birds spiral within the safety of the high sky, watching as the magic-born spring into action, killing the Abyssians. But, along the circumference of the battle, Huginn and Muninn croak despairingly at the approaching armies—a large group of humans wearing bright red hats, and the legion of teal-haired gods, all amassing, marching toward the birds' beloved master.

And within Huginn's right eye and Muninn's left, an ocular transcendence occurs. Staring at the flesh of the dead gods, as well as into the ravens, are the eyes of Sasha. "We are in trouble," she says, feeling the same confusion felt by the ravens who are conjoined in their shared vision.

In remembrance of all which led here, and all which is still to come, the birds croak their elegy from above.

CHAPTER THIRTY-FOUR

Glancing upward, Sasha spies Huginn and Muninn spiraling above. Their croaks muffled by distance. And simultaneously, she views herself from their eyes. There, within her mind, this second perspective watches her every move. As well as the marching steps growing louder and louder, and the ever-increasing brightness of the Abyssians' teal hair. Amassing in the sky and approaching fast is the entire legion of gods.

Yet she cannot help but wonder: *What is going on with the ravens?*

{Yes, Zarathustra's Lust. Stand strong against the coming gods and the death they will surely cause. This faith in yourself—this belief that you can lead the charge, protect your own, this belief that you can rather than you cannot—it is thriving within you while it falters within your husband.}

Though it has been a while, she recognizes its voice. And understands that it only speaks when necessary.

My husband is fine. We are human—this is what we do. Especially in a marriage. When one struggles, another shoulders the weight. I will have faith enough for both of us, and we will prevail.

And this faith—I assume it's the cause of this shared sight with the ravens?

{They are your creations. To them, you have always been a god. Your faith is simply deepening your tether to the White Abyss, allowing you to peer through the minds of these living creatures you gifted life to. But be wary, you are not the first to tap into this power of controlling wills. Be steadfast in your marriage, deepen your faith—lest you never make it through the long, bright dark to come.}

The voice ceases. The pressure pounding within her head accompanying the presence of the Abyssal Consciousness vanishes, pulled back into the White Abyss.

Long bright dark? Speaking in riddles again, but one that I do not have time to consider. But how curious that it speaks as if it knows the future.

Sasha glances toward the legion, moments away from striking. The snowstorm, already fierce, somehow grows heavier, as if Nature herself is reacting to the tension in the air. The wind growing harsher, Sasha and Persephone's hair whips around wildly. But they stand firm alongside Misha and the other magic-born. A wall against an existential threat.

Blades gripped and at the ready, the magic-born raise them toward the descending Abyssians. The gods unhinge their jaws and slash their claws downward upon Sasha's Assembly. The sounds of shearing metal, their nails as hard and sharp as the blades they collide against. The elements are flung toward the teal-haired gods, exploding against them, some missing and colliding with others in the air above. Fire bellowing against bolts of lightning, ice shattering against stone, and wind swooshing through it all. The Abyssians emerge from each blast unscathed—as one pushes through the ever-thickening dark smoke, a sword's blade pierces its chest. Persephone gripping the other end, sends abyssal vibrations through the steel. The pulse rippling the god's flesh before bursting outward.

Another Abyssian reaches from behind as Persephone's eyes glow white. Feeling the weight of the god's pressure approach, she twists, ducks her head beneath a slashing claw, then swings upward at its wrist. The Abyssian stumbles back, screeching as it grips the stump. Its hand plummets, embedding deep into the snow. Claws still flexed, reaching skyward.

Sasha lunges toward a towering Abyssian, sidestepping its outstretched arm—the god screeches as Sasha pierces the center of its palm. And as the Abyssian slams its other hand upon her, Sasha lunges the tip of her other knife into it as well. The teal-haired giant grits its sharp teeth, glaring angrily at the woman with teal magic crackling within her eyes. Understanding the implication, but too overwhelmed by a need to survive to care. Its jaw unhinges, its mouth widening as it bites down. Pulling her arms back, Sasha slices through its hands, severing its two middle-most fingers. White blood sprays as the fingers sink into the snow.

Sasha allows the Abyssian to stumble backward, as she takes a moment to assess the situation. Persephone and Misha clash their blades against the claws of the vile gods, growing overwhelmed as more and more of the legion descend from the dark, stormy sky, joining the battle here on the surface. But Sasha doesn't interfere. The children—their eyes wide, their skin perspiring despite the harsh cold of the newly arrived winter. Their hearts—Sasha suddenly realizes she can feel them, their pulses reverberating through the wiring of their minds, through the White Abyss, and into Sasha's mind. Her tether deepens with each passing moment. And she can see it. Despite her daughter's increasing stress, she has learned much from her father, molding her anxiety into focus, her anger into power.

Sasha watches as Persephone and Misha land fatal blows to two more Abyssians. Then she turns from them to the increasing mounds of flesh within the snow, and to the towering giant still stumbling away from her. Wounded, not healing. And memories from Zarathustra resurface—the origin of the Abyssians, what keeps them alive and what fuels their power. Sasha smiles—a bloodcurdling scream tears her attention away.

"Urgh, y-you...bas-stard!" screams the fiery-eyed young man who journeyed with the fae-woman to find Sasha. An Abyssian stretches a wide smile, flashing his sharp teeth below crazed eyes. Its claw piercing through the young man's chest, stretching out his back, slathered crimson—

A sharpened edge of a brown stone slices through the Abyssian's arm, cleaving it. The fae-woman rushes between the god and the fiery-eyed young man, curling her fingers, gesturing them toward the Abyssian. Nature defying itself, vines tear through the ground and the snow blanketing it. Thorns pointing outward hang along the grassy threads and lunge at the god, piercing its flesh, twisting around and piercing again and again and again, until tightly woven through and around its body. The vines let off a green pulse, and the grassy threading expands—plants and tree branches burst from within. White blood spurts as the Abyssian's skin hangs limp. The flora browning, withering in winter's crisp air, as the god's corpse thuds to the ground.

The fae-woman grasps the fiery-eyed young man, lowering him gently. As he coughs up blood, another Abyssian swoops in overhead—a clash of metal rings loudly as the other young man releases the chains around his arms, letting them snap like snakes at the approaching god. Rushing in from behind is also the other young woman, conjuring fairies from her spittle. They burst upon the Abyssian's face, causing it to hiss through the acid burns.

The fiery-eyed young man, anger gripping him fiercely, says to the fae-woman, "S-sorry. F-fuck 'em up for me, will…you…"

His head goes limp, the anger still seared upon his gaze. Glancing upward toward the unending legion of vile gods. Their poison inflicted upon the earth and humanity, branded forever in the young man's face.

Sasha grimaces. Persephone and Misha rush over to the fae-woman's side, clashing with the onslaught of Abyssians, descending heavier by the moment. One in front, to the side, now behind. In a flash, suddenly dozens of the teal-haired gods lunge toward them, dozens more upon the other magic-born. Darting in fast, then hanging in the air like reapers dressed in white.

A god is slashed, obliterated from within, all the while others parry and avoid the magic-born's blades. Retaliating with their unhinged jaws, wrapping around heads and torsos, biting down and devouring body and soul alike. The number of magic-born drops one by one, and Sasha's heart flutters, watching these ghosts, hollow shells of what they once were, become a tragedy now as they have long relinquished their need to provide blessings.

And watching the horror unfold, Sasha's mind wanders even more. *They still haven't healed*—a gunshot echoes, a bullet whistling overhead as Sasha ducks. Heading straight for her, Misha lunges her hand forward. Orange flame spirals down her arms, growing hotter as it pools into her palms. And bursting outward, Misha winces, turning her head as a shell of blue fire enshrouds her, melting the bullet.

The armies, magic-born and Abyssians alike, turn to face those who dare to trespass upon this grand battle.

Marching forward is an army of humans wearing red hats. Donning plaid shirts, t-shirts, jeans, and other such average apparel, their army outmatches the size of Sasha's, but is still minuscule in the face of the Abyssian legion. Yet, they stare forward, eyes masked in a dull, golden sheen, smiling with a sort of confidence known only by those who lack all awareness, while housing an immense amount of blind faith for the one they fight for.

"We are here to *Make God Great Again*," says a man of the cloth, raising his rifle skyward, then pointing it at Sasha. As if by his command, the others also raise and point their guns at the magic-born. "We will slay the witch and her kin, and then we will allow these angels to liberate us, to send us home!"

Recognizing that dull, golden sheen in their eyes, Sasha grits her teeth in unease. And she ponders the nature of faith—the faith which amplifies magic when placed in oneself—is the same faith these surprise soldiers place not within themselves, but in their god. And by doing so, they deny life and fight for everything unearthly, for a heaven which does not exist. Rushing blindly onward with their religious ideologies, with no awareness of the repercussions, of the toxicity they spew, or any knowledge that is tangible and true. And to all things earthly and human and real, this makes them profoundly dangerous.

The greatest poison ever known to humankind.

CHAPTER THIRTY-FIVE

The air is smothered by the sounds of blades clashing against Abyssian claws, in tandem with the firing of guns, the whistling of bullets. The bellowing of fire, the crackle of electricity, the whooshing of wind, the snapping of ice and stone. Flesh and splintering bone rupturing over the battlefield. The Abyssians care not for the arrival of the gun-toting Red Hat army. To the teal-haired gods, they are merely more humans to consume.

Chaos increasing, Sasha watches as the priest's gun fires, kicked back from the force as a bullet whistles through the air, piercing the throat of a young woman. Unnoticed, her back turned, having raised a sword toward the throat of an Abyssian. Dropping her weapon, she clutches at her neck wound, blood spilling through the cracks of her fingers. The light leaving her eyes, the Abyssian smirks, and bites down. Her lower half tears away at her abdomen, strands of skin stretching as it slumps into the snowy ground.

Sasha lunges toward the priest, who raises his rifle, guarding himself from the slash of her knives. "What is the point of this?"

she shouts. "The world is in ruins, and you attack the ones trying to save it?"

"All we do is for the glory of God!" the priest says. "This world is null and void—none of it matters once we find our home in Heaven—and you find yours in Hell!"

Gritting her teeth, she kicks the priest away, knocking the gun from his hands. *These idiots. The likelihood of our survival was low enough against the Abyssians! Now they make matters even worse. And for what? A heaven that doesn't exist anymore and was never the heaven they imagined anyway.*

Eyes furious and wide, she rushes toward the priest. "You know not what you do. Your god is dead. And the dead are buried for a reason. Do not add any more lives to its antiquated grave by invoking its name!" Bringing the knife down upon his neck, she yanks and tears the bone, decapitating him.

Gasping, not merely from exhaustion but from fury, she catches a glimpse of the priest's eyes. Their dull, gold sheen erupts brilliantly, and as the light fades, the man's teal soul filters through his eyes, conjoining on the other side, before rocketing away toward the obscured mountain's summit, mired in the blackness of night.

What was that? Souls drift naturally into the White Abyss upon death, but where did that one go?

As she glances around at the chaos of the blood-splattered battlefield, she watches as the magic-born continue to be slaughtered, devoured—or shot dead before the Abyssians can feed. Their souls, either digested or simply vanish into the White Abyss, never to be seen. But as the red-hatted army shouts "Make God Great Again" in their final moments, Sasha watches as each soul springs toward the mountain instead.

"Enough of this," says a low, bellowing voice from above. As soon as the words slither through his lips, the battle ceases, all eyes placed upon him. Unable to resist the gravity of his aura.

Glancing upward, Sasha finds the Abyssian War Chief, his long mane fluttering wildly as he hovers, arms crossed beneath a furious scowl.

There he is—the one who ripped Dima's hand off with ease, and destroyed Japan.

At one moment, the Abyssian War Chief tethers his gaze to Sasha, the next he moves so swiftly the human eye cannot catch it, and—Sasha feels a pressure around her throat, and a crushing weight upon her back. Slammed downward, she can feel the ground fissure beneath her weight. Hidden by the snow, which begins to melt from the heat caused by the Abyssian's intense speed.

"You. Female," he says, staring into her eyes, catching a glimpse of the teal magic crackling around within their whites. "How is it you have Zarathustra's power of creation?"

Eyes wide and frenzied, Sasha coughs, blood dripping from her lips. "Why...y-you j-jealous?" The Abyssian's eyes grow in astonishment, as Sasha continues, "You all—you're not the gods you...used to be. What? All these years consuming sentient life, just for it to amount to the same as nourishing oneself with food. There's no one left to provide faith in you—you, empty slates! You've bolstered your lifespans with souls, but they do not give you faith..." Sasha gives a knowing smirk, "...and this makes you vulnerable."

A large shadow emerges from the dark outskirts of the battlefield. Swiftly lunging, reaching out with clawed, metal gauntlets, Seth grips the head of the Abyssian, freeing Sasha from the god's weight.

Every muscle in his body implores him to act, to leap into the fray, to fight alongside them and protect his family. But this was the plan, Sasha's plan, the woman he trusts more than anything in the world—the woman who holds all his faith. And so, upon the arrival of the Abyssian War Chief, Seth abides by her instructions and makes his assault.

Leaping for the muscular and imposing god, the sharp tips of his gauntlet's claws dig into the Abyssian's scalp. Yanking him off Sasha and plowing him to the ground. White flame erupts along Seth's arms, funneling into the grooves of his gauntlets. The Abyssian War Chief swats Seth's arm away and rolls over to gaze upon his surprise assailant. As Seth's arm springs upward from the force, a pillar of abyssal flames erupts skyward. Cutting through the darkness with blinding light. All parties raise arms over their eyes, wincing.

"Zarathustra? No—who are you?" the god asks.

Seth glares with a stoic fury as he brings his fist down upon the Abyssian's face. Upon collision, white flames burst outward upon the ground, creating a portal. The force of his punch hurtles both Seth and the teal-haired god through it. Sasha and the others vanish as reality is torn away and replaced with another—the Abyssian's head slams into the icy peak of Mount Everest, unbothered by the frigid temperature and thin air. Seth bashes fist after fist into the god's face, as white particles drift into the air alongside the snow. Abyssal skin sheared away into a glimmering white haze. Fissures form within the mountain's peak, breaking it apart, rocks and snow alike tumbling down the mountain's side, as a loud rumble grows below them. An avalanche plummets its way toward the foot of the mountain, increasing exponentially in size with each passing second. And with each bash to the face, the Abyssian War Chief whips his furious eyes back to Seth, and yells, "Where is he? Answer me, where is he? Where is Zarathustra!"

Seth's raging white flames spill from the confines of his eyes, as he brings both fists back down upon the god's chest, opening another portal—a flat dusty brown desert contrasted with the sublime verticality of massive red-rock formations lies miles below them—*The Valley of the Gods, Utah*. And spiraling through the air, the Abyssian knees Seth in the abdomen, lands his fist under his chin, claws and pushes at Seth, attempting to get away. But through it all, Seth bears the pain, returning a flurry of punches back at the god with his left hand while gripping his chest—the gauntlet's nails sinking deeply into the skin, causing the Abyssian to groan painfully, loudly, his eyes wide with agony above a furrowed nose and clenched, bared teeth.

Colliding with a monolithic rock formation, the red stone bursts out the opposite side. Spraying the area in a dusty mist.

Seth's fist bashes against the god's face once more, all the while pushing his gauntlet's clawed tips further into the god's chest. Eyes wide, bright with abyssal flame, Seth shouts, "You're here looking for Zarathustra? Just what is it with you gods—harboring eons-long grudges over supernatural quarrels taking place an incomprehensible amount of time before the Earth was ever a thought, which have nothing to do with sentient life, with humanity—" Gripping the god's head by its long teal mane, Seth rapidly bashes it into the stone. Embedding him deeper and deeper and— "These quarrels have nothing to do with us, yet you make it our problem! And all because you want revenge on a god who no longer exists! This is pointless! This is lunacy! Humanity could live in peace, if only gods would stop manipulating *everything!*"

Using both gauntlets to pierce the god's face and chest, white flames coil down Seth's arms, and he continues, "We've triumphed over gods before, and let me assure you, we'll do it again."

Weary of the white flames, having watched his kind die from having magic channeled into their beings, the Abyssian War Chief squirms, kicking and kneeing Seth's abdomen. Knocked off, Seth grunts in pain, his claws ripped from the god's skin, leaving gaping wounds spurting blood in his wake.

The Abyssian launches at Seth, gripping his neck in mid-air, and with a swing of his arm, he hurls Seth toward the ground.

Eyes aglow with white flame, Seth opens a portal behind him, falling through and appearing atop the Abyssian. Another pulse opens a new portal, and slamming his fists into the god, sends him through.

A smoldering red blaze appears below them, as they fall into the mouth of a volcano. The god plummets and sinks into the bubbling magma, while Seth catches himself upon the stony edge.

Springing from the lava is a large white fist, stretching along an elastic arm, lashing toward Seth like a whip—gripping his neck, the hand begins to pull. The cliffside fissures from the pressure of his gauntlet, Seth's heart throbbing as he feels the grip loosening—a pulse of his eyes opens a portal, this one around the Abyssian's wrist, slicing through as the space holding it is severed, creating a window elsewhere. The hand plops into the boiling magma.

As the god retracts his elongated arm, Seth peers across space to find Sasha, Persephone, Misha, and the others, still alive, but struggling against the two armies they are sandwiched between. Shots fired, claws and fangs bared. Souls disappearing into the gullets of gods, with more springing off into the dark.

The brief window closes as Seth climbs the edge of the volcano's mouth. The magma torrents upward, a pillar of flame rising as the Abyssian launches toward Seth, toppling over the edge, rolling down the volcano's incline. Seth's head bashes against the stony ground. The teal-haired god raises a fist, roaring—

Seth's eyes pulse, as chains of abyssal flame wrap around the god. Manipulating their density, Seth uppercuts the god's solar plexus, springing him high into the air. Another pulse and the density changes again, causing the white shackles to grow exponentially heavier, causing the god to plummet. Seth remains on his back, pulses his eyes once more, spreading an oval of white flames directly above him. A portal opens right before the Abyssian collides.

A gurgling scream is heard as the portal closes. Seth stands, catching his breath for a moment. But wanting to remove himself from the volcanic heat, he opens another portal and walks on through.

The Abyssian War Chief awaits him, lying horizontal, the point of a triangle having pierced his chest. Seth glances around the Western Sahara Desert. His feet are slanted, his back hunched to compensate for the angle, as he stands atop the Great Pyramid of Khufu.

"Do you see this beautiful world you're bent on destroying? All its sublime wonders?" asks Seth. "I will not allow it. This is our home, one that has no need for gods."

Lunging his claws toward the Abyssian, their nails pierce his face as Seth's thumbs press into his eyes. The god screams, writhes, twists and pulls, and—swinging his arms down, he cracks the pyramid's tip, shaking himself free of Seth, who stumbles backward within a haze of dust and stone. Rising, heaving, the Abyssian kicks Seth hard in the abdomen, toppling him over. The god, angrier than ever, watches as his assailant rolls to the desert below.

Heaving, Seth clutches his stomach as he slowly rises, gasping, his eyes spring open, twitching with pain. The Abyssian's knee hits the same spot as before. Seth hunches over. The god grips Seth's wild black hair, weaving it through his fingers like rope, and thrusts Seth's head into the ground.

Dazed, Seth glances upward through blurred vision.

"I see now," says the Abyssian, lingering over Seth. "You're quite impressive. So, Zarathustra died before we got here, you claim? No matter. Our goal remains the same—for no one is truly dead while they are still remembered. You cannot kill an idea, and that is what Zarathustra has become in the wake of his life. Concept transcending form. For he may be gone, but he lies before me now—your power, the way you manipulate *The Womb of the One Mind* to your own purposes. Those portals, the amplification of your feeble body's strength and durability...and that woman who has somehow been granted Zarathustra's power of creation." Seth winces at the mention of Sasha. Noticing, the Abyssian smiles manically below frenzied eyes and says, "Somehow Zarathustra has bypassed the Abyssian limitation of being unable to procreate. And thus, here you are—and that woman...and one other."

Seth's unblinking gaze grows in fury, struggling to rise. The weight of the Abyssian's foot now pressing heavily upon him.

"That one," continues the Abyssian, "is special indeed. While you laid in wake like a coward for me to arrive, I watched from above. The way her magic appears similar to yours, but is so much more. I'm sure of it. She is the power that drew us here, and while I would prefer to devour both of them, the prospect of tormenting Zarathustra's offspring is too alluring.

"I'm done with you. You tried to disorient me by pushing me through all these portals. But I feel my kin, and can fly to every corner of Zarathustra's little world far faster than you can create a portal to save them. Watch now as I fly into them with such intense speed that they vaporize from the sheer pressure!"

"*No!*" says Seth, but he shouts after a teal blur. The Abyssian already rocketing away.

Head cloudy, vision wobbling and unclear, Seth rises slowly to his feet. Eyes pulsing white, a portal tears open before him, and he sprints into it. Blackness overtakes his vision, cutting in and out as he collapses to the ground.

"Daddy!" shouts Persephone, noticing her father stumble through a portal, but separated by dozens of Assembly members, Abyssians, and Red-Hat soldiers. Sasha, standing by her side, turns to face Seth as she throws a knife into the chest of a Red-Hat, while simultaneously lodging a knife into an Abyssian's throat, rupturing from within are stones, roots, plastics, and metals—her attention is yanked toward an overwhelming bright teal light, rocketing toward them with immense speed—

Seth's wide eyes burst with abyssal energy as he reaches toward Sasha and Persephone. A whirlwind of white light engulfs them as Seth hopes to whisk them away—a high-pitched whistle transmutes into a thunderous roar as an explosion of teal energy blows a hole in the center of the battlefield. Devouring Assembly, Red-Hats, and Abyssians alike.

Seth stares onward, tears in his eyes, hoping he was not too late.

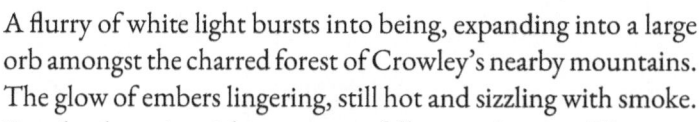

A flurry of white light bursts into being, expanding into a large orb amongst the charred forest of Crowley's nearby mountains. The glow of embers lingering, still hot and sizzling with smoke. But slowly extinguishing as snowfall grows heavier. The air is still, with all wildlife either ravaged by the flames or having run off, attempting to survive. And as the dome of white light disperses, scattering its abyssal particles amongst the ash-coated forest, Sasha and Persephone clutch at their mouths as the stench of unlucky animals seeps into their nostrils.

"Wait..." says Sasha, thinking of the flash of teal light about to collide with her, as she glances at her surroundings. A warmth overtakes her as she realizes Seth warped them away to save them from the Abyssian War Chief. A pit opens within her stomach, devouring that warmth as she imagines Seth, Misha, and the others not surviving.

And another pang assaults her, as she realizes where they are. The dilapidated remains of their cabin atop the mountain summit lay before them. And sitting upon the porch steps is a face she had hoped would never return.

A deranged smirk greets them with a face half melted. Shirtless, he stands, opening his arms wide as a cross, hanging his head back and letting his golden locks dangle behind as a barrage of souls are flung from the town of Crowley and into his mouth.

Whipping his head forward, he says, "And so, witch, we meet again. You and your damned offspring." He flashes his purple-stained teeth as widely as he can, glaring manically.

"Welcome home."

PART FOUR

White Cataclysm

"Dante, as it seems to me, made a crass mistake when with awe-inspiring ingenuity he placed that inscription over the gate of his hell, "Me too made eternal love": at any rate the following inscription would have a much better right to stand over the gate of the Christian Paradise and its "eternal blessedness"—"Me too made eternal hate"—granted of course that a truth may rightly stand over the gate to a lie! For what is the blessed-ness of that Paradise? Possibly we could quickly sur-mise it; but it is better that it should be explicitly attested by an authority who in such matters is not to be disparaged, Thomas of Aquinas, the great teacher and saint. "Beati in regno celesti," says he, as gently as a lamb, "videbunt pcenas damnatorum, ut beatitudo Mismagis complaceat." [In the kingdom of heaven the blessed will see the punishment of the damned, so that they will derive all the more pleasure from their heavenly bliss.]"
—Friedrich Nietzsche, *The Genealogy of Morals*

CHAPTER THIRTY-SIX

MONTHS AGO, THE END OF SUMMER.

The earth roared, quaking as Japan was torn asunder. The Abyssian War Chief's blast of energy ripping through the ground with fury, nothing to impede it. The sound, ever-deafening, but muffled slightly, as it stretched past the confines of Tokyo and through the rest of the country.

The Abyssian legion spread out, zipping across the globe, devouring the souls of humankind along their search for Zarathustra. And as the commotion within the Shibuya Crossing quiets, with only the sound of rushing ocean water spilling through fissures made by the warmongering god, a rustling sound emerged beneath a pile of rubble.

A heavy gray slab of stone laid atop. Pressing severely upon the bricks, metal, and broken glass—the ocean water passing through the fissures rising, the crevasse crumbling along its edges, caused the pile of debris to shift, the side nearest the water spilling away, and—a hand reached out, dropping into the raging, salty water. It twitched and fluttered, pulled into consciousness by the water's warm tide. And, gripping the edge, the hand tried to pull itself free—more debris crumbled to the ground as another arm emerged, pushing the stone and glass away. Yanking with all their might—long golden locks pulled into the bright, sweltering sun—Damien heaved.

Pulling himself free, he rose to his feet. Vision wobbling before him, his head ached. His face and chest melted by Seth, he trudged forward, limping, his torn shirt fluttering off behind him. He glanced skyward. In his blurred vision, he saw not the Abyssians, but mere streaks of teal. Zipping back and forth, as if devouring the blue sky glaring oppressively bright above him. His vision swirled rapidly as he collapsed to the ground.

Seven heartbeats thud sporadically within his chest. Screaming his reason for survival—born from the souls of the sins and their collective power, he narrowly escaped annihilation. The Abyssian War Chief's blast of energy—*we are lucky not to have taken the full brunt of it.* But, lying there, he feared it was only a matter of time before his dream died prematurely. Beckoning him, his eyes fluttered amidst the pull of sleep, his hand dropping—his eyes shot open, as his palm fell into the hand of another. Yanking his head upward, he finds—

"S-Sergei?" Damien groaned, lips wet with saliva, as he reached toward his loyal servant. But his eyes dulled upon finding Sergei dead before him. His lower half crushed by rubble but having been dead before impact. A stone spire of his own creation embedded within his heart. Slain by Sasha, only his soulless husk laid there. Now useless to Damien.

"M-my...Lor-rd," spoke a raspy voice in a Russian accent. Six feet away laid Dima, reaching out for Damien. His intestines sprawled outward like a mass of long snakes in the absence of his lower half, laid within a pool of blood. His heaving lungs protruding from an open chest cavity.

Turning toward the Russian, on the fringe of life and death, Damien smiled. Pushing himself to his feet, Damien trudged toward Dima, hand clutching his side. "You...how strong your soul is…to cling to life even in this pathetic state." Damien's eyes grew wide, frenzied, hungry, his smile stretching wide, flashing his crimson-stained teeth. "Come now. Join Us. For through Us, riding within our bowels, you will be one of the blessed and will have your seat in a heaven of my own creation."

Dima spoke not a word. The light in his eyes faded further behind the dull gold sheen of Damien's soul manipulation. And as the echo of Yahweh trudged forward with arms wide open, his pupils spread into his eyes as they became inky black pools of tar.

Dima's eyes flashed bright gold before the teal glow of his soul spilled out from his eyes, conjoining on the other end, before sinking into Damien's mouth. The Russian's hand dropped hard against the ground. Damien smiled, his vision clearing, steadying. And as he turned, facing west, he walked on, weaving his way through the ruins of Tokyo, being weary of the Abyssian gods scouring the air above.

"Yes, it is almost time. To be the One True God! The Abyssians are an unexpected problem, but it doesn't matter! Even they will bow and offer their wills unto us, once we bolster the hearts of the blessed…and after the crucifixion of the damned."

An airplane circled around Fukuoka, needing to land, but unsure of what to make of the country split in two. As the teal light of the gods streaked their way across the sky, a mother hugging her young boy and girl cowered behind a canoe balanced against a food stand upon a nearby beach. Fear was branded into them after watching from afar, the glowing eyes of an Abyssian sucking the soul out of their father. The woman and children screamed as an explosion roared above them. Bright teal magic colliding with the plane, causing it to spiral through the air. They screamed again as they watched the aircraft smash into the Fukuoka Tower. The city close by, the sound of the explosion, of bending metal and shattering glass echoed loudly in their ears.

Footsteps sounded from a nearby path, disappearing as they sank into the sandy shore. Emerging onto the beach was a teenage boy with golden blond hair.

The woman rose from behind the canoe, a child's hand in each palm. Rushing over, they stumbled upon the loose sand, but met the teenage boy, gasping for air. "You must hide!" the woman yelled in English, "The airport's not running. There's nowhere to go, nothing to do, but hide. Come with us," she said.

Damien turned toward her with a smile and frenzied eyes. The kindness in the woman's face sank into uncertainty as she met his gaze. Stepping back, she pushed both children behind her.

"Do you believe in us?" asked Damien.

"Hmm? I don't know what you—" The woman's soul ejected from her eyes alongside her children, all three sinking into the depths of Damien's bowels. Their bodies thudded against the sand as Damien walked over them. Gripping the canoe and paddles, he drifted off into the Sea of Japan, heading toward the coast of South Korea.

A trail of bodies left in his wake, from the streets of Tokyo to Fukuoka to the shore, and yet still upon the roads ahead. Making the most of the global chaos, he stole as many vehicles as he needed to make his way across Asia and Europe, and eventually the Atlantic, through the sweltering summer heat, where he then stumbled his way back to where this all first began.

Now, winter's beginning.

Damien stares through the heavy storm. From the porch steps of the dilapidated cabin, staring, unblinking, down the path leading to the cliff's edge. Snow covering the mountain's summit, extinguishing the remains of the embers and their surrounding ash. A world set ablaze, but winter now freezing everything over. A white crust killing, and chilling, all that resides within nature.

Glancing skyward, the world, as seen from the mountains of Crowley, is shrouded in dark grey clouds. And flapping wildly above the cabin are the two massive ravens that greeted his first visit to Seth and Sasha's cabin. The birds, which he remembers from their conception. Watching from beyond the veil, after his seven souls were flung back into the White Abyss, before consciousness was lost to him, for a time. He saw it then, his past self, Yahweh, and the ravens plucking out her eyes. Mere birds, yet, in resonating with his past self, their image irks him. Creatures which blinded god and aided in her felling.

Damien winces, groaning, feeling a pressure build around his eyes as he remembers. The rage builds within him as he ponders all the ways he plans to make them suffer.

It ends here, and we are going to make it hurt...how many times must I die and suffer at the hands of that monster? Who killed my seven essences, and then killed my progenitor? The pain from each death ravages me, implores me to see to their torturous end! And from my seat in Heaven...I will relish in their screams.

Manic eyes gleam above a crooked smile as Damien chuckles to himself. Squeezing his hands into tight fists, his knuckles crack loudly as they curl inward. Tension building, as the atom splits—

A whooshing noise whips his head toward the cliffside, as a flurry of white light bursts into being. An egg-shaped dome spirals rapidly before bursting outward into a haze of white particles. Scattering about into obscurity, as they disappear into the snow and ash-carpeted mountains.

His lips quiver, curving into a deranged smirk as he rises to address familiar faces. "And so, witch, we meet again. You and your damned offspring." He flashes his crimson-stained teeth as widely as he can, glaring manically at Sasha and Persephone.

"Welcome home."

CHAPTER THIRTY-SEVEN

Damien's feet sink into the ever-deepening snow, trudging slowly forward as the ravens circling above croak with increasing pace and volume. His eyes become dark pits of tar. A haze of blackness filtering out from their corners. An overflowing, overwhelming black mist. The air ripples around his legs, squeezing the muscles as they press inward, bulging but remaining slim—the skin grows taut as his calves and thighs grow in density.

Sasha takes a fighting stance, her daggers held up and ready. "How the fuck are you alive?"

A gust of air bellows heavily against Sasha, her hair fluttering wildly before her. Wiping the greying stands from her face, she turns, gasps—having rushed by her, Damien's hand grips Persephone's neck, plowing her through the trunk of a large pine tree—the air forced from her lungs, Persephone heaves, eyes wide and bloodshot as the tree snaps, cracks, tumbles over from the impact.

Gripping harder, his nails slice into her neck. Blood pools upon the skin and drips slowly—streams burst into rivers as the flow gushes, his sharp, dirty fingernails sinking deeply into her. Damien flashes a crooked smirk, lips glistening with saliva, relishing in her pain. The skin of his arm ripples, his muscles bulging as he lifts Persephone over his head and swings her into the cliffside. The stone fracturing beneath her weight, the teenage girl ejects blood from her mouth.

"Get the *fuck away from her*!" says Sasha, lunging at Damien with the point of a dagger outstretched. The boy yanks his crooked smile at her. His teeth dripping with a saliva, below a scrunched nose and the ever-widening black haze flowing from his eyes. Stretching his other arm toward Sasha, the air begins to ripple outward.

Sasha's eyes pulse, her pupils sinking into their whites. An abyssal glow enraptures them—diving swiftly at Damien from the other side is Huginn, pecking and clawing until Damien releases Persephone, stumbling backward onto the splintered trunk of the collapsed tree. The jagged wood piercing his right side.

Sasha jabs her dagger into his left hand in tandem with Huginn's beak plunging into his right. Tethered to the ground, Damien's black eyes transition back to their bright icy blues, as he tugs his head away from the horse-sized raven. Face twitching, he scowls.

"Not a fan of birds, huh?" asks Sasha.

Damien jerks his furious countenance at her, spitting in her face. "We remember what these horrid creatures did to us—to Yahweh."

Wiping away his spittle, Sasha drops her other dagger and lifts her palm skyward. "So, you saw that, even after your seven souls were taken by the Abyss?" she says, as teal magic crackles into being above her hand, spiraling, twisting together like snakes before erupting into bright orange flames. Weaving into themselves, they amass into a tiny orb of fire—a miniature sun held within her palm. "Remember seeing this as well?"

Damien struggles away from her approaching hand. The sun's scalding heat melting the untarnished side of his face—the skin boiling, wrinkling, peeling—

Persephone slowly pushes her torso off the ground, one arm bearing her weight, as her other clutches her throbbing forehead. Her eyes pulse alongside the thud of her heart, as she shouts, "Mom, watch out!"

Damien's eyes become swathed with that dark mist once more. Whipping his head backward, a pulse of black static bursts from his eyes, enveloping his body, reaching Sasha's knife and Huginn's beak, the blade rings as energy surges through it. The steel, sheared away in an instant—Huginn lets out a shrill screech, as he stumbles backward, fluttering his wings as fissures form within his beak. Startled, Sasha shouts, "Huginn!" as she retracts her sun-wielding palm, ejecting it to the side amidst her surprise. A bellowing, fiery crash warms them as ash-filled gusts and solar flares burst from the impact somewhere nearby.

Another black pulse from Damien's eyes.

And another—

Another—

More and more—

Another. Black. Pulse.

Tension rises alongside a roaring hum, as the static surrounding his body grows unsteady, bubbling, ready to rupture.

Huggin leaps toward Sasha, his massive body knocking her away and into Persephone's lap—Damien's black static erupts outward. The air rips and tears, slicing through the ground beneath his feet, the surrounding trees—first the feathers and then the flesh in quick succession, blood sprays as Huginn is sheared to the bone.

"*Huginn!*" Persephone shouts through tears. Sasha clasps her mouth as she watches her avian friend's hulking skeleton thud against the ground, sliding into the crater, halting at Damien's feet.

Eyes still swathed in blackness, Damien turns toward Sasha and Persephone. The distant screeching of Muninn mourning his brother from the clouds above. Damien smirks. Raising his arms outward like a cross, blood gushing from the holes in his wrists and from his pierced side, he bursts out laughing and says, "*Yes,* suffer. *Suffer,* like I have *suffered*! Only once you experience the appropriate amount of torment...will I finally solidify your crucifixion upon the Will of the world."

A bright teal glow engulfs and overwhelms as Misha hurtles through the air. The ground upon impact cracks, fissures, and vaporizes within a moment, with Misha far enough from the epicenter to survive, but not to avoid being swept up in the shockwave. Knocking against Abyssian and the Red-Hat army alike, she plummets to the ground, tumbling away until her back slams against an abandoned car.

Her ears ring, her vision wobbles and blurs. Slowly steadying into focus, she glances toward the sudden teal explosion. A crater lies where the energy collided. The concrete, upturned dirt, and stone seared and melted, the surrounding air hazy with heat—a teal mist glistening as it rises. And walking up the crater's incline is an Abyssian with a wild mane and beard. White blood spilling from his stump of a wrist, but stomping furiously toward—*Uncle Seth!*

Misha wants to cry out, but a searing ache presses deeply into her head.

"You insolent—these powers of yours are pesky indeed," says the Abyssian. "But do not worry. I shall kill them yet...after I deal with you."

A shrill screech sounds from overhead, whipping Seth's gaze toward the mountain. Muninn circles the summit in his lonesome, croaking and screeching in a way Seth has never heard before. He feels it—the grief felt by this creature so close to him.

Seth's eyes widen with terror, and as the Abyssian stomps toward him, unhinging his jaw, Seth's eyes burst with Abyssal flame. Overtaken by a white dome, he vanishes. Leaving nothing but dispersed white particles drifting into the deep snow, amidst the clash of blades and nails, and gunshots echoing loudly. The war continues, as the survivors from the teal explosion rush at each other. Caring for nothing but their hate for one another, wanting to engrave the erasure of their foes into the Will of the world.

"Vermin," mutters the Abyssian War Chief, as his gaze turns slowly toward the mountains, tracking Seth's energy signature. "There you are," he says, rocketing away from the streets of Crowley.

Misha's head still aching, she pushes through the pain and rises to her feet. Glancing around her, she finds that Persephone and Sasha are also gone. Grimacing, she looks for anyone to lead them through this catastrophe—and, clutching her spear, she thinks of her father. The always joyful, always prideful man, a loyal servant to Sasha, but a leader all the same. *The Assembly always respected him, and the stories he told me of the days before the Assembly, as a soldier amidst a guild of demon slayers. Heroic tales of triumph over evil.*

Misha glances over the remaining Assembly members. The fae-woman, the girl who creates life from spittle, the boy with chains around his arms. And all the others. Fear shrouds their vision as they struggle against the opposing armies. Taking a deep breath, Misha raises her spear toward a nearby Abyssian and shouts, "Troops! Do not waver! We will see this through to the end, and until then, let's make Sasha, our Assembly leader, proud of our strength!"

Lunging her spear into a god's neck, spiraling flames into its being, engulfing it from within, the Assembly members amass in cheers, rushing toward their enemies with a tenacious glint in their eyes.

And Misha smiles, thinking, *Persephone, please be okay. And Dad, if you were here...I think you'd be proud.*

Amidst the dispersion of white particles, Seth whips his head around. Snow blankets the forests, resting upon the roots rising into charred bark. Embers run like veins up the trunks of surrounding trees. The silence, thick with the absence of wildlife, provides a calm so unblemished that if it were not for the dead trees, the mounds of ash beneath the heavy snow, one might think these mountains serene.

This isn't right—where am I?

Seth pans his gaze, seeking familiarity within the mountain where he has spent much of his life. Made foreign to him by death and destruction. No hope or life lingering in these woods once so full of it.

A whooshing gale, followed by the sound of wood creaking. Tumbling into the earth as it erupts from behind him. And, glancing through the branches, Seth just barely spies the hulking form of Muninn hovering above where the sound emerged. Seth turns, sprinting toward it.

His vision blurs as his face collides with tree after tree, each splintering apart upon impact. His hair is gripped from behind as he's propelled forward. Skin bruises and tears, teeth knocked from his mouth. Blood sprays alongside the trees, reduced to sawdust. Seth's eyes overflow with abyssal flame to account for the pain, amplifying his body's density, its ability to endure, and, gritting his teeth, jerks his elbow backward, thudding against a hard mass—but freeing his head from his assailant's grasp. Swinging his body around with a punch, he—the Abyssian War Chief—glares maniacally, as he tilts his head back, dodging the blow.

Gasping, Seth shouts, "Zarathustra is dead! There's no vengeance for you to have—just go back to your world! Enough already! Just leave us be—my daughter, my wife—something is wrong, they're in danger. So, get the *fuck out of my way!*"

Already bursting with Abyssal light, there in the center of his eyes, bright teal pupils form, thumping with the rapid intensity of a billion hearts. The skin of Seth's arms bubbles furiously like boiling water, sizzling with heat—an animal backed into a corner, growing unhinged with nothing left to lose. And in this moment of desperate fury, there in the depths of his soul, rises the power of many. Lunging toward the Abyssian, Seth raises his fist—

Wrapped in his gauntlet, the air around his arm ignites into a haze of flame, as if melting the very air. Moving so swiftly, the tension creates a stream of fire—bright orange, red, blue—as it weaves around his knuckles, slamming against the Abyssian's face, fissures forming within his white skin, as he's hurtled through a thicket of trees.

Sprawled across the ground, the Abyssian lets out a roar of laughter. And, pushing himself up with his one hand, he says, "I'll give you this. The sentient lifeforms of all other dimensions—they never put up a fight. They could only struggle, like vermin stuck in a barbed trap. The more they squirmed, the more they bled…you have *that* in common with them though."

Seth stands on the other side of the wide row of toppled trees. Heaving, grunting, his mouth clenched beneath wide, furious eyes. The abyssal flames rupturing beyond, stretching out from his pupils, radiating a blinding teal light. And surrounding the power overflowing from his eyes is mangled flesh. Skin torn, face muscles freed into the open air. Bones fractured, held firm by abyssal pressure. The crimson source of life melting and staining the dead forest's blanket of snow.

"I wonder if you would die if you relinquished that power. I wonder if this world would," says the Abyssian, rising firmly to his feet. "But no matter, as I will soon kill you myself."

Seth glances at the fissures creasing deeper into the god's face, and at the stump of his wrist. "Big talk, coming from a fallen god. My wife was right. Despite your speed and strength, you can't heal anymore, can you? For regeneration belongs to the realm of creation—without that, you are no god."

"An unforeseen side effect of our conquest. But an idea has struck me, just now—why devour sentient life but not the world they live upon?"

Seth's heart stirs with arrhythmia. "What are you—"

"Yes, I see it now—why Zarathustra's little world feels so peculiar. The power radiating from the ground...it's the same as yours! Self-sustaining, with no impact upon the dimensional stack! It is the Womb—no, it's a facet of the Womb, a branch belonging to Zarathustra, his life essence—he bled it out from within himself!" The Abyssian smirks. "Well, we are of the same kin—

"I am also a branch of the Womb."

His head whips upward, jaw unhinging. Reaching toward his mouth with his one hand, he tears at the flesh, rapidly clawing it away in strands down to the neck—his head rolls off his shoulders, the necessary support no longer there. And scraps of skin flutter to the snow at his feet, alongside a splattering of white blood and teal hair, obscured by the heavy storm. The headless god continues tearing away at his flesh until only a wide hole between his shoulders remains.

Seth watches in horror as the Abyssian totters forward, as stark white fingers reach out from within, clasping the edge of the fleshy hole. Pulling itself upward is the white scalp of an otherwise featureless form. An evolution birthed through a vaginal canal of its own creation—ejecting from its fleshy confines, a faceless, white form radiates in the air, pulsating with a white aura.

{*Abomination!*} shouts the Abyssal Consciousness from across dimensions. And as Seth glares upward at the god, he hears another telepathic voice reach his mind, resembling the Abyssian War Chief:

{**I. Am.** *Limitless!*} The god roars, and with each word, a pulse of white light bursts outward from its form, stretching slowly, increasing in size. **{And with my infinite mass, I shall wrap my being around Zarathustra's peculiar little world, and it will become one with me. There on...I will be eternal.}**

Tears cloud her eyes as Persephone watches the skeletal husk of Huginn collapse into the snow. A whimper becomes a soft growl as tension builds within her. A hatred for this stranger, this echo of a god who seeks to ruin her life for reasons stemming from before either of their lives began. Persephone was not even a thought when her parents slayed Yahweh, and the vile god first had to be felled before Damien could ever come to be. And yet the boy seeks out their torment at every turn, and has killed Huginn, the loyal raven who has been there for Persephone since her conception.

Sasha's head rises from her daughter's lap, pushing herself to her feet. Glaring, she says, "Just what is it you want, really? You claimed to seek what Yahweh sought—a new world to escape to. But for what purpose? What good is a world where only you exist?"

Damien, his arms still stretched wide like a cross, laughs maniacally as blood drips into the snow from his wrists. "We do not need anyone, for We are a collective. We have ourselves. And besides, Yahweh created her angels. And while we may not be Yahweh, not really, who's to say we won't grow into that power as well?"

Sasha scoffs and says, "I can say with certainty you won't. Put aside for the moment that Yahweh created angels from a perversion of human souls, while you have devoured them fully, nullifying their wills. I can also be certain that won't happen because you're not leaving this cliffside alive."

Damien chuckles, and says, "The ones we consumed are nullified, sure, but the thousands fighting for our cause," he tilts his head toward the cliffside and to the town lying below it. "Perhaps they will be my angels."

A radiant white aura flashes from behind him, from somewhere far off in the mountain's forests. Persephone's eyes glow white in tandem with the light, feeling the pulse of something sinister alongside the sensation of a spider carrying a massive egg sac, ready to hatch, to burst.

"Daddy..." she mutters.

Catching her words, Damien chuckles. "Seems another quarrel is commencing as we speak...it won't be long now. We are at the fulcrum of the world's destiny. It is time to set the world's Will into motion. For you see, absconding to another world may be the ultimate result. But we just want to punish you for what you've done to us and our others—we want your murderous husband to reap the consequences he deserves." His eyes grow wide with fury, his smirk crumbles into a frown. "We are the blessed. We are an eternal recurrence. Kill us if you can—we will then plague you in the hereafter, until through your deaths, we bring upon the desecration of your wills. You three, the damned, have your own faiths only, while We have captured the faiths of thousands! You cannot kill a god, so long as they linger within the minds of the masses. We will always rise again."

"You are *no* god!" shouts Sasha.

Damien shrugs and says, "What does it matter? When in the minds of Our believers, We are exactly that. An omnipotent, all-seeing, all-knowing, *one true God!* And through their Wills, it shall become Truth."

Sasha trudges toward him, ready to end things—a tunnel of wind rushes by her, blurring the fabric of the world. Persephone, with abyssal white light weaving around her body, appears before her mother, her left hand fiercely gripping Damien's throat.

"Persephone, no! Stay away from him!"

Ignoring her mother, and with a swing of her arm, the teenage boy is flung toward the dilapidated cabin, his golden locks fluttering in the air as he plummets to the ground. Tumbling and rolling until slamming against the abandoned home.

"Urgk—" Damien winces, as a collapsed and a splintered pillar pierces the wound in his side—the blood rushes freer. Glancing in the direction he flew from, he finds the air distorted, ripping and tearing slowly like drifting ash. The momentum of his ascent through the air having loosened the world's structure. And, peeking through the slits is the blackness beneath, filtering through as dark motes of dust.

Persephone sprints toward him. He smirks and lifts his right arm—teal magic crackles behind Damien, as the cabin's wall stretches outward like arms eager to embrace him. Reaching out and gripping his wrist. Snapping backward, his shoulder shatters. Damien screams as he watches Sasha rush to Persephone's side, yanking her away.

"Persephone—"

"Mom, I could have had him!"

"No—please don't, just don't," says Sasha, turning to her daughter with vision clouded by tears. "He's too dangerous and, and...and I cannot lose you, too."

Her mother's words yank Persephone from her fury, as memories of Andes come to mind. Of Huginn, too, amidst all which was shown to her by the Abyssal Consciousness—all the heavy loss her mother has endured. And Sasha's love for her, clear in the agony scrunched into her face, by eyes fuller with tears than Persephone has ever seen—her mother's love sinks in fully, finally, for perhaps the first time.

And amidst this loving union, Damien's eyes sink into their inky black tar pits once more. Stumbling backward, Persephone and Sasha watch as the air ripples and tears, shredding the wall of the cabin—a chunk torn from its foundation. The destroyed home crumbles further, slides, and plummets off the edge of the cliff.

"Yes," says Damien, rising to his feet, "Feel for one another. Feel deeply, feel strongly—so I can relish in *tearing you both apart!*"

CHAPTER THIRTY-EIGHT

Damien stumbles toward them, blood gushing from his side and wrists. The cabin behind scrapes against the mountain's rocky summit as it continues to slide off the cliffside. And now stretching well beyond his eyes is a tar-colored aura enveloping his entire body, fluttering like flame. Evidence of the souls he has devoured—the original seven which comprised him having grown dense and large, ready to erupt and end all things in their wake.

Sasha bars Persephone with her arm, pushing the girl back and behind her, and says:

"You want to punish us, but think *yourself* a god and therefore above all criticism. In fact, you're actively trying—with all your lies and fearmongering—to constitute a new ruling: one that will force the hand of the White Abyss to validate you being above criticism, above everything, as it would become Truth that you are God. An act of Will-enforcing, Will-strengthening...an act of erasure.

"You're embodying the role well. I'll give you that. Truly very Christian of you—so imperialistic in its nature, overwriting the cultures which preceded it by means of conquest, of genocide and hate, all the while speaking of love. But while the love you promise to your soulless, mindless followers is a lie, you do hold love—I've seen it firsthand when Seth and I and our friends eradicated the Sins those many years ago. The Sins, evil as they were, still cared for one another as family. You feel that same love, don't you? But appealing to that common human trait would serve no purpose, for your love is selfish and knows only you. Christian love—there is no crueler, more perverse form of love than Christian love, and it is a love entirely derived from self-centeredness. I would know better than most..."

Sasha thinks back to her early childhood, before being saved by Virdeus and the Guild, to when her biological father spoke of love and Christian values, all the while molesting her every single night. "I will not allow your poison to harm humanity any longer. You want to become an eternal recurrence? Well, I declare that my values already are—a world for humanity, with no need for gods. You will not win this battle—you and all you stand for cannot be allowed to endure."

As Sasha unsheathes and grips her knives, her eyes pulsate with abyssal light. And glimmering in tandem is the swirl of white and teal held within her engagement ring. Their blinding glow piercing the dark of night, glittering upon the snow.

Watching with stoic, focused intensity within his eyes, Damien smirks.

"Yes, *yes!*" Damien shouts, purple-stained spittle ejecting from his mouth. "A clash of Wills—through which a birthing of a new guiding principle arises! The stone beneath our feet is now ripe with creative potential! The Abyss now watches, pondering which direction fate will lead..."

This cannot go on.

On the verge of collapsing, held up by abyssal power alone, these are the only words his mind can conjure. *This cannot go on*—Seth's eyes grow wide as he chokes, the Abyssian's new white form gripping his neck. The evolved god having lunged toward him, rendering Seth immobile as his airflow ceases, his left arm pinned to the ground beside his head. The weight of the Abyssian's grip amplifies to intense degrees—Seth's bones fracture, as he stares past the white, featureless being and to the waxing crescent moon peeking through the clouds. Just now on its way out. Sinking into the horizon, obscured by the mountain's trees. The finality of its cycle—when it next rises, it will be a new moon. Harbinger of things yet to come. Yet, with the Abyssian holding Seth down, it feels as if the moon itself is pressing down upon him.

This cannot go on.

And while pondering the cyclical nature of life, Seth is worn down by the realization that he is once more fighting an unearthly being—one which seeks to be a god, calls itself a god, but one that remains blind to its hypocrisies. For gods are of the highest tier and therefore would never cast off themselves, become an entirely new being. A god, a perfect being, would never adapt, become something new, born of necessity, for fear of being tossed away into obscurity. A denial of life and identity after failing to grow and change, throughout their pointless squabbles for power—their incessant need to be in charge. Therefore, gods are lesser than a human at their peak, for humanity is a creature that can truly grow and learn and mature, without discarding who they are and while cohabitating with others. This urge for community over solidarity allows humans to enhance themselves as well as those around them. Reaching sublime heights together, and therefore not falling from the peak, but rising above it. For, to be human is to overcome humanity, to become more than the conglomeration of basic instincts gifted by Nature. To overwrite their modus operandi and engage in artful living, together, creating in ways no other creature can. Not even a god. *This cannot go on*—this is something Zarathustra taught Seth long ago.

This cannot go on.

A raspy scream breaks through as Seth's bones fracture further. Swatting at the featureless face of the Abyssian feels like slapping a brick wall. The sheer density of its body outclasses even Seth's abyssal flames—*and it looks just like the Abyssal Consciousness.*

The Abyssian's body begins stretching skyward in tandem with widening at its sides. Dangling growths form before elongating into tendrils. Wrapping around Seth's ankles, knees, thighs—Seth grunts loudly, as waves of a piercing sensation surges through him. The light from his eyes dulling, fatigue rapidly setting in—Seth brings his left fist down upon the Abyssian's arm—blood vessels in both of Seth's eyes burst alongside muffled screams, as every bone in his hand shatters into dust.

{Yes, vermin.} says the Abyssian War Chief. {**Struggle—then I'll do the same to those women you are so concerned about...and it will be the most exquisite of deaths.**}

As his eyes grow increasingly bloodshot, Seth tosses, flailing with fury. He feels it—as every bone in his body is reduced further to dust, he feels it: the White Abyss squirming beneath his feet like agitated, writhing snakes. His death and the deaths to follow, would no longer be inconsequential deaths, as all deaths are. Live, die, return to the collective pool of power that is the White Abyss. This is the norm, and it is beautiful. To live artfully and to provide well for future generations to live out their lives. Nothing more can be asked. But Seth feels it—the collective souls within the White Abyss are reacting to a power calling out—*much like at the end of Heaven, when I breathed new life into the Earth—but so much more this time!*

We have reached a fulcrum—a moment where one's amor fati, the love of their fate, no longer applies. A handful of powerful souls are all fighting at once to determine the outcome of the future, where any one of us can set the trajectory for things to come—our wills, about to burst apart like the splitting of an atom. Engulfing everything with our desires. And all I desire is...

Seth's eyes shimmer and quake, their bright teal pulsing, once more rising from the depths of abyssal white. And as the god who shed its skin continues to strangle his prey, memories flash into Seth's mind: Sasha peering into his eyes for the first time, when he was still a raging demon. Fighting alongside her, growing and learning from her—and falling in love with her. Her rounded belly, the arrival of Persephone. Her screeching wails as she emerged from the womb, her childish laughter as she pranked Misha. Even her unmanageable teenage angst warms Seth's heart as the life is squeezed from him—and at the thought of his family, those teal orbs quake wildly—and he remembers one other thing heavier than his own abyssal flames.

The power of a True-Born God.

With Persephone in mind, and pain searing through nerves like fire, Seth's neck muscles convulse, as a pressure surges outward—the Abyssian's hands shatters into white particles. **{What, how?}** he says, and as he glances from his wrists to Seth, he finds the human's eyes overflowing with abyssal power, his neck veins convulsing like a pile of snakes and—

"*This cannot go on!*" Seth roars, as a white blast ejects like a cannon from his mouth—a long stretch of abyssal energy surges through the god's white form, through the surrounding trees, and toward the horizon. The Abyssian's scream blares within Seth's mind as the god is fried by the pure stream of abyssal power, until fading to a hiss and then nothing more. As the abyssal beam dissipates shortly after, the crescent moon above vanishes not beyond the horizon, but in a silent explosion of white light.

Body broken and crippled, Seth heaves as blood gushes from every open seam of his skin. A deep crimson pool has long enveloped his body, and with the Abyssian gone, Seth's arms splash into the murky redness. Deepened by the melted snow.

Glancing toward the moon, no longer there, severe winds are spurred, the climate set out of alignment. And Seth weeps. After years of discipline, a long vow to never use the Omni Magic festering within him is now obscured by a trail of blackness torn into the fabric of the world. A chunk of the forest and sky lost forever. The blackness beyond seeping into tangible reality. Through the Omni Magic, Seth has tapped into the powers of a True-Born God, and the tears fall heavier, knowing that—

Abyssal flames wrap around his mangled body, holding it firm like a full-body brace. And, trudging toward their broken home upon the cliffside, Seth laments knowing that he will have to do it again.

―――●○●―――

Adhering to her mother's wishes, Persephone steps back. Though the impulse to disobey is strong. Her powers rippling beneath the surface, squirming like snakes, just like the Abyss beneath her feet. Reacting to something inevitable and momentous. Alongside this sensation is an ever-growing concern—*I've come into my powers these past few months, but the Abyss...it feels volatile, it's creative energy strong, ripe, but chaotic in tandem. I've seen what my powers can do...and have been warned that it's because I am too young. Perhaps this once, I'll listen to Mom. Besides, I felt it—that power within Dad...I'm worried.*

She watches her mother step toward Damien, arms rising, palms turned upward. And alongside their skyward motion, teal sparks burst into long, crackling bolts of lightning, squirming above the stony cliffside. The teal bolts sink into the rocky surface, and slither into the roots of trees surrounding the mountain's plateau—Damien jerks his head toward two bolts surging past him and into pillars of wood, the few remaining pieces of the destroyed cabin, and says, "What are you trying to—" Hands made of stone erupt from the rocky cliffside, gripping Damien's feet, ankles, thighs, as the rounded scalp of a stone golem rises from the ground like surfacing from water. Humanoid forms break free from the shackles of bark and wood, creeping toward Damien from the edge of the mountain's summit. Their long arms carved into spears, rising overhead as they rush toward Damien. New life appearing as all life does. Suddenly, without apparent origin. Into reality from the Abyss, and into which it will dissipate again upon the end of its life—from nothing to something, to nothing once more.

Struggling, feeling the weight of the stone grips around his legs, Damien shouts, "These powers of yours are growing! Or you're adapting and learning—I will put a stop to tha—" Gritting his teeth hard, a loud, anguished groan ejects from his mouth...a wooden spike pierces his throat, slicing through his larynx.

"I told you before, you aren't leaving this cliffside alive. We've killed you before, and we will kill you again," says Sasha, her eyes aglow with abyssal white light. Simultaneously seeing through the eyes of the dozens of earthen creatures swarming Damien. Controlling their movements, their impulses, thoughts, and every ounce of rage as Damien is repeatedly stabbed by the wooden creatures. "You call yourself an eternal recurrence?

Then so are we and so is your death!" she screams, backing away as she allows her earthen familiars to continue their assault.

Watching her mother fight, Persephone cannot help but be in awe. The continual growth of her mother's magic—she knows this is a commonality amongst all magic, that humanity's creative spirit is ever-increasing in potential. Such is the way of the White Abyss's collective pool of power. But this is different. Her mother is a god. *Perhaps not a True-Born God like the Abyssal Consciousness claims I am, but with her power of creation, well, what can't she do?* Magic does what the mind wills it to do. And as Persephone watches her mother, she feels it, the flow of the White Abyss—*she is willing so ferociously right now, with all her might.*

And alongside this awe she feels for her mother, Persephone feels the White Abyss quake beneath her feet. As if it is reacting to her mother's Will.

Damien screams, but no sound emerges. Only a gargled mesh of grunts and wheezing as his body is torn asunder. Sasha's earthen familiars continually pierce his skin, blood oozing into a puddle beneath him, streaming away from his dangling intestines. Bombarded by this surprise, the echo of a god is left with no choice but to let it happen.

His rageful eyes glare skyward as he's disemboweled, spying the lone familiar Sasha has kept at a distance. The second raven, one of the beasts who had pecked out his progenitor's eyes. Damien's heart thumps heavily in his chest, as a mixture of ecstasy and rage ravishes him. Pleasure in knowing he caused Sasha grief by killing one of them—a life that, now at the end of it, was well lived. Everything he has ever wanted, everything he has lived for, has been for this. To have his enemies suffer.

But the rage mingling with that pleasure quakes wildly within his chest. Discontent with leaving one alive, with not maximizing his murderers' torment.

His eyes pulse, swirling into blackness once more.

A tempest of black fog erupts from his body, engulfing the cliffside. Sasha stumbles, catching herself on a tree. Crouching at its side, she grips the bark with all her strength, struggling not to be brushed away by the pressure. About ten feet away, beneath the burnt, snow-covered branches of an evergreen, Persephone stands erect. Her eyes aglow with abyssal white light, anchoring her feet firmly into the ground. The dirt beneath the snow folding in upon itself from the weight. Enduring where the evergreen's pine needles could not, having been thwarted by ravaging fire.

Sasha sighs in relief, seeing her daughter safe, and turns back to the swirling blackness. Ripping through the air so fiercely, the surrounding snow melts, revealing the stony surface of the cliffside, now wet and slick. Sparks and embers whip outward as the black spiral refuses to slow, the friction in the air erupting from the intense speed—a shockwave of black mist bursts outward, followed by sheared wood and stone. The shrapnel scatters, piercing into trees with ease like glass shards embedded in skin. Persephone takes cover behind a thicket of evergreens, as Sasha, made unsteady from the blast, raises her free arm over her face—she screams as blood sprays like a hose over the surrounding snow, her arm blown clean off.

"*Mom!*" Persephone screams, not noticing the form emerging from the dispersed tempest—Damien's right arm, the muscles massively bloated, emerge from the dust of Sasha's earthen familiars, elongating well beyond his body's confines, and had rocketed toward Sasha.

Grown large enough to wrap his fingers around her torso, gripping her tight, Damien's arm hurtles her into the air horizontally, plowing her into a large evergreen, its needles burnt, but still holding strong. Sasha's eyes grow wide, a surging pain splitting down her center. Her spine and lower hip shatter. As she glances toward Damien, obscured by the mist of stone and dirt and wood, she catches sight of her other arm, dangling free of her, its nails dug deeply into the bark of the tree she clung to. And above the massive arm extending twenty feet, she can just barely catch sight of a maniacal grin relishing in her end.

And her vision blurs into nothingness.

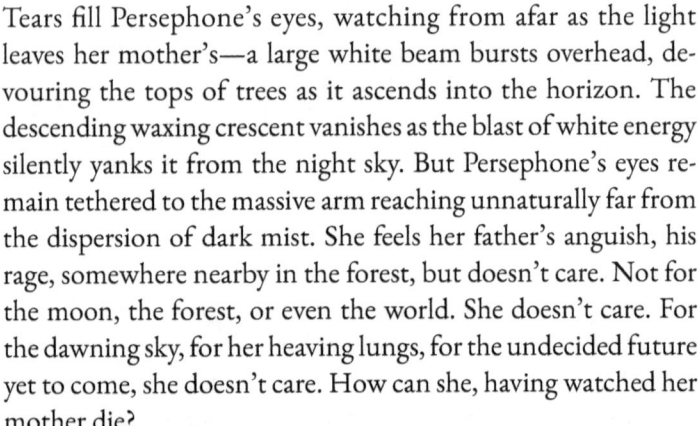

Tears fill Persephone's eyes, watching from afar as the light leaves her mother's—a large white beam bursts overhead, devouring the tops of trees as it ascends into the horizon. The descending waxing crescent vanishes as the blast of white energy silently yanks it from the night sky. But Persephone's eyes remain tethered to the massive arm reaching unnaturally far from the dispersion of dark mist. She feels her father's anguish, his rage, somewhere nearby in the forest, but doesn't care. Not for the moon, the forest, or even the world. She doesn't care. For the dawning sky, for her heaving lungs, for the undecided future yet to come, she doesn't care. How can she, having watched her mother die?

"*I'll fucking kill you!*" she screams, and as she sprints forward, the wind grows harsh and volatile. The atmosphere is set askew in the absence of Earth's lunar companion. So, it screams in its mourning of the moon, fiercely alongside Persephone.

Basking in an abyssal glow, white light wraps around her fists as she leaps forward, bringing her arm down upon the face of Damien—the mist dispersing enough to reveal his maniacal grin. Her fist slams against his nose, but his face doesn't wince, twitch, or move in the slightest. Aside from the subtle sensation of his skin sliding against her fist.

Seven snakelike heads emerge from the mist, towering over her as the haze dissipates completely. Stumbling back, she glances from Damien's face to the black snakes writhing ten feet above her. "What the fuck?" she says, as one of the snakes opens its jaws, snapping toward her—tumbling over, the snake bites down upon the cliffside, mere inches from her feet. A swift jerking motion as the hulking beast whips its backside toward her—seven tails collide into the ground, upheaving stone as Persephone rolls out of the way, and crawls to her feet.

Gaining some distance, she glances at the monster from top to bottom. It's seven bloated heads slither into a conjoined torso, with two small, bony arms with sharp, clawed hands. Descending its waist, it separates again into its tails. And at the fused neck, Damien's maniacal grin slides off its black body, fluttering away furiously within the harsh winds. The enormous arm and its bloated muscles also fall off, thumping heavily into the snow, as the beast sheds its skin. Having altered his muscle mass to such a degree, his souls could not maintain the sheer force of power exerted within this moment of unadorned rage.

It's true being, slithering into the world, just as it did on the accursed day it was born.

The volatile gusts bellow harshly atop the mountain's summit. With the moon's disappearance, all hurtles into chaos. Water levels rise, flooding all the cities of the world, followed by a barrage of other climate disasters. The Earth cannot maintain life without the moon. This integral balance, the fulcrum of human life. An equilibrium, which Seth has broken. And soon, now death shall wash over everything.

And yet he moves forward.

Trudging onward with armor made of abyssal material, he wearily makes his way to the cabin. His home, a place bursting with memories, with love and adoration for—

His feet stand still. The harsh wind pelting his side, as a chill overcomes him, followed by a raging heat. Turning toward an evergreen—its needles burnt, but hanging strong—he notices a dent in the bark. Eyes slinking downward, he sighs heavily as his fists rattle and shake.

Moving onward through the bleak forest, the mountain's summit comes into view—as does his daughter, and a towering seven-headed grotesquerie.

The snow lies high, reaching his knees. And, lifting his left foot, wrapped in abyssal energy, he crashes it down with all his might—white flames burst outward as his sole thumps against the hard, icy ground, engulfing the trees and bushes and—the fire spreads so wide, the summit, the forest, the entirety of the mountain's mass is set ablaze, awash in his fury.

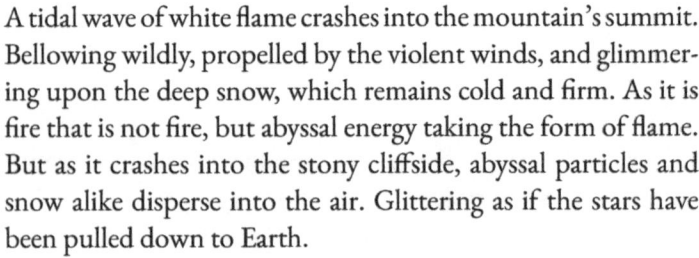

A tidal wave of white flame crashes into the mountain's summit. Bellowing wildly, propelled by the violent winds, and glimmering upon the deep snow, which remains cold and firm. As it is fire that is not fire, but abyssal energy taking the form of flame. But as it crashes into the stony cliffside, abyssal particles and snow alike disperse into the air. Glittering as if the stars have been pulled down to Earth.

Persephone, tumbled to the ground and watching the snake's many tails descend upon her again, covers her face with her arms as the blinding white flame rushes toward her—

Splitting like the Red Sea, the abyssal flames spread and encircle her. A strange, otherworldly sound erupts from Damien's new form, a screech and hiss fused together, creating an ear-piercing static, amplified and echoing as if bursting from massive sound speakers. The seven-headed beast writhes as the tidal wave of abyssal flame collides with it. Its arms squirm about, its heads wobbling, tumbling over and crashing into the ground.

"You killed my wife."

Persephone turns toward her father, finding him clad in abyssal white flames, weaving together to form a bright, glowing armor. But with a face mangled and bloodied—all flesh, with little to no skin to wrap it. Her eyes aglow with abyssal light, she peers beyond the surface into his soul—an unhinged chaos squirms about within, his fists shaking with rage alongside what feels to Persephone as an endless legion of newborn spiders bursting free from their sac. She looks upon her father, feeling her heart *thump* in tandem with his as she spies teal orbs within his abyssal white eyes. Quaking, as their confines expand, larger and larger as they slowly rupture.

"I know you. You're shaped differently, conjoined as one. But I remember those bulbous black heads—the souls of the Sins. You are a soul residing free from flesh, outside of the White Abyss?"

A memory triggers, of when his soul ejected from his body at the split second between being killed by Yahweh and having his soul return to the White Abyss. And returning still, but as one retaining his form, his sentience, a first of such an occurrence. But he stands here now, a flesh-and-blood human. "Echo of

Yahweh. You are a failure," he says. "Your soul has transcended its body, but lost itself in the process."

A soul? Persephone's eyes widen, understanding now what they're up against. *A body can bleed and die, but a human soul is immortal. And existing here, outside the White Abyss, how can it be possible to kill it?*

The seven-headed pitch-black snake snarls and screeches from its featureless face. Thus, confirming Seth's claims. And standing there amidst the white fire, man and monster glare at each other with a rage transcending lifetimes.

Seth lunges at the beast with intense speed, gripping its neck with his right hand and bashing his left into the middle-most head. Seth's eyes appear wider, angrier, amidst the loose and open flesh of his face. His clenched teeth appear massive, no longer hidden by his fleshy lips or long black beard. "*You are only a soul. The boy you once were, dead and gone—all the better!*" he screams. "*For this cannot go on—the lineage of gods ends here!*"

The seven heads thrash about as Seth pummels his fist into another, and another as it lunges toward him with an open mouth. Its throat leading to a shadowy black pit. The same color as the grotesquery's tar-like body. Soul made solid, but without the divine, shimmering teal held by human souls—no, Damien's was tainted long ago, when Yahweh made a monster of herself.

The beast's bony, black arms claw at Seth, scraping against his armor-plated chest, and digging into his fleshy, skinless face—but no reaction is elicited, only the fury in his eyes intensifying. The tails whip at him—Seth catches the meaty tendrils in his right arm, swinging his other into the left-most head. Flinging backward, another head lunges toward him—the wind catches fire as Seth plows his grip into the head's upper neck. Pulling fiercely upward, as one would uproot a weed from a garden. The head squeals and, one by one, the rightmost heads collide into Seth, the first knocking him back, the next breaking his hand free, the other slithers around, colliding into his chest, followed by the rest. Forced from Damien's body, the seven heads plow Seth into the stony cliffside, upheaving chunks of snow and stone.

The seven-headed grotesquery slithers with the flow and consistency of an ocean's tide, slamming *again and again and again* into Seth. Fissures forming in the cliffside beneath their weight—Seth catches the middlemost head as it lunges toward him. Sharp fangs clamping down, but clutched open by Seth, an inch from his face. A foul stench rising from the soul's gullet only increases Seth's fury.

His neck wouldn't budge—but only because a soul, even brought into the world, isn't a tangible thing. That boy—Damien—is dead. This...thing. It's just an idea of him, a concept, his fury outliving his corporeal form.

Pushing the snake's mouth to the right and letting go of its jaw, it clamps down on a mouthful of snow and stone, ejecting both into the air as dust as Seth kicks at the beast's core, sending it tumbling back. But no wound left as evidence.

"You are just a soul. Shall I send you back to the White Abyss, as I have done before?" Seth's eyes glow with abyssal light, as orbs of white flame create a doorway. A vast white space slowly spirals into being. Seth grunts as the pressure of forcing a portal into the White Abyss weighs him down, his teal eyes pulsating ever brighter and—growing wide, they fade, as the portal dissolves into ash and embers. The blackened snake steadies itself and its seven bloated heads, readying to lunge once more, as Seth says, "No. I cannot send you back. Your collective Wills resisted the fate of all souls...and were reborn." He glares at the hulking grotesquery before him. "Who's to say you won't return again?"

The beast slithers forcefully toward him, quivering unnaturally as it glides forward. Each movement inducing a queasy feeling within Seth, overwhelmed by the monster's terrifying aura. Weary of its strength and the edge of the cliff behind him, Seth's eyes glow bright with teal once more—the billions of souls writhing within him, ready to burst—his attention yanks toward the outer edge of the cliffside, at the corpse of his wife slumped horizontally against a tree. A glimmer of white and teal particles hover around her like mist, rising from the shattered gemstone atop her engagement ring—

Seth's eyes dull as he pushes the Omni Magic down, before lighting again with searing pain. The snake's two middle-most heads clamp down on his chest and left side.

No, I cannot—I cannot use this power, with what it may lead to. I promised her I would be better, remain better—after what I did to her people in Magistrum, when I was no better than this beast before me.

The grotesquerie whips Seth back and forth, slamming him into the hard stone padded by snow, before hurtling him through the air toward the forest.

"Daddy!" Persephone shouts. Eyes aglow, the white flames dissipate before her. With the cliffside as the epicenter, the fire disperses into a white mist, slowly creeping back, extinguishing the mountain. Rushing forward, with abyssal tendrils flowing around her, she catches her father.

Spitting up blood, Seth says, "Per-seph-one. Wh-at-ever hap-pens...know that I—I am so proud of you."

"Stop. Don't talk."

The hulking snake monster rampages toward them, as Persephone lays her father in the snow beneath a tree. His head resting against the trunk, watching as his daughter stomps forward, stretching out her left hand, palm facing the beast. A flash of white light engulfs their vision, as a beam of abyssal energy surges toward Damien's soul—a hole burns away at its center as the beam pierces through. Each of the seven heads screeches as they thrash around. And at the edge of the hole, black tendrils slither toward the center. Slowly weaving together, healing the wound.

Seth's eyes grow in astonishment. With all his strength, he was still ineffectual against the beast, leaving no wounds. But Persephone—*that's it!* Blood gushing from his chest and side, his abyssal armor flickering, fading, he struggles to his feet while his daughter's back is turned to him. *A True-Born God has mastery over all things—why not souls?*

Slithering forward again, snow and stone spring into the air at its side. Angrier than ever before. Persephone raises her palm again—the snake's fangs plunge toward her quickly, but she catches its mouth. Feeling herself sink further into the snow, the cliffside begins to crumble—the outer edge is lost to the forest floor beneath. Her eyes set aglow, abyssal energy weaves around her arms to compensate—the beast's tails whip around in surprise, colliding hard against her side, flinging her into a tree. The back of her head slams against the bark, and vision blurs as a concussion takes hold. The hulking beast towers over her, as its seven heads draw closer to each other. The sun, now rising slowly over the horizon, sheds a ray of light on the beast as a blackened orb of energy forms around its seven mouths—growing, intensifying, ready to burst—ejecting toward Persephone, the tar-color laser obliterates the spot where she lay. Engulfing her now steadying vision is nothing but blackness...

Amidst a fluttering white light...

And a splash of crimson...

Persephone's eyes grow wide, amidst a face splattered in blood—an eviscerating, hollowing sensation fills her core with such severity, her insides feel as if they are spilling out of her. Losing all life within her, leaving nothing but a husk beneath a face overwhelmed with horror.

A pair of legs stand deep within the snow in front of her, rising into a bloodied hip severed from its other half. Tears flood her eyes as Persephone shouts, "*Daddy!*" as she watches her father's torso fling through the air in an arch of blood and entrails, his arms stretched wide, but flailing in the air. He thuds into the snow at her side. Crawling up to him on her knees, conscious of the hulking monster slowly approaching, Persephone cups Seth's cheek in her left hand. Smiling up at her, a shaky voice wheezes past his lips in a barely audible whisper. "You...can do it..." Dusk settles upon his eyes, as they flutter to a close.

His eyes peel open in a burst of teal light, his soul ejecting from within, a hazy teal mist flinging into the air. Persephone's shaky hands grab at his soul, trying desperately to clutch him to her chest. But he rockets past her, knocking into the seven-headed grotesquery, tumbling about in the air chaotically, and—the intangible teal mass sprouts a head and two arms. Clawing at itself, twisting and tearing as two more arms and another head protrude from the other side. Swatting at the one trying to tear the two apart. The soul's dual essences fighting for control, one trying to split apart, as the other tries to mend the connection. The fury and the calm—

The furious essence bashes its head against its calm counterpart, which wilts and dies as the furious one cleaves the two apart. The calm one dissipates, returning to the White Abyss's collective pool of power, as the furious one springs higher into the air, spiraling rapidly until flinging off to the side—

The fabric of the world shatters, forcing open a wormhole as the soul flings itself into the space above Persephone and the beast. Severed from its other half, left incomplete—

A loud croak echoes from above the rift, yanking Persephone's attention. Muninn plummets, darting after its master's soul. The two in union, both reeling from the pain of losing their other halves, disappear together, now set adrift into realms unknown.

Persephone screams in agony, hanging her head in despair, tears dripping onto her chest and legs. All the while, the replicant of a god's echo yanks its head back, readying to plunge its fangs into her—

{Is this what your parents would have wanted? Giving in to despair and hopelessness? Or would they have wanted you to stand tall and strong, as the powerful woman they knew you to be? Go on, now. Be a True-Born God...and put an end to things—administer your control over souls, as is your birthright.}

Souls?

Persephone yanks her gaze up, furious and wet—a blaring white light blasts out from her eyes, as pressure builds beneath her skin. Not only that hollowing evisceration from before, from losing her parents, but also from the sheer weight of the Abyss's entirety flowing through her still young mind, as she taps into a power rightfully hers for the first time—all seven heads lunge at her in tandem, as she rises with grace, awash with an abyssal white glow, touching the snout of the nearest head—the hulking beast ceases, frozen in place. And as she stands there, glowing with the same intensity as the stars above, she says, "Be no more."

Seven white fissures crease their way between the necks of the beast, through its core, and between its tails—whiteness envelopes the mountain's summit, as the beast is split apart into seven separate souls. Floating there, unmoving, reduced to their original hazy blackness, as they are crusted over in abyssal white light. Hardening, bursting outward, filling the mountain air with ash which shimmers like starlight, but obscured into nothingness.

And with the sheer pressure of the entire White Abyss flowing through her, it is known that she was not yet ready, that her parents were right, that she was too young. The abyssal power bursting from her eyes begins eroding her skin, crusting over into dense stone—the wind brushes against her, and Persephone is whisked away like sand.

A haze of white ash, amidst a twinkling teal light plopping into the deep snow where she no longer stands.

Now bifurcated, half of Seth's soul is flung furiously between realms. Lamenting in his impotence, his hesitance, his lack of commitment to using whatever means necessary to eradicate the monsters threatening his family and home. Through severing himself from his balanced and disciplined half, his fury now descends through the space between realms where no one but gods can travel—and in this abstract, intangible crossroads, Seth's soul flings itself downward.

One by one, the fabric of each universe shatters as he blasts through the dimensional stack like a cannonball. Each world quakes in terror as he punctures a hole through one after another. Which lay withered and dead in the wake of the Abyssian gods, with no life to be found.

But following in his wake—a river of teal. Breaking off into streams is a crackle of creative magic. His soul bleeding out the billions of others within him, covering each world with Omni Magic.

And while the wormholes created as he bursts through each world remain, the veins of Omni Magic sprinkle themselves into the dead earth, which then glow with teal light. The plants grow green, the soil fertile, and amidst each world's refreshed vigor, new life spawns. First, bugs hatch from teal eggs, then rodents run wild through the high grasses, and birds fling themselves into the air. Followed by bipedal creatures, created in his image. They rise naked from the ground, rejoicing to be alive.

All the while their creator continues his descent of mutual destruction and creation, piercing holes in each dimension until—a grandiose, white city sprawls out below. A world Seth recognizes through memories gifted to him from Zarathustra. The stray god's home, his origin. Abyssia. Seth's soul takes it all in, its pompous, self-important aura, but empty with its legions ravishing the Earth. And at its center rises the highest tower, the church housing the Womb of the One Mind.

His furious soul plummeting like a comet collides with the holy Abyssian chapel, the tower bursting apart as Seth's soul blasts through and—fissures form within the church's walls, spreading outward, enveloping the city as Seth's fury breaks through the holy chapel's foundation, sinking into this world's crust and out the dimension's bottom side. The church's walls swiftly bend inward before an overwhelming white light bursts out from within—the Womb breaking free and born again.

And in his wake, the Womb of the One Mind stretches its tendrils toward the interdimensional fractures. Stretching the broken edges toward each other, performing a dimensional skin graft. Thus, beginning *a long, bright dark.* An era of healing, in these worlds without gods.

And bursting through the lowest realms, Seth's soul arrives at the first to be devoured by the Abyssians. Its condition severe, with dark, black holes slit open across the sky. The void's taint has eaten away at this world for eons since the Abyssians first descended upon a civilization now long gone. But as Seth continues his descent, he hurtles toward the ground and—

An explosion of teal engulfs the entire lowest dimension, causing magic particles to erupt into the air, shattering outward from the large crater formed by his collision. Like the dimensions in the stack above, new life blooms, bustling about beneath the fractured space above, until the glowing particles condense into a bright teal haze, obscuring the many black rifts and replacing the broken sky with a new veil of blue and a warm, bright sun.

At the center of the crater, Seth's furious soul thrashes about, screaming in agony, missing his wife and daughter. Set adrift to a world unknown, and unable to cope, his teal soul grows, rounding out into a massive, towering oval dome.

And, hardening amidst the silence of a newly created world, Seth loses himself to a hazy hibernation, left there as an egg-shaped stone.

As the light faded from her eyes, that searing pain lingered down her shattered spine and hip.

Her soul succumbing to the flow, returning to the Abyss—the sound of shattered stone arrives in tandem with a bright teal glow, dancing before her eyes with abyssal particles. Mingling together as a haze of magic energy—the snapping of bone, as her spine realigns, healing its fractures. She wants to scream out in pain, but she remains on the threshold of life and death, within a hazy state of mind, marrying the two together. The shattered pieces of her hip regrows, her spine tethering to it, unwounded—her eyes reanimating, they light with their bright copper-colored pupils, staring ahead at the teal and white mist.

Unable to move, she glances left to right, finding the bone of her shoulder elongating into a new arm, clamping into place, she again wants to scream. But despite her soul having been yanked back from the Abyss and returned to her body, she remains too fatigued to move.

How can this be? She glances at her ring, noticing something missing. The translucent gemstone lay shattered in the snow, as a haze of white and teal rise from the ring's basket. *The power of creation alongside abyssal potential creating a marriage of life and death.*

With feeling returning to her nerves, her eyes well with tears. At the miracle created from Seth's love for her, and at—

A soft cry emerges from her mouth. Too weak to scream, she can only whimper, as she watches her husband's body encrust with abyssal power. One second, he leans against a tree, the next he warps himself in front of the monster's blast of dark energy, pushing their daughter behind him with arms stretched wide as a cross. Before his torso is launched into the air, severed from his legs. Thudding into the ground, his souls erupt into a fit of fury before severing and banishing itself through a fissure blown into the fabric of the world.

Sasha's arms drop. Hunched over, she claws with all her might at the snow. Attempting to pull herself toward her Persephone. Her legs refusing to move, and the snow offering no grip. Only frigidness strikes the newly formed nerve endings.

The monster lunges at Persephone, and she stands, shining like a goddess, before bursting both the monster and herself into a veil of white ash.

Sasha screams, her voice returning as she stumbles to her feet. Collapsing into the snow again and again, until tumbling into Seth's torso, and the snow so deeply stained with his blood.

Rolling onto her back, she pulls Seth's head to her breasts, hugging him tight—a teal glimmer where Persephone stood pulls her attention. Frantically clutching for it, she pulls her fist close, revealing a teal gemstone with white energy floating within it like water, despite being solid.

Sasha sobs, wailing into the morning hours as clouds break overhead, with the rising sun announcing a brand-new day. Hugging her husband tight, and clutching her daughter's soul essence, Sasha yanks her head back. Glaring skyward with furious bloodshot eyes, she lets out a primal, guttural howl.

CHAPTER THIRTY-NINE

Set adrift into memory, Sasha ventures back about eighteen years. The ring held by Seth's large and callused, but gentle hands. Glimmering in the moonlight alongside its swirl of teal and white, of creation and abyssal power:

Gasping, she raised her left hand to her throat. "Abyssal flames and divine energy, mingling together. A marriage of life and death?"

Seth smiled widely, his cheeks rising high beneath eyes so full of longing and compassion. "In the spirit of everything we've done, of everything we're working toward, will you be wed to me in life and in death?"

Her eyes, glazed over and dull, emerge from memory as she glances toward her ring—the gemstone shattered, its powers having revived her. A miracle performed by Seth from beyond the grave. *Had he planned this? Or was it a fluke of magic beyond even his understanding?* She nods in agreement.

Her eyes flow with tears as she watches her husband join with the stony cliffside. The crackle of teal magic splits the stone apart, cracked by the battle with Damien. And laying Seth's body into the crevasse—his torso aligned with his severed legs as well as she could manage—the teal magic crackles once more, enclosing the ground over him.

"Your remains belong with the Earth, Seth, with the Abyss that is forever tethered to it. But our daughter—" Sasha glances down at her left fist, uncurling her fingers, revealing Persephone's crystalized soul. "I'm sorry, but I want her with me. Though I know you would want the same."

Struck silent by the moment, eviscerated by the tragedy, her body grows still as statues. Her mind spiraling through a tempest of thoughts, meandering toward an uncertain future, built by grotesque gods with the corpses of her loved ones used as bricks and stones.

What do I do now?

{Yes, what will you?}

You...you dare speak to me now? You've been silent all this time, watching this chaos unfold. Now you want to offer your advice and vagaries? When my daughter and husband are dead?

{At this point, there is little to be done, and no room for intervention. And I know your fury, Spawn of Zarathustra. You were the god's lust, and yet you hold such a great anger yourself. Lust goes hand in hand with frustration—rage, if the need is left unmet. And lust and anger—these are two of the strongest emotions that fuel the act of creation. The fuel itself—and the audacity to act. I have no advice for you, Spawn of Zarathustra, for you do not need it. Peering into your soul, I can see the makings of the end already in motion. And you feel it, too, don't you? The White Abyss still squirms, despite the felling of the echo of Yahweh and the Abyssians' leader, the collective pool of Wills still await an answer. *Your answer.* As the strongest god still left alive. So, can you do it? Will you follow through?}

Sasha glances overhead, finding the portal left by Seth lingering above. Unlike his usual portals, this one has been forced open, shattering the fabric of the world.

Just fucking watch me.

Outstretching her arms wide as a cross, her eyes pool with abyssal light, so fiercely it flows upward, extending past her head as fiery, white horns. Yanking her arms together, a crackle of teal magic bursts from her palms—the air before her shatters like glass as fissures tear through the fabric of the world. Squirming along the edges are pitch-black tendrils, but straight through, she finds a familiar sight—the world shatters on the other side, causing Misha's alarmed face to yank behind her as a portal is forced open.

"Sasha?" says Misha. "How did you—what is this?" She eyes the shattered air and the tendrils rising from the broken edges, as her aunt trudges through.

Glancing around at the battlefield, the silence of tragedy is replaced by the cacophony of blades clashing with Abyssian claws, and ear-piercing gunshots rapidly fired off. The Red-Hat Army has diminished, but still outnumbers the Assembly by a great margin. And high in the sky awaits a legion of Abyssians, calculating their most opportune moments to descend and slaughter.

"It's never ending," says Sasha, and Misha frowns.

Their leaders are dead, and yet their Wills persist. Is this what Damien meant by it not mattering if we killed him? Look how spiritedly his army of religious simpletons charge forward with guns in their hands. They will believe in their god's existence until their dying breath, won't they? The cognitive dissonance so strong, nothing could change their minds. Just as I never could with Sergei. But if left alive, unchecked—will Damien be proved right? Will he rise again? As an echo of an echo of an echo...and so on for eternity.

Sasha sighs, unable to care, barely having the energy necessary to maintain her tether to life.

Enough of it all—this cannot go on.

"Misha."

"Yes?"

"Send a message to all international Assembly members. Tell them to head to their bunkers, gather as many civilians as they can find, and meet me in the crevasse below Crowley."

Misha gives her aunt an inquisitive glare. "Sure, but how do you expect them to get there?"

"I will open a path forward," says Sasha, glancing at the fissures in the world's fabric, and turns away from her niece.

"Of course. I'll take care of it right away," says Misha, reaching for the radio clipped to her belt. "But Sasha? What about Persephone and uncle—"

Sasha turns, glancing over her shoulder with eyes wide, quivering, with furious tears. The destruction of all around them, the clash of weapons, and the barrage of shots and screams as soldiers on both sides breathe their last—the cacophony of warfare emphasizes the severe pain creased into Sasha's face.

Misha's jaw drops, her eyes flooding. Turning away, she wipes the tears with the back of her left hand and says, "Understood. I'll alert the Assembly to join you—and Aunt Sasha, don't worry. I'll lead the charge here and hold off these—these monsters."

Sasha breathes deeply and says, "Thank you, Misha. Know that your father would be proud."

Misha nods and rushes off into the uncertain foray. As Sasha turns, eyes aglow with abyssal white, clashing her palms together once more, creating another portal.

IN THE WAKE OF GODS

We wanted to exist as normal humans and treat ourselves as if we aren't gods. But despite our desires, Seth, that's exactly what we are. Not like our daughter, but we are gods. And this world, the Earth—it is magic. And as the last of the human gods, I should be able to do whatever I like with it.

The lights flash on, revealing the towering, massive spacecraft sitting in the center of the cave's floor. Sasha stares up at it with dead eyes. The fruits of labor, finished over the past few months, just barely before they had to abandon this place.

Her heart aches at the words branded along its side: *Project Persephone*. Exhaling deeply, Sasha trudges to the far edge of the room. The ship towers directly behind her. And, whipping her arms outward, sparks of teal magic explode forth, colliding into the rocky cave walls—a shearing noise erupts through the cavern, as a hole for every branch of the Assembly bursts open, shattering the fabric of reality. The world itself obeying her Will.

Hundreds of civilians spill into the cavern at once, led by uniformed members of the Assembly. Mothers holding infants, others gripping the hands of little boys and little girls. Fathers follow close behind. People of every race and culture fill the open space of the cavern. All clamoring as it quickly becomes claustrophobic. Large as it is, the cave is still hard-pressed to fit just under one thousand people within it, amongst the size of the spacecraft.

Sasha stares ahead at the Abyssal Root, stoically ignoring the flood of strangers knocking against her. Their presence, unknown to her.

The Assembly members direct the civilians up the steps leading into the spacecraft, climbing aboard as instructed by Misha.

Sasha sighs in relief that the girl is so observant, so intuitive. As she has given Sasha less to do, less to care for. The turmoil too heavy, it takes every ounce of her to remain standing.

The ship's hatch clamps shut. Screeching women and shouting men fling curses into the air. A handful of Assembly members board alongside the civilians, trying desperately to calm their anxieties. Multiple languages meshing and grinding loudly together, creating a grating, overstimulating effect on Sasha's ears. Her nose quivers and scrunches, she clenches her mouth and bares her teeth. The outrage is slowly quieted as the remaining Assembly members herd the excess civilians back into the shattered holes they arrived from.

"The craft is full. We are sorry. So sorry. Please understand," says an Assembly member. A woman screams as she bashes a fist atop the Assembly member's head, and a young boy, afraid and agitated by herd mentality, conjures lightning in his palms. Immediately, the Assembly members swarm the boy, with multiple elements swirling down their arms—the boy stumbles back, his magic dissipating as his mother screams in fear.

And as they succumb to their fate, they vanish beyond the shattered portals. With nothing left for them, but to hide from the horrors again.

Sasha grimaces, the screaming mother's pain resonating with her.

Silence. No one left in the chamber but Sasha and the hundreds of lucky civilians within the safety of *Project Persephone*. Sasha feels the rage within bubbling, ready to burst—alongside a throbbing ache and desire, a longing, a thirst which can no longer be quenched. She uncurls her fist, glancing into Persephone's crystallized soul-essence, wishing she could see her daughter's face. And Sasha sobs, wishing also to feel Seth's gentle touch, his loving embrace once more.

Turning around, she ascends the steps into Project Persephone. A door directly to the left leads deep inside, until reaching an engine room. Awaiting her is the Abyssal Drive. Sasha spies a groove at the top, in the center of the engine. Not created for any purpose, but simply resting where two pieces of metal were bonded and wedded together. Sasha places Persephone's soul-stone into it. Placing her palm over the stone, teal sparks crackle, fusing her daughter's soul essence into the metal groove.

"I wanted to see the stars, but I'm happy to pass that role along to you."

Tears clouding her vision, she leaves the engine room, making her way back to the cavern outside, shutting the hatch again. And, walking toward the Abyssal Root, she says:

"It must be done, there is no other way—isn't that right, Seth?" She speaks his name aloud, across the boundary of death, to comfort her soul and strengthen her resolve. "After all that, there's still too many of our enemies standing. Without you, without our daughter, how could we possibly overcome this? When the others are not yet human gods.

"But where's the time to grow, to flourish, to ripen into the power Zarathustra foresaw in us? We were almost there. If only we had a fraction of time more. But we do not. Strength of Will takes time, and far too many of us linger behind. Though it is alright. We may lose our home, but not our hope. The hope that stray god placed in you, Seth, as well as in all humankind, it *will* live on. Zarathustra created this world to be our domain, and I will do what I must." Her furious, bloodshot eyes flood with tears, streaming down her wrinkled cheeks. "So, as I commit this destructive act, *listen to my will!* Seth, our daughter *will* rise again, and so *will* we, in spirit, be at her side once more. *Do you hear me, Abyss?* I *Will* this eternal return. For the hope of humankind is...*far greater than wretched, vile gods!*

Eyes awash with divine power, Sasha slams her palm upon the Abyssal Root's control mechanism—tapping into the White Abyss, calling forth all its power and—

The ground cracks between her feet, and as Project Persephone's engines fire, it's not the flames and exhaust overtaking the cavern, but a vast whiteness bursting forward, engulfing the entire cave, swallowing everything—and as it tears through Sasha's body, a burst of teal flashes into a strand of light, being pulled alongside the sheer force and depth of the Abyss.

And on the surface above, the eyes of the Red Hat Army are awash with gold light, triggering a symbiotic glow of white in the eyes of the Abyssians. A fusion of desires—a love of gods and a love of conquest. Watching this, unsure of what it means, the Assembly members are basked in teal light, their bodies joining in the rapturous abyssal power, exploding forth and devouring all.

A collection of Wills weaving together with the full potential of the White Abyss...and becoming one with its future.

The black expanse of space. Far off stars and planets twinkle steadily, insistent on making themselves known, evidence of so much more awaiting those brave enough to endure the darkness, the black unknown.

And Earth, robbed of its green from global fires, spins on faster than it should. Without the moon's gravitational pull to steady it, humanity's home spirals into imbalance.

A thunderous roar fills its atmosphere, but nullified by the silence of space—large white fissures crack outward upon the earth, with North America as its epicenter, and stretching further and further—chunks of earth flings into space as the planet cracks open like an egg—the northern hemisphere lost in an instance of vast, white light.

And hurtling toward the vacuum of space is *Project Persephone*. Riding a wave of pressure from the white cataclysm, the ship quakes violently and is propelled toward the unknown. Breaking through the atmosphere, a white shimmer encases itself around the massive ship, enshrouding its name, windows, and all defining features—the white light pulses outward before rapidly pulling inward—the shockwave colliding into itself, the ship blips out of view. Simply vanishing, leaving nothing but a short stream of glimmering white particles along the ship's trajectory.

And, watching it go, is a massive white form emerging from the Earth's shattered core. Reaching out after it, eager to know what has come of the last of humanity. For tragedy may have struck here, a loss in the war to come. But humanity is a phenomenon of procedural learning, of growth and improvement. And their magic grows substantially with time...as it will, *after a long, bright dark*.

But until then, the white cataclysm continues to tear its way through the Earth, and the white form emerging from with it roars in tandem with the Will of those gods who want nothing more than to share in their loving embrace.

And the Will of the world...
Moves forever onward.

"In the middle of winter, I, at last, discovered that there was in me an invincible summer."
—Albert Camus, *The Myth of Sisyphus*

Special Thanks:

A part of me thought I'd never make it this far. Publishing is a competitive field, and to be published at all is a lofty dream. So, to publish not one book but two, well, I have a handful of people to thank for helping this come to fruition.

First off, thank you to Rowan Prose Publishing for not only publishing my debut, but my sophomore publication as well. For that, and for allowing me to go wild with my imagination and craft a narrative that adheres to my original vision. Not every publisher would allow this, with their many critiques and demanded changes. So, I'm grateful to have gotten my start with Rowan Prose. And don't you worry. As is implied by the ending, there is more to come.

I need to thank my Bard College family as well. If it weren't for my time spent at Bard, I would have never sharpened my writing ability to the degree I have, and I might also be creatively stifled if not for the Written Arts program imploring its students to be inventive, to push the boundaries of the craft. I particularly need to thank my advisor Joseph O'Neill, who guided me in the process of writing "The Monsters Among Us." If that book wasn't as grand and vastly inventive as it is, I would never have gone on to write this sequel or the sequels to come. So, thank you for aiding me in sharpening my vision, in helping this world become as real and beautifully, delightfully broken as we know humanity to be. I also must thank Cole Heinowitz, another mentor of mine while at Bard, who tragically and abruptly passed away. She, like Joseph O'Neill, helped me see how beautiful this world is—despite how dark it can often be.

Thank you also to everyone who read "The Monsters Among Us," and especially to those who have taken the time to tell me how much they loved the book. Truly, that means the world to me and makes all the hard work feel worthwhile.

A big thank you to Jacob Lang, who tragically passed away at the too early age of twenty-six. I've gotten this far thanks to your constant validation and support of me and my art. You believed in "The Monsters Among Us" even when the Sisyphean struggle that is publishing wore me out to the point of despair, when I could no longer believe in my own work. If it wasn't for your belief in me, I would never have written this sequel. Thank you, my friend. Not a day goes by that I do not think about you. Your voice and influence have been part of this book the entire way through.

Lastly, thank you to my future wife, Katarina Markota, to whom this book is dedicated. I truly would not be able to handle the stresses of the publishing industry if I was still unlucky enough to not have you by my side. Thankfully, that will never be the case again. My love, my one-day bride. My pillar of support and the entire reason I have been able to push forward and fight for my spot within the world of publishing. The Sasha to my Seth, to whom I will be married to in life and in death. I can only hope these books reach enough people and the world at large can be inspired to live more kindly, more empathetically, to be a more loving place for those with neurodivergence (as well as for all people), because that is the kind of world I would like our potential future children to be raised in. Lofty as it may be, but then again, so is getting a book published. As was, if you asked me a few years ago, the chance of me falling in love and being truly happy and fulfilled for the first time in my life. Yet here I am, marching toward the future with you, hand in hand.

CHECK OUT MORE GREAT READS FROM ROWAN PROSE:

Kent Priore writes dark literature where romanticism meets modern psychology for a macabre but hopeful depiction of inner struggle, and the human ability to endure. He is a fierce advocate for mental health awareness and for greater acceptance of neurodivergence. For this reason, themes of mental health are pronounced and ever present in his work, both the devastating and the hopeful aspects of it. He graduated with honors from Bard College with a BA in the Written Arts, and is a proud marginalized voice in the neurodivergent community.
www.kentpriore.com

www.ingramcontent.com/pod-product-compliance
Lightning Source LLC
LaVergne TN
LVHW041653060526
838201LV00043B/423